CODE JUGGERNAUT

A Novel

Sherman E. Ross

Copyright © Sherman E. Ross 2024

All rights Reserved

No reproduction, copy, or transmission of this publication may be made without written permission. No paragraph of this publication may be reproduced, copied, transmitted save with the written permission of the publisher.

ISBN: 978-1-917736-08-4 (Ebook)
ISBN: 978-1-917736-09-1 (Paperback)
ISBN: 978-1-917736-10-7 (Hardcover)

This is a work of fiction. The names, characters, places and incidents originate from the writer's imagination. Any resemblance to actual persons, living or dead, is purely coincidental.

Table of Contents

Prologue: White Noise i

Home Fires Burning 1

Holy War in The Heartland 29

Deus 'Sex' Machina 54

Night of the Long Knives 78

Goin' Fission 109

Clear and Present Danger 138

Off To See the Wizard 161

Collision Course 188

The Fourth Horseman 211

Stab-In-The-Back 237

Shatterer of Worlds 271

Marching As to War 293

Barbarians At the Gate 310

Götterdämmerung 333

Epilogue: The Circle Unbroken 360

Dedication 369

Code Name: Juggernaut

Prologue: White Noise

The sprawling compound was stark and barren. More fortress than community, more prison than commune, with peeling paint and rusting nails, row upon row the dilapidated wooden cabins lay in a monotonous arrangement. Like a military installation, the drab gray barracks stood, imposing and monolithic in an endless duplication. Towards the center of the compound were large buildings starkly designated as a "School" and a "Chapel," while armed with toy rifles, noisy blond children at play were involved in games that had an ominous war-like theme.

Near the enclosure's northwest corner stood the shooting range. There, several bearded men and an attractive twenty-one-year-old blonde were busy blazing away with an arsenal of AK-47 Kalashnikov and AR-15 assault rifles. Many of the faded, bullet-riddled silhouettes, crude caricatures of prominent black or Jewish people, stood as grim testament to their marksmanship. There was a large pen-like kennel situated at the opposite end, home to the compound's twelve large Rottweiler and German Shepherd guard dogs. The dogs, all trained to kill, were routinely turned loose and allowed to roam freely in the compound after curfew.

Around the encampment's perimeter was a six-foot fence topped with coils of rather poorly placed concertina wire. Just beyond the fence was the area known as the "deadline," with its carefully concealed holes lined with razor sharp "Punji stakes." On any given night, one could hear the pitiful howl of some poor coyote freshly impaled in the "Punji pits." At the compound's southern entrance, a faded sign hung overhead, starkly stenciled in bold letters,

"ONE GOD, ONE RACE, ONE NATION: WHITES ONLY"

Along the inner perimeter, more heavily armed men were patrolling. Wearing a hodgepodge of camouflage fatigues and castoff army surplus uniforms, grim-faced men stood watch, constantly on guard against an unseen enemy, while just outside of the compound more uniformed men shuffled along, engaged in a ragged close-order drill.

Two of the compound's four corners were occupied by imposing guard towers, manned by hooded men nervously cradling their weapons. Distant memories of the federal fifty-two-day standoff at Waco had prompted a greater vigilance almost paranoia — by the guards in their makeshift machinegun nests. To them, the enemy was all around, merely waiting for a lapse in security. Indeed, the previous year very nearly brought confrontation with federal agents searching for stolen weapons; a clash was only narrowly averted by last-minute negotiation by the US Attorney General. The last thing the FBI needed was a repeat of those distant public relations *debacles* at Ruby Ridge or Waco.

This was "JerUSAlem," the fortified bastion of the white supremacist Aryan Church of Yahweh the Creator, thought by some to be a bizarre racist, survivalist cult waiting for the apocalypse. Local journalists had called the encampment "Kook town" and "the Bunker," having dismissed all its inhabitants as a bunch of "weirdoes," "troglodytes" and "screwballs." It was situated thirty miles southwest of Provo, Utah between the towns of Fairfield and Eureka on approximately one hundred and fifty-five acres of land originally thought cursed by God; pioneers referred to as being barren, bitter cold in the winter, and yet so hot and dry in summer that the Devil couldn't raise Hell on it.

This was home, the "promised land" to some four hundred and fifty-five of God's "Aryan chosen people"— one hundred and fifty-two men, two hundred and twenty-two women, and eighty-one children, all stockpiling an awesome array of weapons and foodstuffs, all eagerly awaiting what they felt was the eventual racial apocalypse. In their leader's vision, they were to be the 'seed corn' of a new nation.

In the school were bookcases crammed with the Bible, as well as copies of *The Protocols of the Elders of Zion, Mein Kampf, The Carson Diaries, The Holy Book of Adolph Hitler*, assorted Ku Klux Klan newspapers, and other racist hate literature filled with standard fare depicting blacks, Jews and other minorities as satanic monsters. The children of several church members were in attendance, their young minds slowly being poisoned with the illusion that they were "Aryan supermen," and that other "inferior mud races" had no right to live in American society and therefore should be eliminated.

In a bizarre "lesson" a dark-haired, matronly- looking woman quizzed them.

"Jonathan, can you please tell me who Jesus the Christ was?" she said softly to a skinny, blond youth.

"He is the immortal leader of our race! He once returned to us as Adolph Hitler!" The child robotically snapped to attention. "He's the greatest white man that ever lived."

"Very good… What happened to our great leader, Tammy?"

"He was murdered by the Jews, Reverend Mother. They're all Christ-killers. They mess up everything. I hate them. I hate them all," the pouting little blonde girl said in terse reply.

"That's right, Lambs. You see, for the second time in history, our beloved savior was murdered by the Satanic Jew. The Evil One wants to use the mud people to destroy us… Lambs, now I'm going to tell you something wonderful," the woman said, smiling. "The Book says that if we're good, one day Christ will return to kill all the dirty blacks and Jews... and all the other mud people... We'll have a wonderful white world."

The children, their tiny faces now distorted with racial hatred, erupted with applause and cheers. The woman continued.

"This is what our Lord Jesus has promised us. Now remember, Lambs, that we are all young warriors of our God, Yahweh... Mary, can you tell me who the Devil is?"

"The Jew! The Jew!" The child's eyes furrowed with hate.

"And who are the seed of Satan?"

"Niggers! Dirty niggers... and all the mud races!"

"And what should we do with the enemies of Yahweh and all their seed?"

"Kill them! Kill them all!" the children began chanting wildly and thrusting their tiny arms out in the Nazi salute. Indoctrination, this passed for education in the Jerusalem compound. For any who would dare stray from *The Word,* discipline was maintained with a cleated strap.

The profile of someone who belonged to the Church was the middle-aged white male who faced job termination because of the deteriorating economy, or the young working-class white man in his twenties who saw around him nothing but diminished opportunity. He resented the rising tide of ethnic and religious diversity which, demographically speaking, was transforming *him* into a minority. He was a person who perceived that "all the breaks" were going to African Americans, Hispanics and others through a host of affirmative action programs and "quotas." He did not understand that the worsening economic situation had, if anything, impacted harder upon these groups than on himself.

He who joined fit the profile of the laid-off white factory worker who had watched in frustration as his career had moved to Mexico or Japan or Taiwan, 'out-sourced,' all in the name of "free trade" and "globalization." All of the earlier populist rhetoric of "Make America Great Again", "America First" and "Build Back Better" had changed nothing. The economic deterioration was only exacerbated by the recent COVID pandemic. He who joined was frustrated by a society apparently unable to punish criminals. He was angered by the new militancy of the LGBTQ community, who in his eyes were "AIDS carriers" who now clamored for same-sex marriage, other "special rights," and an acceptance of what he considered to be a perverted lifestyle. Above all, he was disgusted with the seemingly endless stream of Washington politicians: Democrats or Republicans, who constantly promised the moon and yet always failed to deliver. Someone must be to blame.

This was the man who had grown to early adulthood in an era of seemingly boundless prosperity. Having worked hard all his life he now felt entitled to his reward — well-paying, meaningful employment and a secure future. His argument was a familiar one: "I can't get that job I wanted or a promotion at work because of affirmative action and reverse discrimination" or "the blacks and Mexicans are taking all of *our* jobs away".

As the nation's economy sank deeper into recession, he was now forced to look into the tearful eyes of his children at Christmastime and explain to them that Santa wouldn't be coming this year because Daddy was naughty: Daddy got laid-off. Consumed with rage, he felt that he had been cheated of the "American Dream." He was losing control. He was angry. Someone must be to blame. He was beginning to hate.

For this man, the Aryan Church of Yahweh the Creator was

suddenly beginning to seem more palatable. For their part, the racists were quick to take advantage of the situation by readily supplying the obligatory scapegoat. Slowly, they came to represent a *safety valve*, a focal point for his anger. For his lack of purpose, they offered direction. For his frustration, they granted an outlet. For his growing hate, they provided a target.

Code Name: Juggernaut

Home Fires Burning

"He lieth in his blood, the father in his face; They have killed him, the Forgiver, the Avenger takes his place…
For they killed him in his kindness, in their madness and their blindness.
And his blood is on their hand…
There is a sobbing of the strong, and a pall upon the land;
But now the People in their weeping, bare the iron hand…
Beware the People weeping when they bare the iron hand."
— Herman Melville, from *The Martyr*

Monday, April 13th
2055 hours
The Watts section of Los Angeles, CA

With the blare of distant police sirens in the background, the pickup truck waited in a clearing near a clump of trees in a poorly lit park two hundred yards from the Mount Zion African Methodist Church. In it, an attractive woman carefully slid a pair of leather gloves over her fingers and tucked her shoulder-length blonde hair under a well-worn, faded *Atlanta Braves* baseball cap. Slowly looking around, she emerged from the vehicle.

"Shit!" the woman said, upon realizing that she was standing in a large mud puddle. It had been raining for most of the day.

Going to the rear of the vehicle, Jacqueline Lynch furtively removed a long brown suitcase. She opened it, unveiling a Russian-made *Dragunov SVD* semiautomatic sniper rifle, mounting a Zeiss 8x power telescopic sight. The weapon had been sighted in at twelve hundred yards. An exceptional rifle, it was lightweight and, with modified ammunition, would allow a 7.62-millimeter projectile less than a three-inch drop over nine hundred yards. Reaching into her purse, she extracted a plump silencer and slowly screwed it onto the end of the weapon's barrel. In addition to acting to muffle the sound, the silencer doubled as a flash-suppressor; the assassin would remain invisible as well as unheard. It was a reliable weapon; she had used it twice before. The woman carefully inserted a seven-round clip into the rifle's action, manually inserting a round into the chamber by working the slide mechanism. Each Russian- made 7.62-millimeter round was wicked looking: a missile in miniature, more than three inches long having a titanium jacket and a two hundred-grain explosive mercury-fulminate hollow-point "wad-cutter" that upon penetration would shatter into numerous fiberglass fragments called "*flechettes*," creating additional wound tracks and literally eviscerating the target.

Assembly completed, the stealthy assassin crouched behind a tree, bracing herself against a thick branch. She sighted in the weapon at the front door and calmly waited for her prey. While waiting, the young woman began to reflect on her rather unusual life.

For Jacqueline Diane Lynch, twenty-nine, life had been hard. Born into poverty in Stone Mountain, Georgia, during the midst of the Black Lives Matter and other social movements, "Jackie" had been strongly influenced by her ultra-white nationalist parents. Stalwart members of the Forsyth County klavern, they had instilled in their daughter a deep racial hatred for blacks, Jews, Hispanics and other minorities. Although the family was poor, Jacqueline remembered being sent to an expensive all-white "academy" grade school in order to avoid integration. As a child, she was constantly admonished to "stay away from all the dirty mud children." Her hatred became more pronounced as a young teenager; she was briefly expelled from her school when she had referred to then-President Obama as a "nigger."

Jackie had also been fascinated with guns. All kinds of guns. Her grandfather bought her a twenty-two-caliber rifle for her sixth birthday; by fourteen she was an expert shot with a 30.06. Her fondest memories were of when she and the old man would go off deer hunting with their rifles in the forests of northwestern Georgia. She made a game of it, pretending that she was in the army or tracking Yankees or runaway slaves or marauding Indians. During these trips, the old man regaled her constantly with exciting stories of the exploits of Confederate generals or Ty Cobb's baseball records, or about his own younger days when he had been active as a Grand Exalted Hobgoblin in the mighty Stone Mountain Georgia Klan during the late nineteen-eighties.

A high school dropout and troublemaker, Jackie had drifted aimlessly, tending to blame others for her failures. She joined the Marines at twenty and seemed to find a niche. Having been an excellent markswoman as an adolescent, she quickly became a shooting instructor at the Marine Corps Sniper School at Quantico. Her racist views kept getting her into trouble, however; earlier, she was threatened with court-martial for assaulting a young black marine recruit at Camp Pendleton.

Discharged as a corporal after four years, she continued her slide. While back in Atlanta she was actively involved in prostitution and the sale of illicit narcotics. Later, she became romantically involved with her pimp, a man named David Franklin. Franklin was also a "hitman" for a shadowy white supremacist gang calling itself the *Werewolf*. Eventually they became lovers and began living together. One year later, however, he was killed in a shoot-out with FBI agents in Atlanta during a failed bank robbery attempt.

Having "apprenticed" under her paramour, Jackie Lynch had become an accomplished Werewolf assassin herself. She was code-named *Jack-L*. Already, she had more than twenty confirmed kills. Her first hit, involving the ambush slaying of a black FBI agent in Atlanta, was revenge for her boyfriend's death. From a distance of three hundred and fifty yards she blew his head off with a silenced hunting rifle. Since then, she had been involved in at least eight other sniper killings of prominent black and Jewish men in Philadelphia, Detroit, Washington, DC, Seattle, Buffalo and Montreal.

Her most recent hit had been a black labor union leader and political activist in Detroit. Things didn't go quite right on that job: a black newspaper carrier got a good look at Jacqueline as she ran back to her car. On reflection however, Miss Lynch had reason to be well pleased with herself; besides her successful "career," on top of everything else now she had a new boyfriend.

Suddenly, the church doors opened, jarring her from her thoughts. A crowd slowly emerged, clustered around a large, imposing gray-haired figure. Through a pair of binoculars Jackie Lynch could see the object of her stalk, Reverend Darius Thomas Williams. Williams, at eighty-three, was a prominent black civil rights activist who had at another time and place marched with Reverend Martin Luther King, Jr. from Selma to Montgomery. More recently, he had been involved in such issues ranging from gay rights to homelessness. He had also been instrumental in helping to calm the black community in the wake of the bloody LA race riots several years earlier. Williams was already being compared to Dr. King for his adherence to nonviolence. He had just finished delivering a sermon to the church's congregation entitled "A Time for Martyrs," which stressed the importance of education, parental responsibility and black voter registration. For all this, he had been marked for death by the Werewolf.

Smiling, the large black man was vigorously pumping extended hands as he meandered slowly across the church's dimly lit parking lot. The evening air was crisp and clean after the rain shower earlier; there was almost no wind.

This is perfect, Jackie thought as she slowly adjusted the windage and elevation turrets of the telescope. All good snipers longed for ideal conditions such as these. Absence of wind meant that nothing except gravity would affect the bullet's trajectory to the target. The assassin slowly brought the rifle's telescope to her eye; the magnification setting brought the image of Williams' head into full view. She was sighted in, with the crosshairs meeting at the back of the man's head.

Time to die. Kiss your black ass good-bye, Sambo! It's Judgment Day, Judgment Day! Jackie thought to herself as she brought her finger to the trigger. Her Marine training taught her it was better to slowly squeeze off a shot rather than to make a sudden pull. Her heart was racing; she took a deep breath and fired. There were two muffled reports, interspersed by sharp recoils. Two rounds traveling with a terminal velocity of 960 meters per second struck the black man. Through the telescopic sight, the assassin could see Williams jerk violently to the left from the impact, the back of his head momentarily disappearing in a grotesque reddish-pink cloud of brain material and blood. The man's head simply exploded, blossoming like some hideous flower. The victim never knew what hit him. Clean head shots. Clean hit. Certain death.

"He's been shot! Oh Jesus! Please No!" an elderly woman in the crowd screamed hysterically as Williams collapsed in a bloody heap onto the pavement.

For several seconds, there was complete silence as the crowd stared in numbed disbelief. Then slowly the panic set in. Amid growing terror and confusion, a church steward cradled the victim's shattered head in her lap, waiting for an ambulance to arrive at the scene. It was too late. Reverend Williams was dead.

Slowly panning the telescope from left to right, Jackie surveyed the chaos she had caused. The crowd of well-wishers now began screaming and running in panic. Like a great herd of horses, they stampeded wildly down the street. Enjoying the spectacle, the sniper momentarily thought about shooting additional people. It would be easy. It was a perfect, tempting target, a dense mass of humanity, more or less bunched together.

There were four rounds left in the magazine and one in the chamber. She sighted the weapon in on a small child who, bewildered by what was happening, presented a perfect target. The assassin's finger tightened on the trigger, then relaxed. No. Her assignment was to kill Williams, and she had succeeded. Better now to escape. Jackie reached into her pocket, extracting a long envelope. Dropping it where she was sure it would be found, the shadowy female assassin ran back to her vehicle, hiding the weapon in the back seat under a blanket. In an instant, the truck roared off into the night.

In the moments after the shooting, Los Angeles Police units had quickly flooded the area. Homicide detectives Alan Baker and Orson Davies began by mounting a careful search of the scene. The two cops, a pair of somewhat heavyset veterans with a combined twenty-seven years on the force quickly secured the area. Their preliminary investigation revealed the only clues to the murder: impressions made in the soft ground by the sniper and her vehicle, two spent shell casings, and a cryptic note in the envelope left behind by the killer. The note was crudely typed on standard printer paper. It read:

"Since The Jew-Nigger Criminal Conspiracy Known As ZOG Has Failed To Respond To The Just Claims Of The WHITE NATION We, The Christian, Aryan Storm Troopers Of The WEREWOLF BROTHERHOOD Are Now Compelled To Make An Expression Of WHITE POWER Through An Act Of Revolutionary Violence. The Subhuman Negroid Primate Known as Darius Thomas Williams Was Successfully Liquidated Tonight In Accordance With The Laws Of YAHWEH. Let His Death Stand As A Declaration Of RACE WAR Against All The Agents Of ZION And Their Colored Puppets! HAIL VICTORY! The WEREWOLF Will Kill Again!

The Jack-L is Loose!

Warnung! Unsere Vergeltung ist tödlich!"

"Aw shit!" Davies mumbled upon examining the note. "Looks like some sick racist fuck did the killing. Prominent black guy...Williams no less." He gave a long, audible sigh. "After the riots we had couple of years ago, this is the last thing this city needs."

"You know, I think this was a hit. No way is this a lone psycho gunman. It's got 'pro' written all over it." Baker surveyed the crime scene. "Head shots from a fairly long range... a professional job."

"How you figure that, I mean, a pro?"

Baker bent over and picked up one of the spent shell casings with a pencil. "Well, nobody heard anything...that means a silencer." He shined his flashlight on it. "See this? Looks like a seven-point-six-two-millimeter, titanium maybe."

"Hey, look at all this writing," he said on closer inspection. "I make that out as Cyrillic; those are Russian markings. I'd say that our killer probably used a *Dragunov-SVD*."

"A what?"

"*Snyperskaya Vintovka Dragunova.*" Baker again stooped over beside the tree to recover the other spent cartridge. "It's a Russian sniper rifle. A real man-stopper. Suckers got a hell of a muzzle velocity. Probably the best in the world. Harder than shit to come by." He stroked his chin as if deep in thought. "Lightweight, the latest models can now easily be retrofitted with a Zeiss or Redfield telescope. Put a silencer on that puppy and you got yourself an awesome takedown rifle. The *Spetznatz* really kicked some serious ass in Chechnya with 'em way back in the late nineties. You know, I'm familiar with all that Russky ordnance."

"So just how do you know all this shit? I mean, all the Russian lingo?" Davies shook his head, staring in awe at his partner.

"Hey, I read *Freebooter Magazine*," Baker grunted in reply. "They got a whole article on sniper rifles in their latest issue. Written by *Ivanoff*."

"Who?"

"*Alexiev Sergievich Ivanoff*. Hard-core *Spetznatz*…the King of the snipers. They say he probably dropped over four hundred Chechen guerrillas during his tours in Chechnya using the latest version of the *Dragunov*," Baker paused, clearing his throat. "He was writing about *Lyudmila Pavlichenko* in World War Two. Total bad ass… he wrote that this Russian chick probably dropped over 300 Nazis using a Dragunov." The pair started back towards the parking lot as the CSI Unit arrived. "During the war, the Chechen *mujihadeen* respected Ivanoff…called him *Whispering Death* or something like that. He's retired now. Got a little dacha outside Moscow. Writes articles about his experiences and historical stuff for *Freebooter* from time to time."

The crowd slowly dispersed. As if almost on cue, they were replaced by hordes of reporters and camera crews. A local TV news team and police began interviewing some members of the still terrified congregation. Investigators scoured the area for additional clues. Later, a hearse from the Coroner's Office arrived to carry the slain man's body away.

Davies's fears about the potential for a riot were not without foundation. The city had hardly recovered from the earlier bloody disturbances as well as the allegations of widespread racism at the LAPD. Only two weeks before, there had been another police shooting of a black youth, this time over allegedly stealing a sandwich.

Almost immediately, rumors began circulating in the black community that the Williams killing had been a racially motivated execution. Now rumor and liquor proved an explosive combination. Within hours, bands of enraged black youths, some of whom had been present when the civil rights activist was murdered, now roamed the streets. Overturning cars, setting fires, looting liquor and appliance stores and attacking white passersby, the mob slowly coalesced and meandered toward the downtown area. Years of high unemployment, systemic racism and pent-up frustration now made "Smash-and-Grab" the order of the day. Surrounded by all the opulence that their empty pockets could not buy, they now resolved that the club, the rock and the Molotov cocktail had become the new media of exchange. Inebriated black youths, arms loaded with stolen big-screen TVs, cellular telephones, spirits, assorted clothing and other plunder, could be seen jumping out of burning downtown stores. Figuratively and literally, the streets ran with liquor.

By morning, a full-scale riot was underway. It seemed as if the City of Angels had suddenly become *Hell Town*. There was a sudden rush on gun shops as frightened whites armed themselves and spoke angrily of retaliation. Ever mindful of the tragic events of the earlier disturbances, the mayor mobilized the LAPD for riot duty; the governor placed units of the California National Guard on standby alert. Meanwhile, the catalyst of this mayhem was reposing peacefully in an Inglewood hotel room.

Tuesday, April 14th
0450 hours. (EDT)
FBI Headquarters, J. Edgar Hoover Bldg., Washington, DC

Having talked to the Los Angeles Regional Field Office about the Williams murder, FBI Director George Longstreet summoned Special Agent Douglas Rabson into his office. Longstreet, a silver-haired, lean "southern gentleman" of sixty-four, was a hard-bitten veteran agent from Biloxi, Mississippi. Having risen through the ranks, he had been picked by the president to head the bureau. During this brief tenure he had become somewhat of a legend. A product of the "new

South," Longstreet's first task as a new agent had been to investigate white supremacist violence during the late nineties. Since then, he had risen steadily through the ranks, finally being granted the directorship in what some called a political appointment. Probably more than anyone else, it was he who had brought the agency out of the shadow of the distant Waco and Ruby Ridge disasters, as well as embarrassing revelations surrounding botched intelligence preceding September 11th, 2001, and January 6th, 2021.

Director Longstreet brought a renewed sense of professionalism to the FBI. Long gone were the days of the Fedora-clad "gumshoe" of Purvis lore. As never before, minorities and women were recruited into the Bureau. Under Longstreet, the agency was now ultra high-tech, placing greater emphasis on counterintelligence, organized and white-collar crime, securities fraud, international and domestic terrorism. Indeed, the Bureau's Domestic Counter-terrorism Strike Force, of which Douglas Rabson was a member, was his own brainchild. Conceived with the passage of the Patriot and National Anti-terrorism Acts, it had come into being from his long-held belief that it was only a matter of time before domestic political terrorism, already rampant in the Middle East and Europe, would come to America. The horrific events at the Atlanta Olympics, the World Trade Center, the Pentagon, Oklahoma City and most recently, the US Capitol had already proven him right.

"Agent Rabson, sorry I called you in here at this God-awful hour, but we think there's been another killing by the Jack-L," the director said as Rabson entered.

"What, you mean she's scored again?" the agent said, suppressing a yawn.

"Yeah. This time it was a minister. I just got off the horn with Dumbrowski's people out in the LA office. We've got to move fast on these killings. Black community's starting to get up in arms, you know, saying cover-up and all. Already we're getting scattered reports of rioting."

"My God, that makes number eight. Let's see... she's got eight confirmed hits in about eleven months." Rabson slowly shook his head.

"Nine," the director said in correction. "This time the sniper apparently shot and killed a black political activist, some local guy named Darius Williams after he addressed a church meeting. The killer popped him twice, two head shots. Just like the other murders. Nobody heard anything because she used a silencer again."

Rabson nodded in response. Longstreet continued.

"The ballistics aren't in yet of course, but they found two spent seven-point-six-two- millimeter shell casings at the scene... just like the Detroit and Philadelphia killings. Get all you have on these murders together."

"Yes sir."

"What is it? You've worked on this kind of assignment before. Those inner-city street gangs for instance, just last year."

"Somehow that was different."

"How so?"

"Motivation. Those gangs were a bunch of street kids who grew up in poverty. They were simply in it for the money. These neo-Nazi assholes are doing it out of *belief*. With the black and Latino gangs, it was all strictly a matter of turf and drugs... plain economics; with these guys it's *political*. We're not talking about a bunch of yahoos who go out at night yelling 'nigger,' painting swastikas on synagogues or burning a cross somewhere. This is different, and something a lot more frightening. Look at what those crazy assholes did right here, ransacking the Capitol way back in twenty-one."

"Yeah, I know... well, tell your wife and kids you're going be gone a while; I'm sending you out on the Red eye to LA to coordinate the investigation with the locals," Longstreet responded in a low, Mississippi drawl. He handed Rabson a coach-class ticket.

"Yes sir." Rabson knew that his taking another trip right now would not go over well at home. Among other things, it meant that he would have to miss his oldest daughter's piano recital on Saturday. Sarah was really looking forward to his being there. Oh well, it came with the territory. Sarah would understand.

Tuesday, April 14th
0855 hours (PDT)
Los Angeles Police Headquarters, Parker Center.

Already the riot's toll had climbed to thirty-nine dead, ninety-eight injured. Three hundred seventy-eight people had been arrested for looting and arson. Black mobs roamed the streets, screaming "Kill Whitey!" in a mood that was chillingly reminiscent of the civil unrest of the nineteen-sixties. Some of the city's most notorious street gangs had suspended their mutual hostility and hastily called an impromptu non-aggression pact in order to share in the looting and pillage. In one particularly savage incident, a white cabdriver was trapped in the Watts section of town when his car broke down. Pleading for his life, he was dragged from the vehicle and savagely stoned to death by the drunken mob.

Angry whites counterattacked. A terrified black thief was cornered in an alley like an animal. "Get him! Kill that nigger! Lynch him! Bring him over here!" someone in the crowd yelled. He was savagely beaten, kicked, stripped, castrated, doused with gasoline and set ablaze. His triumphant attackers, maddened with liquor, danced around his smoldering corpse howling "Burn Nigger! Burn! Look at that nigger burn!" Both grisly scenes of sadistic racial violence were captured on video by courageous television camera crews. The film footage from both incidents would later be used as evidence to identify the hooligans in court, both white and black. The video images, in helping to convict the assailants, provided a measure of grim vengeance for the mutilated dead.

By midmorning, it was estimated that over two hundred fires had been set and were burning out of control. Fire-fighting personnel refused to enter certain areas of town because of reports of snipers. At last, police units, now backed by National Guardsmen, were moving out in force to contain the violence. Meanwhile, after reading the preliminary report on the Williams killing, Homicide Division Chief Captain Murray Thompson summoned Detectives Baker and Davies into his office. Riot or no riot, he had a murder investigation to conduct.

"So, you guys think that the Williams killing was a hit?" Thompson said as the pair entered the office.

"Yes sir, based on what we found, we do," Baker said, clearing his throat. "And a professional job too."

"Well, so do I." Thompson settled back into his chair. "And so does the FBI. I've been talking to their field office here. It seems that over the past ten months there have been similar killings in Seattle, Atlanta, Washington DC, Detroit, Philadelphia, and now here. All the victims were prominent black or Jewish men: a minister, labor union leader, a politician, an African ambassador, an FBI agent, radio talk-show host, lawyer, gynecologist and a judge, at least nine hits in all, counting Williams. All apparently racially motivated," he finished, reading from a hastily scribbled note.

"Goddamn!" Baker took a seat. "So, looks like some psycho asshole is out trying to start his own private little race war."

"Wait, there's more… The feds think the hitter is a woman. A female they're calling 'Jack- L,'" Thompson paused, allowing the thought to set in. "A professional assassin. We've got a hitwoman on the loose."

"A woman's doing all this killing? No shit?" Davies said.

"Yup. They've apparently even got a witness to the Detroit killing. It's a white woman, that much they know for sure, and she used the same weapon in both the Detroit and Philadelphia murders. Cryptic notes were found at each scene, just like this one," the captain said. He handed the killer's note to Baker.

"A woman… Guess that explains the small shoe prints CSI found in the muddy ground. I'd say that the killer wears a size six-and-a-half." Davies began looking over one of the crime scene photographs.

"Sounds like she's a real sweetheart," Baker said. "And now looks like we got a full-scale race riot on our hands…I mean, it's like the freakin' Wild West out there!"

"The FBI has been working on the case for several months. They've got some hot-shot counter- terrorism agent coming out here tomorrow; you guys be ready to brief him on what you have when he gets here. That's all."

Tuesday, April 14th
0930 hours
Hyatt Hotel lobby, Inglewood, CA

"Hey, Fatso! You got anything for me? I'm Ginger Kereluk, the woman in Room two twenty-four," Jacqueline shouted to the portly hotel clerk behind the desk. The man was absorbed with the riot coverage on a small television.

"Let me see…Ah, yes ma'am, here's something," the clerk said, eyes still fixed on the TV. He reached down and pulled out a large Manila envelope from a slot in a large mail bin beneath the desk.

"Well, then give it to me!" Jackie barked, rudely snatching the envelope from the startled clerk's hands. "I think your service here sucks!"

"Have you heard the news? Someone shot and killed Reverend Williams last night. It's all on TV," the clerk said, recovering his composure and trying to make conversation. "Be careful if you go out today... Whole lot of rioting going on in Watts and downtown... It's just awful, he was such a good man. He worked so hard to bring the races together. Now some twisted nut killed him."

"So? Some ugly, melon-head coon gets his ass burned. Hey, ask me if I care. Who gives a fuck? If you ask me, the colored guy had it coming." Jackie glanced at the scenes of looting and mayhem on the television. "Look at all them coons. Why they ain't three generations since swinging from trees. Niggers are all just a bunch of savages. Wouldn't bother me none if the law locked up all the coons in this city," she murmured with a scowl as she turned and walked back to her room.

"Bitch," the stunned clerk mumbled to himself as Jackie walked away.

Back in her room, she turned on the TV to watch coverage of the rioting. Reclining on the bed, Jackie proceeded to open the envelope. In it was $10,000 in cash. As the assassin flipped through the money the telephone rang. A familiar voice was on the other end.

"Hello? This is Miss Kereluk."

"Jackie, this is Howard," the voice on the other end said.

"Ah, Howie! I sure wish you were here right now lover," she said, rolling over and playing with her hair. "Assignment successfully completed, as per your instructions. I did your thing for you."

"Yeah, I know. Nice work last night. One less spook. It's the lead story on all the morning news shows. We're having the rest of the money delivered to your hotel room."

"I'm counting it now. Ten grand... Dirty...Sexy... Money. Are you watching the riot?"

"Yeah, I'm looking at it now, it's really something. It's all over the TV. *CNA News* is giving expanded coverage. The race war is really coming down fast! And to think that it was you who started all this."

"Cool, huh?" Jackie began to laugh.

"Get packed. Leave your weapon at the safe- house in Simi Valley. They'll send it to you later. We want you to go LAX and grab a flight to Salt Lake," the mysterious voice said. "We'll pick you up there. Be here by the twentieth. I think we've got another job lined up for you to do."

"Good. I'm ready to blow this lousy piece of shit town anyway. Before the niggers burn it down. Had a little problem with one of the staff earlier, but I took care of it. I'll see you soon." Jackie softly placed the receiver back in its cradle.

Wednesday, April 15th
1330 hours
LAPD Headquarters, Parker Center

It had been an uneventful five-hour flight to Los Angeles. By the time Rabson's plane had touched down at LAX Airport, the rioting was for the most part over. Heavily armed National Guardsmen now patrolled the streets, relieving LAPD units in enforcing a no-nonsense dusk-to-dawn curfew while an exhausted city paused to bury the slain civil rights leader. Rabson arrived, and, after checking in with the Bureau's Assistant Director for Los Angeles, was met by a policewoman and taken straight to Police Headquarters at Parker Center. He entered and took the elevator to the third floor where Captain Thompson rose to greet him. The captain immediately led the agent to the squad room where Detectives Baker and Davies were waiting.

Rabson, at thirty-nine, was married to a beautiful lawyer, the father of two precocious girls, and a rising star in the bureau. Viewed as being high-strung, he was one of the agency's "whiz kids." Born in Boston, scion of a federal judge, Rabson had been raised under the aegis of New England liberalism. After obtaining a bachelor's degree in psychology from Harvard, he went on to pursue an advanced degree in criminal justice. After that he joined the FBI, breezing through the Academy at Quantico. An agent for twelve years, he was now a member of the Bureau's elite Domestic Counter-terrorism Strike Force assigned to the Washington DC area.

The unit had come into existence as a result of passage of the National Anti-terrorism Act. This legislation, passed in the wake of the New York and Washington tragedies, had been controversial; it had given the president and Attorney General sweeping new powers to quash domestic sedition. Over the past several years in this position, Rabson had investigated everything from the World Trade Center to inner city gang activity to abortion clinic violence. Now, he was investigating the activities of various white supremacist and neo-Nazi groups, most notably a new and particularly vicious one calling itself *Werewolf*. For the last seven months, Rabson and members of CSF had been involved in tracking the mysterious female racist sniper.

Rabson, a Jew, aside from his professional attitude, had a special motivation for this assignment; both his maternal great-grandparents had been murdered by the Nazis during the Holocaust, and he was concerned by the disturbing resurgence of racism and anti-Semitism in the country, as well as ongoing political violence.

"Good afternoon, gentlemen. I'm Special Agent Douglas Rabson, FBI." The agent deposited his briefcase beside the desk. "I'm here to investigate the possibility that the Williams murder may be part of a much wider conspiracy involving white supremacists."

"Okay. Nine people have been brutally murdered. All black or Jewish. So, who all's involved? Who's behind all this killing?" Baker said. "The Klan? Skinheads? The Nazis?"

"None of the above. We think it's a relatively new group that calls itself the Werewolf."

"Werewolf? That was the name on the note we found at the scene of the killing," Davies recalled. Baker began rummaging over some papers on the desk to retrieve the note.

"Right. They call themselves the 'Werewolf' after the secret Nazi guerrilla army Hitler tried to form near the end of the Second World War. It's a racist gang that started right here in California about five years ago," Rabson said, beginning to give them some insight. "Since then, it's spread to Georgia, Texas, Utah, Idaho and several other states. They're so violent that even other more traditional white supremacist groups shun them. They'll even beat each other up. We think that they've got about seven-to-eight hundred hardcore members both inside and outside of the prison system, plus several thousand sympathizers and wannabes. Bureau Intelligence suspects there may also be Werewolf activity in the military."

"Son-of-a-bitch," Davies murmured to himself.

"One more thing," the agent added. "These assholes don't play. They pride themselves on being the baddest of the bad. They're heavily armed and won't back down in a fight. We understand that you have to commit murder to get in. They killed at least thirty-two people last year. All the victims were minorities. Remember that Texas prison riot earlier this year? We think it all got started when a black inmate was cornered by a Werewolf death squad. They slit his throat... and castrated him with a homemade shank... Painted a crude swastika on the wall in the guy's own blood."

"Yeah, I remember, something like thirteen people were killed in that riot." Thompson said, slowly nodding. "So, where do these sonsabitches get all their money? How do they finance their operations?"

"Extortion, bank robbery, drugs and prostitution mostly. They've also used strong-arm tactics to shakedown small businesses. The Bureau thinks the gang was also involved in that $6.2 million armored car heist in Denver last year. Two guards were shot to death in cold blood. That case remains unsolved," Rabson continued reading from a thick file folder.

"On this note we found at the scene of the murder, what exactly do the letters Z-O-G mean?" Baker passed the note to the agent.

Rabson carefully examined the note. "Yeah…Zionist Occupation Government, or ZOG. These groups all seem to have the opinion that the country is somehow controlled by the Jews." He handed it back to Baker.

"Ha! You mean it ain't?" Davies blurted out jokingly in ignorant reply, not realizing that Rabson was Jewish. Thompson blushed.

"What's all this stuff at the bottom mean?" Baker said, waving the note around. "Some kinda kraut mumbo-jumbo, right?" He pointed it out to Rabson.

Rabson brought his finger to his chin and paused. "My German is a little rusty… *'Unsere Vergeltung ist tödlich'*… It's German all right. It roughly translates, 'Our vengeance is deadly'… The calling card of Werewolf."

"Has the Bureau had any luck infiltrating this gang?"

"Not much," Rabson said with a sigh. "That's what makes these bastards so dangerous. They're changing their tactics… they mostly operate in small cells or even as lone wolves. In a large group somebody eventually always talks… But if you're dealing with a single nut case or a few isolated crazies it's different… How do you infiltrate a person's mind?"

"Well, what about this mystery woman, this female assassin? How exactly does she fit in?" Thompson interrupted. He picked up the preliminary crime report.

"I was just getting to that." Rabson pulled another folder from his briefcase and began reading. "Apparently, she's a first-rate assassin who's got at least nine hits that we can't prove. We've code- named her, *Jack-L*. We know that she was an ex-hooker who was shacking up with her pimp, a Werewolf hit man named Franklin couple years back. Franklin was killed in a shootout, but his girlfriend vanished."

"Vanished?"

"Yup. But it looks like she took up his business."

"Have a name?" Baker said.

"Only some of the aliases that she's used in the Detroit and Philadelphia killings… Diane Sydney Wilson, Sydney Lake, Lynne Kereluk, Jacqueline Lake, Ginger Stratten and some others, but nothing definite. The name she gave at her last arrest apparently was a phony…Interesting… it says here that her fingerprint records from both the Atlanta PD and NCIC databases have somehow disappeared."

"Got any pictures?" Thompson said.

"The photos we got are dated, about four years old, from Atlanta when they picked her up for hooking." Rabson again opened his briefcase, displaying several of the black-and-white mugshots of Jacqueline Lynch that had been taken after her arrest for prostitution in Atlanta.

"She's a torpedo? Boy, this chick's really stacked! Nice! A real looker. I think she could kill me anytime," Davies blurted out tactlessly while examining one of the photos.

"She might just do that. We know she's already killed one law enforcement officer," the agent replied, becoming increasingly annoyed at the antics. "Black FBI agent in Atlanta. Abel Willis. I knew him. He had a family. This bitch drilled him through the head with a high-powered rifle while he was playing with his dog and young son in their backyard... Let's cut the smart-ass remarks, okay?"

"Oh... eh, sorry, I didn't mean to be so flip," Davies said sheepishly, visibly embarrassed.

"The Bureau thinks that the Werewolf is involved in a conspiracy to eliminate prominent blacks and that they're using this female assassin. We want to find her before she makes another hit. That's why I'm here." Rabson closed the briefcase. "I'll need to see the autopsy report on Williams to compare the bullet fragments with those taken from the Detroit and Philadelphia murders. I suspect that they'll match."

As the meeting broke up Thompson came over to Rabson, placing his hand on his shoulder. "Don't mind Orson Davies. I know that he's an asshole sometimes, but he's a good cop."

Thursday, April 16th
1230 hours
LAPD Headquarters, Parker Center

Agent Rabson was out of the office. The bullet fragments taken from Williams' body during autopsy had been examined and the preliminary report was in. Captain Thompson assembled his detectives in the squad room. Forensic Pathologist Carl Fischer was giving the report, complete with the grisly photos taken during the autopsy.

"Well, gentlemen, here's *mein* report," Dr Fischer said in a heavy

German accent as he passed out copies of the document. "*Herr* Darius Williams was killed by two massive gunshot wounds to the head. There were two wounds of entry high up on the back of the skull to the right, about one-point-two millimeters apart. Upon entry, both projectiles exploded into numerous fiberglass *flechettes*. These proceeded to traverse the victim's brain. As you know, *flechettes*, being fiberglass, aren't readily detected on X-rays. These projectiles are called wad-cutters. They've been used often by professional assassins to cause maximum damage in their victims by tremendous hydrostatic displacement of tissue."

"Jesus Christ! You can kill a goddamned elephant with artillery like that," Thompson whispered to Baker.

The investigators shook their heads. Dr Fischer continued.

"There was a massive wound of exit at the top right of the skull. The numerous fragments, traveling at a high speed, carried roughly seventy percent of the subject's right cerebral hemisphere through the port of exit. In short, the man's head literally exploded." The doctor looked up and slowly surveyed the room, as if gauging the response of his audience. "Fragments of the metal jacket that enclosed the *flechettes* were retrieved from the dead man's skull. They were titanium. We had them subjected to neutron activation analysis. We faxed the results to the FBI laboratory in Washington to compare with those taken from the scenes of the Detroit and Philadelphia murders. We just received their reply. *Mein Herren*, they are a perfect match. The same weapon was used in all three killings."

"You're sure?" Thompson said, flipping through the report.

"*Genau*... uh, yes. The bullets used in the murders came from the same lot of ammunition, neutron activation analysis leaves no doubt. They are probably Russian or Eastern bloc. The weapon's rifling left identical marks on the projectile's jackets in the Detroit case and here. It's almost as good as a fingerprint... *Jawohl*, we are sure," Dr Fischer replied. He unconsciously kept lapsing into German. "That's *alles*, gentlemen."

Later in the day Rabson returned to LAPD headquarters. Brimming with nervous energy, he had a break, the first real solid lead in the case. He rushed into the captain's office.

"Sir," he said as Thompson turned around. "I took the liberty of having several of your uniformed officers distribute copies of the suspect's mugshots to various area hotel personnel, figuring that our assassin is probably hold up somewhere. I got lucky, well sort of lucky."

"What did you find out?" Thompson sat as Rabson pulled out a thick notepad.

"Officer Bidwell stopped at a Hyatt Hotel over in Inglewood and showed them to one of the clerks there. He recognized her immediately. She was in Room Two-Twenty-Four, under the name of, let's see, Kereluk. Ginger Kereluk," the agent said while reading from the scribbled notes.

"Hmm, that hotel must be one the busiest in the city… I'll bet they have dozens of guests in and out every day. Wonder how the clerk was able to remember her in particular," Thompson said in a skeptical reply.

"Apparently it was no trouble at all. He said that she was always complaining, a real bitch. Real attitude case. She was rude to the staff. Left the room in a mess… and no tip either. Bidwell also says here the clerk remarked that this Kereluk woman seemed glad about the Williams killing. She apparently kept making racist slurs during the riots."

Thompson suddenly looked up gravely.

"Wait, did you say, the Hyatt?"

"Yes sir. Is something wrong?"

Thompson leaned back in his chair.

"About an hour ago, Davies and Baker reported that they were at the Hyatt responding to a call. Apparently, this morning a janitor found the body of one of the black maids hidden under a pile of linen in a utility closet on the second floor... a dump job. Baker said her windpipe had been crushed. She had been strangled... Okay, anything else?"

Absorbing the information, Rabson continued. "The clerk told Bidwell that this Kereluk checked out around noon on Tuesday... And anyway, Kereluk is the alias she used last in the Detroit killing. I talked to Regional Director Jim Dumbrowski. He's sending over a print and photog team to the Hyatt. We must have gotten lucky. Room Two-Twenty-Four hadn't been rented out since the suspect left. The hotel staff was just getting ready to clean it when I got there. Finally, I had a hunch that she was heading for LAX, and I was right."

"Go on," Thompson grunted while pouring a cup of coffee.

"Most professional killers don't hang around long after a hit. I circulated the photos and the name around the terminals. It seems our suspect took a United flight, number eh, Seven-fourteen to Salt Lake City. She bought her ticket with cash," Rabson finished, closing the notepad.

"So, what's in Salt Lake?"

"Lot of white supremacist activity in the Provo area. There's a bunch of paramilitary crazies there who call themselves the Aryan Church of Yahweh or some nonsense like that. Maybe she's meeting her employer there, maybe she's going to do another hit, or maybe it's just her idea of a vacation. I'm going to contact the Bureau and our field office in Salt Lake." Rabson slowly began thumbing through the suspect's photographs.

"Well, while you were out, we got the preliminary autopsy report on the Williams' murder. Among other things, they concluded that he was killed by the same weapon used in some of the other slayings. A Russian sniper rifle," Thompson said. Rabson nodded sagely.

Friday, April 17th
0910 hours
LAPD Headquarters

Agent Rabson rushed into Captain Thompson's office. In his hand was a briefcase with documents he had picked up from the Bureau's Field Office. He had a satisfied look on his face.

"We got our break," the beaming FBI agent said, opening his briefcase and displaying its contents. He practically thrust some papers into the startled police captain's hands. "Our suspect has got a name. Jacqueline Diane Lynch."

Thompson glanced at the documents and looked up. "You're sure?"

"Our forensics people got several good sets of prints from the room she rented at the Hyatt. Ten- point masterpieces! They were sent to the Bureau overnight. I got the reply here."

Thompson again studied the documents.

"The prints were compared to those the Bureau has on computer file in our database." Rabson produced another document. "It seems our shooter has served in the Marines. And get this: her service record indicates that she had been an excellent marksman, rated expert sharpshooter. The suspect was an instructor at the Marine Corps Sniper School for a year and a half, a woman named Corporal Jacqueline Diane Lynch."

"So, what you're telling me is we're after a woman who's probably the most famous Marine sniper since Lee Harvey Oswald,"

Thompson said, rising from his desk.

"Wait, there's more," Rabson said, walking over to the other side of the desk. "Managed to phone one of the DI's at Camp Pendleton. He said that she apparently really hated blacks. Her service record here shows that she had been reprimanded twice for her conduct with black recruits; the Corps once even threatened her with a court-martial."

"Uh-huh."

"Director Longstreet has ordered me to proceed to Salt Lake City and coordinate the investigation from there. The Jack-L may have another assignment. We've got to try and find her before she makes another hit... It's been a pleasure working with you, Captain Thompson."

"And you... Hey, nail that murdering bitch for me!"

"Yes sir... I'll try," the agent said with a jaunty wave.

Saturday, April 18th
1040 hours
FBI Regional Headquarters, Salt Lake City, UT

It took Rabson's flight just under two hours to get to the capital of Utah, arriving at Salt Lake City's International Airport. He was looking forward to meeting the Bureau's Utah Special Agent in Charge Kelly. Tom Kelly, a towering figure at six-five, was part of the so-called "new FBI." Still youthful looking at sixty, Kelly was a no-nonsense investigator who had attained the position of Station Chief at the Salt Lake office two years earlier. He was one of only two African Americans to have reached this position within the Bureau.

"So Rabson, you think this Jacqueline Lynch character is in my neck of the woods?" Kelly said, examining the assassin's photograph.

"Yes sir, I do. She killed Williams in LA on the thirteenth, right after he addressed a church meeting. Head shots with a Russian sniper rifle. That much we know for sure. Left town on or about Tuesday, took a United flight into Salt Lake City."

"Yeah, I got your message… Well, she may be here for that big Hitler shindig being held at the Church of Yahweh Monday night." Kelly went to a file cabinet and returned with a plump folder marked *Aryan Church*. "It's going to be a hell of a big powwow I hear. Bureau Intelligence informs me that they got Klan, Nazis, skinheads, and other right-wing kooks coming from all over the country to celebrate Hitler's birthday on Monday."

"Oh yeah, Hitler's birthday… So, exactly what's with these people?" Rabson said, slowly shaking his head.

"They're a bunch of crazies who believe all that Hitler nonsense about race wars between them and the blacks and Jews, world coming to an end, you know, crazy, apocalyptic stuff like that," Kelly continued reading from one of the file's memos. "The people of Provo are getting tired of 'em. They're giving the place a bad name and all," he finished. He handed the memo to Rabson.

Rabson scanned the document and placed it on the desk. He cleared his throat. "Sir, I've heard about all the death threats."

There was a long silence as Kelly settled back in his chair.

"Agents from my office have had several run- ins with these people," Kelly said slowly, now leaning forward. "Last year back we managed to get old Malachi Hollander put away for killing two IRS agents in cold blood. He was being investigated for tax evasion. Hollander shot them both from ambush with a machinegun when they arrived for work at the Ogden office. An informant we had at the church fingered him. We got his ass up in Florence in Supermax, doing double life."

"All right, that helps. Anything else?"

"Well anyway, that must have pissed off a lot of his people in the Yahweh church. After all, Malachi is the church's founder. They just couldn't handle their leader being put away by a black guy. Before long, I started receiving the death threats. Nothing ever came of 'em. These assholes are just a bunch of cowards."

"Well, I'm wondering if this Lynch character is here on a hit." Rabson glanced down at the woman's photo. "Maybe those Yahweh crazies have put out a contract on you and she's the hitter."

Kelly stroked his chin, pondering the thought. "So, you think this woman was brought in here to kill me?"

"Maybe. We know that she's got at least nine hits already. These Werewolf assholes are natural killers. She's a professional assassin who obviously enjoys her work. We think she's already killed one FBI agent, just last year in Atlanta."

"Yeah, Abel Willis. I knew him. He did a rotation with me about five years ago, just before he got transferred to the Atlanta office… So, the Bureau thinks that she's the hitter?"

"Yes sir. All I'm saying is watch your back."

"Don't worry, I will," Kelly said in a reassuring tone. He got up and placed his arm on Rabson's shoulder. "The Bureau's got several agents watching my house and family… Besides, I grew up in an East St Louis ghetto with people a hell of a lot scarier than these clowns."

"I'm going to start distributing copies of this woman's mugshots to local law enforcement, get some more eyes out there working for us," Rabson said, gathering up the photos. Kelly watched him leave the office.

Code Name: Juggernaut

Holy War in The Heartland

"We will incite the people; we will lash them to a frenzy…"

— Adolph Hitler

"There is nothing more terrible than ignorance in action."

—Johann Wolfgang von Goethe

Monday, April 20th
2000 hours
The Aryan Church of Yahweh the Creator, near Provo, UT.

The chapel building itself was large; the inner walls, dimly lit with torches, were festooned with early American, Nazi and Confederate battle flags. At the front of the room stood an altar, imposing and monolithic. Upon the altar rested a bible, a revolver and a sword. Copies of the treatises of Joseph de Gobineau and Houston Stewart Chamberlain, as well as other white supremacist and anti-Semitic hate literature, all filled with gory details of Jewish "ritual sacrifice" and black savagery, lay stacked neatly to one side. Hanging on the wall behind the altar were large pictures of Jesus Christ, George Washington and Adolph Hitler. In front of the altar, stretching almost the length of the chapel lay neat rows of chairs. Outside, scowling guards, armed with AR-16 semiautomatic weapons and wearing camouflage fatigues with swastika armbands, stood stiffly at attention in the entrance. Above the chapel's entryway was a large sign with the word "JerUSAlem" printed starkly in black letters.

The doors opened. A large number of people began to assemble, eagerly awaiting the arrival of their leader. Earlier in the day there had been a large hate rally, with bombastic speeches and a barbecue which culminated with a book burning on the hill just overlooking the compound. This day marked a truly festive event: it was the gathering of the Aryan white tribes, the coming of the *Herrenvolk* — the Master Race, all having come together to mark the birthday of their spiritual leader, Adolph Hitler.

Among the seven hundred or so individuals present, were some of the most dangerous people in America. Misfits, hoodlums, thugs and just plain rowdies they represented the broad spectrum of the white supremacy movement: hooded klansmen of the *Konfederate Knights,* violent teenage neo-Nazi "skinheads" from the Salt Lake City-based *Aryan BoyZ* and *White Nation,* "Identity" Christians from Idaho and Utah, far right-wing survivalists from various citizen "militias," violent anti-tax protesters, white ex-convicts who had given their allegiance to racist gangs while in prison, and a group of desperate farmers in danger of losing their lands to foreclosure. Diverse in their backgrounds, all had come together with a common hate for African Americans, Jews, Hispanics, other minorities, homosexuals, radical feminism, the banking system, and, above all, the political leadership in Washington, DC, which they referred to as the "Zionist Occupation Government" or "ZOG."

While waiting, some of the racists discussed what they perceived to be growing problems in America: drugs, illegal immigration, big-city crime, the BLM Movement, affirmative action programs that gave "special rights" to blacks, gays and other minorities, various social welfare programs and a general moral decay as seen in the popular medium. Others passed the time before the meeting by telling racist jokes or casually perusing through the stacks of hate literature. All of the problems seemed to confirm the central message of the assembly: that the whole of American society was on the verge of collapse. In their own logic, this was the end result of what they referred to as the "World Jewish Conspiracy."

A woman arrived. She was clad in an elaborate white robe which bore the hooked cross of the swastika on the right arm. The frail, fifty-two-year-old brunette quietly took her place in a chair beside the altar. Her piercing, jet-black eyes slowly panned around the room, surveying the assembled throng. As if on cue, the people rose to their feet. With solemnity they acknowledged the appearance of their leader by extending their arms forward in the stiff Nazi salute and began chanting, "Hail Victory!" and "White Power!"

An avowed white supremacist, Dagmar Judith Hollander was as enigmatic as her church. A Colorado native, the ex-housewife had angrily pulled her daughter out of the Denver Public Schools when she once saw a picture of Martin Luther King, Jr. on the wall. She had become convinced that the public schools were "nests of immorality" preaching the doctrine of "race-mixing."

Several years earlier, she had written *The Aryan Manifesto: The Coming Race War in America*, *Yahweh's Way* and *Eternal Jew*, books which, by using biblical themes and symbolism, predicted the apocalypse as a futuristic racial bloodbath. In them, she espoused the notion that the world was ruled by a secret committee run by the UN, the Federal Reserve and the Jews. According to Hollander, this cabal planned a "New World Order Domination" through gun-control, abortion, taxes and racial miscegenation. To her, this conspiracy was the "beast" foretold in the Book of Revelation. In establishing her church, she and Malachi had admonished her followers that the Aryans must leave the cities, stockpile weapons and food, and prepare for the coming race war. According to Hollander, only the pure Aryan race — the "elect of Yahweh" — would survive the terrible tribulations and become rulers of the entire world. From humble beginnings, the ACYC now had metastasized into several additional chapters in Texas, Montana, West Virginia, Oregon, California and Idaho. Earlier during the year, it had even acquired a website on social media.

Extending her hands, Hollander softly motioned for quiet. The self-styled "Reverend Mother" was visibly moved by the spontaneous display of support from her congregation. A gifted speaker, she was about to give her greatest oration. Over seven hundred people, a large number of them children, had crowded into the chapel. Her message was a simple one: the time of the great tumult was near. As the room became quiet, she began to address the throng.

"Which way, Aryan man?" she opened. "We, the children of Yahweh are now at the crossroads. The battle with the Evil One is about to be joined. Is it our destiny to follow the path of the materialistic, socialistic, capitalistic Jew and all his degenerate doctrines of secular Humanism, abortion, communism, homosexualism, and mud-race-mixing miscegenation? Is this the path of the Aryan?"

"No! No!" the crowd thundered in response.

Hollander continued. "The subhuman mud races are degenerate beasts who our Lord Yahweh has cursed. Unwashed and impure, they carry AIDS, COVID, syphilis and other racial diseases. They are the mortal enemy of the Aryan and must be destroyed! However, the satanic Jew, whose mask is ZOG, teaches us that the colored races are our equals. The mud peoples our social, political, and racial equal! The false prophet states that we must sit down with them, break bread with them, send our precious children to school with them… sleep with them… Is this the way of the Aryan?"

"No! No! Kill the mud-niggers! Death to the niggers! Death to the Jews!" the frenzied crowd shouted, now howling for blood. "Persecute them all!"

Hollander continued, her voice becoming more guttural and harsher. She began pounding on the altar to stress her points. Beads of sweat glistened on her forehead.

"The corrupt Jew government in Washington known as ZOG — tells the Aryan that through all this communistic affirmative action garbage that we must be *replaced* and give our jobs and livelihoods to the coloreds and other mud races, that *you* labor to have your taxes stolen to support all the lazy minorities, illegals, faggots, queers and other human garbage through social welfare programs... Is this the way of the Aryan?"

Again, the crowd responded in the negative, now chanting in unison, "No! No! The Jew will not replace us! The Jew will not replace us! The Jew will not replace us!"

As her voice rose Hollander, like some avenging prophet, raised her forefinger high in the air, bringing it down in a sweeping motion. "ZOG spreads the lie of a so-called 'Holocaust', while at the same time it has perpetrated the greatest, most monstrous crime in all human history," she paused. "It is the Jew who has used abortion as the means of genocide to eliminate the most creative, intelligent and inventive race in history — the Aryan," she said, again raising the finger. "And yet at the same time they encourage the uncontrolled breeding of inferior peoples, as well as the polluting of the Aryan with the blood of non-Aryans. They have attempted, through illegal confiscation and gun control, to even deny us of our basic right to bear arms to defend ourselves. Finally, they force us to set aside a day to honor the communistic traitor *Martin Lucifer Coon*... Is this the path of the Anglo- Saxon-Teutonic Aryan?"

"No! No!" the throng roared in response. "They'll never take away our guns!"

Hollander was pleased that she was "finding the words." She matted the sweat from her forehead and continued.

"The Bible is a racist book. It's the ways of the pure Aryan race." She lifted the bible and revolver from the altar, raising them high above her head. "These are what made our people great... the Holy Bible and the gun! I ask you now, who is the Devil? Who is the Devil? *Wer ist der Teufel?*"

The crowd, now on its feet as one, responded in a savage, almost pagan frenzy of chanting, "The Jew! The Jew! Kill the niggers! Kill the satanic Jew!"

Having worked the crowd to a level of raw excitement, Hollander had arrived at the object of her diatribe. Her face was furrowed with hate and anger. "Tonight, our God Yahweh has brought us together for a sacred task. I tell you now that the end time is near. I call on you to prepare. Very soon our people shall be going into battle. The battle, as foretold by the Apostle John in the Book of Revelation. It will be a *holy war* unlike any in all of recorded human history. It shall be a struggle of epic proportion. A *holy war* of good versus evil. Light versus the darkness. A battle to save the last, best hope of mankind... our Aryan, Christian civilization from the inferior, ape-like subhuman mud races, as well as the despotic ZOG tyranny of the puppet Tel-Aviv Jew government in Washington!"

"It shall be as you say Reverend!" a fat woman in the back of the hall yelled. "This we swear to you!"

"Give 'em Hell!" another voice cried out, clenched fist raised in anger.

"In a swift stroke, the eternal mask of the Jew Devil... the rump ZOG-Jew government shall lay prostrate and helpless from our blow. It shall be a castrated giant. In the coming racial holy war, we, the Celts, Lombards and Teutons — the true Nordic Aryan tribes of Israel — shall take back the homeland that our God, Yahweh has promised our Aryan forefathers. This we must do for the sake of our children. We owe this to our ancestry as well as our posterity."

She momentarily stopped, waiting for the applause to die down.

She sipped some ice water. The audience was spellbound, completely in her power. She was again at the point of screaming, and had to pause, allowing her eyes to drift upwards, as if searching for divine guidance.

"The hour of sacred vengeance is near!" she roared. "It shall be as a great cleansing! Hear thy humble servant Oh Yahweh! We shall purge thy land with blood! On thy holy day of judgment, the filthy mud-nigger beast and the Jew Devil shall perish in a sea of blood! This we swear to you Oh Yahweh, Oh King of the Universe and Light of the Aryans! For thou art a mighty and terrible God!" She now raised a clenched fist. "We art thy terrible right hand… With thy right hand thou shall dash in pieces the enemy! We shall be the terrible, swift sword of Jehovah-Yahweh!" She now brought the fist against her open palm with a loud crack.

Hollander stepped in front of the podium, trembling, as if possessed by some demonic force. "My friends, we are… at war! We must slay the enemies of God! In this great struggle our creed is the depth of our hate… Our uniform is the color of our skin… and our weapon is the *Word* of Yahweh!" She again picked up the bible and waved it above her head.

The crowd was now again on its feet, arms thrust forward in the Nazi salute. Several of the women in the audience, overcome with emotion, fainted dead away. Like a skilled actress Dagmar Hollander had her audience utterly captivated. With her voice again rising, she delivered the cataclysmic finale.

"My Aryan brothers and sisters, hear me! The battle is nearly joined! Prepare thyself to strike! Strike the blow and Babylon-ZOG shall fall! In the name of *unser Aryan Volk*, Strike! In the name of your Aryan children's future… Strike! In the name of all of the sacred dead who have fallen for the freedom and salvation of our people… Strike! Finally, in the name of the immortal leader of our race Adolph

Hitler, whose blessed birthday we humbly observe today... Strike! *Meine lieber Aryan Volk, Sieg Heil!* Hail Victory! White Power! White Power! *Sieg Heil Adolph Hitler*!"

Concluding her address, Hollander thrust her arm out, returning the salute of the cheering throng. With a look of grim satisfaction, she lowered the arm and slowly left the podium. The woman waded into the crowd, basking in their adulation. The speech had been hypnotic; the racist throng followed her outside and exploded in a thunderous frenzy, chanting "White Power!", "Racial Holy War!" and "Hail Victory!" On cue, a massive thirty- five-foot cross was ignited. In a Wagnerian scene starkly reminiscent of the Nuremberg rallies, the pagan spectacle unfolded. Grown men and women, and small children among them, chanted as one. The spontaneous demonstration continued for nearly ten minutes before subsiding. As the meeting broke up, Hollander disappeared into the chapel office, exhausted but triumphant. This was her finest hour. The room, adorned with Nazi swastika and Confederate battle flags, was her private refuge. A large portrait of Adolph Hitler glared menacingly from the wall behind a massive oak desk. Inside the office a visitor was waiting. It was Jacqueline Diane Lynch.

"You spoke with such fire tonight Reverend Mother. Can anyone doubt our conviction and purpose? Our ultimate victory is assured. As you said, Babylon-ZOG will fall," Jacqueline said, hugging the Reverend.

"I think that it's wonderful to see such a people so alive with the Holy Spirit — the spirit of Yahweh. And they're all just so full of love for our people. It's just beautiful," Hollander said. "So nice to see you again, Jacqueline. I see that you had a little success the other night. Very good. Brother Howard will see you in the morning."

Monday, April 20th
2310 hours
Salt Lake City, UT

Jason Chalmers, Ariadne Beausoleil, Nick Hoover and Franklin Corbett were driving down a darkened street, dropping Quaaludes and chasing them with cheap wine. Earlier, the four teenage "skinheads" had been in attendance at the church's Hitler Rally. Now they were cruising "Nigger Town," looking for trouble. The men were all decked out in standard skinhead regalia: shaved heads, braces, faded jeans, bomber jackets adorned with SS runes and swastikas, Doc Marten "shitkicker" boots and razor- sharp knives that they called "nigger-stickers" and "coon-openers." High school dropouts, the skinheads were members of a violent racist gang. Just the previous night Corbett and Chalmers had beaten and knifed a homeless black man because of his race. The pair was "bummed" to learn later that their victim had survived.

Jason Nathan Chalmers, nineteen, a.k.a. "Skull-Head" and "NumbNutZ," had been arrested for ethnic intimidation in connection with a cross-burning at a black minister's home. He spent most of his days selling drugs, watching white power music videos or looking for black pimps he could beat up and rob. A hulking bodybuilder, the drifter and high school dropout had recently started a skinhead gang called *"Fascisti BoyZ"* in his native Utah. His girlfriend, Ariadne Tatiana Beausoleil, alias "Skin-Girl" and "Zyklon-(B)itch," had come a long way in her eighteen years. A runaway from a broken home in Slidell, Louisiana, the petite brunette drifter quickly adapted to life on the streets. By age seventeen, she had a lengthy arrest record for prostitution, shoplifting and assault.

Franklin Corbett had acquired the moniker of "Psycho" after recently killing a stray cat in a microwave oven. At twenty, he was the oldest. He already had an extensive police record for pimping, assault and drug possession. Corbett was a natural sadist. Tall and slender, like Cassius of Shakespearean drama, the Alabama-born Corbett had a cadaverous "lean and hungry" look about him. Finally, Nick Hoover, eighteen, called "Eight-Ball" by his friends, was a newcomer about to undergo initiation into the group.

"So, what do I have to do?" Hoover said, taking the wine bottle from Chalmers.

"If you want to join us, all new members gotta pass some tests we call the Terrible Terrors," Chalmers said in reply. "You know, to prove your loyalty to your race. To see if you're man enough to fight for your own kind, for Aryan people."

"I'm listening," Hoover answered, bolting down a swig of wine.

"Each time you complete a mission you get a number of points. When you get enough you become a full-fledged Aryan Warrior," Chalmers said, removing his jacket, revealing a skull tattoo on his massive left arm. "You get to wear a true badge of honor… the Skull-bone, the Blood and Honor Aryan Death Skull of the *Waffen-SS*."

"Yeah man, like last week me and NumbNutZ beat up some candy-ass faggot outside a gay bar. I just went ape shit on his ass. Wish I'd killed him now. Fucker probably had AIDS or some other fuckin' fag disease," Corbett interjected. "Last night, we fucked up some ugly black guy in an alley. You shoulda seen it. Kept stabbin' that nigger 'til my arm was tired."

"Too bad they both lived," Chalmers said in a tone of dejection. He took the wine bottle back from Hoover. "Got my Skull-bone couple months ago after wasting some black hooker chick. Stupid, skanky-assed bitch spat on me and called me a fucking Nazi. Ain't takin' that shit from nobody, especially no nigger. Wasted her ass… slit the ugly bitch's throat."

Corbett smiled. "We decided to take Skin- Girl out tonight… It's her turn."

The quartet turned onto a dimly lit street. Further ahead, they spied a young black man. Demetrius Bones had just finished his shift at a nearby convenience store and was now walking home, listening to rap music on his portable "boombox" CD player. After involvement with various local gangs and drugs, Bones was finally getting his life in order. But now fate had placed Demetrius Bones at the wrong place at the wrong time. Absorbed in his music, he failed to take notice of the green sports car stopped at the intersection behind him.

"Hey! There's a stinking nigger over there!" Chalmers rasped, pointing towards the youth. "Hey man, look over there... that's the reason you can't find a job. That fucking affirmative action shit! Jobs all go to his kind... 'cause of the color of his fucking skin!" he said, turning to Hoover. "How do you like that? Fucking niggers taking jobs from the white Christian man. They take food right outta the white man's mouth!"

"Yeah," Hoover said, nodding slowly in a detached, inebriated agreement.

"Hey Skin-Girl," Chalmers said, turning to Ariadne. "What about it? Wanna get back at all the fucking niggers who raped your kid sister back in Slidell? Now's your chance."

"Yeah... Let's get him! Let's cap his ugly black ass! Let me waste him! I want to do him!" Ariadne snarled, seething with hate and bouncing up and down on the back seat. The petite young woman was now suddenly emboldened by liquor and drugs. "It's my turn... Pull up over there."

"Yeah... It's Skin-Girl's turn!" Corbett said. He reached into his jacket pocket, producing a silver-plated thirty-two caliber semiautomatic handgun and a seven-shot clip.

"Skin-Girl, are you ready to carry out your holy mission... to eliminate all racial enemies of the Aryans?"

"I am!" the woman said in reply, trembling with anticipation.

"Swear to Yahweh your sacred racial allegiance! Recite the Twenty-One Words of the Sacred Aryan Blood Oath," Chalmers said with a penetrating leer.

Ariadne paused briefly, then gave her response.

"I know what to do and I know what is right… to fight the Jew Way and keep my land White!"

"Let's do it," Chalmers said, draining the wine bottle and belching loudly.

Corbett drove past the unsuspecting Bones and parked further up the street. He pulled the weapon's slide back, chambering a round with a hollow click. He handed it to Ariadne. She placed it in her purse and opened the car door. Clad in cut-off jeans, sandals and a black halter the slender young brunette was dressed to kill.

"Okay baby, ready to go coon hunting? You know what to do. We'll wait here and cover you," Chalmers said. "Just turn on the sex. Act like a hooker. You know what to do." Ariadne kissed him on the lips and slid out into the street.

"Oou-Oou-Oou-Oou! It's monkey-slapping time again! Do it Skin-Girl! Do it! Kill the black spear chucker! Race War! C'mon, if you won't do it for me, do it for Yahweh!" Corbett hooted as Ariadne sauntered out onto the sidewalk. With the provocative gait of an experienced hooker, she casually leaned up against a large tree as the black youth approached.

"Hey baby, wanna party with Skin-Girl?" Ariadne said in a low, sexy Cajun accent while furtively reaching into her purse. "Wanna get your wiener sucked? Wanna get a blowjob from a white girl? Wanna fuck me? Cost you thirty bucks."

"No baby. Not tonight," Bones said. He smiled.

"Then fuck you, nigger!" She turned and pulled the weapon out of her bag. Before the startled youth could react, the young woman pressed it against his groin and pulled the trigger. The pistol discharged with a loud crack. With a look of stunned disbelief, Bones grimaced and slowly collapsed to the ground, holding a bloody crotch. The bullet had plowed into his genitals.

"How do you like me now, huh nigger? You wanna rape me like my sister? How sexy am I now, huh? How sexy am I now?" Ariadne screamed, looming over the wounded man. Her heart was racing. "You don't look dead yet... Want some more?"

"No Jesus, No! Please," Bones yelped pitifully, spitting up blood. The black man curled in a fetal position, slowly writhing in agony. Ariadne took careful aim and fired again, this time hitting her victim in the face. The shot ripped into the roof of his open mouth, ricocheted off the hard palate and severed his brain stem. Bloody bubbles slowly gurgled up in a frothy foam from the gaping mouth wound.

"Nigger... Nigger! Nigger!" the woman screamed at the dying man, as she kicked the broken CD player into the street. "I hate niggers!"

"Skin-Girl, Come on! Leave him! Let's get the fuck out of here!" Chalmers yelled as his girlfriend ran back to the car.

"Fuck you, asshole nigger! White Power! Heil Hitler!" she yelled as the car screeched up the road. Startled local residents rushed into the street, attempting to assist the wounded man. Bones lay in the road in a rapidly expanding pool of blood, slowly bleeding to death. Thick puddles of coagulating blood slowly welled under his body. The man's heart was beating on automatic with an increasingly irregular pulse. By the time the ambulance had arrived on the scene it was too late. Paramedics pronounced Bones dead: Death by exsanguination. Ariadne Tatiana Beausoleil had passed her test. She had earned her Skull-bone.

"I seen it man!" an irate black man in the growing crowd yelled as the police arrived. "I seen it all. Couple motherfuckin' skinheads... white chick just shot the brutha. No reason... Just yelled 'niggah' and shot him like a dog in the street!" he said, motioning with his hand as if it was a gun.

"Yeah man... knocked him down, shot his ass dead! Bitch be yelling some crazy shit bout Hitler," another said. Others in the crowd slowly nodded in mute affirmation.

"Calm down please. Now can any of you describe the assailant?" one of the officers said while pulling a notepad and pen from his pocket.

"Skinny-assed, boney-butt white bitch. Dark hair... five-four... hundred-five pounds maybe. Wearing cutoff jeans and flip-flops... Honky bitch just shot him!" the first man said, quivering with rage. "Also saw couple skinheads... They was in a dark sports car!"

"Able to get a license or the car's make?"

"No man," the man said dejectedly, slowly turning away. "It happened too fast."

The police quickly went to work dispersing the crowds, retrieving the two spent shell casings and taking statements from other witnesses.

Laughing, the killers arrived back at Chalmers' "crash pad" apartment in time for the late local news. The lead story was of an apparently racially motivated drive-by slaying of a young black man. Under a large Confederate battle flag that hung loosely on the wall Corbett, Chalmers and Ariadne were all piled on a waterbed, snorting cocaine and feasting on beer and leftover take-out pizza.

"Holy Shit! You wasted that asshole! Hey Skin- Girl, you blew that niggah away! I mean fuck, it's on TV and shit!" Corbett said gleefully while listening to the news report. He began playing with the murder weapon.

Ariadne was delirious, laughing and in a cocaine-induced stupor, as she wolfed down a slice of pizza. "I killed a nigger! I killed a nigger! You see it? Pop! Pop! Shot him in the nuts! Put a bullet right in that ugly coon's balls! Blood all over him!" She smiled broadly. "Reckon I done got away with murder. Proud of what I done."

"Yeah baby, the fucking race war's begun! You're now a true Aryan warrior of Christ," Chalmers said. "Tonight, you struck a courageous blow for our people! Awesome, man!" The two men exchanged "high-fives" as Ariadne giggled hysterically.

Nick Hoover wasn't sharing in the celebration, however. A social misfit, he had joined the gang for free booze, drugs and chicks and just "to belong." While he had no use for blacks or Jews he wasn't into murder. As his friends partied and joked, he was in the bathroom, visibly sickened by his involvement in the killing. With a heave he vomited into the toilet. Corbett walked in.

"Hey man, what are you doing? Let's party! Skin-Girl wasted that nigger! He's fucking dead. She wasted his ass! They're showing it right now…on TV! Way Cool! That ugly nigger had his balls splattered all over the front of his pants!" Corbett said with a demonic, savage grin.

"I feel sick… Shit man, we just killed somebody," Hoover slurred, slowly shaking his head and wiping residue of vomit from his chin.

"Hey man, you a pussy or something? I mean, got to send a message," Corbett said, leaning against the door. "That was a wake-up call… now everybody knows they better not fuck with the White Nation."

"Shit Man, I didn't know you was gonna kill him," Hoover stammered, shaking uncontrollably.

"Better get used to it. That's what we're all about," Corbett answered, pulling out the murder weapon and twirling it around like a western gunfighter. "By the way, next time we go out, it's gonna be *your* turn... Are you ready to kill a coon?"

Now quivering in fear Hoover looked up and murmured, "Are you?"

Franklin Corbett returned a penetrating leer and said, "Fuck it, man, I already have. You're looking at hundred forty-six pounds of murderer. Me and my crew kidnapped some ugly ass homeless nigger last year. Bashed in his head with a fuckin' claw hammer. Went apeshit upside that motherfucker's head!"

Hoover's eyes flashed, transfixed in fear. Corbett continued. "That was back in Biloxi. We took his body out in the bayou. With the chainsaw. Made dog food outta that coon for my dog. Yep, Ol' Duke ate real good for a solid month!"

Corbett walked out. Pale and still trembling, Hoover turned back to the commode and vomited again.

Just before turning in that night Ariadne gleefully scribbled the day's events into her journal.

April 20: Jason got us some real good toot. Went to the big Hitler Unite the White rally at the church today. It was awesome! Went out later and killed me a nigger. I think we should do that again sometime. It was lots of fun!

The race war had begun.

Tuesday, April 21st
0845 hours
Aryan Church of Yahweh the Creator, near Provo, UT

Dagmar Hollander and Jacqueline Lynch were waiting in the chapel office when a man entered. With a ponderous gait of someone considerably older than his fifty-nine years approached the two women. Twenty-five years in the Air Force had left Howard Brennan physically broken. Almost completely gray, his face was without expression, a mask wizened with the frailty of premature aging. The stresses of his previous work had left him afflicted with a pronounced tachycardia and heart block, which in turn hobbled him with a potentially life-threatening hypertension.

Howard Brennan was a bitter, frustrated man. His life was falling apart. Besides a marriage that was clearly on the rocks, he had seen a promising career in Air Force nuclear weapons design ended because of his outspoken opposition to government policy: particularly that of the current administration. Two years earlier saw the now ex-colonel being cashiered by the president himself. To him, this was the government's thanks for years of service.

Having fled to Utah, he sat seething in his anger at the government. There, he became active in the Christian Identity movement and other white supremacist groups, finally gravitating to the Aryan Church of Yahweh the Creator. The distant Oklahoma City bombing in 1995 had been a real tonic to Howard. Recounting the details of the attack the terrorist bombing had given him an idea for "payback" to the government that had wrecked his health and destroyed his career.

Jackie watched Howard as he entered the room. Since his coming to the group the two had become lovers. After a seductive tryst she eventually became Howard's girlfriend. Now he had come to the church with a bizarre plan. In front of him lay a recent copy of the *Los Angeles Times* newspaper. On the front page was the screaming headline:

FBI PROBES MURDER OF CIVIL RIGHTS ACTIVIST
NINTH KILLING IN LAST SEVERAL MONTHS
NO BLACK MAN IN AMERICA IS SAFE

He momentarily scanned the front page and nodded in satisfaction.

"Impressive hit last week. That makes nine. Nine hits."

"Yeah. Asshole never knew what hit him."

"Like I said, impressive."

"It's like they say about the female of the species… That's why I really like the SVD sniper rifle. It's got lots of really good knockdown power. And the fucking cops don't know shit."

"You almost screwed up in Detroit though. Somebody saw you waste that black guy there. Should've killed that witness."

"Look, that wasn't my fault. Tried to kill him. But that lousy colored guy just ran too fast. Couldn't get off a shot. That's all… Understand that you got another job for me."

"Yeah, one that requires your uh, special talents and delicate touch." Howard slowly brought his finger to his lips. Upon hearing this, the hit assassin's eyes lit up. The thought of another murder so soon clearly had excited her.

"Who's the mark?"

"White guy named McClintock. George McClintock. Guy's a DOE official. He's head of security at Rocky Flats. I knew him when I was doing some work there several years ago." Howard handed the assassin a large packet. In it were several black-and-white photographs of George McClintock as well as information of his habits and last known address. She began to study the material.

"Hey, he's kind of cute... So, when do you want him hit, lover?"

"I don't want him hit! At least not yet. I want you to get some information from him. Get close to him. Seduce him. Sleep with him. Have sex with him. Fuck him. Anything it takes, but we need information about the present security conditions and location of nuclear material storage at the Rocky Flats facility." Howard slowly took the packet from her hands and placed it to one side. "It should be easy. Our people in Denver tell me that McClintock is in the process of getting a divorce. Just turn on the sex."

"Mmmm... Weaponized sex! Don't worry, there ain't a man alive I can't seduce," the svelte assassin said, licking her lips. Howard took her in his arms.

"I'll be in Denver on May twenty-fifth. I'll need the info when I arrive. I'll see you soon." They kissed passionately. Jackie departed from the office, passing Brennan's wife, Suzanne. They exchanged cold stares. Inside, Howard turned to Reverend Hollander.

"There, I've just set in motion the events that are going to bring down this corrupt government. Jackie won't fail. She's the best in the business." Leaving the room, he passed Suzanne without a word.

It was nearly closing time at the Red Dog Lounge, a seedy dive of a bar at the corner of Colfax and Broadway. There, amid the usual flotsam and jetsam of drunks and losers sat George David McClintock. For the last year and a half, McClintock's life had been steadily falling apart, a living hell. Aside from the considerable pressures of being the head of security for the Rocky Flats Nuclear Facility he was in the midst of a very ugly divorce from his wife, Theresa. Indeed, the divorce had become a financial bloodbath in itself: as compensation for fifteen years of a stormy marriage Theresa McClintock now expected half of her husband's present assets plus maintenance payments.

Her lawyer, a divorcee herself, wasn't taking any prisoners. In addition, his own attorney's fees had at $250 an hour, already run into thousands of dollars. As a final insult, in order to get away from Theresa, George McClintock had finally moved out of his house and rented a cheap apartment in the crime-ridden Capitol Hill section of town.

His work at "The Flats" added yet another layer of frustration. As the Head of Security at the facility, he oversaw a shrinking budget and a sullen staff. Morale among his subordinates was never lower. *And why not?* he thought. It was an open secret that Rocky Flats would eventually close like all those other military facilities.

Depressed, George McClintock had become withdrawn from friends and family members. He found himself spending more and more time at the Red Dog. Detached from life it had become his only refuge, his last pleasure. The bartender and alcohol were fast becoming his only companions. George once seriously thought about hiring someone to kill his wife but couldn't bring himself up to it. At forty-eight, it seemed that he had hit rock bottom. He was depressed. He was broke. He was vulnerable. He had just finished his third drink when he heard a woman's voice behind him.

"Excuse me mister, but is this seat taken?"

Startled, George turned around. A slim woman was standing behind him. She had shoulder-length blonde hair that looked almost like silk, so fine was the texture. At about five feet, eight inches tall in a slinky black, backless leather blouse, matching miniskirt and stiletto "fuck-me pumps," she seemed like an oasis admit the human flotsam huddled in the bar.

"No not at all. Please sit down," George stammered, clumsily removing his jacket from the stool. "May I buy you a drink?"

"That would be nice… Vodka martini, dry," the woman said as

she sat down next to him.

"Bartender, a vodka martini for the lady," he snapped authoritatively, recovering his composure.

"Right away George," the bartender said, turning to the counter and smiling sheepishly.

The pair spent the next several hours at the bar talking. It seemed odd to George that all the conversation was centered about him: his work at the Flats and the ongoing divorce. The woman, while revealing little about herself, appeared impressed. Around midnight the couple left together as the bar was closing.

"I just realized that we haven't been introduced. Uh... I'm George. George McClintock. Listen uh, you're not seeing anybody, are you? Maybe we can see each other again," George said. His tone was almost pleading.

"Hi George, my name is Jacqueline. *Available* Jacqueline," the woman said smiling, drawing up close and gazing into his eyes. She took George's hand and pressed it firmly against her breast. "Listen, you want to be alone tonight, George? Neither do I. Do you want me, George? Do you want me now? Do you want to go to bed with me? Let's go to your place where we can *do it*."

The pair walked slowly down Colfax Avenue toward McClintock's apartment. There they made love into the night. George thought that perhaps his luck had finally changed.

Monday, May 4th
0835 hours
Aryan Church of Yahweh the Creator, near Provo, UT

"Excuse me, Reverend Mother. I have a problem," Nick Hoover said, gently tapping on the door and peeking into the chapel office.

"Yes?" Hollander answered, looking up from her work. She

motioned for him to enter the room. "You're Brother Hoover, right?"

"Yeah… Reverend Mother, I don't like blacks and all, but it's about that guy Skin-Girl killed. I mean, he wasn't doing nothing, just walking down the street. She just shot him," Hoover mumbled in a rambling monotone.

"Brother Hoover, please don't bother me with this. I'm working on next Sunday's sermon. You must realize that we are at war with the forces of darkness. We must slay the enemies of Yahweh. You knew this when you joined our little community. Accept what has happened as the will of Yahweh."

"I joined 'cause I didn't want to be forced to mix with the other races and all. But I don't think that we should kill 'em for no reason! We should leave 'em alone!"

"Don't you raise your voice at me, young man," Hollander said, now rising from the desk. "You call it murder? The elimination of the enemies of Yahweh is not murder. It's an act of faith. Part of the great cleansing foretold in scripture. Whatever Sister Beausoleil has done was the work of God. Now if you can't accept the will of Yahweh then I suggest that you—"

"I don't think we should just kill 'em for nothing!" Hoover repeated, somewhat surprised at himself to be arguing with the church elder. A small crowd had gathered, attracted by the commotion inside the chapel.

"Brother Hoover," she said softly. "You're obviously confused. You've been listening to the ZOG-controlled media. Don't believe all their damned lies. You see, that's what makes the Jew so dangerous. They're all so crafty… and cunning," she finished, placing her hand on Hoover's shoulder. The youth's head dropped.

"Let's not speak of this again," she said soothingly. Hoover turned and shuffled out. Watching the youth leave Dagmar Hollander gestured to one of the church members, a tall, muscular blond. The man had a chiseled, cat-like face. Massive arms covered with racist tattoos, he caressed a large truncheon, almost lovingly, as one would hold a small dog.

"Brother Hoover is showing weakness. Follow him. Keep an eye on him. I don't trust him. See where he goes and who he talks with," Hollander said to the husky member of the congregation.

"What if he strays from the fold, Reverend Mother?"

Hollander pursed her lips and looked away.

"If he strays from the fold, he shall have to be disciplined in accordance with the laws of Yahweh… Just like what you and the others did with that traitor Leach. We don't need problems here."

"I understand. It shall be as you say, Reverend Mother." The man turned and left the room. Hoover realized that he was in trouble; he noticed that his friends had suddenly begun to avoid him. Others looked at him with silent contempt or just turned away. He was frightened.

Saturday, May 16th
2033 hours
The Red Dog Bar, Denver, CO

Jackie and George had been dating for two weeks. Their relationship seemed to have blossomed into a full-blown romance. Jackie, aware of her assignment knew that she didn't have much time. Howard was due to arrive in Denver in nine days. Meeting George at the Red Dog, she was determined to make her move. She was waiting in one of the booths as her date arrived.

"George, uh, I have a favor to ask of you," she said as he sat down.

"Sure sweetheart, anything," George said. He smiled.

"Gee, how do I ask this?" Jackie pondered. She rolled her eyes around the room. "I represent an environmental awareness group called *Earth First,* and we decided that we want to hold a protest rally at Rocky Flats."

"You want to do what?"

"We want to come on base and hold our rally! It would be a protest against the conditions there and the government's slow response to cleaning up the facility," she said, pouting.

"But Jackie, the plant is off limits to all unauthorized personnel. You know that."

"But aren't you Chief of Security there? All that we would want is to come inside the gate and conduct a peaceful demonstration. That's all… If you loved me, you would do it. We have no right to poison this planet. That place is poisoning the environment, animals, all of the small children. Don't you even care?"

"Listen. I can't. So let's drop it."

"You make it sound like we're a bunch of Russian spies or something! I mean, the Cold War is over… besides, we could make it worth your while." Jackie slowly began rubbing George's hand. Looking into George's eyes she realized that statement hit a receptive chord. As things were, he had just received another bill from his lawyer earlier in the day concerning the ongoing divorce.

"What do you mean by that?"

"The group I belong to has lots of money. It would be worth it if we could get on base to hold our rally for the TV cameras. Besides, I would be very grateful. More grateful than you could ever imagine," Jackie replied smoothly, gently caressing his cheek. She could sense that the man's greed had been stimulated.

Perhaps there is a way to get out from all these money problems.

And besides, she's right. The place is a mess, a real shithole. If only it could be done right, he thought to himself. "I'll think about it Jackie. Maybe you're right. Perhaps something like this could be pulled off. Maybe a little publicity like that could stir up those assholes in Washington to do something about that place… How much worth my while?" he said. Jackie simply smiled. She knew the fish had been hooked and was ready to be reeled in.

Deus 'Sex' Machina

"...The female of the species is more deadly than the male..."
—Rudyard Kipling, from *The Female of the Species*

"*Cher-chez la femme*" ("Look for the woman")
— French expression

Monday, May 25th
1130 hours
Denver International Airport

Howard had arrived in Denver after having had a miserable flight. The plane was almost thirty minutes late, a stewardess had accidentally spilled a cup of hot coffee over him and, much to his chagrin, a large, very loquacious black man had been assigned the seat next to him. *It just ain't my day,* he thought.

A beaming Jacqueline Lynch was waiting for him at the terminal. Everything was going according to plan. For the past several weeks, Jackie had been dating George McClintock. Her seduction was nearly complete.

"Welcome to Denver," Jackie said, warmly embracing her boyfriend. "How was your flight, lover?" The couple walked over to a rental car at the curb.

"Don't ask... So, what's the status of our little project? Our people in Salt Lake have been all over my ass for information. Have you got the stuff from that McClintock guy yet?" Howard was noticeably on edge.

"Not yet. He's primed. McClintock's going to cooperate, but I think I'll need another day or two." Jackie said, fixing her hair in the rearview mirror.

"I need it now! We can't wait. I—"

"Look Howie, I do things my way! Now I said I'd get you what you want shortly. I said it'll take another day and I meant it. So don't fuck with me, okay? I really don't need this shit."

"Well, what's all this about an extra ten grand?" Howard said, attempting to change the subject.

"McClintock says he'll do it if we give him twenty grand. That bitch he's divorcing is really taking his ass to the cleaners. She ain't going to leave him with a pot to piss in. He wants twenty grand out of the deal. The stupid asshole's desperate. I've already given him the first installment... Have you got the rest of the money?"

Howard pulled out a bulging suitcase. In it were several large envelopes, each containing one hundred crisp $100 bills. "Guess the price of treason doesn't come cheap," he muttered while placing the envelopes in Jackie's purse.

"Don't worry lover, I'll take care of your money. I'm meeting McClintock tomorrow night at the Hyatt Regency at the Tech Center. I'll get the stuff you want. That fool actually thinks that I'm some environmentalist wanting to hold a rally at the Flats. I'm going to have to take care of McClintock my own way... Listen, uh, I'm sorry that I was such a bitch, okay? I've just been uptight lately," she said in a low voice. "I'm glad this assignment is almost over."

"Thought you enjoyed this kind of work."

"Not with this McClintock asshole," she sighed. "Jeez! He's nothing but an over-sexed claw machine. I swear it's just like sleeping with an octopus. You know, I think the dumb fucker has actually fallen in love with me."

"Well, that is the idea."

The pair drove through Denver. As they turned onto Colfax Avenue, Howard observed some depressing signs of what he considered the moral and racial decay in the country: a scantily-clad black prostitute was standing on the street trying to "turn a trick," desperate for some "crack money," while in an alley a drug deal was hastily being concluded. Further up the street an alcoholic staggered about, having casually just urinated in the gutter, oblivious to his surroundings. An elderly Hispanic lady stood on the curb, doing a brisk business selling burritos from a vendor's wagon, while two youths were arguing with each other in Spanish. The little market on the street corner was almost completely covered with gang graffiti. Driving along he was further disgusted upon seeing that many of the local shops and businesses were Mexican, Ethiopian and Vietnamese restaurants.

"There! Now you see what sixty years of integration and all that diversity bullshit have done to this country. Goddamned race-mixers! Nothing but colored pimps, illegal aliens, faggots, hookers, bums, drugs, disease! Makes you sick! I swear, it's like being in an African city. You can see where we're heading… Straight to Hell!" Howard ranted angrily, pounding his fist against the car's dashboard. "You give the White Man a pile of bricks and in no time he'll build you a great city… You give the colored races a city and they'll leave you a pile of bricks."

"Yeah, bummer. Everything the mud races and Jews touch turns to shit!" Jackie replied, turning her head in time to see a bearded, elderly man wearing a black yarmulke waiting at the bus stop.

"Well don't worry, shortly we're gonna shake things up a bit. Get this country back on track! Once we get the stuff from McClintock, we're gonna take this country back. All of it! Pretty goddamned quick!"

While stopped at a traffic light, a black teenager driving a sports car pulled up beside them. Loud rap music was blaring from the speakers while the youth's head slowly bobbed to the beat of the music.

"Take a look at that goddamned ugly chimp over there!" Howard snarled as the light changed. "Ignorant, nappy-headed monkey... Probably stole that sports car." He made an obscene gesture with his middle finger as the youth drove on.

Later, the couple arrived at a Holiday Inn Hotel in north Denver and checked into room two- thirteen under the name of Clement. While unpacking, Howard reached into his suitcase and pulled out one of Jackie's mugshots.

"I want to show you something. Ever seen this?" Howard handed her the picture.

She studied it for several seconds and smiled. "That's my mugshot. From Atlanta, when I was tricking for Dave couple of years back... Boy, I sure looked like shit back then... Where'd you dig up this old relic?"

"Skin-Girl was busted again for DUI last week in Salt Lake. While the cops had her downtown, she saw several of these lying around the station. She stole one of them when they weren't looking. She got it to us when they turned her loose... We may be in trouble."

"Oh shit! Great! How the fuck did they find me?" she said in disbelief. "I covered my trail."

"Our people did some checking," Howard said, taking the photo from her hands. "It seems some FBI agent named Rabson has been passing out copies of these around in the Salt Lake area." He sat down on the bed beside her. "What gets me is that this asshole apparently even knows your name. ZOG is on to you. They must also know about the Williams hit. You must've screwed up somehow."

"That's bullshit! No way Howie!" she said, forcefully shaking her head. "No way I screwed up! I'll bet the FBI has a rat in JerUSAlem who fingered me. It's a standard ZOG tactic. You know, that's how those assholes operate."

"Hmm. You may be right," Howard said, slowly nodding in agreement. "The Church rooted out one ZOG agent about six weeks ago, just before you got there. There may have been another. It's good that you were here in Denver for the last few weeks, but they may come looking here, especially if ZOG has a spy in JerUSAlem."

"Well, if this Rabson guy gets too close, my little friend here will be ready for him," Jackie said, slowly raising her skirt to reveal a single-shot, twenty-two caliber derringer, strapped to her thigh with a lacy black garter.

"Very sexy, Jackie."

"*Very deadly,* Howie. Explosive twenty-two caliber, Teflon hollow-point, with a magnum load. Remember, I've already killed one FBI agent, so another one don't mean shit." The couple finished unpacking and relaxed in their room.

Tuesday, May 26th
2215 hours
Denver Hyatt Regency Hotel, Room 1412

Coming straight from work, George McClintock arrived back at the room he rented earlier. He was carrying a thin leather valise. Overlooking the atrium, the room he selected was one of the more expensive ones. There, one had an excellent view of the mountains. He nervously opened the suitcase, examining the documents inside. They were all marked **TOP SECRET**.

Better know what I'm getting into, he thought, flipping through the papers. In addition to a map of Rocky Flats, there were photocopies of detailed shipment schedules for nuclear weapons transport from the facility. *If I get caught it's not only my job… it's jail.* He pulled out the map of the sprawling facility.

"Wonder why Jackie's group needs all this info…? Crazy environmentalists," he muttered to himself. "Fuck do I care… long as she's got the rest of the twenty grand and my ass don't get caught. Anything to end this divorce and get away from Theresa."

There was a soft knock at the door. George placed the map back in the valise and nervously looked through the peephole. Relieved to see his girlfriend, he slowly opened the door. Jackie entered, carrying a large briefcase and purse. She was stunning, wearing the same black leather miniskirt and stiletto heels that she wore when they first met at the bar.

"Hello lover, you got something for me?" the woman murmured with a sexy grin. George placed the valise on the table. Opening it he began spreading the papers in front of her.

"I had a hell of a time stealing all this shit. Jesus Christ, this must be quite a rally your people are planning," he said. Jackie carefully began examining the contents.

"We got to get a few things straight first. The ground rules." George slowly took the papers from her hand.

"I'm listening."

"I'll arrange for you to get in. You and your people are going to remain near the fence. Keep away from the Weapons Storage Area," George said forcefully. He began pointing out the location on the map.

"What are all these buildings?" Jackie pointed to a cluster of structures near the east gate.

"That's the Plutonium Processing Area… Off limits, *comprende*? You can't go near there… Don't even think about it," George said, slowly waving his finger in Jackie's face. The woman slowly nodded, taking in all the information.

"Don't obstruct normal plant operations. Hold your little protest in front of the cameras and leave… Agreed? Now I've got to get these maps back to the Flats before they're missed."

"You're very thorough. My people will be impressed. Our rally is going to be great. And it's all thanks to you."

"And another thing, this rally can't happen around the eighth of next month. We got a big shipment heading out to Amarillo then. I don't want your people in the way"

"Not a problem. We want to go on the third."

"Good… Okay. It's all here. I kept up my part of the bargain. Now where's the rest of my money? Ten big ones," George said, rubbing his hands together. His eyes were fixed on Jackie's briefcase.

Jackie dropped the satchel and slowly unbuttoned her blouse and miniskirt, striking a seductive pose.

"There's plenty of time for that later… It's such a beautiful night, maybe we can find a way to kill a little time first."

"Bullshit! First the goddamned money… We can fuck later," he said. With that, Jackie, now livid, opened her briefcase and flung the two large envelopes with the $100 bills at George's head.

"And all the time I thought you loved me! Here's the rest of your fucking money, asshole! Ten grand… Fuck you!"

George bent over and picked up the envelopes, inspecting the contents. He felt bad over what he had said. Apologetic and contrite, he went over to the woman, gently caressing her shoulder.

"Look baby, I'm sorry. My damned nerves are shot. Theresa's lawyer is really playing hardball with the divorce. They're cleaning me out. I guess I'm just getting uptight 'cause I need money. You understand. Besides, I'm a little nervous about taking all this stuff. I kept thinking my secretary was watching me while I was taking all this. I don't want to lose my job."

"George, did you fuck up? Did anybody see you?"

"No. Nobody suspects. Everything's cool…Listen, I ain't been out of my shoes in twenty-four hours. You wanna get laid?" He stared at Jackie's open blouse.

"Wait here for a minute, lover. Let me get comfortable, okay?" Jackie sashayed provocatively toward the bedroom, slowly performing an erotic striptease. George meekly followed, finding the woman's miniskirt and heels lying on the floor leading to the bedroom. Just inside the doorway he retrieved the woman's blouse. There, stretched out on the bed and slowly rubbing her crotch, lay Jacqueline Lynch, clad only in a lacy garter and bikini panties. She slowly peeled the bikini, playfully tossing it into the man's face. He took notice of the grotesque Death's Head tattoo on her left shoulder.

"I've been meaning to ask you, what the hell's that hideous thing for?"

"You like it? That's from when I was in the Marines… As you can see, I'm not carrying any concealed weapons." Jackie propped herself up on the bed. "What's the matter Georgie? You've seen me naked before… I feel erotic. C'mon, I want to feel you in me. It's such a beautiful night. Open the window for me, lover. I want to feel the night air coming in from off of the balcony. Let me send you to heaven… Make love to me…Rape me."

"Let's do it."

George opened the heavy sliding door that led to the balcony, feeling a warm gust of air on his face. He gazed out, momentarily looking at all the traffic far below. *That's quite a drop,* he thought to himself.

He went back inside to the nude woman. Overcome with raw desire, he slowly opened his pants and climbed on top of her, savagely kissing and caressing Jackie's large breasts. She slowly enveloped him with a muscular leg as the bed swayed rhythmically back and forth.

"Ohhh… that's right lover, stick it in me," Jackie moaned. "Do it hard! Ah yes! Do I feel good to you, lover?"

George merely grunted in reply, nuzzling her moist, soft nipples. Locked in a passionate embrace, he didn't take notice as his paramour furtively reached under the pillow.

"Ohhh… Ah! That's it! Stay hard! Easy lover… Now wait for me. Wait for me! Ah… Yes! Yes! I love you," Jackie moaned in an orgasm as she pierced the side of the man's neck behind the ear with a tiny hypodermic syringe, injecting an oily substance into the base of his neck. George spontaneously ejaculated and recoiled violently from the sharp pain.

"Ah! Bitch… Pussy's claws are sharp… You like it rough? You wanna get raped, huh bitch? Wanna get fuckin' raped?" George snarled, grasping the side of his neck. "Little cat-bitch… scratched me, it's not nice to scratch."

"Oh, did poor Georgie get scratched? Here, let Mommy make it better." Jackie kissed him on the lips.

The primal lovemaking continued for a minute while the assassin waited for her venom to take effect. Slowly, George began to feel light-headed and dizzy. In an instant he began noticing a tingling sensation in his hands and feet, followed by a creeping numbness. Realizing that something was terribly wrong, he tried to push away from the woman, scratching her shoulder in the process.

"Was it good for you too, lover? Get off of me!" She pushed the now paralyzed man to one side and got up.

"What the fuck's happening to me? I... can't... move! Please...Help me," George slurred softly as he stiffened on the bed, suddenly overcome by a strange paralysis. For a moment he thought that he had just suffered a stroke. He was fully conscious, but completely immobilized. Out of the corner of his eye he could vaguely make out Jackie putting the syringe into her purse. The nude woman loomed over him. Slipping back into her bikini panties the assassin spoke to him softly.

"Poor Mr. McClintock. You're my bitch now. It's a pity that you have to die, but you're of no further use to me. I kill people for a living. I'm what you might call a hitwoman, a torpedo for a white organization that calls itself the 'Werewolf.' My boyfriend and me are going to steal some plutonium from your facility. You know Howard Brennan, you worked with him... We're going to build a bomb."

She sauntered over to the doorway, retrieving her shoes and miniskirt.

"Poor George. You're paralyzed... You can see, hear... and you can feel. But you can't move. You see, I drugged you with a little something that leaves you helpless. The drug lasts about ten minutes and is very difficult to trace."

George was completely limp and pale. The man's breathing became shallow and labored as the drug began to paralyze his diaphragm. Gasping for breath, he felt he was suffocating. His eyes were glazed over, but filled with terror. Jackie retrieved her blouse.

"You've been a very naughty little boy tonight George... Look at this mess you're making all over yourself... and these clean sheets." She knelt beside the terrified man. "Bad, bad George! You're going to have to be punished." Jackie slowly rose to her feet and walked around the other side of the bed.

"You actually thought I was in love with you… You dumb fuck, I used you!" She gently caressed his forehead.

"You know, I could castrate you right now," she said tauntingly with a laugh, now stroking his testicles. "That would be fun… cut your balls off… and watch you slowly bleed to death all over the bed." She now grasped his still erect penis. A volcanic eruption of thick semen pulsed out of the organ onto his stomach, before rolling onto the sheets.

"But no. Your death has to look like an accident… or suicide." She again reached into her purse, this time removing a small flask of whiskey. "I've got it! You were so depressed about the divorce you started screwing some cheap Colfax hooker, got drunk, and fell over the balcony while she was giving you a blowjob. Or maybe when you're found, everyone will think that you simply couldn't take it anymore. That you committed suicide because of the divorce from that bitch Theresa."

She slowly unscrewed the cap. "Don't worry, it's going to be quick. I'm gonna throw you over the balcony. Over one hundred and fifty feet… straight down to the pavement. You'll be able to see everything. I really hope you enjoy your flight." She slowly began pouring the liquor on George's clothing and inserted the bottle in his pocket.

"I'm so sorry George, but the Werewolf wants no survivors to tell tales… By the way, I think you're a lousy lover." She gently closed his pants, kissed him on the lips and slowly dragged him over to the balcony.

By the time Denver Police had arrived at the hotel, a small crowd of people had already gathered around the prostrate figure that lay in a bloody heap on the pavement. It was George McClintock. He had fallen fourteen floors to his death, narrowly missing an elderly couple that had just passed by and crashing head-first onto the asphalt at ninety- five feet per second — roughly sixty-five miles an hour. A thin rivulet of blood and brains slowly traced a convoluted path from his shattered skull into the street. Witnesses told the police that upon impact, his head had split open like a slaughtered animal. While his partner questioned members of the assembled crowd a patrolman took note of the victim's ID, covered the body with a sheet and radioed in the report.

"One-Bravo-Six to Central Dispatch, be advised we're at the Hyatt Regency. Looks like we got a jumper here. A birdman... One middle-aged, male Caucasian... very dead... Drunk as a skunk from the looks of it. Guy named George McClintock. He really made a mess... Christ Jesus! He's all over the sidewalk."

Another policeman arrived and began the grim task of laying a spool of bright yellow tape with stark black lettering labeled **CRIME SCENE — DO NOT CROSS** around the body while a departmental camera crew began shooting black-and-white photos of the deceased. An ambulance pulled up; the corpse was placed on a gurney and carefully removed. As the crowd slowly dispersed, a svelte blonde woman in a black leather miniskirt strolled by. She was carrying a valise.

"What happened here?" she said to an elderly lady in the shrinking crowd.

"It's horrible. I — think that some poor man must've jumped out of a window and killed himself or something. Suicide," the frail woman stammered in reply.

"How tragic. What a pity." Jacqueline Lynch walked around the corner to where she had parked the rental car. In an instant, she loaded the stolen documents on the back seat and drove off into the night.

Wednesday, May 27th
0830 hours
Holiday Inn Hotel, Room 213, Denver, CO

Howard was listening to the local morning news on the radio, having taken a break from studying the stolen diagrams. Jackie came in from her morning jog and started preparing breakfast in the hotel room's makeshift kitchen.

"I did your thing for you last night. Sorry about George. He fell," Jackie said, smiling.

"Yeah, I just heard it on the news. The damn stupid cops think it was a suicide. That he jumped out the window. How'd you do it? You fuck him?"

"Yeah, fucked his brains out... Poor Mr. McClintock, I drugged his ass with that whatever- you-call it shit. It works real good. I did it while we was doing the nasty in bed. No one will ever know."

"Pavulon...curare...methoxetamine...succinylcholine chloride... and ketamine. Goddamned animal tranquilizers. Well, they'll be hard to trace," he said, nodding thoughtfully.

"And then I gave him some flying lessons. Off the fucking balcony... fourteen floors. He hit the pavement. Headfirst. Whoosh... Splaaaat! You should have seen it. His brains were all over the sidewalk. The cops'll think he committed suicide." The sexy assassin cracked an egg into a frying pan.

"Why'd you have to waste him? I thought I told you I didn't want him hit yet. Why'd you kill him?"

"Because I wanted to," she said with a shrug. "Told you I was going to take care of him my own way. You know how I operate... seduce and destroy." She kissed Howard's forehead. "He knew too much... Did you know McClintock was under surveillance? I mean, his own secretary was watching him like a fucking animal in the zoo. So, I just killed him, while we were doing the *mattress mambo*... I had to. That's all. Besides, I got you your money back." She reached down into her purse and retrieved the envelopes. Howard greedily fingered through the cash.

He managed a smile.

"Are you sure that McClintock's death will standup as a suicide? Remember, we're at a critical stage. We don't need no cops."

Jackie removed her windbreaker and sat down in Howard's lap. "Everything's taken care of, Sweetie. I wasn't wearing any lipstick, make-up or perfume. No way they can tell a woman did it. I drugged him behind the ear... They'll never find it. Got rid of the syringe. No one will ever know. So don't be so uptight." Jackie began gently caressing Howard's cheek. "Made it look like he got drunk and killed himself. Relax, Mommy has taken care of everything."

Howard took notice of the deep scratches on her arm. "Well, what happened to your shoulder?"

"Oh, it's nothing, that lousy fucker just scratched me when I drugged him." Jackie slowly rubbed the sore spot on her arm. She got up as her paramour began again sorting through the papers.

"Well, McClintock was very thorough. The maps you stole are excellent. They show the location of plutonium storage, tamper material, even the beryllium/polonium neutron initiators. All the ingredients we'll need to make a thermonuclear trigger. Good."

"Huh? Uh, right."

"Also, the complete layout of their security arrangements and shipment schedules... Impressive. You did a good job."

"Thanks. Now why don't we discuss my fee?" Jackie began removing her shoes. Like a dominatrix the seductive woman planted her foot on his lap, revealing a lace bikini through her jogging shorts. "Wanna get laid? You can fuck me now. Come on lover, I feel sexy… Do me right here. Right now… On the floor."

The couple got up and moved to the center of the room. "You know I always like to have sex right after I've killed someone. Besides, that bitch you married doesn't love you. You don't love Suzanne. Why don't you just divorce her. Then we can be together…Take your clothes off… Rape me." Howard slowly opened her blouse.

"No. Don't unbutton it… Rip it off!"

"I like it when you talk like a slutty little sexpot. You know it gets me all excited… The last guy to get laid by you don't feel so good though. He lost his balls… fell off a balcony I hear."

"Fuck you Howie… You think you can handle a castrating bitch like me?" Jackie began playfully spanking her bottom and threw her jog bra and panties into the corner.

The pair slowly finished removing their clothes. Sexually aroused, Jackie gently began rubbing up against his body, moaning in ecstasy. She quivered with raw excitement, collapsing into her paramour's arms. In an instant, her body was slippery with saliva, sweat and semen.

"Ah…Your nails are sharp. That's right, scratch me, little Aryan sex cat."

"Yes. Scratch out your eyes!"

"Do you feel my power? White Power. Our strength comes from our sacred Aryan blood… and our white skin. Yesterday, you took a man's life…now you must replace what you have taken. It is the Will of Yahweh…Give me your sexy Aryan body to enjoy."

Howard hungrily began suckling Jackie's large breasts while in the background a love song was softly playing on the radio. By the time the song had finished, the couple's clothing lay in a pile on the floor. So did Howard and Jackie. Sexual combat. The couple spent the next several hours making love like a pair of crazed animals.

Thursday, May 28th
1545 hours
University Hospital, Forensic Pathology Dept., Morgue, Denver, Colorado

Doctors Madeline Cain and David Parker had completed their preliminary examination of tissues taken from McClintock's corpse. What initially appeared suicide now suddenly was beginning to look suspicious.

"Dave, that guy they brought in last night, some VIP who worked for Rocky Flats or something like that. They're calling it a suicide, right?"

"Yeah. Something McClintock."

"Things just don't add up. Okay, there was a large bruise under the left ear," Dr. Cain said, pulling several spectral traces out of her desk. "I managed to extract several microliters of fluid from it and had my technician perform HPLC, IR, NMR and mass spectrometry testing on it. You know what he found? I'll give you the official IUPAC, name: *2,2-chlorophenyl-2-methylamino-cyclohexanone*," Cain said, opening and reading from the dog-eared page of a ponderous chemical reference book.

"Hmm... you mean ketamine? You're kidding?" Parker said as he studied the traces. "Isn't that some kind of a dissociative anesthetic... what they use in animal tranquilizers? It's sometimes used in combination with Pavulon in surgical procedures. It's very popular on the street; the junkies call it *Special K*. At high enough doses it'll cause paralysis of voluntary muscles... He was drugged! Murdered?

My God, what a sadistic way to kill someone. He was probably fully conscious."

"Wait, there's more. The victim's blood chemistry revealed elevated levels of succinic acid and choline. Got the HPLC traces and mass spec data over here."

Parker nodded slowly. Cain walked over to a large battery of scientific equipment on the lab bench. She retrieved a computer printout.

"And here's the kicker... There was some skin, dried blood and blonde hair strands under the dead man's fingernails on the right hand. Some of the hairs had complete follicles. We should be able to get DNA. I sent it all to the Cell Bio Lab for analysis. Got the results here. You know what they found from the skin samples?"

"What?"

"Barr bodies," she said, briefly pausing to let the thought sink in. "The karyotype analysis is conclusive. That means this McClintock guy probably scratched his killer before he died... He was killed by a woman. A woman who uses a hypo."

"That could probably explain the dried semen stains they found on the dead man's pants and on the sheets at the hotel," Parker said, slowly nodding. "He was probably making it with the woman who killed him, but why use ketamine and succinylcholine?"

"Who knows? Good way to cover-up a murder though. Hard to trace. The victim is completely helpless, paralyzed. He was probably thrown out the window to look like a suicide. It was dumb luck that I found it. Better tell the cops no way is this case a suicide. Looks like that they're dealing with a homicide... and the killer is a woman."

Early the next morning, Dr. Parker contacted the Denver PD. Summoned to the morgue, Denver Police Homicide Detective Sgt.

Joseph Bishop met with Doctor Cain. As they talked, the body of George McClintock was wheeled in on a gurney. The victim's face was unrecognizable, the result of massive cranial damage upon impact. Sgt. Bishop, a seasoned homicide cop with over twelve years on the force, grimaced at the sight.

"So, you think that this McClintock guy was murdered?" Bishop said while momentarily turning away. Cain slowly unzipped the green tinted plastic body bag.

"Absolutely. Upon impact the victim's vertebra collapsed into each other, like an accordion... Detective, you see this hematoma, that's—"

"Wait doc, wait," Bishop said while pulling out a pad of paper. "Remember, I'm a beat cop, not a chemist. Don't give me all that *hematoma* stuff. Slow down and speak English, okay?" He smiled.

"Sorry... Okay, see this bruise below the left ear?" the doctor continued, pointing out the area on the corpse with a long probe. "It was caused by an injection with a hypodermic needle. A hypodermic needle containing a mixture of drugs... ketamine, succinylcholine and Pavulon."

Bishop bent over and examined the area on the corpse. He slowly nodded.

"These drugs are normally used to tranquilize animals or as muscle relaxants during surgery. Indians in South America sometimes used Pavulon on their poison-tipped arrows while hunting. It can cause temporary paralysis at low doses, even though the patient is fully awake... Higher doses can kill by paralyzing the diaphragm. I'd say he was probably injected while he was making love."

"Just how do you know all that, doc, I mean, about the lovemaking?" Bishop said, scratching his head.

"We found blonde hair strands and fresh skin tissue under the dead man's fingernails. Analysis of the tissues revealed substances called *Barr bodies*. Barr bodies are found only in women. It's the X chromosome which is inactivated during gestational development. From this and the position of the neck wound, it seems to indicate that the killer was a woman; the wound was probably made by the killer as they were embracing, like in a kiss for example. There was also other physical evidence as well."

"Like?"

"They found evidence of fresh, dried semen and vaginal discharge on the dead man's penis, underwear and pants…Lots of it. He probably ejaculated when the killer made the injection."

"Uh-huh, and you think that once he was immobilized, this woman with the X- what's-his-names dragged him over to the window and pushed him out to look like a suicide." Bishop said. He suddenly remembered from the preliminary investigation that McClintock was in a very ugly divorce proceeding with his wife.

"That's right. It's sure a clever way to cover up a murder. Some of the drugs are known to be relatively unstable and broken down rapidly by the liver. Undoubtedly the killer was aware of this," Dr. Cain said, slowly nodding. She handed Bishop a file folder with the data. "You'll probably want to take all this to your crime lab people. I'd say that you're looking for a female, Caucasian, early thirties, blonde and with type AB negative blood."

Bishop took the folder. "But officers at the scene said McClintock had apparently been drinking. What about all the liquor they found on the body?"

"It was all just for show. Blood tests were almost negative. Alcohol levels less than point-Oh- five. No way he was drunk." Dr. Cain read from the toxicology report. "And another thing… a drunk would pour liquor in his mouth. Not all over himself."

"Hmm, all this would explain a lot. Witnesses said they didn't hear McClintock scream as he fell, and there was no sign of a struggle in the hotel room… Nice piece of detective work doc."

"Just doing my job… I'd say that yours is cut-out for you. One thing's for sure. Whoever this woman is I'd say she's very, very dangerous."

"Yeah… Thank you, Dr. Cain," Bishop said, slowly nodding. "You know, there's a future for you in police work." He left the morgue and called his boss Homicide Division Commander Lieutenant Al Bundy on his cell phone.

"Al? Joe. Listen, I been talking to the doc here at the morgue. Looks like we may have a homicide here on the McClintock case after all. He was in the middle of a dog mean divorce with his wife, wasn't he? Maybe we should pick her up for questioning. Also, can you contact the FBI? See if they got anything on a woman hit killer who uses a hypo."

Friday, May 29th
1440 hours
Denver Police Headquarters

"Mrs. McClintock, I think you know why you were asked to come down here. Detective Bishop has given you your rights and you've waived your right to the presence of an attorney," Al Bundy said as Theresa McClintock sat down.

"Officer, am I under arrest?"

"No ma'am, this is only just a few routine questions for right now. I'll try to keep it brief." Bundy pulled a well-worn notepad from his pocket.

"Shoot," she said, smiling, although nervous.

"Where were you around ten p.m. on the night of May twenty-sixth?"

"Let's see, I was at home, watching *Star Trek* I think. God, you know I just love that show."

"Got any corroborating witnesses?"

"Only the Klingons."

Bundy looked up with an impatient scowl. "Ma'am, how would you describe how you felt about your husband?"

"Let's see, I hated him… he hated me… and we hated each other." Theresa said, playing with her hair and staring at the ceiling.

Bundy abruptly closed the notepad. "Look lady, this is a serious investigation. We can make things pretty hot for you. So let's try to cut out all the smart-ass answers, Okay?"

"Listen, I don't need this crap!" Theresa said, now livid. "Frankly, I ain't sorry he's dead, but I didn't kill my soon-to-be ex-husband. I didn't need to, because my attorney was going to kick his ass in court… You make things hot for me? Then charge me! Here and now! Right now! Otherwise get the fuck out of my face!" Theresa got up to go to the door. She turned and continued.

"You want to know who killed George? Why don't you just go find that blonde bimbo he was sleeping with?"

Bundy leaned forward in his chair.

"What? Who?"

"Who knows. Some blonde bitch he had stashed away. I'll bet he was screwing this chick and her boyfriend probably freaked. Figure he must have been hammering on her ass real good. Big Time. I saw 'em couple times together at the Red Dog bar. If you don't believe me, then go talk to Zach Duncan, he'll tell you. He tends the bar at the Red Dog."

"I see... I've got just one more question, Mrs. McClintock."

"Oh, what is it? And I prefer to be called by my maiden name, Johnson."

"What's your blood type?"

"How the fuck should I know? Type A, I think." A uniformed officer escorted Theresa to the front desk to take the rest of her statement. Bundy remembered the morgue's report on McClintock's death, particularly the part about the blonde hair strands found under the dead man's fingernails. In his mind, it was beginning to look like George McClintock's killer was this mysterious blonde.

After a quick lunch, Detective Bundy drove over to the Red Dog Bar on East Colfax. Isaac "Zach" Duncan, twenty-six, was a part-time bartender at the Red Dog Lounge. Blond and fit from daily workouts, he looked as if he could have stepped out of one of those TV commercials selling jeans. His body seemed to ripple with muscles. The bar was almost empty as the usual lunchtime crowd had departed. He had just sat down for a break when Bundy walked in.

"Isaac Duncan? I'm Al Bundy, Denver PD. I'd like to ask you a few questions about one of your regulars. Guy named George David McClintock."

"Call me Zach... Too bad about Ol' George. I kind of liked him."

"When did you last see Mr. McClintock?"

"Let's see, last Sunday afternoon, around eh, six p.m. I guess."

"Can you remember how he acted? Anything strange? Did he seem depressed or upset at all?"

"You kidding? Not George. He was Good-Time Charlie. Swear

he had a roll of bills on him that could choke a horse. Bought rounds for the house. Way he was spending money I figured he hit the lottery or something. Slipped me a ten-buck tip." Zach removed his apron and walked over to the other side of the bar. "Thought he was strapped for cash 'cause of the divorce... You'd never figure that the way he was spending money."

"Was he alone?"

"No way man. He was with that blonde babe again," Zach said with a wolf-like grin.

"Can you describe her?" Bundy pulled out the notepad.

"For sure. This chick was a real fox. Maybe late twenties, five-eight, about one hundred-twenty pounds... blonde hair off the shoulder... sea blue eyes, nice boobs... killer ass, great legs to die for. Like I said, a real babe. Man, I get a hard-on just thinking about her. She put all those other bimbos to shame."

"I see. Anything else?"

"George and this chick were quite an item. Way I always seen them acting, they couldn't keep their hands offa each other. I figure they was really doing the nasty. I mean, we're talking major league."

"You've got a very graphic memory. Did you by any chance get her name?" Bundy said, writing hurriedly.

"Ahh... Jackie! Yeah, that's it. Jackie. Didn't catch the last name though."

"We're going to send a police artist down here to try and get a sketch. Okay?"

"Sketch? Hey! What's this all about? What you think this chick do, kill somebody?"

"Routine investigation. You sure know a lot about McClintock."

"Hey I'm a bartender, remember? I hear all the shit. Everybody's stupid problems. You know what they say about regulars at a bar, the booze goes in, and the info comes out."

"I'll have to remember that during my next interrogation of a suspect." Bundy smiled, closing his notepad.

"Come on, level with me. Was George banging on some guy's old lady? Did he piss somebody off or something?"

"We're just investigating Mr. McClintock's death. These questions are part of the standard procedure."

"I just can't figure George out," Zach said, shaking his head.

"What do you mean?"

"I knew he was depressed about the divorce and all but, with a chick like that on his arm, why would he jump out of a fourteen-storey window and kill himself?"

"I don't know, maybe he had a little help," Bundy said, handing Zach a business card. "I'll send the police artist out to see you tomorrow. Thank you for your time, Mr. Duncan, eh, Zach."

Night of the Long Knives

"…A child shall be born of a poor family, who with his tongue shall seduce many people…"
— Nostradamus, *Century III, Quatrain XXXV*.

"Cry Havock [*sic*] and let slip the Dogs of War!"
—Antony's soliloquy, from Shakespeare's, *Julius Caesar*

"I shall shrink from nothing, I shall destroy everyone who dare oppose me…"
— Adolf Hitler

Monday, June 1st
2030 hours
A private residence, Aurora, CO

After a forty-minute drive, Howard and Jackie arrived at the home of Nick and Stacey Manson. Situated in a quiet and secluded area of town it was anything but innocuous. There, besides the Mansons, "skinheads" Jason Chalmers, Ariadne Beausoleil, Franklin Corbett, and twelve other Aryans were waiting in the basement. The Mansons had turned their home into a Werewolf "safe house," part of a vast network of hideouts across the country the Aryans referred to as their "Underground Railroad" where, like the runaway slaves before the Civil War, the white supremacist fugitives could find safety and sanctuary from the authorities. Now, it was the scene of an ominous meeting.

On the dining room table lay the detailed map of the Rocky Flats Nuclear Processing Facility that Jackie had stolen. She began speaking to the assembly,

"Quiet... This is the Rocky Flats facility," she said, pointing to the map. "You all know how much Howie loves history; he's code-named it *Harper's Ferry*. Six thousand, five hundred acres. Here is our target: Plutonium Processing and Storage Building, number one-oh-three. It's got bomb-grade plutonium, triggers for hydrogen bombs. We're going to steal one of them and kick some ass! McClintock has let on that a shipment to Amarillo is scheduled for the eighth, so we ain't got a lot of time to get what we want."

"What about the fucking guards?" Nick Manson said.

"You worry too much, Nick. We've got nine- millimeter Beretta semiautomatics, with silencers. MAC-10s and an AR-15, also silenced. I'll bring the SVD. Nobody's going to hear shit. Hollow-point ammunition. Anybody that fucks with me is gonna get hit. If necessary, we'll kill them all. Just like that," Jackie said, snapping her fingers.

"Simple enough," Nick said with a nod.

"After Stace and me pop the guards, Chalmers, Jake, Night-Hawk, Red Becky and the Cyclops are gonna get the stuff. Right here, in Building one-oh-three," Jackie said while gesturing to a rectangular figure on the map. "The rest of us will secure the perimeter. Some of us will be wearing those DOE security uniforms they made for us at JerUSAlem," she said, now pointing to a closet.

"We've got five vehicles, all with DOE markings. Trojan Horse is on the inside. She's going to take out Communications in here, building number one-oh-one and shut down the security system. In and out... just like sex! In a few days the Werewolf will become the world's newest nuclear power."

"Like the way you got such detailed info so quickly," Chalmers said.

"It was easy to get from McClintock, just before I killed him," she said with a smirk. "Hey, you want good info, try fucking a DOE cop."

At that point Howard, wearing his Air Force colonel's insignia, walked into the room and started talking. His voice was somber, almost choked with hate and emotion.

"I think it's important that you all understand what is at stake here," he began slowly. "This ain't gonna be no ordinary fucking guerrilla raid. We, the Aryan *Stürmabteilungen,* are going to light a fire in the belly of the beast that'll serve as a beacon for our race! With this device that you're going to steal, we're going to bring down this corrupt, Godless ZOG regime. But I ain't gonna bullshit none of you, some of us are probably going to die. So if you want out now, there's the door. But you had better keep your mouth shut!" Howard made a sweeping gesture to the door. None moved. The room was absolutely quiet.

"You like the way this country is headed?" he continued, becoming more animated. "I don't. Don't any of you realize that in just fifty years *white people* are going to be a minority group in this country? Shit, the goddamned Democrats and Republicans have fucked up everything! I don't even recognize America anymore. Nothing but Kikes and Gooks, Spics and Spooks! Food stamps! Welfare bullshit! Goddamned nigger jungle *crap* music! Gangs... *Everywhere!*" he paused, anger building. "Fag rights! Jew rights! Nigger rights! Hell, what about white rights? Ain't no justice for the Aryan man anymore. In fact, ain't nothing left for the white man! Too many Jews! Too many spics and niggers! Too many queers! And those lousy piece of shit fuckers in the government just don't care. Well, all I can say is that soon, very soon, we're gonna give this country its wake-up call, a reality check. Going to start setting things right!" Howard was almost at the point of screaming. He was beside himself with rage and hate.

"Those fucking race traitors in Washington ain't doing shit for their own kind! I'm tired of talk! 'Cause talk don't get you shit! I just can't take it anymore. Something's got to be done…" he again trailed off. Slowly, he said, "You'll make the hit day after tomorrow. Jackie's in charge. We'll get sufficient plutonium to make a small bomb… Then we're gonna kick some ZOG ass! Big Time! When the big one goes, I'm going with it. Just like Ed Carson in *The Diaries*. I'm ready to die for my race. I don't give a damn. Fuck it. Got to take out ZOG! Going to solve the all-important *Nigger Question*… Now! Race war!" Howard droned, slamming his fist on the table.

"So, we gonna kill the president?" Stacey said.

"We're gonna waste out the whole fucking ZOG! Think of it Stace, a small nuclear implosion device with maybe forty-to-fifty kiloton yield in a van parked a few blocks from the Capitol and White House and is detonated…during the State of the Union speech where the whole ZOG is assembled! Kill 'em all! The Justice Department, State Department, the Supreme Court, the Post Office Building, Treasury Department, the goddamned IRS and FBI buildings, everything! The whole federal government apparatus will be completely destroyed!" Howard's voice was rising in an almost hysterical, savage joy.

"What's more, whole lot of colored in D.C. They're all going to die. You see, this'll make the niggers all over America go ape! They're going to riot and steal, just like all those crazy Black Power Mau-Mau Zulus did in LA back in April! Then, the Aryan white man is going to stand up, and just start killing the niggers like crazy!"

"You can see it all around," he said, slowly pacing. "Since the fall of Communism in the early nineties, conflicts are becoming less ideological… more tribal and racial."

The others in the room nodded in agreement.

"Rwanda... the Congo... Syria... Lebanon... Iraq...Afghanistan," he continued, walking over to a counter and retrieving a book. "I intend to trigger a race war here! Just like in the *Diaries*!" Howard began waving the book over his head. "Hey, the ethnic war in Syria couple years back was nothing compared to what I'm going to start! You'll see, even the liberals and Jew-lovers are going to have to join in... Just like the book says!"

The others nodded approvingly. Howard continued his harangue.

"Or even better yet, maybe they'll all think that President Petrov went nuts and the Russians did it... and start a nuclear war! Either way this'll bring total chaos and societal collapse! Race War!" Howard screamed triumphantly. Foamy droplets of spittle dribbled down along the edges of his mouth.

"But can you really build a bomb?" Nick Manson said, almost trembling in awe of such fury. It was like seeing Hitler reborn.

"I've got advanced degrees in engineering and nuclear physics. I was actively involved in nuclear weapons design and development for years when I was a colonel in the Air Force... before those goddamned ZOG pricks cashiered my ass...*Fuck yes,* I can build a bomb! Twice as destructive as the one they dropped on the Japs! You just steal the plutonium and all the shit I need. Then we'll use it to bring down that wicked Sodom and Gomorrah in Washington!"

"What exactly are we going to steal?" Stacey said.

"First, we want the plutonium," Howard said, placing his finger to his chin. "As Jackie said, they have it in Building one-oh-three... There. After those major fires at Los Alamos way back in two-thousand, they've had to move a lot of it out of New Mexico up here for storage." He began pounding his finger on the map. "It's finely machined metal stored in special vaults in air-tight, lead-lined canisters with argon gas to prevent degradation. They're in ingots.

We'll need six."

"Anything else?" Chalmers said.

"Beryllium-polonium initiator... reflector and neutron source. That's what we're going to trigger the bomb with. They're probably in Building two-oh-three. We'll also need tamper material."

"Tamper? What's that?" Stacey said.

"It's the depleted uranium jacket for the plutonium core," Howard concluded. He paused and slowly panned his steely eyes around the room. "Okay, that's all."

With that, the assembled group rose to their feet, extended their arms forward in the Nazi salute and exploded in a frenzy of chanting:

"Race War! Race War! Race War! Hail Victory! Werewolf! Werewolf! Werewolf!" The room was suddenly alive with hate. The spectacle continued for several minutes after Howard and Jackie departed. As they drove away, he noticed that Jackie was crying softly.

"You don't have to die, please. Live for me. I don't want you to die. I love you so much!"

"No! Babylon-ZOG will fall... and I shall fall with it. For the Werewolf, day after tomorrow will be *die Nacht der langer Messer*," he said, trailing off. "I got a seven-year-old nephew. What do I leave for him? Way things are headed in this shit country, he's going to be a blond, blue-eyed Aryan stranger in his own land. You think I want him to grow up with all this shit? I'm doing it all for him. I'm going to go down and take the government with me, like Samson in the temple of the Philistines... Death is a small price to pay for immortality."

"I can't imagine a life without you... I think I want to die with you. We'll die together. I'll be just like Eva Braun. I would gladly die for you, my *führer*… God bless you… I love you so much," Jackie whimpered, with tears in her eyes.

"No! You're too valuable to the movement," Howard said, touched by her words. "You're going to be needed to fight when the racial tribulation begins. I love you, Jackie, but you must live for the movement, for the cause. I want you to be a sort of Aryan Joan of Arc, the matriarch of a new, white nation." He kissed her on the cheek.

Tuesday, June 2nd
2335 hours, Zero Hour
The Manson residence, Aurora, CO

It was a warm, cloudless late spring night. The temperature hovered around sixty-nine degrees. The peaceful stillness of the night was disturbed only by the occasional croaking of frogs. Beyond the apparent tranquility however, feverish activity was underway. The Aryans prepared for battle.

Besides herself, Jackie had carefully selected fourteen other Aryans as her *Stürmabteilung* to accompany her on the raid. Jefferson Davis Collins, a.k.a. "Night-Hawk" was a 33-year old murderer and ex-Klansman from Fort Smith, Arkansas. Church of Yahweh members Lee and Jake Franklin were two skinhead brothers suspected of the recent rape and murder of a black prostitute in Salt Lake City. Stacey Manson was an Aurora housewife who, along with her husband Nick, ran the safe house. The Mansons had been involved in several bombings in the Denver area. Rebecca Stephens of Stone Mountain, Georgia, a.k.a. "Red Becky" was a close friend of Jackie's. She had endeared herself to the Werewolf in the previous year by shooting and killing a black policeman in Atlanta.

David Safely also had been picked. He knew Jackie from the days they both served in the Marines; just recently he had been thrown out as a section-eight case. Since then, he had acquired the nickname of "Bat-Man" after beating a homeless, wheelchair-bound black man to death with a baseball bat. Franklin Corbett, Ariadne Beausoleil and Jason Chalmers, who had proved their devotion to the movement with the Bones murder in April were recent inductees to the Werewolf who were also selected.

Joseph Paul Recke, nicknamed "JR" and "Old Shatterhand," after the character in the old Karl May western dime novels, was a racist ex-convict from Fredericksburg, Virginia, recently questioned in the firebombing of a Richmond synagogue. He was now working as a hit man for the Werewolf.

Joseph Horan, twenty-nine, having the moniker "Skull," was a racist killer wanted for the recent murder of a black highway patrol officer in Florida. He had left the Klan because *it* wasn't violent enough for him. Nathan Mantooth, thirty-five, alias "Cyclops," was a bearded, 335-pound murderer from Tuscaloosa, Alabama who had lost an eye in a bar fight. The hulking ex-farmer had been described as being a congenital racist; he once shot a black cow. He was wanted for questioning about an armored car robbery in Denver the year before.

Joachim Klimper, thirty-four, a.k.a. "Outlaw," was a former member of the South African Defense Forces. An unreconstructed Afrikaner, he had been formerly employed as a sniper during the Second Namibian Civil War. He had fifty confirmed "kills" of guerrillas during the conflict. Klimper was wanted for questioning by the authorities in South Africa in connection with the fire-bombing of black churches in Cape Town. With the arrival of black rule in South Africa, he fled to America, where he became active in a variety of neo-Nazi groups, including Werewolf. Klimper had accompanied Jackie to Washington, DC as her spotter when she murdered Zimbabwean ambassador Miloko several months earlier. Finally, the Werewolf had an operative, a sleeper, inside the Rocky Flats facility itself. Pamela Mae Haney, a petite thirty-two-year-old blonde also known as "Trojan Horse" who had been working as a custodian at the

Flats for the last six months.

Lynch, Safely, Chalmers and Recke all donned several custom-made DOE security guard uniforms as the others loaded the weapons into three large trucks. All of the vehicles were white with DOE markings. As the work proceeded Jackie Lynch and Howard Brennan looked on approvingly. The couple embraced and kissed affectionately. A tear slowly ran down Howard's face. He was about to embark on his dream.

"Don't worry lover, we're waging the battle of the Lord; Yahweh shall be with us this night… I love you," Jackie said tenderly. She climbed into the lead vehicle. The caravan slowly pulled out, in a line, like circus elephants. Its destination was the Rocky Flats Nuclear Facility. *Die Nacht der langer Messer*—The Night of the Long Knives, had come.

For the past several years, the Rocky Flats Nuclear Weapons Facility had been in the news. Nestled in the shadow of the Rocky Mountains 16 miles northwest of Denver the sprawling, six-thousand-five-hundred-acre plant had for decades been the primary site for the production of "trigger" devices — atomic bombs — needed to provide sufficient heat and pressure for the detonation of thermonuclear weapons. Its heyday was during the Reagan Presidency of the 1980s, the era of fat defense expenditures. Well into the new millennium, however, the year that the plant stopped the processing of plutonium to triggers, all had changed. The Soviet Union was no more and Communism was in retreat. A Democrat sat in the White House, elected in part on the promise that there would be more butter and fewer guns. Even the most ardent hawk could acknowledge that a "reduction in force" of the nation's nuclear arsenal was probably in order. Henceforward the plant, in need of massive a clean-up anyway, would serve primarily for storage of weapons as well as more than fourteen tons of unprocessed plutonium.

It was after the end of the Cold War, but not the end the controversy that surrounded the Rocky Flats facility. Now there were heightened concerns by environmentalists and residents in the nearby communities of Superior, Louisville and Arvada about the safety of tons of plutonium in the neighborhood. Billions of dollars had been slated by the Department of Energy for cleaning up the plant, budget cutbacks and "politics as usual" forced seemingly endless delays. Journalists from local Denver papers were having a field day with stories ranging from lax security to improper storage techniques for plutonium and other toxic by-products. Stories abounded of radiation leaks and oxidized plutonium slowly eating through corroding metal containers and poisoning the water table.

Low morale at the Flats was another matter. Budgetary cutbacks and layoffs had decimated plant personnel. Only a skeleton crew of technicians, supported by a thin garrison of DOE security people remained to staff the immense facility. The staff grumbled over low wages and extended work assignments. With regards to the security force, the sudden 'suicide' of Security Chief McClintock had only served to make things worse. His temporary successor, Elison Ames was almost universally loathed by the rank and file. Insubordination bordering on mutiny, alcoholism and even drug abuse were becoming serious problems. Bored and depressed, the guards conversed among themselves with a fatalistic expectation of eventually being victims of "down-sizing."

Wednesday, June 3rd
0005 hours
Plant Protection Building #101, Rocky Flats Nuclear Facility, Jefferson County, CO

Their shifts completed, DOE security guards Clarence Barker and Jon Bent were leisurely walking down a dimly lit corridor, exchanging small talk.

"I see they got you pulling this shift too," Barker said.

"Yeah man. Bummer. That Elison Ames sure is an asshole," Bent said with a sigh. "Too bad we're stuck with him as Head of Security. Fucking slavedriver… Sure sorry McClintock killed himself."

"Hell, I don't blame him," Barker said, nodding. "With that crazy bitch he was divorcing and all, plus working in this shithole, hell, I'd probably kill myself too."

The two men went into a men's room to grab a joint. The plant's lavatories had become ideal spots for clandestine drug deals. Inside, the pair was startled to find the body of Technician George Caldwell sprawled face-down in a pool of warm vomit. A faint smell of almonds was rising from the man's corpse.

"Oh my God! I think he's dead!" Barker dropped his unlit marijuana cigarette and rushed over to the prostrate form.

"Shit, man, what do you think? Heart attack?" Bent said excitedly.

"I don't know man. Get on the horn — Get someone down here, fast!" Bent ran down the hallway to a paging telephone. He started dialing the plant's infirmary when Pamela Mae Haney, one of the plant custodians and the Werewolf mole, suddenly appeared behind him.

"Pam, whatever you do, don't go in there," he said, pointing toward the men's room. Suddenly, out of the corner of his eye he could see what resembled a child's water pistol in the woman's gloved right hand. An instant later, he felt a warm, oily liquid splash into his face. Grimacing, he collapsed to the floor, twitching momentarily. Bent gave out a sigh and then lay still. He was dead. Without emotion, Pam casually stepped over the corpse and walked over to the men's room. Barker was standing over Caldwell's body.

"What's the matter? I just saw Jon in the hallway. He looked like dog shit."

"It's George here. I think he's dead. Heart attack maybe. Looks like we got a problem here," the man said, looking up.

"I'm the problem, asshole!" Pam leveled the pistol at the startled guard's head and shot a stream of the oily substance into his eyes. Barker stiffened and collapsed on top of Caldwell, foaming at the mouth. In just over a minute, he was dead. The air was heavy with the aroma of almonds.

"Fucking asshole," the woman muttered as she exited, dumping the now empty water pistol in the trash bin. Leaving the scene of carnage, Pamela pushed a trash cart toward the main communications room. The communications room of the Plant Protection Building was truly a marvel of technology. Sensors, alarms, motion detectors and sophisticated surveillance cameras could all be monitored by one person using computers operated from this room. There, the acting Security Chief Elison Ames was reclining. He was all alone. Munching on a chicken sandwich, Ames was casually flipping through a copy of the June issue of *PlayMate Magazine*. Pamela quietly came up behind him. She reached into the cart and furtively pulled out a silenced Beretta nine- millimeter pistol.

"Why do you read all that shit?" she said, quietly chambering a round.

"Hey, I'm just getting all the volleyball scores," Ames said jokingly, as he thoughtfully examined the Miss June centerfold. The woman suddenly fired a single round through the back of Ames's chair. With a bullet between the shoulder blades, he flopped forward, dead. Pressing the weapon against the base of the man's skull Pam fired again. Ames's blood and brains splattered all over the computer terminal console. Next, the killer proceeded to shoot up the banks of computers, crippling the security system. The numerous surveillance cameras and sensors along the perimeter, one by one, began to shut down.

0011 hours

Security guard Nicholas Sutherland was standing in the sentry box at the main entrance when he spotted a caravan of trucks turn off of Indiana Street and slowly approach the fence. Seeing DOE markings on all the vehicles he wasn't concerned. With his AR-16 rifle casually hanging from a sling he motioned to the lead vehicle to stop.

Boy, wish they'd hire more guards like her, he thought to himself, seeing an attractive blonde woman in a DOE Security uniform step out of the lead truck.

"Hello, I'm Ginger Kereluk. Me and my people here have been assigned as a security detail at this facility. Open up," Jackie said, smiling. She handed the guard her security badge and false papers.

"What? Security detail? Nobody tells me nothing anymore," Sutherland muttered. He shined a flashlight on the documents. "Everything looks in order, but I'll have to check it out."

Sutherland turned toward the sentry box, reaching for the telephone. Jackie pulled out a silenced Beretta handgun and rammed it into Sutherland's back.

"Okay pal, nice and easy… drop the telephone. Now open the gate or I'll kill you."

"Hey! What…? Hey little girl, you got to be kidding me," the guard said in a disbelieving voice. "Come on, quit fucking around, before Ames sees you."

"Do it, asshole… Now! Open the fucking gate, or I'll blow your head off!" Jackie pulled the slide back on the pistol.

"Sure lady, take it easy." The terrified guard relented. Sutherland hurriedly punched in the access code. The gate slowly slid open.

"See, now was that hard? You're fucked, asshole." Jackie fired a round into the guard's back. As the man flopped onto the ground, she took aim at his head and fired again, execution-style.

"Skin-Girl, you and Psycho stash the body. Now! Come on, Move it!" Jackie barked as she wiped Sutherland's blood off of the silencer. Ariadne and Corbett dragged the man's corpse behind some bushes near the front entrance. The caravan slowly rumbled onto the plant grounds. Looking around, Jackie was pleased by the almost military precision they had begun their mission.

"Okay, Trojan Horse should have secured the Communications hooch by now... Let's go!" Jackie said to Stacey, as she glanced at her watch. Klimper and Jake Franklin, armed with the silenced Dragunov and a MAC-10, sprinted across the compound and took up positions covering the perimeter. Clad in one of the DOE uniforms, Dave Safely remained at the sentry box, watching the entrance. As Jackie and Stacey ran towards the Communication area Pam Haney emerged from the building.

"Security's shut down. They're blind! I killed them all!" Pamela announced triumphantly, with the smoking, silenced Beretta handgun hanging ostentatiously from her belt. Jackie motioned the trucks to move toward the Weapons Storage Area.

"Stace, take out the Security Annex!" Jackie said. Stacey Manson loped over to the small Quonset hut adjacent to the Processing and Storage Building, screwing a plump silencer onto a MAC-10 machine pistol as she ran. Entering quietly, she noticed three DOE security guards fast asleep on their cots. Their shifts weren't to begin for another hour. Methodically, the silent killer moved from cot to cot, pumping a single .45 caliber hollow-point round into each sleeping man's head. A moment later she emerged, waving to Jackie.

"Lee, you, Joe and Skin-Girl cover those buildings over there." Jackie pointed to a row of buildings in the distance. "If anybody comes out, waste them!"

0020 hours

The killing continued. Security guard Ames Willis was slowly approaching along the far side of the perimeter. With a cool eye, Klimper tracked him with the telescopic sight of the *Dragunov*. A single 7.62-millimeter round through the brain sent him sprawling to the ground, dead. With bolt cutters, Jackie snipped open the locks around the fence of the Processing Building. Before her stood the imposing concrete edifices of the Component Fabrication Building #203 and Plutonium Processing and Storage Building #103. She walked to the entrance of Building 103, encountering DOE security guards Nick Cooper and Oscar McCracken.

"Who are you?" McCracken said, yawning.

"Ginger Kereluk, DOE. I've got a security detail. Ames sent me." She furtively reached into her purse.

"What's going on out there?"

"Our people are deploying now. I'm afraid it looks like there's been a little trouble at the Main Gate."

"Oh? What kind of trouble?" McCracken began craning his neck for a better view of the main entrance.

"This kind." Jackie dropped into a combat stance with the silenced Beretta, shooting McCracken twice through the heart. He was dead before he hit the floor. Cooper started to draw his service revolver. Jackie pointed her weapon at him.

"No you don't. Drop it asshole! Do it... Now!" she snarled. Cooper dropped his gun. "Now get inside... Becky, Cyclops, Night-Hawk, Jake, follow me!" With the frightened security guard in tow Jackie Lynch, Rebecca Stephens, Nathan Mantooth, Jeff Collins and Jake Franklin entered Building 103.

0032 hours

The perimeter, communications center and compound around the Weapons Storage Area had been secured. The security system was neutralized, and Jackie had positioned her commandos near other buildings with orders to eliminate anyone else who might interfere. In just twenty-seven minutes, the Werewolf storm troopers had seized complete control of the Weapons Storage Area. Now Phase Two, the most sensitive part of the operation, the actual theft of fissionable components commenced. Jackie came up to Cooper roughly. Without warning, she suddenly gave him a karate kick in the groin and pressed the barrel of her handgun against the side of his head. With a groan the guard doubled over and vomited.

"Okay asshole, which of these rooms has the plutonium?" she said impatiently. "Don't fuck with me. I've already killed two people tonight; they can't hang my ass any higher for one more."

"Down the hall, to your left. It's in vaults. Please! I got a family!" the frightened guard said, pointing.

"Are there any motion detectors or sensors in this building? Talk fast!"

"Yeah, but they stopped working about fifteen minutes ago. I was going to check it out in the Communications hooch."

Jackie looked along the wall. "You'd better not be lying. Cyclops, you and the others get the stuff. Becky and I'll watch him."

Mantooth, Collins and Franklin squeezed into protective white "space suits" that were hanging on the wall next to the entrance. While the two women kept an eye on Cooper, the trio jimmied open the locks and entered. Moments later, they emerged carrying several cylindrical lead-lined canisters adorned with Day-Glo orange stickers labeled "**RADIOACTIVE**-Pu^{239}." The containers, referred to as "birdcages" in DOE jargon, each were hermetically sealed and had an ingot wedge of one kilogram of finely machined and casted weapons-grade plutonium that had been stored under argon gas.

The terrorists carried the containers outside to the waiting vehicles. Moments later they returned, quickly removing several large crates marked "**DEPLETED URANIUM**." While the loading was underway, Jackie again came up to Cooper.

"Okay, asshole, where are the neutron initiators kept?" Jackie said to the guard impatiently. "Hey, I'll blow your head off right now!"

"They're shipped separately for security reasons; we got 'em stored in another building," the guard said. Without warning, Jackie slammed the butt of her gun down on Cooper's wrist, breaking it. As the injured man writhed in agony she said, "Goddammit, which building?"

"Ah! Building Two-Oh-Three... You're going to build a bomb, aren't you?" the guard mumbled.

"That's right... Lights out, asshole." Jackie slugged Cooper across the face with her pistol. As the injured man collapsed to the floor she aimed and shot him once through the chest. The guard stiffened and lay motionless on the floor in a pool of blood. The terrorists ran out of the building.

"Okay, Building Two-Oh-Three. Howard said we want something called 'beryllium/polonium initiators.' If anybody's in there, kill them! Kill 'em quick and kill 'em dead." Jackie examined a crude diagram that Howard had given her earlier. After forcing the lock, the terrorists entered Building 203 and began a hasty search. The building was completely deserted. Several initiator assembly units, being readied for dispatch to Pantex, were already crated for shipment.

It's great that we don't have to spend a lot of time searching for all this shit, Jackie thought to herself. *We simply couldn't ask for better service.* In preparation for shipment to the Pantex facility, all of the desired components had been cataloged, inspected, crated and were ready to steal.

0105 hours

With tamper materials, neutron initiators and the weapons-grade plutonium loaded into the trucks, it was time to go. Four of the terrorists proceeded to drive off in the first two vehicles, laden with loot. Jackie and Pamela watched with a grim satisfaction as they rumbled through the main entrance past a rather faded, weather-beaten sign:

ROCKY FLATS NUCLEAR FACILITY
UNITED STATES GOVERNMENT
PROPERTY
DEPARTMENT OF ENERGY
VIOLATORS WILL BE PROSECUTED

"Jake, start gathering the others, time to saddle up. Let's get the fuck out of here!" she said, pointing to the last vehicle.

The others clambered onto the remaining truck and slowly pulled out. Cradling a silenced MAC-10, Jackie scanned the perimeter for any last-ditch opposition from the remaining garrison. There was none. As the last of the caravan drove through the gate, they all relaxed, giving each other a "thumbs-up" sign. Jackie offered up a silent prayer of thanksgiving to Yahweh on the success of the operation.

In the lead vehicles, now cruising through sleeping Denver neighborhoods, we have the means to bring down the Zionist government and launch a race war... the heart of an atomic bomb, she thought to herself, glancing back. The scene of horrible carnage slowly faded into the distance. The Weapons Storage Area of the Rocky Flats Nuclear Facility had been left to the dead.

0115 hours

Why did I ever take this lousy, dog shit job? Harvey Roach thought to himself as he slowly walked the perimeter; his thoughts were clearly elsewhere. Indeed, he was in a job he absolutely abhorred. A DOE security guard for less than seven months, Roach had already been reprimanded twice for insubordination and absenteeism by his supervisor. Anyway, he felt that his boss Elison Ames was an asshole. He didn't care. In a couple more months he'd be out of this job and going back to school. As he began walking down the eastern boundary of the facility, he suddenly noticed what appeared to be a mannequin lying next to the fence. On closer inspection, he was horrified to discover that the body was that of his friend, Ames Willis. The man's face had literally been blown apart.

"Holy Shit!" Roach muttered as he unlimbered his AR-16, clumsily inserting a 32- round magazine into the weapon's action. Alert for sudden danger Roach moved purposefully toward the main entrance. Willis's killers could be lurking in the darkness. He was puzzled to see the gate wide open and the sentry box unmanned. He picked up the telephone in the sentry area and punched in the number of the communications building. No answer. Turning around, he saw what appeared to be a human hand protruding from under a bush. He shined his flashlight onto the bush and recoiled in horror.

Oh my God! It's Nick! What the fuck's going on here? Roach thought as he viewed Nicholas Sutherland's lifeless body. There was blood all over it, and the back of the head was missing. Realizing that the plant security had been breached and at least two men were dead, he momentarily considered entering the facility, AR-16 rifle in hand, round up the killers. Be a hero.

Yeah, right. Dead hero. All that shit works well enough in Hollywood, with Stallone or Norris or Swartzenegger in all those Rambo-type action movies, he thought to himself. *Why get my ass killed for this place anyway?* For him, common sense won out over raw courage. He turned and started running down the road to a nearby convenience store. The clerk on duty almost fainted at the sudden sight of the wild-eyed man waving an AR-16 bursting into his store.

"Hey! I've got to use your phone! There's trouble at Rocky Flats," Roach said, panting. He dialed 9-1-1 to the Westminster police department, gave a hurried description of the scene to the dispatcher and collapsed in exhaustion on a bench inside the store.

0132 hours

Seven police cruisers and a SWAT van arrived at the Flats. Heavily armed men in riot gear and Kevlar vests were led by Roach through the main entrance while others began to surround the facility. Technicians working at the far side of the plant in the other buildings were rounded up and questioned. They, working the graveyard shift opposite the Weapons Storage Area, knew nothing as yet of the night's terror.

Roach and the SWAT team leader entered the Plant Protection Building. There, amid the row of shot-up computers, they found Elison Ames slumped over his terminal in a pool of blood, with a half-eaten chicken sandwich and a blood-splattered copy of the June issue of *PlayMate* still clutched in his fingers. Down the hallway lay Jon Bent, dead with the paging telephone receiver dangling beside him. The men's lavatory yielded still more carnage. The bodies of Barker and Caldwell lay twisted in attitudes of violent death while giving off a strong odor of almonds.

"Keep away from those bodies," the SWAT leader barked to his men. "That smell, I think it might be cyanide."

"Lieutenant," one of the SWAT members called out. "I think you better come over to the security building. You'd better take a look at this."

Roach and the lieutenant left the building and went over to the Security Annex. There, Roach vomited at the sight. There was blood everywhere. Lying on their cots were the bodies of the three security guards, all having been shot through the head as they slept. Three spent forty-five caliber shell casings were lying on the floor next to one of the slain men's cot.

"My God! What kind of an animal would do this? Head shots. Shot 'em in their beds!" the police lieutenant muttered in a low, pensive voice. Eleven years as a police veteran had not prepared him for horror like this.

"Christ Jesus Skipper, there's another one over here!" a SWAT member yelled, pointing to the entrance of the Weapon's Storage Area. There, the body of Oscar McCracken lay sprawled in bloody heap in the doorway to Building #103, shot through the heart. Weapons drawn, the police cautiously entered the building. Turning the corner, they encountered yet another body. It was Nick Cooper.

"Hey, this one's still alive!" an officer noted while checking Cooper's pulse. Jackie's bullet missed Cooper's heart by a few millimeters, grazing the aorta and finally lodging in his back. He had a collapsed lung and had lost a lot of blood, but he was still alive.

"Better get an ambulance here for this one, he's going into shock," Horowitz said to his team. "And get us some back-up to secure the area."

"You'd better get the DOE and the FBI here also. We got trouble. Big trouble," Roach said as he glanced into the storage room. He noticed that the plutonium vaults had been opened. "They keep weapons-grade plutonium in there. Looks like some of the birdcages have been monkeyed with." Roach would know; he had been present the previous week as the materials were being readied for shipment. He could see the lieutenant mulling over the implications of what had happened.

0155 hours
The Manson residence, Aurora, CO

In a mood of celebration, the terrorists had arrived back at the safe house. In a large storage shed, the stolen booty was quickly unloaded and hidden. Meanwhile, the Franklin brothers were busy spray-painting the getaway vehicles, obliterating any telltale DOE markings. As the work proceeded Jackie and Howard inventoried the haul: six and a half kilograms of weapon-grade plutonium, one beryllium/polonium neutron initiator stored in platinum foil in a sealed container, and dense uranium tamper material.

"Sieg Heil Adolph Hitler! We slaughtered them! We slaughtered those lousy, stupid assholes!" Jackie announced with an almost childlike glee. "And now we can build a bomb! An A-Bomb!"

"No Jackie, not yet." Howard could see the crestfallen expression on her face. "First, I have to construct the explosive lens."

"The what?"

"The lens. I have to build the implosion mechanism so the weapon can be detonated. I'll need you for another errand." Howard picked up one of the plutonium canisters. "Don't worry; I'm going to need a little time to assemble this thing. Remember, we're going to use it in January and blow up the Zionist regime in Washington."

The storage shed also served as a bank. Here, carefully hidden away in watertight pouches was the $6.2 million that the Werewolf had stolen in the armored car heist the previous year. Howard distributed envelopes containing $6000 to each of the terrorists. The money was a "salary" for those who participated in the raid. As the terrorists counted their money Howard began to speak in a hushed tone.

"Before you all leave, I want to read something to you," he began, pulling a crumpled piece of paper out of his pocket. "Governments are instituted among men, deriving their just powers from the consent of the governed; that, whenever any form of government becomes destructive of these ends, it is the right of the people to alter or abolish it, and to institute a new government... I was quoting the words of a great man: Thomas Jefferson, in the Declaration of Independence. I want you all to understand that today ours was an act of patriotism, sanctioned by the Founding Fathers of our country and by our God, Yahweh. Tomorrow the ZOG-controlled press will call us terrorists and criminals. The great battle to liberate our people from the yoke of the ZOG has begun! It has begun with an act of revolutionary violence. There can be no turning back now. The first blow has been struck. It now must be victory or death! May God bless you all." Howard turned and slowly walked away; tears rolled down his cheek.

With that, Collins, Mantooth, Stephens, Klimper and the Franklin brothers departed. The other terrorists remained behind to help guard the stolen materials. Jackie and Howard got into the rented car and reflected over the night's work.

"Well, we're on our way," he said, wiping his face with a handkerchief. "There's nothing can stop us now. It's actually begun... ZOG will die! I love you." He gazed into her eyes.

"It's such a beautiful night. Yahweh has blessed us with a great victory... and each other. I want to be with you tonight, lover."

They headed back to their hotel room.

0204 hours
Rocky Flats Nuclear Facility

The commotion around the Flats had attracted unwanted attention. Already, elements of the local press, suspecting that something was up, had begun to arrive. Police and plant officials quickly threw a cordon around the facility, seeking to prevent news of the massacre from leaking out as well as preserve the crime scene. At this point,

Denver FBI Regional Director Frank Bledsoe and Special Agent Al Gordon arrived on the scene. As the grisly task of removal of the dead commenced the pair was greeted by Plant Manager George Gillian.

"This is awful. A goddamned disaster," Gillian said to the agents as they arrived. "We got ten dead, and one critical. I just finished a preliminary search. Looks like some of the weapons-grade plutonium is missing."

"Shit!" Bledsoe said, kicking the ground in frustration. "How much is missing?"

"We don't know yet. I've got my staff going through the records, but some was definitely taken. At least two birdcages," Gillian said, lowering his head. The trio watched solemnly as the first of the slain men was carried out into a waiting coroner's van.

"We've got to notify the WMD Directorate," Bledsoe said. "Al, you contact local law enforcement. And NEST. We got to close this city up tight, airport and main roads. And for Christ's sakes, keep the damned press away. Last thing we need are a bunch of reporters running around getting in the way. If they ask, give 'em bullshit. Don't let 'em snow you with any First Amendment-freedom- of-the-press crap. Tell 'em that we'll make a statement later."

0215 hours

After some difficulty, Frank Bledsoe had finally gotten through to FBI Director Longstreet. He was clearly agitated.

"Frank, what the hell's going on in Denver?" the director said.

"Sir, there's been a terrorist raid at the Rocky Flats Nuclear Facility. A bloody one, I'm afraid," Bledsoe said as he watched another gurney covered with a blood-splattered sheet being wheeled out of the Security Annex.

"Casualties?"

"Sir, it was a massacre. Pure and simple," Bledsoe said, sighing. "Looks like we there's ten dead, one critical, and he probably won't last the night. The DOE guards never had a chance. I'm told that some of the victims were found shot to death in their beds. Their very beds for Christ's sake! Understand one victim was even found with food in his hands."

"And the plutonium, what about that? Is it intact?"

Bledsoe took a deep breath before answering. "Plant Manager Gillian thinks that some is missing."

The Director paused. "Frank, I've got to meet the president and the NSC within the hour. Do you have anything at all that I can tell them?"

"I'm afraid not sir."

0419 hours (EDT)
FBI Headquarters, Washington, D.C.

Having conferred with Bledsoe, Director Longstreet issued an urgent coded message to all ATF, FBI, AEC and DOE field offices:

TERRORIST RAID ROCKY FLATS THIS MORNING. MANY CASUALTIES. WEAPONS PLANT SECURITY SEVERELY COMPROMISED. THEFT OF FISSIONABLE MATERIALS BY TERRORISTS' PROBABLE. THE IDENTITY OF TERRORISTS UNKNOWN. PRESIDENT AND NSC HAVE BEEN ADVISED.
<MOST SECRET>

0440 hours (EDT)
The White House, Washington, D. C.

Upon notification of the developing situation at Rocky Flats, the president called an emergency meeting of the National Security Council. In the middle of his third year in office, the president could still remember how his Republican opponent had trashed his record during the bitter campaign. The stinging labels of being "wishy-washy" and "weak" on foreign policy and crime were hard for him to expunge. To silence the critics who were concerned with his decisiveness he knew he had to deal with the developing crisis in a firm way.

The meeting came to order. In addition to the FBI and CIA directors and members of the Joint Chiefs, Secretary of Energy Marilyn Snider was in attendance. She began speaking.

"Mr. President, I fear that we are faced with the ultimate nightmare, the theft of fissionable materials from one of our nuclear storage facilities. As you know, several hours ago the processing plant at Rocky Flats in Colorado was attacked by as of yet unknown terrorists. There's been a number of casualties among plant staff personnel."

"Exactly what was stolen?" the president said.

"Reports are still sketchy. It appears that weapons-grade plutonium and various trigger components were stolen." Snider said amid hushed gasps from others in attendance.

"Jesus, Mary and Joseph!" the CIA Director said excitedly. "So, you're telling us they got a goddamned atomic bomb!"

"How many of your people were murdered?"

"Mr. President," the Energy Secretary stammered, fighting back tears. "It was a massacre. I understand at least ten of the plant staff were murdered."

"George," the president said, turning to Longstreet. "This is your baby now... What have you implemented?"

"Sir, I've notified ATF and DOE field offices. Frank Bledsoe has got several agents at the scene. Airport personnel at Denver's DIA and satellite airfields have been alerted in case the terrorists try to move the stuff. NEST's got a team on the way. Finally, I'm activating my Counter- terrorism unit to spearhead the investigation."

"Any evidence to go on as to who the terrorists are?"

"No sir. Nothing yet. I suspect that the terrorists will make a claim of responsibility within a day or two."

"This was obviously a well-planned assault. George, level with me, do you think these terrorists are going to attempt to build a bomb?" the president said grimly.

George Longstreet paused briefly while clearing his throat. He then gave his answer. "No sir, I don't."

"Why not?"

"The atomic bomb is an extremely precise instrument. It requires detailed knowledge of engineering and physics. The construction of such a weapon is probably beyond the capacity of many terrorist groups, both here and abroad. Frankly, I'm personally more concerned about the other possibility."

"And what might that be, George?"

"That the missing plutonium will wind up in places like Baghdad, Tripoli or God forbid, Pyongyang," Longstreet said, looking away. There was a muffled groan from the others at the prospect of the mad North Korean dictator Kim Chi acquiring additional nuclear capability.

"So, you believe that foreign terrorists are involved?"

"Maybe. I'm sorry sir, I just can't give you anything more definitive until the preliminary investigation is completed."

"Well people, we're going to have to pull out all the stops on this on. I don't have to tell you that we have to maintain secrecy about what has happened. My press secretary will provide you with a sanitized version of events to give to the press. This version will be one in which there's been a radiation leak at the facility and several people died. The news shows will get the truth soon enough anyway."

"Why don't we tell the truth now?" Snider said.

"Marilyn, if we tell the people that bomb-grade plutonium was stolen from a nuclear processing plant by unknown terrorists there'll be wholesale panic. That's the ultimate goal of terrorism: to spread fear and suspicion amongst the population. We're not going to give those bastards what they want. You understand… Thank you all. Meeting's adjourned."

0600 hours. (MDT)
Room 213, Holiday Inn Hotel, Denver, CO.

Dawn was slowly breaking. Jackie and Howard were lying in bed watching TV, exhausted after the previous night's work. Slowly flipping through the various channels, the pair alternated between children's cartoons and morning news broadcasts. All the lead stories on the news concerned an *accident* at the Rocky Flats Nuclear Facility. The "sanitized" version of events, as released by the Department of Energy, was that a number of workers had been exposed to lethal levels of radiation during clean-up operations at the plant's plutonium storage area. While admitting that several of the workers had died, the DOE stressed that the nuclear material at the facility was intact. On listening to the lie Howard smiled broadly.

"Everything is going according to plan."

"But why are they giving us this horseshit explanation on what happened?" Jackie said, puzzled.

"Because they don't want to create a panic. If they said what really happened all hell would break loose. But don't worry. All of this we shall turn to our own advantage. We shall use ZOG's own lies against them."

0745 hours
Denver General Hospital

After a three-hour touch-and-go surgery, Nick Cooper, the surviving DOE security guard, was moved to a recovery room. He was in the best of hands. The DGH Trauma Unit, nicknamed the "Knife and Gun Club" was rated one of the best in the country; they were experts in the treatment of penetrating missile wounds. A delicate surgical procedure was performed to remove fragments of the projectile and repair the aortic aneurysm caused by the bullet. He lay under the heavy sedation of a drug-induced coma while a veritable phalanx of federal and state law enforcement officials stood watch outside his door. In the lounge, two of the surgeons who treated Cooper were watching news broadcasts that repeated the government's version of events.

"What's all this crap they're trying to feed us about this being some kind of nuclear accident?" one of the physicians said in amazement. "Bullshit! That guy Cooper in there, wasn't he from Rocky Flats?"

"Yeah, that bloody uniform I cut off of him was DOE and he's got a Rocky Flats ID in his wallet," his exhausted colleague said in reply, trying to suppress a yawn.

"Where do they come up with this fantasy about radiation leaks? He's got gunshot wounds, not radiation sickness."

By mid-morning, the investigation was well underway. Frank Bledsoe's FBI advance team, as well as members of the BATF began questioning plant staff and analyzing what evidence that was available.

"You guys be careful handling those bodies! Put on some gloves and lab jackets!" Bledsoe yelled at county morgue personnel as they went through the grim task of removing the corpses of Bent, Caldwell, Barker and Ames from the Communications Building. Plant Manager Gillian walked over to him. The two men entered the building.

"So, how's the investigation proceeding?" Gillian said.

Bledsoe raised his head and began sniffing the air in the room. "You smell that? Almonds, right?"

"Yeah, what about it?"

"That almond smell... probably cyanide. I'd say your people in there were murdered with sodium cyanide." Bledsoe spied a child's water pistol lying in the trash. "You see this? Bet the killer used cyanide to kill those men, I'd say probably dissolved it in DMSO."

"What?"

"Dimethyl Sulfoxide, or DMSO," Bledsoe said, gingerly retrieving the toy from the trash with a pencil. "It's readily absorbed through the skin. Looks like the killer probably used this kid's squirt gun to spray a cyanide-laced solution into the men's faces. Clever way to kill somebody without leaving any wounds on the body. Cyanide works fairly quickly. Rather potent blood-gas poison. Those poor devils never had a chance."

"Uh-huh, I'm impressed."

"Don't be. It's an old Soviet assassination technique. No obvious wounds... and real quick. The victim appears to have died from cardiac arrest... a heart attack, although using cyanide is rather crude." He carefully placed the toy in a plastic bag marked *EVIDENCE* and handed it to an aide. "There are quite a number of various shellfish toxins are much more effective... It's starting to look like the terrorists had help, a man on the inside."

"How do you figure that?"

"Well, looks like your communications and security systems were neutralized from Building One-Oh-One. It's a cinch that whoever did it must have had someone on the inside who simply killed all these people and shut everything down."

"I see."

"What's more, the killers apparently knew when you were preparing to make a shipment to Pantex. Knew exactly when to strike," Bledsoe added. "I'll need a list of all the people who were scheduled to work here last night. And let me know if anybody's missing. Also, it's probably a long shot, but we'll need anything you got on the perimeter surveillance cameras."

"You got it."

Additional FBI teams were arriving. The painstaking task of retrieving evidence had commenced. Agents took impressions of the tire tracks and made plaster casts, assisted by members of the federal Nuclear Emergency Search Team (NEST) and the FBI's Weapons of Mass Destruction Directorate (WMDD). The bodies of the slain men were photographed and removed; the numerous shell casings were collected for further analysis. Frank Bledsoe slowly paced toward the Main Entrance, and worried.

Goin' Fission

Thursday, June 4th
1046 hours
FBI Regional Headquarters, Salt Lake City, UT

Doug Rabson had received instructions from Director Longstreet to proceed to Denver to help coordinate the Rocky Flats investigation. In the several weeks since his arrival in Salt Lake City, the search for Jackie Lynch had been fruitless. While sightings of the suspect were reported, nothing panned out. As before, the suspect had simply vanished. There had been no murders in the city that one could tie to the Jack-L. In fact, things had been so quiet that Rabson had been told he could fly back to Washington to spend a little time with his family. Besides, Jacqueline Lynch could wait. The theft of plutonium was much more important. He was in the process of informing Kelly of his departure when the Station Chief called him to his office.

"Rabson, can you come in here? There's someone here I think you should see."

"Certainly sir." Rabson followed the Station Chief into the office. There, seated in a chair, was a trembling, shabbily dressed teenage youth with a clean-shaven head, thin, bony arms and a mouthful of dirty, rotten teeth. It was Nick Hoover.

Rabson stared at the youth. "What's your name, son?"

"Nick. Nick Hoover."

"All right, Nick," Kelly said. He pulled a chair over beside the youth. "Tell Agent Rabson what you just told me."

Hoover wetted his lips and slowly began speaking. "First of all, I want you to know that I ain't killed nobody. It was the others. They done it. It was Skin-Girl, Psycho and NumbNutZ. They done it all. They're crazy, man. I tried to stop 'em. I want out."

"Now who was killed?"

"Some black guy... last April... she just shot him and laughed. He was just a kid. They're all fucking crazy! I want out!" Hoover said. His eyes were nervously darting around the room.

"What else?"

"The others said they was going to steal some kind of nuclear shit. Make a bomb." Hoover now nervously began rocking back and forth in the chair. On hearing this, Rabson froze.

"What? Say that again."

"I heard 'em talking. They was going to rip-off some kind of nuclear shit somewhere in Colorado and try and make a bomb. They want to start a race war. They stopped talking when they saw me."

"Who was going to do all this, Nick? Come on!" Rabson said. He began shaking the youth.

"Anything else? Tell me about the woman."

"Some really weird chick... Don't know her name. But folks in JerUSAlem was saying that she wasted some black civil rights dude in LA back in April."

Rabson nodded, absorbing the information.

"Can you describe her?"

"I'd say she was about thirty. Blonde hair, maybe five-eight, one hundred twenty pounds or so I guess. Hey, man, I only seen her once, at the big Hitler rally we had back in April. I heard 'em talk."

Rabson reached into his briefcase and pulled out a copy of Jacqueline Lynch's photo. He showed it to him. "Nick, I want you to look carefully at this picture… Is this the woman?"

Hoover took a long look at the photograph. "Yeah… That's her," he said, nodding.

"Where is this woman now?"

"Somewhere in Colorado. I think… I don't know where."

On that, Hoover was rushed out of the office into another room. Kelly and Rabson began talking.

"Well, you think this kid's bullshitting us? You believe this skinhead asshole?" Kelly said while pouring a cup of coffee.

"The DOE issued a statement concerning Rocky Flats as being a nuclear accident. Nothing at all was mentioned about the theft of plutonium — only ATF, DOE, FBI and NEST were informed of the details. Yet somehow that punk kid Hitler Youth in there knows all about it — *Hell yes* I believe him!"

"Yeah, and it looks like that little hit lady you're tracking is somehow involved again."

"Sir, what other information do we have on this guy?"

"The usual," Kelly said, picking up Hoover's Salt Lake City Police file. "Reared in a dysfunctional family environment, hung out with the wrong crowd, skipped school, experimented with drugs, got his girlfriend pregnant. Says here he's got a record for shoplifting and burglary… he generally raised hell."

Rabson slowly nodded in response. Kelly continued.

"Apparently hooked up with a gang of local skins called *White Nation*. We think they may be connected with all those crazies up in JerUSAlem. This is all they got on him." Kelly closed the file.

"Have you got any informants at JerUSAlem?"

"Had one, good one, up until about almost two months ago. Guy named Leach. Isadore Leach."

"Had? What happened to him?"

"Don't know for sure. He was the one who fingered Malachi Hollander in the IRS killings… he also told us about the Hitler Rally back in April. Then, he just disappeared," Kelly said, opening a manila folder marked *Leach*. "We never heard from him again. Local police found a badly decomposed body near Lake Utah about two weeks back. It was completely nude. There were signs of mutilation; looked like the animals got to it first. Fit Leach's general description though. Guy had been shot twice through the head and had his testicles and penis cut off. We're still waiting for a positive ID from fingerprints and DNA."

"Hmm. Disappeared almost two months ago you say… about the same time that Jacqueline Lynch arrived in the Salt Lake area," Rabson said, slowly nodding. "Think that skinhead in there would be up to being an informant?"

"I doubt it, but bring him back in. I got an idea. Want to try something. You know, good cop-bad cop." Hoover was summoned back into the Station Chief's office. Kelly sighed and began talking to the youth.

"Listen Nick, we want you to go back to JerUSAlem. We've got to find out what's happening there."

"Uh-huh, yeah right," Hoover said with a nod, abruptly standing. "You want me to spy. You must be fucking crazy! Ain't no nigger

FBI cop gonna get my ass killed! Nobody rats on the Werewolf! Forget it man!"

"You better set yo' dumb ass back down," Kelly interrupted. Hoover cowered back in the chair. The black ex-linebacker loomed over him. "If there's any niggers 'round here it's you! I've handled you dumb-shit skinhead assholes before. Just like scrapping shit off of my shoe." Kelly pulled his chair over to Nick, glaring at the trembling youth. "You know, I could just turn your sorry ass over to the local cops on that murder last April. And this is a death penalty state, they'll fry your dumb white ass. They don't play that shit here! Or even better, maybe we'll let on to the kluckers at JerUSAlem that you were here talking to us FBI. Either way, your sorry ass is history, chump! So, what's it gonna be?"

Kelly got up and walked over to the window. Hoover sat motionless with a pensive expression. A tear slowly welled up in the corner of his eye. Rabson placed his hand on the youth's shoulder.

"I guess I really fucked up again, huh."

"Look Nick," Rabson said gently. "I'm going to level with you. We've got to find the material those people have stolen. You're not like the others. Your very being here proves that. You saw a young man brutally murdered simply because of the color of his skin. You had the decency to speak out."

"I just don't know… Like the black guy said, either way, I'm fucked."

"Nick, that woman you saw has already killed at least nine people; she has to be stopped. More importantly, the material she stole can be used to kill thousands. We can give you protection. If you cooperate with us, we've got what's called the Witness Protection Program… Besides, there's a fifty-thousand-dollar reward for information leading to the recovery of the stolen material."

"Fifty grand? No shit?" Hoover said, now keenly interested. As he was escorted out, Kelly pulled Rabson aside.

"Doug, when did the Bureau authorize a fifty-thousand-dollar reward for the missing plutonium? This is news to me."

"They didn't, but I had to say something to get that asshole to cooperate with us. These sonsabitches always open up when you dangle cash in front of 'em. Works every time," Rabson said. Kelly smiled broadly.

1330 hours

"Rabson, weren't you instructed to go to Denver and assist the WMD people in the Rocky Flats investigation?" Director Longstreet said in an angry voice over the telephone. "What in Hell are you still doing in Salt Lake?"

"Sir, I am investigating the terrorist incident. In fact, I may know who the terrorists are."

"What? How?"

"I think the Werewolf was behind this. We have a young skinhead defector here. I think he's going to cooperate. Apparently, the woman I've been tracking is somehow involved."

"I see, some skinhead told you. Don't you know those racist pricks will say anything to—"

"Sir, this kid knew details of the terrorist raid that nobody else could. Remember, no information concerning the theft of plutonium was released, yet somehow this kid knew all about it."

"Go on," the director said, now somewhat calmer.

"Apparently Jacqueline Lynch left Salt Lake City a couple of weeks ago. Somehow, she's mixed up in this."

"You better be right on this one. I'm meeting with the president and Attorney General in thirty minutes. I'll pass on the information that you have to them... All right, I want you to fly to Denver and coordinate with Frank Bledsoe and the locals."

"Yes sir."

"The DOE has completed its inspection of the facility. I just got off the horn with the plant manager there. It's a hell of a lot worse than we thought; the terrorists have apparently made off with various other components for a nuclear device besides the plutonium."

1600 hours (EDT)
The White House, Washington, DC

"I called this meeting in order to be brought up to speed on the Rocky Flats situation," the president said. "George, you have the floor."

"Mr. President," Longstreet began, gesturing to an Air Force officer standing in the doorway. "I've taken the liberty to ask Air Force Colonel David Travis to accompany me. He's an expert on nuclear weapons design and I think we should hear what he has to say. In the last twelve hours, I have been informed that in addition to the kilogram of plutonium, other nuclear components were stolen by the terrorists."

"What other components, George?" Attorney General Jen McCormick said.

"Specifically, tamper materials and neutron source. Col. Travis will elaborate," Longstreet said. The colonel dimmed the lights and turned on a slide projector. He began to speak.

"The first slide here shows a schematic diagram of a plutonium atom. As you can see, there are ninety-four positively charged particles called protons in the nucleus. The natural repulsive forces of these charges on each other are cancelled out by the presence of neutrons and a tremendous amount of energy. The next slide gives a diagram of an implosion-type atomic bomb. The tamper consists of depleted uranium metal," he said as he pointed out the details on the image.

"It surrounds a sub-critical sphere of plutonium. The plutonium itself is fabricated into a hollow sphere with either polonium and beryllium or a deuterium initiator at the core."

The NSC members all watched with a worried fascination as Colonel Travis proceeded to the next slide.

"To detonate this type of weapon, conventional high explosives surrounding this structure have to be simultaneously exploded against an inclusion of Baratol. This causes the so-called lens effect. The lens changes or focuses if you will the detonation shockwave from normal convex to concave. This is known as *implosion*. The detonation wave symmetrically compresses the tamper, which in turn crushes the plutonium core into what is called a *critical mass*. Tensile strength as well as uniform compression of the core is provided by the uranium tamper."

"And that causes the explosion?" the Energy Secretary said.

"Not quite. The detonation wave also causes the beryllium and polonium of the initiator to interact and generate neutrons. Millions of neutrons in a fraction of a second. As the plutonium core becomes critical, these neutrons begin the fission process by colliding with and splitting the plutonium nuclei, releasing the intra-nuclear energy I spoke of. This in turn releases still more neutrons and so on. The reaction becomes self-sustaining," the colonel said, moving to the next slide.

"The tamper design also retards loss of neutrons by containment and reflection, making the process more efficient. The virtually instantaneous splitting of tens of trillions of plutonium nuclei in turn results in the release of all that vast amount of electromagnetic and thermal energy. The result is the chain reaction that causes the atomic explosion, the sudden and violent release of this energy."

"Colonel, what does all this mean?" DOE Secretary Snider said with a tone that bordered on panic.

"Madam Secretary," he began with a sigh. "It means that the terrorists have at least several of the components required to build a functional atomic bomb. With what was stolen one or maybe two bombs of forty-to-fifty kiloton yield can be produced."

"Colonel, roughly how much destruction could result from the detonation of such a device," the president said.

The colonel paused before answering.

"Sir," he said in a measured tone. "A fifty-kiloton device would be approximately four times more destructive than the one dropped on Hiroshima in nineteen forty-five. I helped in the design of the fission device on our advanced W-88 warhead. The trigger you could build with the plutonium stolen, expertly designed, would be at least as destructive. Placed in the heart of a major city, say New York at rush hour, at least five hundred thousand casualties, is a conservative estimate."

There was a collective gasp in the room. The colonel continued.

"Property destruction is another thing; it would probably run into the hundreds of billions, perhaps trillions of dollars. The disruption of the country's economy would be, as you could imagine, tremendous. You all remember the terrorist attack on the World Trade Center back in 2001. That was nothing compared to what this type of device could do." The colonel laid his pointer down and looked away. "On the other hand, if these terrorists got hold of lithium-6-deuteride or tritium and know what to do they could go *thermonuclear*... A hydrogen bomb.

At the very least, with a source of tritium or deuterium in the core we're talking about a boosted fission-fusion-fission blast in the low-to-mid megaton-range."

"Oh my God!" Secretary Snider said loudly, burying her head in her hands.

"Such a device detonated in say, the lower Manhattan section of New York to continue my example, would completely destroy the city. The effect would be devastating. The country's economy would almost certainly collapse," the colonel finished, turning up the lights.

"George, I don't understand. At our last meeting you practically assured me that the terrorists lacked the capacity to build such a bomb," the president said in a somewhat angry tone.

"Sir, my original assessment of the situation was made on the information that was available at the time. I've just become aware of the new developments, the theft of all the additional components," the FBI Director said, looking down.

"Marilyn," President said, turning now to the DOE secretary. "Why were all of these components together in the first place? It seems to me that we sure made things easy for the terrorists."

"Mr. President, there was a shipment of triggers to Pantex that was scheduled for the eighth. It's standard procedure to run an inspection on the components prior to shipment. We felt that any danger was of hijacking while enroute to Texas. We simply couldn't conceive of a terrorist raid on the plant facility itself," she replied dejectedly.

"May I add," the colonel interjected, "The conventional explosives must be precisely engineered and triggered simultaneously in order for the detonation to occur. Otherwise, all you have is a big firecracker."

"Nevertheless, we must assume that the terrorists intend to build a bomb… George, have the terrorists made any attempt to contact us with demands?"

"No sir… Sir… eh, we think we may have a line on who the terrorists are," Longstreet said. All eyes in the room turned to the FBI Director.

"Who?"

"One of my Counter-terrorism Section team believes that a white supremacist group that calls itself the Werewolf was involved."

"The Werewolf?"

"Yes sir," Longstreet said, opening a file. "A racist gang that has been suspected of a number of racially motivated murders over the last year."

"Yes George, we know who they are," McCormick said. "Do you believe that these people have the sophistication to have pulled off this raid, as well as to build a bomb?"

Longstreet took a long pause before answering. "Yes, ma'am, I do."

"Based on what?"

"An informant. One of my Counter-terrorism people has contact with an informant close to the organization. The very fact that these people knew exactly what components to steal indicates to me that they probably have the knowledge and means to construct a bomb."

The Attorney General simply turned her head. Longstreet knew that it wasn't a very satisfactory answer. She had been a hard-nosed, no-nonsense prosecutor in Texas before being selected as one of only two women members of the president's cabinet. It was not for nothing that she had been nicknamed "General Jen" McCormick. As tempers were beginning to rise, the president adjourned the meeting.

Friday, June 5th
0914 hours
Denver International Airport

"Douglas Rabson? I'm Station Chief Frank Bledsoe."

"Good morning, sir. I appreciate your having come here to pick me up." Rabson extended his hand. The pair walked through the airport terminal to retrieve the rest of the agent's luggage.

"No problem… Well, as you know, all hell broke out at Rocky Flats two nights ago. Plant personnel were massacred and components of an atomic bomb stolen."

"Yes sir, I know the general details. How's the wounded man doing?"

"Not good. It was touch-and-go last time we checked. He's still unconscious. We got him under constant guard. He's the only witness to the massacre… I understand that you may know who the terrorists were."

"It's pretty shaky right now, but we may be up against a neo-Nazi group calling itself the Werewolf," Rabson said as he pulled out Lynch's photograph. "This woman may be involved. We think she's a professional assassin for the gang."

"Hmm, Denver cops are looking for a woman in the McClintock case," Bledsoe said, examining the picture.

"McClintock? Who's that?"

"About nine days ago, the plant's Head of Security, one George McClintock, fell out of a fourteen-story window. The locals at first dismissed the case as a suicide because of his ongoing divorce; now they're calling it suspicious," Bledsoe said. He handed the photograph back to Rabson.

"Oh?"

"They now say he may have been killed by a woman."

"Really? I think I'd like to start by talking to the police involved in this case if that's all right."

"Fine, you can go as soon as you get settled."

The two law officers drove into the city.

1135 hours
Denver Police Headquarters

"Lieutenant Bundy? I'm Special Agent Doug Rabson, FBI," the agent said, cautiously rapping on the door and peering inside the office. "I'm involved in an investigation of George McClintock's death. I understand that you're calling the case suspicious and that a woman may have been involved."

"Yeah, my captain told me to be expecting you... that's correct," Bundy said, rising from his desk and extending his hand. Rabson could see that the detective was a little surprised that the feds would be so concerned about a local murder case.

"McClintock was an important federal official. It's routine procedure that we would investigate his death," the agent went on, careful not to reveal details of Rocky Flats.

"McClintock was apparently in the middle of a rough-and-tumble divorce," Bundy said. He turned and reached for a plump folder. "At first it looked like he was depressed and simply committed suicide; now we're not so sure."

"How so Lieutenant?"

"McClintock was found with a needle mark in the back of his neck. Traces of some drugs that cause paralysis were found in the wound. The doctors at the morgue found other physical evidence that point to his being with a woman at the time of his death."

"Maybe the woman he was divorcing killed him."

"Nope, Theresa McClintock is a real bitch but checks out clean. Besides, she was having too much fun torturing him with the divorce."

"Well, can anybody identify the woman?"

"We've talked to a bartender and people at the hotel who've all seen her. Got a general description to go on… blonde, slender build, about five-seven, late twenties maybe."

"Maybe this is her." Rabson produced Lynch's mugshot.

"Maybe. Who's this?"

"We think she's a hitwoman for a gang that calls itself the Werewolf. She's got at least nine hits that we can't prove. Name's Jacqueline Diane Lynch."

"Let's take a ride," Bundy said, getting his jacket. "I want you to show this picture to a guy named Zach Duncan. He tends bar on Colfax at a place called the Red Dog. He's supposedly seen McClintock and some mystery woman together about two nights before his death."

1250 hours
The Red Dog Bar, Denver, CO

Bundy and Rabson drove over to the East Colfax bar. Isaac Duncan had just begun his shift. The lunch crowd had thinned out considerably; only a man and woman were seated in a booth near the front. The bartender came over to the two lawmen.

"Afternoon Lieutenant, uh — Bundy, right? I never forget a face!" Zach Duncan said with a smile. He was as loquacious as ever. "Who's your friend?"

"Douglas Rabson, FBI. I'd like to ask you a few questions Mr. Duncan," Rabson said, displaying his identification badge.

"Holy shit!" Zach said. Startled, he dropped the empty glass he was carrying. "Is this about Georgie McClintock and that Jacqueline chick? Hey, I told the cop here everything I know."

"This shouldn't take very long, Mr. Duncan."

"Call me Zach."

"Okay Zach... have you ever seen this woman before?" The agent reached into his pocket and displayed Lynch's photograph. The bartender recognized her immediately.

"Shit! That's her!" Zach said loudly. Curious about the commotion, the other patrons in the bar turned around. "That's Jackie, the chick I seen with George!"

"You're sure?"

"No doubt man, I mean, her hair is longer in this picture but that's her! No way I'd forget a body like that."

"When did you last see her?"

"The twenty-fourth, I think. Sunday. Yeah. She was with George. They came in here a lot."

"Thank you, Zach. Lieutenant Bundy and I will leave you copies of our business cards. I'd appreciate it if you would give us a call if this person shows up here again."

"Come on G-man, clue me in, what's this chick done?" Zach said, stuffing the business card into his apron. "You think she killed George or something?"

"It's just a routine investigation. Thank you for your time."

Bundy and Rabson left the bartender and slowly walked toward the exit. The two men paused at the door.

"Ol' Zach's in rare form today," Bundy said, shaking his head.

"I kind of like Zach. He's so uh, colorful."

"Well Agent Rabson, seems like this Jackie Lynch character is the woman we're looking for, but I still don't see what you feds want with her. This is a local killing."

"It's like I said, we think that Lynch is a professional assassin for a racist gang. We suspect that she's killed at least nine men, all black or Jewish."

"But McClintock was white, and he wasn't Jewish either."

Rabson paused and took a deep breath. He decided to trust Bundy.

"Lieutenant, I'm going to level with you. A few nights ago, there was a-uh, incident at the Rocky Flats Nuclear Facility."

"Yeah, I read about it in the papers, some kind of bad nuclear accident or something I hear. Couple guys died. What does that have to do with the McClintock case?"

"That was just the cover story the DOE gave the press to prevent a panic."

"Panic?"

"The plant was attacked by a gang of terrorists. They practically slaughtered everyone there. We think this Jacqueline Lynch was involved."

"What?" the lieutenant was now genuinely confused.

"I think the assassin seduced McClintock to gain information or access to the facility. When she got what she wanted, she simply killed him and tried to cover it up by making it look like he committed suicide."

"Well, what were the terrorists after?"

Rabson paused at the question, then reluctantly he gave his answer.

"Plutonium. Bomb-grade plutonium," he said, almost forcing the words out.

"Jeeeezus!" Bundy murmured.

"For obvious reasons, I have to ask you not to repeat any of this. The Bureau and DOE will release detailed information in time." Bundy slowly nodded his consent.

Rabson was satisfied that he had a solid connection between Jackie Lynch and the Rocky Flats raid. Exiting, he and Bundy took no notice of the couple at the booth. Pamela Haney and her boyfriend Bruce Davies quietly finished their drinks and left the bar. They watched the two lawmen as they drove off.

1420 hours
FBI Field Office, Byron Rodgers Federal Building, Denver, CO

Section Chief Bledsoe was waiting when Rabson arrived back at the office.

"The preliminary investigation of the Rocky Flats raid is finished. We have at least one suspect, we're looking for a woman named Pamela Mae Haney."

"Oh?"

"Just now finished talking to the plant manager there," Bledsoe said. "Apparently Miss Haney had been a custodian at the Flats for about six months. When she never showed up for work after the massacre, plant officials became suspicious. Local cops went to her Arvada address. She had moved out a couple of days earlier." Bledsoe pulled out an Arvada Police mugshot of the woman.

"I see."

"Our people searched the apartment. They found a bottle of some chemical called dimethyl- sulfoxide, rubber gloves and a half empty container of sodium cyanide under the bathroom sink — same stuff used to kill the three men in the Communications Building."

"Didn't anyone at DOE bother to conduct any kind of a security background check on this woman before she was hired?" Rabson said, somewhat incredulous.

"Apparently not. I guess they thought that she wasn't in a sensitive enough position to warrant it. I mean Hell, she was only the goddamned janitor," Bledsoe grunted in reply, shaking his head.

"Do the local cops have anything on her?"

"One item from a few years back. She was arrested for assault with a deadly weapon," Bledsoe said, reading from the police file. "It seems that this Haney was involved in a minor automobile accident way back in twenty-twenty-three… real minor accident. It says here that she apparently jumped out of her car and shot the other driver in the arm with a twenty-two-caliber handgun."

"For a fender-bender? Boy, talk about road rage. People sure are crazy. Now I think I've heard everything," Rabson said, slowly shaking his head.

"At her arrest, Haney gave a different reason for the shooting."

"And what was that?"

"The arresting officer's report says she apparently shot him because he was black," Bledsoe said, closing the file. "You able to get anything from the Denver PD?"

"Yes sir. Talked to a local bartender." The agent pulled out a pad of notes. "He gave us a positive ID on Jackie Lynch. Apparently both she and McClintock were at his bar several times. It's beginning to look like she killed him."

"Director Longstreet's been riding my ass. I'm going to call Washington and fill him in on the investigation so far. I want you to get copies of this woman's picture out to hotels, bars, anywhere you can think of. See if we can find this killer before someone else is murdered."

"Yes sir." Rabson watched Bledsoe leave the room. He opened his briefcase and added Pam Haney's photograph to those of Jackie.

Saturday, June 6th
0849 hours
Holiday Inn Hotel, Room 213, Denver, CO

Jackie returned to the room carrying a bag of breakfast items she had purchased from a nearby McDonald's. The room itself was a mess. Books on nuclear physics, integral calculus and engineering, calculators, and sheets of paper with soccer ball-like drawings as well as complex mathematical equations were scattered all over the floor. Amid the chaotic scene sat a pensive Howard.

"Howie, what is all this shit?" the woman surveyed all the chaos. "You're just like a little kid… I'm gone for half an hour, and you make a mess."

"They're diagrams. I'm designing the implosion mechanism that's going to detonate the bomb."

"Hmm, looks like you're designing soccer balls to me… Well, did you have to tear the place up so?"

"Couldn't be helped." He rose and embraced her. "Never mind that now, we got a problem."

"What's the matter now?"

"I just got off the phone with Pamie. The FBI is on to you. The Werewolf is blown. We've been betrayed."

"Calm down. Now, what happened?"

"Yesterday, Pamie and Davies were at that bar you met McClintock in. They heard the bartender there talking to some cop and an FBI agent named Rabson. The FBI man had your picture. The bartender fingered you, knew you by name."

"Shit! That lousy, fucking bartender again!" Jackie hurled an egg muffin sandwich across the room in disgust. "Asshole kept trying to hit on me... I just don't get it. How could they have found me? How could they have known?"

"I don't know honey. Pamie talked to the Reverend in JerUSAlem last night. They think that ZOG may have planted an FBI stooge there, but they think they got a good idea who the rat is."

"I hope they cut his balls off!"

"Listen, you want out? I'll understand. We can manage this operation from here without you."

"No way," Jackie said, shaking her head. "I'm going to stay with you. You know I stay at your side. Shhhh... Don't worry lover, I'll fix things." She kissed him on the cheek. "This Rabson guy, isn't he the same agent who was passing my picture around Salt Lake?"

Howard briefly pondered the question.

"Yeah... Hey, that's right!"

"You know, I think I'm going to have to take care of Mr. Rabson."

"What do you mean?"

"I'm going to kill him... Hey Howie, wanna kill a cop?" Jackie began licking her lips as she screwed a plump silencer onto a Beretta nine- millimeter handgun.

"No. Not yet." Howard slowly took the weapon out of her hand. "There's no time for that now. In a few days we have to see *the Professor*. Then I'll have a more important errand for you. In the meantime, pack your things. We're getting the hell out of here. We're going back to Stacey and Nick's."

"Okay... but I got to run a little errand first."

1445 hours
Holiday Inn Hotel, lobby.

In his fifth stop of the day, Rabson had arrived at a Holiday Inn Hotel in north Denver. There, an elderly woman who was working at the clerk's desk greeted him.

"May I help you, sir?" the woman said sweetly.

"Ma'am, I'm Special Agent Rabson, FBI." Rabson showed his badge and ID.

"Oh, my! I used to watch all you people on TV."

Rabson turned to one side, concealing a smile. "Yes ma'am... I wonder have you ever seen this person?" he displayed the assassin's photograph. The old woman slowly extracted a pair of glasses from her purse and examined it.

"Oh my, yes. That's Mrs. Clement. She and her husband were in uh, let me see, Room Two- thirteen. I think. You just missed them. I checked them out just this morning."

"Her husband? Was there a man with her?"

"Yes, Mister FBI Agent. Very nice man. He said he was a doctor. He told me that he worked on secret projects or something like that for the government."

"You say they checked out this morning?"

"Yes, just before noon."

"Well ma'am, will you do me a big favor? Please don't rent that room out or have it cleaned until we've examined it. It's very important."

"Oh, just like they do on television."

"That's right, ma'am, just like on television."

"All right, G-Man! You have a nice day."

"And you too, ma'am." Rabson pulled out his cellular phone and hurriedly called Bledsoe.

"Frank. This is Rabson. I'm at a Holiday Inn here on north Broadway. A clerk here gave me a positive ID on Jackie Lynch, under the name of Clement. She's got an accomplice. A man. I'm going to secure the hotel room they stayed at… Shit! I probably missed 'em by a few hours. They checked out only a short time ago. Send a latent print team here on the double."

"Okay Doug… Oh, I'm afraid I've got some bad news for you."

"Today's the day for it."

"Just before you called, I talked to a Denver homicide cop named Bundy. It seems about an hour ago they found a body of someone you know, a guy named Isaac Duncan. He was found shot to death in the alley outside of his bar, point-blank range with a nine-millimeter. Whoever did it must have been waiting for him. No witnesses. He was shot twice, one through the heart and one in the genitals. The killer probably used a silencer… Doug? You there?"

"Shit! Yeah, I'm still here. Zach Duncan was a bartender. He was the guy who identified Jacqueline Lynch as being with McClintock at a bar, just before he was murdered… I wonder how she found out that I talked to Zach?"

"Well, I'm sending Al Gordon and a print team out there. You sit tight until they get there. Oh, by the way, good job"

"Yes sir. Thank you, sir." Rabson sat down in the lobby and waited. He mulled over Zach's murder in his mind. It was hard to make sense out of the senseless.

Sunday, June 7th
1045 hours

The latent prints crew had finished their work during the night. A number of incriminating fingerprints had been collected from the room and sent to Washington for analysis and comparison. Rabson and Gordon were assembled in Frank Bledsoe's office. Bledsoe began speaking.

"Well gentlemen, I've got the reply on those prints we got from the hotel room. There were two sets of prints belonging to Jacqueline Lynch and a man named Howard Douglas Brennan."

"Brennan? Who's that?" Gordon said.

"Howard Brennan was a colonel in the Air Force." Bledsoe replied. His voice became tense as he read the file. "He was thrown out as a nut case a few years ago… Oh my God! It says here that he had been involved in nuclear weapons design at Hanford, Los Alamos and Rocky Flats."

"Jesus! So now we got a goddamned psycho on the loose with an atomic bomb?" Gordon said.

"What's this man's affiliation with the Werewolf?" Rabson said.

"The report doesn't say," Bledsoe said, "But apparently this guy really hates blacks and Jews. Says here that he's suspected of having associated with known white supremacist and neo-Nazi groups while in the Air Force. They finally kicked his ass out of the service after he publicly threatened the president."

"So, what does this guy look like?" Rabson said.

"Five-eleven, about hundred eighty-five pounds, sandy colored hair. It's only a general description. The Bureau is sending us photos of Brennan from when he was in the service. That's all, gentlemen. I've got to call the director." As the meeting was breaking up, a secretary came running over to Rabson.

"Sir, there's a young woman who's been calling you… she's on the line now."

"Thank you." Rabson went over to the desk.

"Yes? This is Agent Rabson."

"Is this Mr. Rabson? Douglas Rabson? It's too bad about that little accident Isaac Duncan had yesterday," a woman's voice on the other end said.

"What? Who is this?"

"They call me 'Jack-L'… I'm afraid I had to kill your bartender friend yesterday," the mysterious voice said. "It's a real pity the pathetic asshole had to die, but he talked too much. So, I shot him. I got your name and number from the business card I took off his body."

"Is this Jacqueline? Let's see… which is it today, Jacqueline Lynch, Jacqueline Clement or Ginger Kereluk? By the way, how's your husband, uh, Howard Brennan?" Rabson said, motioning over to Bledsoe.

"Oh, you know my name and everything. You even know about Howie."

"I know that you've killed ten people."

"I've killed a lot more than that. Twenty-eight to be exact… but then again, I don't count niggers. Listen, I kill people for a living. If a man stands in my way, I dispose of him. They say that killing people is a lot like eating potato chips. I know that you're probably trying to trace this call. Don't bother. It's a burner… I just want you to know that you're going to be my next victim if you don't stop chasing me," she said while hanging up. Rabson momentarily froze, clearly stunned by the coldness of the remarks.

"Well Frank, looks like I just made the varsity," Rabson said, turning to Bledsoe. "Guess I'm getting to some people."

"What do you mean?"

"That was the Jack-L. She just threatened to kill me."

"She called… *here*? So, this bitch is coming after you?"

"Sort of looks that way."

"Well, she's going to have to wait her turn. Director Longstreet wants you to give a first-hand account of the investigation to the president and the NSC after his news conference Wednesday. Here's your ticket." Bledsoe handed Rabson a coach-class plane ticket to Washington, DC.

"Maybe I can spend a little time with Rachel and the kids."

1600 hours (EDT)
The White House Situation Room, Washington, DC

In a somber atmosphere, the president and members of the National Security Council met. The first of the funerals for the murdered men was scheduled for the next day. The President took his place at the head of the table and started the meeting.

"Where's Marilyn?" he said, noticing the absence of the Energy

Secretary. "I asked her to prepare a list of improved security measures to be implemented at these nuclear facilities. Oh well, we'll get to her later. Ahh... George, what do you have?"

"Sir, we know the identity of some of the terrorists involved," the FBI Director said somewhat apprehensively. "As you remember, I told you that a racist gang called the Werewolf was involved. It looks like they had a mole inside the facility."

"Very unlikely, George," the Attorney General said. "Top level personnel are always vigorously screened in the background check and security clearance procedure. You know the guidelines."

"That's correct ma'am. But the mole wasn't top level. We think she was a janitor!"

"She? A woman? A woman is mixed up in this?" the president said in amazement.

"That's right, sir. A woman named Pamela Haney. No background check was done with this person. Apparently, the Werewolf managed to get her into the plant. When they were ready, she enabled the facility to be penetrated. We're looking for her now."

"Go on," the president said.

"There's another woman involved. A professional assassin named Jacqueline Lynch. The head of security at the Flats facility, one George McClintock was apparently seduced and murdered by this Lynch."

"Why?"

"To get information about security procedures, timing of trigger shipments to Pantex, the works. Apparently when she got what she wanted she simply killed him and tried to make it look like a suicide."

With the NSC now completely captivated, Director Longstreet

delivered the most shocking revelation of all. He cleared his throat and continued.

"We think that the leader of the terrorists is an ex-Air Force colonel named Howard Douglas Brennan."

"Howard Brennan? Not that crazy son-of-a-bitch," the president winced.

"Yes sir. Colonel Brennan was involved in the design of primary triggers for thermonuclear warheads. He was actively involved in the design of the improved Mark 12A warheads on our Peacekeeper missiles while doing research at Livermore and Los Alamos. He was cashiered from the Air Force because of his racism and personality clashes with government officials."

"That's not the half of it, George," the president interjected angrily. "This man is obviously a psychotic. He disagreed with administration policy right down the line. And he was a racist. I finally fired his insubordinate ass when he said publicly that the country would be better off if a hijacked seven-forty-seven were to be crashed into the White House. With all the events of nine-eleven still vivid I simply couldn't tolerate crap like that."

"Yes sir, I remember the big article they did in *Newsweek*. The press compared you to Harry Truman."

"So do you know where these people are now?"

"Not quite, ma'am. Our investigation has revealed that Brennan and his wife settled on a ranch somewhere in Utah. He became associated with various sects of Identity Christianity. Tom Kelly's Office in Utah has reported that there's a particularly militant group in the Provo area which calls itself the Aryan Church of Yahweh the Creator," Longstreet said.

"Aryan Church of Yahweh, you say?" McCormick said. "Hell, I

remember dealing with those crazies just last year. They were stockpiling weapons for years. Last year there was almost a shoot-out between those people and federal agents. We backed off a bit. Nobody wanted another Waco."

"Something about stolen weapons, wasn't it?" the president said.

"Yes sir. ATF traced them to the Provo area, but we couldn't prove anything. The weapons were never recovered."

"Well, if Brennan is involved in the theft of the plutonium, we're in trouble. He's got all the background to build a bomb as well as the motivation — and a wide range of vulnerable targets. Inasmuch as he lives in Utah and associates with this racist sect, I'd say that this Aryan Church of Yahweh is the place to start looking for the stolen material," the president said, glancing down at his watch. "I wonder where the devil Marilyn is, I wanted everybody to see her security report… All right people, I think that's enough for today."

As the meeting was breaking up, a secretary came up and handed the president a sealed envelope bearing the letterhead of the Energy Department. Recognizing Marilyn Snider's handwriting on the envelope he slowly walked toward the Oval Office to read it. In reading the opening lines he suddenly froze.

Sir,

By the time you read this I shall be no more. The events of the last two weeks, of which I am completely and solely responsible have burdened me with a profound sense of guilt which my death cannot compensate. I feel that I can no longer bear this burden, either as your Energy Secretary or in life itself. It has been a pleasure to have served you these years.

Because of my failures, ten of the loyal and faithful individuals under my charge have been brutally murdered and a dangerous material has been abducted. I have failed myself, I have failed my President, and lastly, I have failed the country. In closing, permit me to recommend that Assistant

Energy Secretary Nils Larson be elevated to the position of Secretary. God bless you, Mr. President, and God bless the American people.

Marilyn Snider.

"No! God, no! Why Marilyn? Why? It wasn't your fault! It wasn't your fault!" the president sobbed softly, slowly shaking his head and pounding his fist against the wall. "My God! What will the country say? What will the country say?"

"Is anything wrong, sir?" a female White House Secret Service agent said to him in the hallway. Without answering, the president handed her the letter and shuffled into the Oval Office, closing the door. There he laid his head on the desk and wept like a child.

… Sherman E. Ross

Clear and Present Danger

"…Now we are engaged in a great civil war, testing whether that nation, or any nation so conceived and so dedicated, can long endure…"

— Abraham Lincoln, from the *Gettysburg Address*

By midweek, in spite of frantic efforts by the administration, the government's cover story regarding Rocky Flats was crumbling. From the beginning, the State Department was inundated with inquiries from foreign countries on the whereabouts of the stolen materials. The Israelis were especially concerned should the plutonium suddenly appear in the hands of radical Islamic extremists. The Russian ambassador spoke publicly on how ironic it was that only several weeks earlier that the Americans expressed concern of the security of plutonium in the Russian Federation.

The local Denver news organizations had been naturally suspicious of the heightened activity around the facility; they had literally flocked to the plant like vultures around carrion. At the Denver General Hospital various medical people had informed the media that Nick Cooper, the surviving guard, had sustained wounds from gunshots rather than radiation exposure. As for Cooper's condition itself the prognosis was worsening by the hour. Despite the apparently successful surgery, Cooper was dying. By Tuesday, his condition had been downgraded from critical to grave. Evidence of septicemia, or blood poisoning, had manifested itself in rapidly falling blood pressure and ominous signs of major organ failure.

Cable Network Agency was the first to break the story that the facility had in fact, been attacked by terrorists. Having now been 'scooped' by the competition, the other networks scrambled to make up lost ground. By Tuesday, Rocky Flats was the lead story on all the major news programs. Finally, the fact that the Energy Secretary had been dead found in the bathtub of her Washington, DC townhouse next to an empty bottle of sleeping pills only fueled still further the speculation that the plant's security had been severely compromised. Financial markets began to react. On the strength of the *CNA* report, the DOW Industrials tumbled 1,990 points in a wave of panic selling before recovering forty-six by the end of the trading day. 'Black Tuesday' was the third worst day in the history of Wall Street. Resolving to control events rather than be controlled by them, the president obtained time on all four major networks for a primetime news conference.

Wednesday, June 10th
1900 hours
The White House Press Room

"Ladies and gentlemen, the president of the United States," the White House Press Secretary announced amid the throng of reporters and correspondents.

"Ladies and gentlemen of the press, and my fellow citizens," the president said while nervously donning a pair of reading glasses and shuffling a small pad of papers. "Before I begin this news conference, I would like to make a brief statement concerning the events of the last several days." Although a gifted public speaker, the president seemed strangely ill at ease. He almost had to struggle through his prepared text.

"Last week, a gang of terrorists attacked the nuclear facility at Rocky Flats, Colorado near Denver. A number of Department of Energy personnel stationed at the plant were savagely murdered by these cowards. In addition, small amounts of nuclear material were stolen." The President slowly scanned the room for any signs of emotion, as if to gauge the response of the audience from his words.

"Let me assure you, and let me assure the nation, that the cowards who carried out this senseless crime shall be brought to justice, and that the security of this republic shall never be compromised. I have instructed the National Security Council and various federal law enforcement agencies to act in concert to bring about the speedy recovery of the materials. In closing my statement, let me further say that this has been a difficult time for the Administration. The First Lady and I have lost a first-class Energy Secretary and dear personal friend in Marilyn Snider," the president said, wiping a tear from the corner of his eye and softly clearing his throat. "All right, I'll take the first question." He pointed to a female reporter in the first row.

"Mr. President, you said that nuclear materials were taken by the thieves. Do you mean plutonium or other bomb-making materials?"

"Yes."

"Exactly how much was taken?"

"We don't know yet. An inventory is still underway. However, I am informed that at least several pounds of plutonium may be missing."

"Any way that it could be fabricated into a bomb?" a reporter from the *Times* said.

"You get right to the point. No, not very likely. Nuclear weapons production requires a sophistication that is beyond most terrorist groups today."

"But Mr. President, what other reason would terrorists have to steal these materials but to build a bomb?" another reporter said.

"Probably to sell on the arms black market," the president replied. "You all must understand that the real danger lies in these materials winding up in Iran, North Korea, Iraq or some other unstable, rogue nation." He took a question from another reporter.

"Mr. President, there's been a lot of terrorist activity in the Middle East recently, you know, radical Islamic fundamentalists and the like, any way this is somehow related?"

"We just don't know yet. investigating. It's best not to draw any conclusions at this time."

"Mr. President, we 'lost' several kilograms of plutonium back in nineteen sixty-eight that somehow *reappeared* in Israel. We don't seem to protect these materials very well," a reporter in the back of the room yelled.

"Well, as you know, I wasn't president then." Nervous laughter rose from the audience. "I've since implemented improved security measures at Hanford, Lawrence Livermore, Rocky Flats and Pantex."

"Looks a little like locking the barn door after the horse has been stolen if you ask me," one correspondent whispered to another.

"Sir, exactly what kind of security measures have you implemented?" a voice said from the back.

"Without going into too much detail, these measures involve better screening and training of security personnel, better, more secure storage of nuclear materials, and so on," the president responded.

"Sir, we've heard conflicting stories. Exactly how many of the plant's personnel were killed by the terrorists?" the same reporter said.

"We have ten dead and one severely injured."

"How's the wounded man doing? Will he recover?"

"He's in serious condition. The doctors are optimistic. We have him hidden away in a secret location and hopefully we'll get valuable information from him shortly."

"Mr. President, I've heard rumors that the murderers are everything from Palestinian commandos to white supremacists. Do you have a line on who any of the terrorists are?" a *CNA* reporter said.

"Nothing definite, but we're working on it."

"Sir," the reporter persisted. "I've received information that you've activated the Counter- terrorism Strike Force of the FBI. Perhaps you do know something definite about the people who did this."

"We're looking at a variety of possibilities. That's all I can say at this time," the president responded in a sharper tone, having just been called a liar.

"Sir, has there been any contact from the terrorists? You know, demands for money or some other ransom, calls for release of prisoners, threats?" a reporter from the *Post* said.

"No, nothing at all. Well, thank you all. My Press Secretary will provide any pertinent information as it becomes available."

The news conference was concluded.

Nick Hoover wasn't much of a spy. Whatever decency may have brought him the Tom Kelly's office back in June, raw greed for FBI reward money turned him informant. He had no sooner returned to the JerUSAlem compound when he began making mistakes. He asked too many questions concerning the whereabouts of Lynch, Beausoleil, Corbett and others who were involved in the Rocky Flats raid. Before long, members of the commune began voicing suspicions about Brother Hoover. These suspicions were communicated to Reverend Hollander.

Hoover was not only an inexperienced spy; he was too obvious to the cult members. Having been given one of Kelly's business cards,

Hoover neglected memorizing the number and destroying it. He carelessly left the card in a shirt pocket where it was discovered in the commune laundry.

2200 hours (MDT)
Aryan Church of Yahweh the Creator, Near Provo, UT

"Brother Hoover, the Reverend Mother wants to see you. Come with me… now," a church member said, rousing a sleeping Nick Hoover from his cot. He was a tall, muscular blond wearing camouflage fatigues and a swastika armband, the same one that the Reverend had assigned to follow him.

"What's this all about? I ain't done nothing," a groggy Hoover muttered as he followed the man outside. As he left the building, another man struck him from behind with a large club. The dazed youth was dragged into a waiting truck. The vehicle sped off into the night.

2218 hours

The truck pulled to a stop in a large clearing near Lake Utah. Another vehicle was already there. The area itself was dimly illuminated with torches and the vehicle's headlights. Dagmar Hollander and three hooded church members waited. One of the men had a large, snarling German shepherd guard dog.

"Do you have him?" Hollander said to the blond man as he emerged from the truck. "Do you have the serpent?"

"Yes, Reverend Mother, I have the serpent."

"Then let us proceed." The two men dragged the dazed youth roughly from the truck into the clearing. Hoover, now realizing what was happening, began to struggle and whimper.

"You the nigger-lover?" one of the other church members said.

"What's this? I ain't done nothing. Please!"

"Silence!" Hollander pulled a piece of paper from her purse. "Brother Hoover, you are now charged with the gravest of crimes: treason against your race. Do you have anything to say before the indictment is read?"

"What did I do? No! I ain't done nothing!" Hoover mumbled, terrified as one of the church members pulled out a large truncheon. Judith Hollander began reading the 'indictment.'

"Several days ago, Sister Connie found this in your pocket while doing the laundry." She pulled out Tom Kelly's business card. The card was worn from repeated washing, but the words *Federal Bureau of Investigation*, along with a telephone number were plain to see.

"You will take note that the card bears the name of our enemy, that FBI nigger Tom Kelly! He's the FBI man who persecuted Malachi." Hollander passed the card to the others present. The youth stood motionless.

"Where did you get this?" Hollander said forcefully. "Answer me!"

"I-uh found it?" Hoover stammered unconvincingly. It was the best lie he could think of. Hollander's lips pursed with anger.

"Liar... Stinking traitor! Judas! Brothers Hood and Avery have been following you ever since you started showing weakness last month. They saw you enter the FBI federal building in Salt Lake City last week. Did you *find* this in there?" Hollander now waved the card in the terrified youth's face.

"Please Reverend Mother, let me explain. I ain't no rat." The two men held the youth as Hollander slapped him across the face. As if on cue, the dog started barking and straining on its leash.

"I warned you to keep your mouth shut, but you had to betray us. Like

Judas… for a handful of silver. I took you in. I gave you food and sanctuary… and this is how you repay me. I helped you and yet I receive treachery in return. You make me sick! White nigger! White Judas!" She spat in his face. "What say you, fellow Aryans?"

"Guilty as sin," the blond man said. "Kill him!" The others nodded in agreement.

"No! It wasn't me! Please, I ain't no rat!" Hoover said. He was crying.

"You're guilty! Guilty of race treason! I cannot help you now. I advise you now to make your peace with your God. You shall be taken to a place of execution where you shall be put to death in accordance with the laws of Yahweh. And may our blessed Father have mercy upon your soul, for I shall have none. Take him!"

"No! Please… It wasn't me! I'm sorry!" Hoover said in a sob. "I don't wanna die!"

"Take this race traitor out of my sight! Leave him where his ZOG friends can find him. Let his death serve as a warning to any others who should wish to live in the world of sin. The Will of Yahweh be done." Hollander turned away.

"Please!"

"Sorry Kemo Sabe, no can do," the man with the dog said with a shrug. "Once you go black you can't go back!"

"Snitches are bitches that wind up in ditches," the other men began chanting.

"I don't want to die! You're all fucking crazy!" Hoover screamed, struggling fitfully as two of the Aryans dragged him off into the distance. Several minutes later, the terrified youth was heard screaming pitifully. Moments later, laughing and joking, the two men returned to the vehicles. There was fresh blood on their clothing.

Thursday, June 11th
1530 hours
FBI Headquarters, J. Edgar Hoover Bldg., Washington, DC

"Good afternoon, sir," Rabson said to Director Longstreet.

"Welcome back to DC. Tell me, how are Rachel and the kids?"

"Everybody's fine, sir. Thank you for asking."

"You see the president's news conference last night."

"Yes sir."

"What did you think about it?"

"He handled things about as well as could be expected, given the situation of wanting to inform the public while at the same time withholding sensitive material so as not to hamper the investigation or create panic."

"Well, as of yesterday Jacqueline Lynch and Howard Brennan were added to the Bureau's 'Ten Most Wanted' list." Longstreet pulled out several copies of the wanted posters.

"These are going up all over the country. We're even trying to get segments on various popular primetime news broadcasts and unsolved crime programs on TV… You ready to brief the president?"

"Yes sir."

"Excuse me, sir," a secretary said. "I have a long-distance call from the Regional Office in Salt Lake City for Agent Rabson."

"Thank you." He followed the secretary to a phone. "This is Agent Rabson."

"Rabson, this is Tom Kelly. Tried to get you in Denver but Bledsoe told me you were back in DC… Doug, I'm afraid we lost our informant last night."

"Shit! What happened?"

"Early this morning a couple joggers found the body of a white male, about twenty. He was tentatively identified as Nick Hoover... Looks like those Yahweh fuckers castrated him. He was found beaten, with his penis and testicles stuffed in his mouth and his throat cut. The body was apparently really mutilated. Out of pure cussedness they even urinated on it."

Rabson paused momentarily and sighed,

"Thank you, sir."

1600 hours
The White House

"Mr. President, this is Special Agent Douglas Rabson, a member of my Counter-terrorism Strike Force," the director said, gesturing Rabson into the room. "He's presently involved in the Rocky Flats investigation."

"I'm very happy to meet you, Agent Rabson. I've heard a lot about your work."

"Thank you, sir."

"I understand that you have discovered the identities of some of the terrorists involved in the Rocky Flats raid."

"Yes sir, we believe that we have."

"Are there any new developments?"

"Sir, I've just been told that our informant at the Yahweh Church in Utah was murdered last night."

"So, we no longer have any eyes or ears at the compound?"

"I'm afraid not sir," Rabson sighed.

"Well, that settles it. George, I'm initiating Operation Thunderbolt," the president said, turning to the FBI Director.

"Thunderbolt?" Rabson said.

"We've decided we're going to enter the JerUSAlem compound, Doug," the FBI Director interjected, "and search for the stolen plutonium. The operation's codenamed Thunderbolt."

Rabson was incredulous. "Sir, the Church of Yahweh is very heavily armed. Tom Kelly in Salt Lake tells me they've got a lot of automatic weapons and even antitank ordnance. Any force attempting to enter there would almost certainly sustain very heavy casualties."

"Don't worry," the president said. "I've instructed Attorney General McCormick to coordinate the operation with General Meade at Fort Carson. Elements of the Fourth Mechanized Infantry Division will be alerted to surround the compound. Right now, we're just waiting for a federal Judge to sign the warrant before we go into action."

"But, sir, this is just the kind of confrontation these people want. You know, the big jack-booted federal government versus the little guy. David versus Goliath. Remember what happened at Waco way back in ninety-three?" Rabson said.

"Goddammit, I know what happened at Waco! But the loss of plutonium and those other components constitute a clear and present danger to the security of this country! We're going to serve the warrant to search the compound. Everything by the numbers. But if resistance is encountered, it's gonna be neutralized. I'm sorry Agent Rabson, but we're going into JerUSAlem."

"Very good, sir," Rabson said in resignation. As the meeting broke up, Director Longstreet pulled the agent aside.

"Hell's the matter with you, Rabson, arguing with the president like that? Can't you see that we don't have any other options? And for Christ's sake, why bring up Waco?"

"Sir, I assumed that the president wanted candor; I told him what I felt. That's all. Besides, I don't think they're going to find the plutonium or the murderers in JerUSAlem. Jacqueline Lynch and Howard Brennan are somewhere in the Denver area, with the plutonium."

Monday, June 15th
0600 hours
The Aryan Church of Yahweh the Creator, near Provo, UT

Under the supervision of Attorney General McCormick and Regional Special Agent in Charge Kelly, preparations were underway for *Thunderbolt*, the assault on the JerUSAlem compound. Two battalions of the 1st Infantry (Mechanized) Brigade, Fourth Mechanized Infantry Division under Colonel Otis Bradford had arrived during the night; they quickly deployed around the commune. The unit had a distinguished history dating back to the Second World War. Nicknamed the 'Iron Brigade' it had fought last during the Gulf War. Bristling with reactive armor, three M3 Bradley AFV's and three M113 APCs offloaded from giant C5A transports at Salt Lake City International and came to take up their positions just before dawn. All throughout the night, Apache AH-64 attack helicopters equipped with Hellfire missiles and 7.62 mm mini-guns buzzed the compound, illuminating it with an eerie light.

All of this activity was noticed by the denizens of JerUSAlem. The message was unmistakable: it was time to do battle with ZOG. At Judith Hollander's command, the commune mobilized for battle. All the menfolk hastily donned camouflage fatigues and assembled along the perimeter, heavily armed with AR-16 assault rifles and LAW antitank rockets. Snarling guard dogs stood ready to be released. The compound's two guard towers suddenly sprouted a brace of M-60 machine guns. A heavily sandbagged machine-gun nest stood near the main entrance while a battery of Claymore antipersonnel mines covered the perimeter near the punji pits. Meanwhile, frightened children were sequestered in the Chapel as the women prepared to assist their husbands on the line of battle.

As the sun rose, the stage was set for an ugly confrontation. Col. Bradford beheld elaborate defensive positions that would have done Erwin Rommel proud. Under instructions to avoid a clash if possible, the Attorney General decided to try diplomacy. She and Tom Kelly slowly walked toward the gate under a crude flag of truce. Seeing this, Hollander and one of the church members went out to meet them.

"Halt!" a voice cried out as the Attorney General approached.

"I am Attorney General McCormick. The President of the United States has charged me to serve you with this warrant. It's signed by Judge Davis and empowers me to conduct a search of these premises."

"Listen, lady, that piece of paper don't cut no ice here," the church member who had accompanied Hollander said menacingly as he fingered his AR-16. "So, why don't you and Buckwheat over there get the hell out of here while you still can!"

Such talk brought out the Texas-sized meanness in Jen McCormick. An old poker player versed in the art of bluffing she wasted no time in responding.

"Young man," she said, staring at the youthful church member. "I've served you this warrant. It's a federal decree. I've got five thousand armored infantrymen behind me. A full brigade! We don't want a confrontation, but Station Chief Kelly and I are going to search this facility, one way or the other. Even if I have to level it first! Now I hope you understand… behave yourself."

At that point Dagmar Hollander entered into the conversation.

"Exactly what are you searching for, Madam Attorney General?"

"Nuclear materials that were stolen from the plant at Rocky Flats."

"You think that we've stolen them? What makes you think that they are here?" Hollander said innocently.

"Our investigation points here."

"Are you a Christian? Why do you persecute the children of Yahweh?"

"Nobody's persecuting your group."

"What do you call all this?" Hollander pointed in the direction of the troops. "Tanks, helicopters and heavily armed soldiers arrayed like the Philistines against our peaceful community filled with unarmed women and children. We are merely practicing our faith. The First Amendment grants us this. We have simply rejected your secular world. Now you come to destroy us… just like the Romans."

The Attorney General was becoming exasperated. The diplomacy angle was clearly getting nowhere. She abruptly stuffed the warrant into the church member's pocket.

"Madam, members of your so-called faith are suspects in over ten brutal murders… as well as other crimes. Now I repeat, you have been served with a federal warrant. You will comply. You have five minutes!" McCormick said, glancing down at her watch.

After a tense moment Hollander stepped back and relented. "Very well, you may conduct your search, but only while accompanied by church members… And not him!" Hollander insisted, glaring now at Tom Kelly. "No Negroes, Jews or dogs allowed. Only Aryans may enter into the sacred Tabernacle of JerUSAlem. This is the word of Yahweh."

Mindful of publicity, Hollander always took pains to use the word

"Negro" or "Jew" when in public. She reserved harsher epithets for whenever the cameras were turned off. Kelly and McCormick stood motionless. The Reverend continued.

"And another thing… We shall not surrender our weapons. We do not have what you're looking for. We are a peaceful people following the word of Yahweh, but, if forced to defend ourselves, we won't go like the Branch Davidians. You're not going to murder us like you did at Ruby Ridge or Waco." Hollander casually gazed back toward the machine-gun nest near the front gate. "You may search for your plutonium or whatever, all you wish. Do not frighten the children and try to remember that this is a holy place."

McCormick and Kelly, although angry, acquiesced. They didn't push the point. The warrant specifically authorized a search for the missing plutonium and various components. For her part, the Attorney General was relieved that the compound was to be searched without bloodshed. No Waco.

As McCormick and Kelly returned to their positions, one of the male church members angrily protested to Hollander.

"Why don't we fight? They don't scare me. What are we waiting for? We can take 'em. Hey, I'm ready!"

"No, Brother Jones. Let them search all they want. They won't find anything. The plutonium isn't here. It's in Colorado. Let ZOG waste its time and energies pursuing a wild goose."

"But Reverend Mother!"

"No! This is not the time or place for battle! We obey no law but the Word of Yahweh… You will do as I command! Let them pass."

With a gesture from Hollander, the Aryans sullenly lowered their weapons and stood back as the federal agents began their search. Under the direction of a gray-haired official from NEST government personnel in navy blue jackets marked *FBI* and *ATF*, some carrying Geiger-Mueller counters as well as other sensitive radiation-detection gear swarmed over the compound in the search of the missing plutonium. The atmosphere was tense. Some of the supremacists stood with weapons at the ready, fully expecting that a clash was imminent. Others taunted the federals, perhaps hoping to provoke an incident.

The search yielded a virtual arsenal of hidden weapons. There were heavy machineguns, assault rifles, explosives, grenades and even a flame-thrower, but no trace of the plutonium. In addition, more than five hundred pounds of enriched fertilizer and several fifty-five-gallon drums of high-octane fuel were discovered hidden in a storage shed. After almost two hours of fruitless searching, the Attorney General reluctantly conceded defeat and ordered it stopped. As the federals withdrew, many of the church members began mocking them with jeers and fascist salutes, but there was no bloodshed. No Waco. As the troops and agents were leaving McCormick came over to Hollander.

"Exactly why do you people need all this ordnance?" the Attorney General said, shaking her head.

"We must be prepared to protect ourselves," Reverend Hollander replied. "The Second Amendment gives us the right to arm… it's right in the Constitution… maybe you should read it."

"Protect yourselves? From whom?"

"From those who would destroy us. Biblical prophecy has foretold of the coming of the Apocalypse. The Antichrist already walks among us. The Evil One resides in Washington D.C. We are merely preparing for the end times, but our Lord Yahweh shall provide for us in the coming struggle… whether it's with rifles or pistols or atomic bombs or the jawbone of an ass… as you can see, we aren't the raving lunatics that the Zionist-controlled press has depicted. You won't find any vats of cyanide-laced soft drinks or drug-crazed zombies around here."

"What about all that fertilizer you've got in that building over there?"

"We use that to grow our own food. We wish to live apart from your sinful world."

"Have you ever heard of Nick Hoover?" McCormick said, changing the subject.

"Why, yes, I believe he left our little community a few days ago. Such a nice boy, are you looking for him too?"

"He was found murdered several nights ago near Lake Utah. I don't suppose you would know anything about that."

"How tragic," Hollander said, trying hard to conceal a smile. "Maybe he was doing something that he should not have… or perhaps he was killed by the Negroes. Cannibals, savages, they're all like that you know. They would kill each other for sports jackets and tennis shoes."

Tom Kelly, having overheard the remarks, walked over and thrust his finger in Hollander's face.

"Tired of this shit! Lady, *you* call us savages? That's very funny." The Attorney General eased in between them.

"Have you seen either of these people?" McCormick opened a valise and produced the FBI wanted posters with Lynch and Brennan's pictures.

"No, I haven't. I told you that we are a peaceful people who only seek to obey the will of Yahweh. We have no criminals here," Hollander said, turning away. "Now please, take your trained Negro and leave us in peace."

Wednesday, June 17th
0805 hours
The Manson residence, Aurora, Colorado

"Come here. I want to show you something," Howard said. He was working on the Manson's PC computer. Jackie, now sporting a brunette wig, entered the room.

"This is a graphic arts design software package... Old as Hell. Now let me show you what it can do." Howard got to the computer's "c" prompt and typed the command *GRAFF.bat*. Momentarily, the computer screen went blank. An instant later a multifaceted spherical image suddenly appeared on the computer's screen.

"Nice, huh?"

"Very nice, it's a soccer ball, right?" Jackie said, only mildly impressed.

"No, this is my design of the implosion mechanism for the bomb. See all these little wedges? That's where the conventional explosives are going", he noted, pointing to the image. He began using the computer's mouse and the menu bar to add more detail.

"You see, when finished, there's going to be forty-eight of these little wedges in the bomb."

"Why are they of two different shapes?"

"That's my own design. I put that feature into the primary fission mechanism of the Mark 12A warheads that I helped to design on our Minuteman and Peacekeeper missiles. Alternating hexagonal and pentagonal wedges of high velocity explosives makes for a very efficient implosion device. I've been reading up on all of Dr Neddermeyer's papers on implosion design from the 1940s. I've improved upon his original designs."

"I see," Jackie said, now interested. She leaned over to get a better view of the screen.

"The explosives are going to form the outer jacket of the bomb. You've heard of shaped charges when you were a Marine. Basically, that's what this is. I have designed them so that the main force of their explosion will be directed inward. This, in turn, will squeeze the tamper around the plutonium and initiator at the core. That's going to trigger the atomic blast." With a click of the mouse the figure began to rotate counterclockwise. "When it goes off, it'll have about fifty kilotons of explosive power. That's fifty thousand tons of TNT! Twice as much as they nuked the Japs with at Nagasaki. That bomb required two-and-a-half tons of conventional explosives: mine will need about sixty or so pounds. You see, it's all so simple."

"Wow!"

He hit a key and the schematic image filled with color and shading. "That nineteen forty-five bomb was crude, downright primitive. Most of its force was wasted. And the Hiroshima bomb was even more of a dog. Goddamned gun-type uranium bomb. Only one-dimensional compression. No true symmetry. Primitive as Hell! You just watch, I'll get four times more destructive power from the same amount of plutonium. And all parked along Pennsylvania Avenue just two blocks from the Capitol and White House!"

Stacey Manson, having heard parts of the conversation, walked in and looked at the computer screen.

"What are all the little dots here in the conventional explosives?"

"Those are holes which are going to be countersunk into the conventional explosives. They're for the blasting caps."

"Blasting caps? You mean that you're really gonna set off an A-bomb with blasting caps?"

"That's right. Forty-eight blasting caps are gonna simultaneously ignite the high explosive C4 wedges," Howard pointed out on the computer. Hitting the *PRINT* command button, he began printing copies of the image.

"Just how are we gonna make all these wedges?"

"That's why you and I are going to see a guy called the 'Professor' on Saturday. He's a kind of expert on explosives. Here, take these out to the garage. They're diagrams I want to take to him in Greeley on Saturday."

He handed her a small suitcase. Jackie went into the garage and placed it in Nick's truck. Suddenly sensing that she wasn't alone, Jackie slowly turned around. She caught the image of a woman in the corner of her eye. It was Suzanne Brennan. She had a pistol in her hand. The woman emerged from out of a shadow and walked over towards Jackie.

"Jacqueline, I've just come here from JerUSAlem. I've come to take my husband. Now where is he?" she said with a menacing tone.

"Inside." Jackie said, slowly gesturing toward the door. "But Howie doesn't love you anymore. He wants only me."

"You lousy man-stealing little bitch! Fucking Jezebel! Why don't you just leave us alone?" Suzanne sobbed, pointing the weapon at Jackie.

"Look, slut, it's not my fault that you can't keep your man. You've got the gun... you wanna kill me, huh, bitch? Then do it!" Jackie barked. On hearing the commotion, Howard and the Mansons quickly ran to the garage.

"Put the gun down, Suzanne!" Howard yelled at his wife upon entering.

"Don't worry, Howie, this bitch ain't got the balls to do shit!" Jackie said. "Come on, kill me, bitch!"

"Put it down!" Howard repeated. Weeping hysterically, Suzanne Brennan slowly sank to her knees. Jackie walked up to her and slowly took the weapon from her hand. Howard came up to his wife.

"Suzanne, why the hell did you come here?"

"I came to take you home Howard. The FBI searched JerUSAlem a few days ago. They're looking for you and this harpy. They're saying that you've killed those people at Rocky Flats! I just can't take it anymore! Maybe if you just give yourself up, everything'll be fine."

Howard looked at Suzanne with a gaze of utter contempt, as if he hated her all his life. He reared back and struck the sobbing woman in the mouth with his clenched fist. She recoiled backwards halfway across the garage.

"Stupid slut! Don't you realize that you may have been followed? ZOG is probably using you to find me!" Howard screamed, grabbing her by the hair.

"Please Howard, no! I wasn't followed! Please. I want to help you. I love you, Howard…Ah! You're hurting me!" the frightened woman screamed. Howard seized her by the throat and slugged her again.

"Shut up! Don't you ever embarrass me like this again! Next time I'll kill you! You hear me! Jackie's my wife now, you understand?" Howard yelled, blood vessels bulging from his neck. Grabbing her hand, he yanked the woman's wedding band off and thrust it into his pocket.

"Please stop!" the terrified woman screamed, nursing a broken finger. "You're sick Howard. Sick in your mind… You're crazy!"

"Kick her ass, Howie!" Jackie snarled. "Do it! She's a fucking race traitor! She tried to betray us. She betrayed the movement! She tried to betray *you*!"

Upon hearing this, Howard seemed to go berserk. Like a wild

man, he slugged the woman again and began kicking her in the stomach and face. He could hear the unmistakable crunch as her jaw broke from the savage blows. As the beating continued, Jackie stood transfixed, delighted at seeing her rival being removed violently from the scene.

"Bitch! Lousy bitch!" Howard screamed, kicking the now unconscious Suzanne in the head. She lay in a bloody heap. Spying a length of heavy galvanized steel pipe lying over in the corner Howard picked it up from the floor and loomed menacingly over Suzanne.

"Do it, Howie! Do it!" Jackie hooted. "Beat her fucking brains out! Kill her! Come on! Do it now!"

"Take it easy Howie," Nick Manson said, edging between the pair.

"Get the fuck out of my way, Nick!" Howard said. He began waving the pipe over his head.

"Come on, I said back off!" Manson repeated. "Before the neighbors hear." Howard slowly backed away, dropping the pipe. It fell to the ground with a loud clang. Exhausted, he was escorted out of the garage by the Mansons. Suzanne was lying sprawled in a heap on the floor, covered with blood. She was barely alive.

"She's not breathing." Stacy performed a perfunctory examination, then following her husband out the door. "I think she's dead."

"Stupid bitch! Lousy whore! I hope you die!" Jackie said as she exited the garage. She went back into the house where the others were seated around the kitchen table.

"So, what are we gonna do with her?" Stacey said. "We just can't leave her body in the garage. I mean, the neighbors might have heard all the screaming."

"I got an idea," Jackie said. "When it gets dark, we can just dump her body in Five Points. Simple."

"What?" Howard said.

"Five Points is the colored part of town. It'll look like a mugging. Why don't we just dump her there and everybody'll think that the niggers did it. The cops will blame it all on the blacks!"

"That's a great idea," Howard nodded in agreement. "If the cops find a white woman beaten to death in a colored neighborhood who knows what might happen. Maybe even a race riot. At any rate, it's a sure thing blacks will get blamed for it all."

"What if she dies?" Stacey said.

"That's what we want… anyway, who cares? As long she dies somewhere else and as someone else gets fingered for it," Jackie said coldly. "So much the better. We never really needed Suzanne anyway. I've always hated that stupid bitch. Now Howie and me can get married."

"Well just wrap her in a blanket or newspapers or something. I don't want her blood all over my truck, it's practically new," Nick said.

Jackie ran to the bedroom and retrieved an old army surplus blanket. Nick and Howard slowly lifted the limp form of Suzanne into the vehicle. The pair got in and slowly pulled out of the garage. Stacey and Jackie remained behind, cleaning up the blood and hiding any incriminating evidence.

Off To See the Wizard

Saturday, June 20th
1120 hours
A McDonald's restaurant in Greeley, CO

"I wonder where the Hell Mitch is. He's twenty minutes late already," an agitated Howard said.

"Calm down. That's the fourth time you've looked at your watch in the last few minutes. Try to relax," Jackie said.

"Yeah, I guess maybe you're right."

"So, just who is the professor that we're meeting anyway?"

"Guy named Mitchell Price. This kid's good, a chemical engineering whiz. And he's just about the best high explosives man in the business I hear. Hell of a chemist, he's got his training at the University of Northern Colorado. And he's devoted to the movement," Howard said, munching on some French fries. "He led an on-campus protest against the university's affirmative action program couple years ago."

Jackie nodded thoughtfully, taking in all the information. Bolting down a cheeseburger Howard continued, "Mitch hooked up with the church and other race-conscious groups through computer bulletin boards and the Internet. He's done a couple of small jobs for us already."

"Sounds like a valuable asset."

"He's more than that. I can't build the bomb without him. He turned his basement into a laboratory after his parents were killed two years ago."

"Just how exactly did he get the nickname of the 'Professor' anyway?"

"We gave him that handle because he's so smart, kind of like that character on the *Gilligan Island* series."

"Ah! Look here," Jackie said while flipping through a copy of a Denver newspaper. "It says, 'unknown woman critical after beating… I guess the cops found poor Suzanne."

"What else does it say?"

"An unknown woman, described as Caucasian, early forties, was found severely beaten in a north Denver alley this morning. She was rushed to Denver General Hospital where her condition was listed as critical… Yup, that's her."

"You mean the lousy slut didn't die?"

"Don't worry. You saw all the blood. You practically split her head open. After the beating you gave her, she ain't gonna be nothing but a fucking vegetable… a goddamned brain-dead zombie. We're in the clear. There's no way that they can tie it to us. They'll probably finger some dumb colored guy."

"Yeah, I know. I'm going to send Skin-Girl and NumbNutZ to the hospital to see if they can find out anything. I think that she's got a busted jaw. Also, her hands are broken. No way she can squeal to the cops even if she lives."

A disheveled-looking man entered the restaurant. It was Mitchell Price. Rail thin, with tufts of red hair sprouting from his head wildly in all directions and thick, horn-rimmed glasses Price gave the appearance of a circus clown. Jackie had to restrain herself from laughing. With a shambling gait — almost a stagger — the bespectacled figure retrieved a food tray and approached the couple.

"Excuse me, I'm in a hurry. May I sit here?" the man said.

Howard examined the figure closely. "That depends. You a student?"

"Yes sir. But if the *chemistry* is right, I hope to become a *professor*," the man answered. Howard smiled.

"Sit down, Mitch."

"Thanks. Who's the chick?"

"Mitch, I want you to meet my girlfriend, Jackie. Jackie Lynch."

"Hi Mitch... Howie, what was all that about?" a perplexed Jackie said as the man took his seat.

"Prearranged greeting. You can't be too careful."

Mitchell Price was a strange man. Only twenty-five, in many respects his life paralleled that of Howard Brennan. Like Howard, he had been a child prodigy who dabbled in white supremacist dogma.

"Mitch, we got a job for you."

"I'm listening."

"Question. What's the best high-velocity explosive available?"

Mitch pondered the question briefly and gave his answer. "Let me see... according to the US Army's Field Manual, it's Composition B. Roughly about twenty-six thousand, five hundred feet per second... real high velocity. But it's strictly military issue. Penta-Erythrothol tetranitrate is almost as good, and it's commercially available, at least if you're a construction company that's doing some demolition work. It's called C4."

"Right!" Howard said, visibly impressed. He opened a briefcase. "I've got some diagrams here I want you to see."

Mitch glanced at the figures. "Looks like some kind of implosion mechanism. You're working on the principal of implosion, the Munroe Effect, right? Holy shit, you guys going to build an atomic bomb or something?"

"Oh, he's quick! I can see why they call him the 'Professor'," Jackie said while munching on a carrot.

"Mitch, I need forty-eight of these wedges you see here: sixteen pentagonal and thirty-two hexagonal ones. Each about a pound in weight, all made out of C4 explosive. Also, I'll need a quarter- inch diameter hole countersunk and centered in them as well," Howard said, pointing to the figure.

Mitch stared off towards the ceiling, as if doing a mathematical computation in his head. "But that's about forty-eight pounds. Shit, I can't make that much C4. My lab's strictly a small operation. I don't think I can help you," Mitch said, shaking his head.

"Don't worry about that. I'll get you the C4. What I need is someone who can do the fabrication." Mitch studied the diagrams.

"Yeah, I can do it… No sweat. I'll have to make ceramic molds and modify my kilns."

"I'll also need you to make us baratol. We're going to use that for the lens."

Mitch nodded. "Yeah. No sweat on that. That's easy to make; it's just a slurry of barium nitrate, aluminum metal filings, nitrocellulose and TNT. All this is going to cost you though."

"How much?"

"Let's see… I'll do the whole job for fifty grand. Half when I start, the balance on delivery."

"Done!" Howard said. "How long for the molds?"

"I've got to do some really fine machining to get them to your specs... Give me about a month."

"Roughly how long for the entire job?"

"If I start around August first, I think I should be able to deliver around Halloween, mid-November at the latest."

"I think Jackie and I can live with that. Another question, for the detonation of the primary C4, which would you recommend, M6 or M7 blasting caps?"

"Oh M6's for sure!"

"Why?"

"Electrically activated. Reliable as Hell, and they use RDX, a real nice, shattering high explosive," Mitch said.

"Yeah, Cyclonite is very powerful. One of the better high explosives," Howard said, nodding in agreement. "You know, that's what the Germans used in their antitank *Panzerfäuste* during the war."

"Mitch," Jackie interjected. "What can you tell us about the Alliance Construction Company?"

"They're just about the biggest construction outfit along the Front Range. They do the really big jobs. During the late seventies they were under contract to help dig the Eisenhower Tunnel through the mountains."

"I see," she nodded.

"If you want C4 I'd say that's the place to get it."

"Mitch," Howard said slowly, measuring his words. "I'm going to let you in on something, but you better keep your mouth shut… remember, the Werewolf doesn't forget and never forgives."

"Yeah, I know. I ain't gonna say nothing."

"You knew about Rocky Flats couple of weeks back?"

"Yeah, it was in all the papers. I also saw the president on TV."

"The Werewolf did it. We got enough plutonium to build a bomb."

"No shit?" Mitch's eyes became wide in amazement.

"That's right."

"What's the target gonna be?"

"That's strictly need-to-know. But there's an extra ten grand in it for you if we can move the stuff up here for a while."

"Sure Howard, no problem."

"Okay Mitch." Howard took the diagrams and placed them back in the satchel. "That's all for now. We'll be seeing you again in about a month. We'll have the C4… and the money."

"Bye Mitch!" Jackie waved. The pair departed. They drove off to a nearby Holiday Inn hotel.

"In a few days, I want you to scope out the Alliance Construction. Try to find out all the information that you can on security arrangements and inventories of high explosives," Howard said as they entered their room.

"We gonna steal the C4 from Alliance?"

"That's kind of what I got in mind." Howard began unpacking his suitcase. "I think you're gonna have to do another hit."

Jackie smiled broadly.

Settling into their room, the couple relaxed and started watching television. Howard's favorite movie, the 1964 nuclear war parody *Dr Strangelove, or How I Finally Stopped Worrying and Learned to Love the Bomb* was on Channel Two. The pair laughed as the mad General Jack D. Ripper ordered the entire SAC B-52 bomber wing to attack Soviet Russia. "That was a man who really knows how to get things done," Howard said. He especially enjoyed the part when Major T. J. "King" Kong rode the H-bomb cowboy-style, during the movie's final scene. In just a few months' time he would finally realize his own fantasy. Like Dr Strangelove, he had finally learned to stop worrying. Like Major Kong, he too, would ride the bomb.

Monday, June 22nd
0930 hours
J. Edgar Hoover FBI Building, Washington DC

"Doug," FBI Special Agent Jim Roberts said, pulling Rabson to one side. "It seems that a Jane Doe was found badly beaten in a Denver alley. Local police sent her fingerprints to us to try and get an identity."

"Yeah, what about it?"

"We were able to make an ID. The woman's name is Suzanne Brennan. She's from Eureka, Utah."

"Suzanne Bren—… she wouldn't happen to be any relation to a Colonel Howard Brennan, would she?" Rabson said.

"She's his wife. Police apparently found her beaten half to death on a Denver street and left to die. I processed the prints from Howard Brennan when the guys in Denver went over that hotel room. I read his file and remembered that he was married to a woman named Suzanne."

"I'd better go see the director. I'll get in touch with Frank Bledsoe in the Denver office. Try and get them to coordinate with local law enforcement."

"What's up?"

"We've got to protect her. Since Nick Cooper died without coming to last week, she may be the only link to the whereabouts of the plutonium," Rabson said.

"You got it."

1015 hours

Rabson and Director Longstreet were conversing in the hall as Jim Roberts approached.

"Excuse me, sir... Doug, I just got off the line with Denver PD. They say that Mrs. Brennan was really beaten up, suffered five broken ribs, a broken jaw, a skull fracture, both hands broken and a punctured lung. It's a miracle she's even still alive. Whoever did it just dumped her in the street."

"Do they think she'll make it?" Longstreet said.

"Her doctors are optimistic. They weren't able to question her. She's being kept in a drugged-induced coma while they look to see if there was any brain damage. One thing, though, the locals say that no way was this a street robbery."

"What do you think?" the director said.

"I think that asshole Brennan tried to kill his wife. She probably pissed him off somehow, or—"

"Or what?"

"...Or maybe she was planning to come see us," Rabson said, stroking his chin. "Picture this... her psycho husband is living with another woman, this Jackie Lynch; he steals weapons-grade plutonium to build a bomb. He intends to detonate it somewhere. She suddenly gets spooked and then tries to contact us. He flips out and beats the hell out of her. They dump her in an alley to make it look like a street mugging, fully expecting that she would die."

"All right. Let's assume that your theory is correct. Get back to Denver. I want you and Bledsoe to question this woman when she comes to. She may be all we have to go on. I'm going to call Bledsoe and have him place a team at the hospital to protect her."

"Yes sir," Rabson said as Longstreet walked away.

Oh shit! I've really crawled out on a limb this time. I'd better be right or it's my ass! And there goes another one of Sarah's piano recitals that I'm going to have to miss, he thought to himself.

1430 hours
The Alliance Construction Company, Greeley, Colorado

Amid scores of bulldozers, earthmovers and other heavy construction equipment Company Manager Tobias Carlan was walking near the main entrance finishing a late lunch of a ham sandwich and soda when he saw an attractive blonde woman emerging from her vehicle. She wearing a navy-blue jacket emblazoned with *ATF* in gold lettering.

ATF? Oh shit... what do these assholes want now? he thought to himself. "Good afternoon. May I help you?"

"Good afternoon, my name is Jacqueline Wilson, ATF." The woman presented her identification. Carlan took it and scrutinized the badge.

"I would like to see an inventory listing of your stocks of high explosives."

"Hell, we didn't know anything about this."

"That's the general idea. The Bureau wants spot inspections in order to confirm compliance with federal standards."

"Well, I just can't get these records right now. I'm busy," Carlan said as he casually licked food residue from his plump fingers. "Besides, you people just inspected us last February."

"Mr. Carlan, I can shut your operation down right now. You're under a federal mandate to present those records to the Bureau upon request. Now I suggest that you get those records... *Now*!" Jackie said with a penetrating stare.

Carlan shrugged and motioned the woman to follow. "Okay, lady, Okay, okay. Don't get all unglued. Follow me." Carlan and Jackie went back to his office. Once there, he went over to a gray metal filing cabinet and produced two plump folders marked *Explosives Records*.

"These are all the records on explosives for the last two years. If necessary, I can go back further. We've got other records on computer disk," Carlan said, presenting her with the files of records. Jackie began looking through the files.

"I don't think that will be necessary, Mr. Carlan... Oh, I see here that you recently got in a large order of C4 explosives."

"Yeah, we got a big job on the Western Slope coming up in the second half of July. We'll need some real heavy stuff."

"Where and how are you storing it?"

"Over there in that shed. We got it in crates. Don't worry, we meet all the federal safety standards. Wanna see?" Carlan said, pointing to a large concrete structure in the center of the compound.

The pair walked over to the building. There, large crates marked *C4 -DANGER High Explosive* were stacked near the doorway. Jackie examined the room's contents, jotting down the quantities on a notepad.

"Everything seems to be in order. You may resume eating your lunch," Jackie said. "Hey, look, I'm sorry that I was such a bitch. My boyfriend and I are having a little trouble, but I shouldn't take it out on you. Okay?"

"Forget it," Carlan shrugged.

"One thing though, you don't seem to have much security around here. What if someone were to come here at night to steal some of your explosives? How would your people respond?"

"We're ready for them. We keep five armed guards at the place overnight. They got service thirty-eights. Plus, a couple trained dogs roam around the yard. The fence is seven feet and topped with barbed wire. We keep the storage area locked up tight. It's safe enough."

"I see... Okay, well thank you Mr. Carlan, and have a nice day. The Bureau really appreciates your cooperation."

"Bitch!" Carlan muttered to himself as the woman walked away.

Tuesday, June 23rd
1805 hours
The Manson residence, Aurora, Colorado

The home of Nick and Stacey Manson was again the scene of clandestine activity. At Jackie Lynch's command Pamela Haney, Ariadne Beausoleil, Bruce Davies and Jeff Collins had assembled in the basement. On the table rested a crude hastily drawn map of the Alliance Construction Company.

"Okay people, listen up," Jackie began. "This is the layout of our next target, the Alliance Construction Company, a construction outfit in Greeley." The others crowded around the table.

"Security's in this building here." Jackie pointed to a square figure near the entrance. "Their security is really pretty lax. I could list at least a hundred things those assholes were doing wrong. I tell you it's wide open."

"How many guards?" Jeff said.

"Five on duty to cover the whole area on any given night. Hardly really enough to guard the whole perimeter."

"Any surveillance equipment?"

"Nope, but they got dogs. Couple shepherds."

"That's it?" Jeff said with a look of disbelief.

"The fence is topped with barbed wire. You'll have to be careful when you go over it. Skin-Girl and me are going to watch the guards while you and Davies go after the C4. Pamie, you'll wait where we park and cover the perimeter."

"Where's the C4?" Davies said.

"It's in here, in this concrete storage bunker in the center of the compound," Jackie said, indicating its location on the map.

"How much do we want?"

"Howie says at least fifty pounds, but I think we should steal a little bit more. Just in case. The stuff comes in crates, roughly ten pounds each. Let's see, I think seven of 'em will more than suffice."

"What about the blasting caps?"

"We want M6 blasting caps. Unfortunately, I don't know where they are. It's a cinch that they aren't in the same building as the explosives. Guess Skin-Girl and me are gonna have to force one of the guards to tell us."

"Looks pretty simple, Jackie. When do we strike?" Jeff said.

"I think we'll hit 'em on the fourth of July."

"How patriotic!" Stacey said, grinning broadly.

"It's more than just that, Stace. We've got to strike on a holiday when everybody's distracted. That way, the job is so much easier. One more thing, we're going to have to kill them all. No witnesses. Even the dogs," Jackie said coldly. "As Howie would say, *'kein Mitleid'*... No Mercy."

"Kill 'em all?"

"You got a problem with that Bruce?" Bruce Davies sank into a monastic silence. The other terrorists stood motionless, Jackie folded the map and wrapped up the meeting. "Finally, we're moving the plutonium up north to Greeley. I think that Howie wants to build the bomb there. Okay, that's all people."

Wednesday, June 24th
0830 hours
Denver Police Headquarters

"Doug? Doug Rabson? You remember me? I'm Lieutenant Bundy. We were working on the McClintock case back in May."

"Oh, yes, I remember," Rabson said, extending his hand. "Too bad about Zach Duncan. I liked him. How's that case going?"

"It's still open. Found him in the alley. Duncan caught two slugs from a nine-millimeter semiautomatic. Second shot killed him. Hit the heart dead center. He was swimming in blood. The first bullet looks like it was just some kind of torture... The killer blew his balls off. In broad daylight, right behind the bar. Hell of the matter is that nobody saw or heard nothing. The killer probably used a silencer or something," Bundy said, pouring a cup of coffee. "Homeless man and his dog found the body."

"Uh-huh."

"No way was this an ordinary street mugging," Bundy continued, sipping his coffee. "Duncan was found with credit cards and thirty bucks in his wallet. He was shot through the balls... Maybe a love triangle. Right now, we're thinking the killer might have been a jealous lover or some kind of a sex nut."

Rabson shook his head. "Jacqueline Lynch killed him. I don't know but somehow, she found out that Zach had been talking to us... and it cost him his life."

"So, what's the status of the stolen plutonium?"

"It and Lynch have simply vanished, no traces. I'm here right now pursuing a potential lead."

"Oh?"

"There was a woman who was found badly beaten on a Denver street a couple of nights ago and—"

Bundy turned his head and looked quizzically at Rabson. "You're investigating that...a street mugging?"

"Not exactly, but we think that she may be involved in the case. By the way, I'm looking for a Lieutenant Mancuso."

"Right this way, Robbery Division." The pair walked to an office on the third floor. The squad room was cluttered with fast food wrappers and empty soft drink containers.

"Lieutenant Mancuso, I'm Douglas Rabson, FBI. I was instructed to meet with you concerning the Suzanne Brennan case."

"Yeah, Frank Bledsoe in your office phoned me. Told me you were coming. Sit down Rabson," the lieutenant said, clearing off trash from the corner of the desk.

"Thank you, sir."

"Now, what's this all about? Some woman gets the living shit beat out of her couple nights ago in Five Points and all of a sudden, the feds are involved."

"Lieutenant, the Bureau feels that this woman may have knowledge in the Rocky Flats case."

"Uh-huh. There was no ID on this woman. Only reason we found out who she was is because we sent a set of her prints to you FBI guys in Washington. How do you figure she's involved with Rocky Flats?"

"We believe that she's the wife of one of the terrorists," Rabson said. Mancuso's eyes suddenly lit up.

"I see," the lieutenant said, stroking his chin. "You think that maybe they beat her up and left her for dead,"

"Right. The Bureau wants a round-the-clock protection for this woman. We want to question her when she wakes up."

"You mean, *if* she wakes up, don't you? I read the medical report on this woman," Mancuso noted. He pulled out a copy of the preliminary medical report. "Says here she's got busted ribs, a jaw broken in two places, both hands broken and a fractured skull. The doctors at Denver General have her in an induced coma while they try to get the brain swelling down."

"She's got to pull through. I'm not exaggerating when I tell you that this is a matter of national security," Rabson said.

"Well, Rabson, let's take a ride to Denver General. We can talk to the doctors who are treating her. They can give you a better opinion of her chances to make it."

1023 hours
Denver General Hospital

"Lieutenant Bundy? Nurse O'Brien tells me that you wish to see me," Dr Milton Abrams said. "Is this concerning the Brennan woman?"

"Yes, doctor. This is Special Agent Douglas Rabson, FBI. He's also involved in the investigation." The trio walked toward the reception area.

"Dr Abrams, please describe for me the types of injuries that Mrs. Brennan sustained."

"Severe trauma wounds to the head and torso region of a particularly savage nature. Apparently, as she attempted to fend off the blows both of her hands were broken. I've never seen a domestic violence case so brutal as this, and I've been practicing this kind of medicine for over twenty-two years."

"I see. Sir, it's imperative that we question this woman as soon as possible. Can you give us an estimate as to when that may be possible?"

"Well, she's out of danger. The brain swelling has gone down considerably and the broken bones have been set. We still have her in a drug-induced coma. Questioning her may be difficult even when we bring her out of it, her jaw was broken during the beating, it's been wired shut."

"I have a way of communicating with her," Rabson said. "We must interrogate her as soon as possible. I'll leave you one of my cards. Thank you, doctor."

"Oh, Mr. Rabson, is it really necessary to have all these police and FBI agents around here? They're interfering with normal hospital procedure."

"I'm afraid so, sir. Mrs. Brennan is a potential government witness and when whoever attacked her finds out she's still alive he may try again. I'll try to have the guards to be a bit less conspicuous."

Saturday, July 4th
1800 hours
The Manson residence, Aurora, Colorado

The fourth of July had come. Amid the growing cacophony of the bursting of firecrackers and rockets, Jackie Lynch, Jeffrey Collins, Bruce Davies, Pamela Haney and Ariadne Beausoleil climbed onto three trucks. Grimly, they checked their weapons: silencer-equipped Ingram MAC-10 machine pistols and nine-millimeter Beretta semi-automatics. The Aryans were going into battle once again. At Jackie's signal, the vehicles began moving north onto the Interstate. Their destination was the Alliance Construction Company of Greeley.

The day before, Howard and Nick moved the plutonium and other components to the Greeley residence of Mitch Price. He decided that the Price laboratory facilities provided a more conducive environment to building the bomb than Nick Manson's garage. In addition, in the back of his mind was Suzanne. He was troubled by the fact that she hadn't died from the beating. If she were to recover, she would probably lead the authorities to the Manson house. Better to move the materials now. Earlier in the day Jackie had received a telephone call from Howard advising her on the successful delivery of the materials. On this, she and the others began their preparations for the night's work.

The journey to Greeley took just over an hour. Upon arriving, the terrorists assembled in a clearing near the main entrance. While the others donned stocking masks and gloves Jackie carefully scanned the perimeter of the facility with a pair of binoculars. She could not believe what she saw.

"Night-Hawk, come and look at this," she said while motioning to Jeff Collins. "There're no security guards anywhere around the perimeter. Looks like they're all in that building over there. Haven't these fuckers ever heard of security?"

"You're right… Ah! I count two… no, three dogs loose in the yard," Jeff said, panning the binoculars slowly around the area. "Shit! This place is wide open."

"Jackie, hurry, I gotta go pee!" Ariadne winced.

"In a minute, Skin-Girl. I told you before not to drink so much beer before we do a job. Now, try to hold it," Jackie said as she sprinted back to one of the trucks. A minute later she returned with the SVD sniper rifle.

"Night-Hawk, I'm going to take out the dogs. You have the others ready to go," she said, screwing a silencer onto the weapon's muzzle. She found a ready-made sniper's nest at an old tree stump. Carefully, Jackie sighted in the weapon on a large German Shepherd in the center of the compound. For a whole minute she slowly tracked the animal's movements in the telescope. An Alsatian bitch, it was a beautiful animal. It pained her to have to kill it. Jackie took a deep breath and slowly pulled the trigger. A 7.62-millimeter round struck the dog square in the chest with the force of a sledgehammer. It spun to the ground, dead. Next, the sniper spied a plump Rottweiler near the fence. Another muffled report. With a pitiful howl the dog went down. Its mate, on hearing the wail, came bounding across the compound to investigate. A third silenced projectile through the head cut the animal down in mid-stride.

When he saw the dogs drop, Jeff began climbing the fence. He was momentarily caught in the barbed wire but managed to free himself. The others waited with mounting anticipation as Jeff cut through the locks on the gate. In a matter of seconds, the terrorists raced into the compound. The perimeter had been breached.

The security personnel guarding the Alliance Construction Company weren't exactly an elite unit. Two had only been on the job a week, having replaced a recently terminated individual. One wasn't even supposed to be there that night; he was subbing for a man whose wife was having a baby. Another was a part-timer. A junior at the nearby University of Northern Colorado; this was the only job he could find. It wasn't bad. It paid twelve-fifty an hour and gave him plenty of time to study since nothing ever happened there anyway. Finally, the fifth guard, a heavyset black man, had been a military policeman in the Army. Too fat for civilian police work, he was forced to settle for the chief security guard position on the graveyard shift at Alliance.

Instead of patrolling the perimeter, all the guards had clustered in the main building, joyfully feasting on beer and chips while watching a baseball game on a brand new nineteen-inch color TV set. The *Colorado Rockies*, were hosting the *Atlanta Braves* for a fourth of July make-up game. The men howled and hooted with delight as the *Rockies* scored the go-ahead run in the bottom of the eighth inning. Suddenly, they were confronted by a pair of silencer-equipped MAC-10's as Jackie and Ariadne stood in the doorway.

"Against the wall gentlemen... *Move!*" Jackie snarled as she forced her way in. Four of the men were stunned, unable or unwilling to grasp what they saw. They sat almost in a daze, motionless in amazement. The fifth, thinking it to be some kind of joke, smiled.

"I said move your ass! You laugh at me and I'll kill all of you right now!" A single shot smashed through the screen of the television. Glass and sparks from the shattered TV showered down on the men. That brought immediate compliance. The frightened guards jumped up, overturning several cans of beer in their haste.

"Night-Hawk, you and Bruce get the stuff. You know where it is. Skin-Girl and I'll cover these assholes," Jackie yelled out to her confederates. Bruce and Jeff loped over to the explosives' storage area.

"All right, gentlemen," Jackie said, turning back to the frightened guards. "Very nice to be with you this evening. If you all just relax and do as I say, nobody'll get hurt. Everybody goes home happy,"

"Who are you?" the fat one said. "What happened to the dogs?"

"I'm sorry, but I'm afraid I had to put your dogs to sleep. Had to use my little hush-puppy on 'em," Jackie said with a smirk, caressing her weapon. "Now all of you face the wall! You too fat boy! Hurry up!"

"Did you have to shoot up my TV? I just bought it. Shit! It ain't even paid for yet," he complained.

"Shut up, nigger!" Jackie said, pressing her weapon into the man's back. "You don't want to see that game anyway... the *Braves* are gonna kick the *Rockies's* ass."

"Hey man, I got a bad feeling 'bout this," one whispered nervously to another.

"I said shut the fuck up!"

Meanwhile, Bruce and Jeff, having broken the locks on the explosives' storage area, were busy loading cases of C4 into the trucks. Inside each were ten rectangular bricks of C4 plastic explosive, each weighing about one pound. All told, the thieves removed seven cases. A jubilant Jeff Collins returned to the security building while Davies momentarily joined Pam in the truck.

"We got the C4, Jackie," Jeff said, sticking his head into the doorway. "It's real high velocity stuff. Fucking primo! We also got some other shit too."

"Very good... all right, gentlemen, I want the M6 blasting caps. Where are they?"

The men said nothing. Jackie, ever impatient, fired another round into the still smoking television. She, again, came up behind the black security guard.

"Turn around! Get in the corner! I said *where* are they? Listen boy, this is a MAC-10. Forty-five caliber hollow points called wad-cutters. It's got a fucking silencer. I could blow your ugly black head clean off and nobody'd hear a thing. On the other hand, try to imagine how painful a bullet in the testicles would feel right now... I'll kill you just like I did those dogs!"

The man moistened his lips. "They're in there," he mumbled, nervously pointing to an adjoining room.

"Bruce, get 'em," she barked. "Then wait for us outside." Bruce went into the room. An instant later he emerged with an armload of blasting caps. He made several trips out to the truck.

Ariadne and Jeff slowly backed away and lined up, as if forming a firing squad.

"Thank you, gentlemen." Jackie eased back next to Ariadne. "You've all been most helpful. Now I need just one more thing from each of you."

"What's that?" the black man said nervously.

"Not much... just your lives. You've seen our faces... You know too much."

"No! Please, no! Wait! Hey, you got what you wanted! You don't have to kill us!" he screamed.

"You actually thought I'd let you live? Even with your low mentality you must know that's impractical," Jackie said, slowly shaking her head.

"We ain't gonna say nothing!"

Jackie again came up to him. "Damn right you ain't... My mama used to play a game with me when I was a little girl," she said with a twisted smile. "It goes something like this, 'Eenie, Meenie, Minie, Moe... Catch a nigger by his toe... and if he hollers, let him go.'"

Jackie's expression suddenly turned cold. "Now I gotta ask you something real important, so try to pay attention... Are you ready to die? Are you ready to die like a nigger?" She set her MAC-10 to full automatic with an ominous click.

"Please... No!" the terrified guard whimpered. Tears were running down his cheeks. "Come on... I got a wife and kid! Please!"

"Fuck you... Now get on your knees, chimp... Do it!" Jackie suddenly kicked the man in the groin. With a moan he doubled over and fell to his knees. "Now suck on it... Suck it! Go on, stick it in your mouth!" She pressed the barrel of the silencer into the man's mouth. "Now bite down on it, Fuck Face... Do it now!"

"Please don't do this," the trembling guard mumbled, slowly closing his eyes.

"I got no love in my heart for you, nigger!"

"Please!"

"Shhhh... Don't try to talk with your mouth full." Jackie pulled the trigger. The man's head disintegrated as the weapon's barrel ejaculated a stream of large caliber bullets. The bloody, now headless corpse stiffened and pitched to the floor with a loud thud. The other terrified men instinctively huddled together.

"Do it!" Jackie shouted. Ariadne and Jeff sprayed the other guards' backs with their MAC-10's. The startled victims twisted like marionettes in the hail of bullets. Jackie quickly reloaded and joined in the massacre. Several beer cans and an empty potato chip bag flew wildly aloft as the men fell. In seconds it was all over; a heavy odor of burnt cordite permeated the room. The wall behind the slain men was pocked and blood-spattered. Three of the bullet-riddled corpses lay sprawled in a grotesque pyramid, animated by only an occasional involuntary twitch. Jeff Collins went outside; the two women slowly walked among the prostrate forms. Ariadne began perfunctorily checking the men for any signs of a pulse; Jackie had a quicker, more direct method of examination: she simply kicked each victim in the groin. If the man reacted, he would be instantly shot through the head.

A man who was only wounded twitched while attempting to feign death. Jackie saw the motion and smiled.

"Hey Skin-Girl, lookie what we got here. This one's playing possum," she said while reloading her weapon.

"Peek-a-boo… You're fucked!"

"No! Jesus No… Please!" the man screamed while attempting to cover his head.

"Are you white? You're a lousy race traitor … Fuck you," Jackie snarled, leveling her weapon at the man's head. A single muffled shot. He twitched no more.

"Gonna piss on your graves!" Ariadne giggled at the prostrate forms as she dropped her shorts, squatted and urinated on the floor.

"*Hasta la vista*, assholes… Okay, let's get the fuck out of here," Jackie said as she ran outside.

Sunday, July 5th
0716 hours
The Price residence, Greeley, CO

"Holy shit!" Mitch said in amazement to Howard as the terrorists unloaded the explosives. "Looks like you got enough C4 here to blow up a goddamned mountain!"

"That's the general idea… How are the ceramic molds coming?"

"They'll be ready next week. Let me test them first and I think they'll be ready to go."

"Excellent!" Howard said, slowly rubbing his hands together.

Mitch walked over to Jackie. She was watching the *Sunday Morning News*. The main story was a bulletin about a massacre in

Greeley the night before. The news camera slowly panned around the macabre scene: members of the Coroner's Office and the CSI Unit from Greeley PD were removing the bodies of the slain guards while the corpse of one of the dogs, covered with flies and already grotesquely bloated in the early morning sun, lay sprawled in the center of the compound.

"Hey, we made the news! Big time!" she yelled over to Howard. "And the stupid assholes think that a disgruntled ex-employee done it."

"You actually wasted those people last night?" Mitch said nervously.

"That's right, killed them all. No big deal… Popped this fat, colored guy. You should've seen it. Ugly monkey. Kicked him in the nuts, made the cowardly fat fucker beg for his life… He was actually crying. He literally pissed his pants! I looked into his stupid, chocolate face, pulled the trigger and his head flew off! Brains went everywhere. Reckon that dumb coon is probably in nigger-heaven shaking hands with the Devil 'bout now," Jackie said laughing, almost giddy at the retelling of the story. "It was too bad that I had to kill the dogs, though. They were pretty cool."

Mitch stared at Jackie and slowly turned back to the television. He looked as if he was going to be sick.

"Why the surprise? Because I'm a woman?" she said angrily. "Grow up Mitch. It's a whole new ballgame… It's like what they said on that cigarette commercial on TV years ago. You know, the one that said, 'we've come a long way, baby' or something like that."

"You're not a very nice lady."

"Hey! I shot a dog!" She turned off the TV and faced Mitch. "You ever hear of a guy called Darius Williams?"

Mitch pondered the question briefly. "Wasn't he some kind of black civil rights church dude who got wasted in LA couple months back? It was all over the news."

"Yeah... I did it Mitch. I hit the preacher- man. Blew his head clean off with a high-powered rifle and silencer. Left his body lying in the street... along with the rest of the fucking garbage."

"You're kidding?"

"Hey, it's just like sex. The more you do it, the more you like it. I'm a working girl... a hitwoman. Remember that race riot in LA last spring? It all started after I wasted that Williams guy back in April. I kill people for a living... You got a problem with that, prick?"

"As you said, no big deal," Mitch shrugged nervously. "Come on, level with me. We both know that Howie wants to build an atomic bomb. Who's he gonna torch? Who's gonna get their asses burned?"

"Listen, you're being paid to provide a service. That's it, nothing more. You'll find out if and when Howie wants you to know. So don't bother me right now, okay?"

"Hey! Don't get all uptight. I mean, we're all on the same side. I was only curious, that's all."

"Well, curiosity can get your ass killed around here. You dig?"

"Yeah, sure. I understand," Mitch shrugged. He started to turn away. Without warning, Jackie suddenly turned, grabbing the startled man in the crotch and backing him against the wall.

"No Mitch, I don't think you do. Listen, about a month ago there was this guy, not much younger than you. Guy named Nick Hoover. He was pathetic. Fucking traitor asked too many questions. Like you. Asshole tried to squeal to the feds. Tried to sell us out. You want to know what the Werewolf did to that fucking Judas? Well, do you?"

"What? Ah! Please, Jackie, you're fucking hurting me."

"Reverend Hollander told Skin-Girl they grabbed him by the gonads... kind of like how I've got you right now," she said, squeezing his genitals harder. "Next, they slit him open. They slit his throat... and cut his balls off... stuffed 'em in his big fat mouth. That's what we do to all fucking race traitors."

"Come on Jackie, let me go... It hurts!"

"Goddammit, look at me when I'm talking to you! There was also this fucking bartender who actually tried to rat on me. He doubled over and folded like a jack-knife when I shot him. I blew his balls into outer space before he even knew what the fuck was happening... Now, look, I like you. Howie really likes you. So don't ask too many questions and do as you're told...and just maybe you'll stay alive." She released him.

"Okay, okay! Ah! Ohhh!" Mitch moaned, holding his groin in pain.

"See this?" Jackie said, rolling up a sleeve and exposing her tattooed left arm. "It's the *Totenkopf*, the Death skull of the SS. It means I've killed somebody... more than thirty people. I'm wanted for murder in Canada... and seven states. So don't fuck with me, Boy Scout. I'll beat your balls off."

Jackie left Mitch and walked back over to Howard; the pair watched as Jeff and Ariadne placed the last of the explosives in the garage.

"Where's Bruce and Pamie?" Howard said.

"We took a hell of a lot more C4 than we need. There might be some other jobs we can use it for. So, after the raid I sent them back to Denver with a couple pounds of the stuff. We'll keep it hidden there."

"Why don't you ease up on Mitch? He's all right."

"Yeah, I know. You're right… he just kind of pissed me off. I guess I'm just a little uptight, that's all. I'd better go apologize to him."

"Well, now I have everything I need. Now at last I can build the bomb. Come next January, we're going to destroy the Zionist regime in Washington, and it's all thanks to you," Howard said, embracing her.

"It's all just so beautiful. In a few months we're gonna kill four hundred thousand people. I love you," she said gleefully, gazing into his eyes. They kissed.

Collision Course

Monday, July 6th
1320 hours
Alliance Construction Company, Greeley, CO

With the discovery of the theft of the explosives' agents from the Bureau of Alcohol, Tobacco and Firearms had been summoned up to Greeley. Amid a chaotic scene a visibly shaken ATF Regional Director Joseph Wheeler paused in his investigation. He momentarily glanced down at an early edition of the local newspaper. In stark, boldface, large point type were the headlines:

HORRIBLE SLAUGHTER PEN
FIVE SLAIN IN GREELEY PLANT MASSACRE

In twenty-seven years in law enforcement, I've never seen anything like this, he thought to himself as workers from the Coroner's Office whisked a sheet-covered gurney past him.

After interviewing the company's plant manager and other employees, Wheeler had contacted the FBI's Denver office, which temporarily pulled Frank Bledsoe from the Rocky Flats case. Upon seeing Bledsoe pull into the parking lot, Wheeler dropped the paper and walked over.

"Agent Bledsoe?" he said, extending his hand. "I'm Joe Wheeler, ATF. Let me fill you in." The pair walked over to the massacre site, pausing at the front door. "Local cops found five guys shot to death in there early yesterday. Multiple gunshots. Jesus Christ! Looks like somebody spilled a couple cans of red paint in there."

Bledsoe stooped over and retrieved a spent shell casing next to the doorway with a pencil.

"Forty-five-caliber... MAC-10 maybe?"

"Yeah. Four of the victims were found in a pile against the wall next to that shot-up TV over there," Wheeler said, pointing to the blood-spattered wall. "We found the black guy slumped in the corner... They blew his head off. Poor devils never had a fucking chance. They even shot the dogs."

"Go on," Bledsoe said, scribbling in a notepad.

"We were called in because the theft of explosives was involved. I was talking to the plant manager before you got here, guy named Tobias Carlan. I think you should hear what he has to say about this." The agents walked over to a small employee lounge. There, a trembling Tobias Carlan waited, staring blankly into space.

"Mr. Carlan? I'm Frank Bledsoe, FBI. Director Wheeler here says you have something to say to me. Please tell me everything you know."

"Somebody just shot them. Shot 'em down! Killed them," the shocked man stammered fitfully. "I found them early this morning. All dead. Even the dogs."

"Please, tell me what happened."

"Mr. Carlan, tell Agent Bledsoe about the woman who came to see you," Wheeler said. Carlan, still visibly shaken, took a deep breath and began to speak.

"Couple of days ago, a woman from the ATF Bureau showed up at the company. She demanded to see the records on our storage and inventory of high explosives we use in our construction projects."

"Go on, sir, please."

"Well, anyway, I showed her the records. She was real interested in our stocks of C4 explosives."

"Did the woman have a name?" Bledsoe said.

"Jacqueline eh-something, I think. Yes, Jacqueline Wilson, she said."

"We have no record of sending anyone here for an inspection, and no woman named Jacqueline Wilson works in the Bureau," Wheeler said. "Besides, the Alliance facility was just inspected back in February and got a clean bill of health. This Wilson woman is a phony."

"She was also interested in our security arrangements," Carlan continued. "I'm afraid I told her everything. And now all my people are dead and at least seventy pounds of high explosives have been stolen! The storage area was picked clean!"

"Please, Mr. Carlan, tell me exactly what was stolen," Bledsoe said.

"Our inventory shows that seven cases of C4 plastic explosive, six dozen M6 blasting caps, adhesive putty and a galvanometer are missing."

"How much C4 was in each case?"

"Ten bricks, each one weighing about one pound. Roughly ten pounds in each case. That comes to about seventy pounds total," Carlan mumbled in reply.

"What would one use a galvanometer for?" Bledsoe said, writing furiously.

"A galvanometer's what is used to test an electric firing system. It's used to test the continuity of the firing circuit between the blasting machine and the explosives," Carlan said. "You always want to make sure you've got a good connection."

"Please, try to calm down sir," Bledsoe said gently. "Can you describe this woman? Her appearance?"

"About thirty, five-eight, maybe... hundred- twenty pounds... short blonde hair. She was really quite striking. I figured she had to be legit; she had an ATF uniform and ID, you know, the whole nine yards."

"Think you can describe her for an FBI artist?"

"Couldn't forget a face like hers."

"I'll get Hal Munday out here," Bledsoe said, turning to Wheeler. "We'll try to get this woman's sketch out to area law enforcement as soon as possible."

"What do you think?" Wheeler said.

"C4, blasting caps, five murders. It all adds up. It's a cinch that somebody wants to blow up something. Wants it so bad they're willing to massacre five innocent people for it. The killers probably used this Wilson woman as a scout," Bledsoe said, slowly closing the notepad.

1330 hours

"That's her!" Tobias Carlan said to the FBI artist as he put the finishing touches to the sketch. "That's the Wilson woman! That's the woman I saw last month! Boy, you guys are good!"

"You're sure? This is the woman you saw here several days ago?" Bledsoe said, examining the sketch.

"Yes sir. That's her. No doubt."

"Okay, we're going to start distributing copies of this sketch to local law enforcement," Bledsoe said, turning to Wheeler. "I'm going to keep a team up here to assist you ATF guys in the investigation."

"That's fine. Just what we need. Nothing like a little interdepartmental cooperation," Wheeler said in response.

Tuesday, July 7th
0829 hours

FBI Field Office, Federal Bldg. Denver, CO

"Welcome back, Frank. How's the Greeley investigation going?" Rabson said as Bledsoe entered the office.

"It's going. Joe Wheeler and the ATF are all over the place. Christ! It was a massacre; five guys were shot to death late Saturday night at a construction company. I guess you could see it coming. From the looks of it, their security was terrible, I mean downright nonexistent," Bledsoe said, gazing up at the ceiling and shaking his head. "Instead of doing their jobs guarding the place, they were drinking beer, eating potato chips and watching a damned ballgame on TV. Looks like the killers made off with at least seventy pounds of C4 explosive plus some other stuff."

"Anything on who might have done it?"

"The company manager told me that a couple of days ago some woman apparently impersonating an ATF official came to the facility, asking about their stocks of C4 and their security."

"Coincidence maybe?"

"Not a chance. Wheeler's people swear that she's a phony. The manager told her about the inventory of explosives — especially the C4."

"Was he able to describe the woman?"

"Well, that's the good news. He gave us a pretty good description of the woman. I got Hal Munday up there yesterday afternoon. He got a good sketch of the woman," Bledsoe said, opening his briefcase and showing Rabson a copy of the sketch.

Rabson studied the sketch and physical description carefully for a full minute. "Frank... you know she kind of looks like Jacqueline Lynch."

"Huh?"

"Sure. Here, look close, see for yourself." Rabson held the sketch up against her mug photo. The two agents examined the images carefully.

"Yeah, I see. I think you may be right."

"Frank, it's all beginning to fit. Let's say that you've stolen weapons-grade plutonium, tamper materials and an initiator neutron source. If you were going to build an implosion-type atomic bomb you'd need conventional explosives, right?"

"Yeah, I suppose."

"Probably real high velocity stuff... something like C4 or Semtex. I think that pretty much settles it. The Werewolf is definitely trying to build a bomb."

"But there's no telling where those sonsabitches will use it... Where are you going?"

"I'm going to Denver General. Around six yesterday I got a call from Dr Abrams. He told me that Suzanne Brennan was lucid and out of danger. She may be our only link. I was getting ready to leave when you arrived."

Rabson immediately got into his car and drove to the hospital. If his theory was correct, the Werewolf was well on its way towards an operational nuclear device. Severe injuries or not, the Brennan woman had to be questioned. As he drove, he devised his method of interrogation.

0901 hours
Denver General Hospital

"Doctor Abrams, I'm Douglas Rabson. We spoke briefly over the phone yesterday afternoon. I understand that Suzanne Brennan is awake now and able to undergo questioning."

"Yes, she is awake. Thank God there was no brain damage. But I don't see how you can question her. Besides, all the other injuries, her jaw was broken in two places; it'll be wired shut for at least the next six to eight weeks. And both of her hands were broken."

"Yes sir, I'm aware of these facts, but there is a way that I can communicate with this woman. I can't go into the details right now but it's imperative that I speak with her."

"Very well, Mr. Rabson," the doctor relented, "but I must insist that you spend no more than thirty minutes with her, less if she gets tired. Her recovery will be very slow and she needs a lot of rest. Understood?"

"Yes sir. Thank you."

Showing his FBI credentials, Rabson walked past a brace of Denver police officers guarding the entrance to Room 312. Inside, he was horrified at the sight: Suzanne Brennan had been savagely beaten. Besides having several broken ribs both of her hands were heavily bandaged, giving a mummy-like appearance. In addition, her broken jaw was securely wrapped, wired shut and restrained in a large harness.

How could anyone do something like this to another human being? What sort of sick mind would do this? Rabson thought to himself, shaking his head in disgust.

"Mrs. Brennan?" he said softly. "I'm Special Agent Douglas Rabson, FBI. I'm investigating the attack that was made on you. We're going to try to find the person who did this to you, but we're going to need your help. I would like to ask you a few questions, if I may. I realize that you can't speak or write anything, but you can still *communicate*. I know that you're probably tired, so I'll try to be as brief as possible." Rabson gazed into the frightened woman's eyes.

"I'm going to ask you questions; you can answer by blinking your eyes — twice for yes and once for no. First of all, can you hear me all right?"

The woman blinked twice.

"Very good. Now Mrs. Brennan, who did this to you? Was it your husband? Did your husband beat you up?"

Suzanne blinked twice. A tear slowly ran down her cheek.

"Several weeks ago, terrorists attacked the facility at Rocky Flats. Eleven men were murdered, and some very dangerous materials were stolen. Was your husband involved?"

Two blinks. Rabson opened his briefcase and pulled out the Lynch mugshot photo. "This woman's name is Jacqueline Lynch. She's wanted for several murders. Was she also involved?"

Two blinks. This time Rabson noticed her eyes furrowed in anger.

"Would you be willing to testify against your husband?"

After some hesitation she blinked twice.

"You're doing fine, Mrs. Brennan. Now, it's important that we find these people before anyone else is murdered. Do you know where your husband and this woman are?"

Two blinks.

"All right. Now I'm going to try and find out where. I'm going to ask you the name of various cities in the area, and you indicate to me when I mention the correct one. Again, two blinks for yes, one for no. Ready? Lakewood?"

The woman blinked once.
"Arvada?"
One blink.
"Westminster?"
One blink.
"Aurora?"

Her eyes suddenly flashed two blinks.

"Excellent. Aurora. Are you holding up okay, Mrs. Brennan?"

Two blinks. He saw that she was becoming more relaxed.

"Fine. Were your husband and Lynch staying in a hotel in Aurora?"

One blink.

"How about a private home?" Two blinks.

"Okay. Mrs. Brennan, eh-may I call you Suzanne?"

She blinked twice approvingly.

"We're going to determine who owns this private home. I'll go through the alphabet. When I get to a letter in the person's name, you'll let me know by blinking. We'll do the last name first."

Rabson's "interrogation" continued for another hour. By a painstaking process, he was able to obtain information on the case. He ended the questioning when Mrs. Brennan started showing fatigue. As he emerged from the room, he was confronted by an angry Doctor Abrams.

"Agent Rabson, I thought I told you no more than thirty minutes with that patient — you were in there more than an hour. You have deliberately violated my orders. Now, I warn you that I'll restrict your access to this patient if you don't follow my instructions!"

"I'm sorry, sir. But the interview was worth it. I learned a great deal of information from Mrs. Brennan."

"Oh, come now. I doubt that. A woman who can neither speak nor write suddenly tells you everything you wish to know."

"That's correct, sir. Mrs. Brennan was exceedingly helpful in this case. I stopped the interview when she became tired. I'll try to return tomorrow to continue my interrogation."

"And what if I refuse to grant you access to this patient?"

"Then in that case, Doctor, I'm afraid that you will be arrested for obstruction of a criminal investigation. The questioning of this woman is now a matter of national security; you will not interfere," Rabson said. "I'm going to contact my superiors now."

1210 hours
FBI Field Office, Federal Building, Denver, CO

"Where in Hell have you been?" Bledsoe said as Rabson arrived. "I've been looking all over for you."

"I was at Denver General, questioning Mrs. Brennan."

"You what? How?"

"Yes sir. That's correct. But I was able to question her. I used a method I remembered from a seminar for interrogation of a victim who cannot speak or do a facial movement. She informed me that Jacqueline Lynch and Howard Brennan are held up in Aurora, in a house owned by a man named Nick Manson. They've got the plutonium there."

"Just how exactly were you able to get her to talk?"

"Not talk. *Communicate*. It was really very simple. I would ask her questions that normally required a yes or no answer; she would communicate the answers with her eyes, two blinks for yes, one blink for no."

"I see. Pretty smart… Academy Interrogation One-oh-One. What about this Manson character?"

"I checked with local law enforcement. You wouldn't believe this guy. Manson has a long record for assault, pimping and burglary. Indicted for murder, no conviction. Did several years in Cañon City earlier. Joined the White Brotherhood while in the joint. He'd probably starve if it wasn't for prison food. His wife isn't much better."

Bledsoe made a long pause. "Okay, I'm going to contact the director on this one. I'll try to get us a surveillance team on the Manson house. This is really your collar; I suppose you'll want in on the raid?"

"Hell yes, you bet I do."

1504 hours
The Manson residence, Aurora, CO

At Bledsoe's order, a six-man FBI stake-out team quickly began a grueling surveillance of the Manson house. Disguised as a roadwork crew and electricians, they monitored activity in the community; whenever someone left the house, that person was followed. They managed to ascertain that besides the Mansons there were two other people inside. Since the Greeley raid, Pamela Haney and her boyfriend Bruce Davies had been staying at the Manson house. The pair were carrying several pounds of the stolen C4 and blasting caps. Jackie had decided that it might be a good idea to use some of the surplus explosives for other jobs.

Thursday, July 9th
0830 hours
FBI Field Office, Denver, CO.

"I've just received the go-ahead from the director," Bledsoe said. "The necessary warrant is being prepared now. This'll probably be the first time in the history of American jurisprudence that a warrant was issued on the basis of an eye-blink. We'll be going in tomorrow morning. We can't wait on this one."

Rabson nodded in reply.

"I understand."

"We'll follow standard procedure. None of that John Wayne shit. We've arranged backup from Aurora and Denver PD. The Bureau is sending us a SWAT unit. They arrive at DIA tonight. The stake-out team informs me that besides the Mansons there are at least two other people in the house. A man and a woman."

"Hmmm, must be Jacqueline Lynch and Howard Brennan," Rabson said, slowly nodding. "Maybe we have the Jack-L cornered at last."

Friday, July 10th
0915 hours
Near the Manson residence, Aurora, CO.

"One-Zulu-Bravo. This is Tango-X-ray, do you copy?" Rabson said, speaking into his portable radio.

"Roger, Tango-X-ray. We're in position," a voice on the other end responded. The SWAT assault team had positioned itself around the back of the house.

"Stand by."

Pamela Haney had just finished her breakfast. Casually peering out the window, she caught a glimpse of a man crouching behind a tree. Looking closer, she noticed the man was wearing a navy-blue Kevlar helmet, matching flak vest with the gold letters *FBI* emblazoned upon it, and a black mask like something a ninja would wear. Panning her eyes up the street she took note of other uniformed men furtively deploying toward the house. She ran to the back of the house to alert the others.

"Nick! Stace! Oh, shit! Get up! The FBI's outside! ZOG's found us!"

Bruce Davies was in the bathroom shaving. He instinctively grabbed his MAC-10 when he heard his girlfriend pounding on the door. The other terrorists, with weapons in hand, rushed to the windows, watching with a nervous apprehension as the trap slowly clamped down on them.

"Yeah, they're all around," Bruce said anxiously. "Jesus Christ! Look, there's some more of 'em coming up the street!"

"They're coming this way all right," Nick said, ramming a 32-round banana clip into his AR-16 assault weapon.

"Shit! I wonder how those assholes found us," Stacey thought aloud.

"It doesn't much matter now. The only thing to do now is to make a stand and fight it out! Let's kick some ZOG ass!" Bruce said, as he grimly took up a position in the bathroom and loaded his weapon. "Christ! Look at 'em come! Stace, you go out back and get us some more ammo!"

From a heavily armored SWAT van Rabson watched with professional admiration as the operation unfolded. He felt that perhaps at last this long and frustrating case was finally coming to an end. The two principal suspects were almost certainly in the house. They could not escape. All the preliminaries had been done. The surrounding homes in the area had been quietly evacuated by local police earlier in the morning. The FBI Special Weapons Assault Team was in position, and all potential exits had been blocked. Much to Rabson's dismay, camera crews from the local TV stations had also arrived and were setting up. A local news helicopter whirled overhead in the distance.

Oh well, freedom of the press and all. I was wondering when they would show up, he thought as a thin cordon of police held the newsmen back. With all in readiness, Rabson picked up a megaphone and began speaking.

"Nick Manson. This is the FBI," he said in a booming voice. "The house is completely surrounded. You and everyone inside drop your weapons to the floor, place your hands behind your heads and exit the premises through the front door! You will not be harmed."

"Fuck you! White Power!" Pam Haney yelled, breaking the front window and spraying the street with her MAC-10. Forty-five caliber bullets ricocheted off of the armor plate of the van or thudded into trees. The other Aryans joined in, firing as fast as they could load. FBI, local police and press all dove for cover from the galling fire.

Above the din of gunfire Rabson repeated his plea for the suspects to surrender. The images of a Waco-style conflagration kept recurring in his mind.

"Your position is hopeless. I repeat, you cannot escape. Drop your weapons!" The volume of fire from the house merely increased.

"Mr. Rabson, shall we return fire, sir?" a youthful-looking SWAT team member said.

Rabson grimly bit his lip and said, "Yes, but try to wing them. We need those people alive. We'll try to keep their attention focused here while the other unit takes 'em from the rear… Commence firing!"

A fusillade of fire poured into the house as the federals opened up. Several teargas grenades sailed through the windows. One FBI man, armed with a large M203 grenade launcher attached to his AR-16 and 40-millimeter "flash-bang" concussion grenades crouched behind a parked car. He fired a grenade into a bathroom window where the fire was especially heavy. The grenade went off with a loud bang. Bruce Davies was knocked down and momentarily blinded by the flash of the bomb but was otherwise unhurt. Meanwhile, a three-man assault unit had stealthily maneuvered itself to the back of the premises. With crowbar-like "hooligan tools" they forced their way into the storage shed. Stacey Manson, having gone to the back of the house for the additional ammunition heard strange noises coming from the shed. She pushed the door open, suddenly confronting a huge black FBI agent.

"Die nigger! This is it!" she screamed as she emptied her MAC-10 into his chest, knocking him down. The other two agents returned fire, hitting Stacey in the arm. She was startled to see her 'victim' suddenly rise from the floor, apparently unhurt. Handcuffed, the screaming woman was taken outside and treated for her wound.

"Hey Jake, you all right man? Shit, you just took eight slugs in the chest from a MAC!" a comrade said.

"Yeah, fine, just got the wind knocked out of me," the dazed FBI agent said, opening his jacket. "This is gonna hurt like hell tomorrow... All I can say is I'd like to kiss the sonofabitch who invented these Kevlar vests!"

The volume of fire from the house abruptly slackened and stopped. Pamela Haney threw her weapon out the window. She was concerned about her boyfriend, who was still rolling around on the floor from the effects of the concussion grenade.

"Cease fire! I think they've surrendered," Rabson said. "All right, you people in there, come out with your hands in the air! Now!"

An instant later, Pamela Haney staggered out, with Bruce Davies on her arm. Rabson and members of the assault team cautiously moved forward, weapons at the ready. "Lie down! Face down, on the ground!" he yelled. The exhausted terrorists meekly complied. Local police were cuffing the suspects when suddenly, from out of the bullet-riddled house Nick Manson emerged, clad in camouflage and AR-16 assault rifle in hand. Like some Viking berserker of old, Manson ran toward the oncoming FBI agents. He let loose a burst of automatic weapons fire that rattled off of the pavement.

"Werewolf! White Power! White Fucking Power!" he yelled as an FBI sniper tracked him in the telescope of a Steyr-Mannlicher 30.06 rifle. A single round in the chest threw him backwards, sprawling to the ground, dead. A moment later, members of the assault team that had been in the shed emerged after a hasty search of the premises. All of the terrorists had been accounted for. Two members of NEST, armed with neutron detectors and a Geiger-Mueller counter began a walk-through to search for the stolen plutonium. Several Aurora firefighters quickly entered the house to extinguish a small blaze in the bathroom that had ignited where the concussion grenade had exploded. The battle was over.

Rabson looked at Haney and Davies and then examined the dead man. He walked back to the van with a disappointed look on his face. Frank Bledsoe, who had arrived as the battle ended came over to meet him.

"Well, Rabson, nice work. No casualties in the assault unit, and only one dead for the bad guys. You can fill me in on all the details when we get back to the office... What's the matter?"

"Frank, the plutonium's not in there."

"How do you know that? Our search has just started."

"Jacqueline Lynch and Howard Brennan aren't here, so neither is the plutonium. I was hoping that those two over there would be the suspects, but no dice. Looks like this investigation is far from finished," Rabson said dejectedly. He started walking towards the house.

"May we have a statement?" a newswoman said, pushing her camcorder in front of Rabson.

"No, please, not right now," the exhausted agent mumbled in reply. "The Bureau will make a statement shortly." In his preparation for the assault, he had absent-mindedly left his ID tag on his vest. The camcorder had captured the image of *RABSON* on the name plate.

Additional ATF and FBI agents swarmed into the now vacant, teargas filled house, beginning a painstaking search. In addition to stacks of white supremacist hate literature a large cache of weapons was uncovered.

"Will you look at all this shit!" Bledsoe mentioned to Rabson as they surveyed the immense haul. "It's a good thing we caught 'em with their pants down. These bastards could have held us off for days with all this stuff."

"Yeah, but, like I said, the plutonium isn't here."

"Mr. Bledsoe? Mr. Rabson?" Agent Al Gordon said. "I think you both should come out here and look at this." The two men followed Gordon out to the storage shed. There they gazed into a makeshift underground vault. In it were stacks of cash hidden in watertight pouches.

"Holy Hell! We hit the jackpot!" Bledsoe said, picking up several of the bundles. "You know what all this is?"

"Yes sir. It's probably the six million bucks that was stolen during that armored car heist here last year. I still remember reading about those two guards who were shot to death, execution-style."

"Right. That money was being transferred from Colorado National Western Bank to one of the casinos up in Central City. Look close, you can still see some of the bank wrappers on the money. I sweated five months investigating that case," Bledsoe said.

"I'll notify Colorado National Western and have them send someone down here. They can make a positive identification by the serial numbers." As the two men walked past Pamela Haney's truck, Rabson saw something partially wrapped in a blanket on the back seat. He opened the door and made a closer inspection.

"Frank, you see what I see?"

Bledsoe pressed against the car windshield.

"Yeah, it looks like some kind of rifle. This place is crawling with weapons, so what?"

"That's a Russian *Dragunov* sniper rifle and telescopic sight."

"Okay. So?"

"It's seven-point-six-two-millimeter. The same type the Bureau suspects was used by the Jack-L in several hits she's made. Didn't Joe Wheeler and the ATF find several seven-point-six- two-millimeter shell casings at the scene of that construction company massacre?"

"Yeah... that's right! Found near the fence. They're saying that at least one of the dogs was killed with a seven-point-six-two-millimeter round."

Rabson and Bledsoe left Gordon to supervise the search. The federal agents spent the day removing the evidence. All in all, it had been a good day. Four Werewolf operatives were out of commission, as well as a huge cache of stolen weapons and money recovered. After weeks of frustration, there was finally a glimmer of good news.

During a hastily arranged primetime news conference, the

Attorney General and the FBI Director made the most of the day's events. In hailing the dramatic results of the raid in Colorado, the pair sought to show the public that 'their FBI' was always alert, ever vigilant. According to their version of events, a racist gang had been smashed, their sedition nipped in the bud. Director Longstreet crowed loudly over the performance of the Bureau's Counter-terrorism Strike Force (and in the process did a little politicking of his own by casually reminding the public that its creation had been, after all, his idea); Rabson was mentioned several times, singled out as a rising star in the Bureau.

1813 hours
The Price residence, Greeley, CO

"Looks like ZOG agents caught up with Nick and Stacey," Jackie said in disgust as she and Howard watched the news conference on television.

"They should've killed themselves rather than get caught," Howard said coldly.

"Well, shouldn't we be getting out of here?"

"Relax. Nothing has changed," Howard said reassuringly. "Nick was the only one who knew exactly where we are, and he's dead. ZOG's hired assassins made sure of that."

"What about the others?"

"Forget them. They have sacrificed themselves for the movement. They won't talk, even under ZOG torture. They all took the oath. Besides, they know that we'll go after their families if they do. The Werewolf lives... I wonder how they found out about the safe house."

"I'll bet I know. Had to be Suzanne. She probably ratted us out somehow. You should've killed her," Jackie said. She had a look on her face that seemed to say, 'I told you so.'

"Yeah," Howard sighed, nodding. The pair continued to watch the broadcast. They listened as the director and Attorney General praised the role of Doug Rabson during the operation.

"That Rabson guy again!" Jackie said. "I wish that you would've let me kill him."

"You have to keep your mind focused on our mission."

"I'm covering the trail that leads to you. This Rabson guy is dangerous. He has to be taken care of."

Howard slowly nodded. "All right. Do it. What do you have in mind?"

"We stole more C4 than you need for the bomb, right?"

"Yeah. And?"

"Let's put some of the excess to good use. Howie, I got an idea." The pair flipped the channel over to the *CNA Evening News* where more coverage of the raid was being shown. They watched the film footage of Doug Rabson directing the operation. "So now we know what he looks like. In a couple weeks I'm going to kill that man. Just you watch," Jackie said, smiling.

1815 hours
FBI Field Office, Federal Building, Denver, CO

In a mood of celebration, various agency personnel clustered around televisions and watched the Attorney General's news conference.

"Well, Doug, looks like you're the man of the hour. Accolades from the director himself, and even from old Stoneface McCormick," Frank Bledsoe said, patting the somewhat modest Rabson on the back.

"Yeah, I guess we got kind of lucky."

"Lucky? Hell, you broke this case open, you and your eye-blink interrogation of Suzanne Brennan. Quit being so damned modest! We've got those assholes on the run!"

"I'm not so sure."

"Can't you be just a little bit happy? We took out four terrorists today, prime suspects in both the Rocky Flats and armored car attacks. Recovered a shitload of stolen money and weapons. Not bad for a day's work."

"Frank, don't get me wrong. Sure, we took out some of their operatives. But the Werewolf is still active. Right now, we've still got a psychopath and his girlfriend loose somewhere with all the elements of an atomic bomb. Let's go down to the holding area. I want to show you something."

The two men took the elevator and descended into the dungeon-like catacombs of the basement of the Federal Building. There, FBI prisoners were held for questioning and processing until trial or transfer to local authorities. There, Pamela Haney, Bruce Davies and Stacey Manson had been housed in separate cells. Far from being downcast over their incarceration, the prisoners seemed strangely at ease, indeed almost jovial. Only Stacey appeared depressed, and that was because her husband was dead.

"Yahweh is King! Sieg Heil Adolph Hitler!" Pam yelled as the two men approached. She stood up and thrust her arm out between the bars in the Nazi salute. A grotesque SS Death's Head tattoo was plainly visible on the out-stretched limb.

"What do all you pigs want? Huh Jew-boy?" Davies snarled, still groggy from the effects of the concussion grenade. "What about it? If I wasn't so damn slow, you'd know how dead feels right now, Jew-boy!" Rabson ignored the insult.

"You have all been read your rights and therefore understand that you don't have to talk to us if you don't want to."

"That's right, Pig! We ain't got to talk!" Pam said, spittle flying from her mouth.

"Each of you is probably going to be charged with, among other things, at least eighteen counts of murder. Does that have an effect on any of you?"

"They had to die, Yahweh has commanded it," Pamela said.

"What?"

"Their lives were of no importance. They had to die for the revolution, the race war. It's all right in the Bible. This is the will of Yahweh."

"You lousy ZOG pigs murdered my husband!" Stacey sobbed, still nursing her wounded arm.

"Don't worry Stace, the Werewolf's gonna have its revenge! Eye for eye! Tooth for tooth! Blood for blood!" Pam yelled.

"What do you clowns mean by that?" Bledsoe said.

"Well, what do you think, asshole! We stole all that nuclear shit in Colorado. Jackie and Howie are going to build a bomb, and all you ZOG assholes are gonna pay when they set it off. ZOG will die!" Pam said.

"Don't bet on it, lady," Bledsoe said. "You're going to be charged with Murder-One, at least four counts in Colorado. They'll probably fry your ass in the chair."

"I'll bet I live long enough to see ZOG destroyed! You stupid assholes are all gonna die in the coming race war! You hear me, Jewboy? Your ass is gonna fry in a nuclear Auschwitz! White Power! Werewolf for Life!" Pam screamed. Her face was twisted with racial hate. "And you better believe that the next time we do a holocaust we're gonna do it right!"

"Hey! You treat us like animals, we gonna act like animals! White Power! Werewolf for Life!" Stacey yelled through the bars of her cell.

"White Power! Werewolf for Life!" the others joined in, flashing the Nazi salute as the two men left the holding area.

"You see what I mean Frank?"

"Yeah, I think so."

"Of all the prisoners I've seen, I've never seen a bunch like these guys. Fanatics, pure and simple. Responsible for the deaths of at least eleven innocent people, and maybe more. They're all going to be charged with capital murder, all facing almost certain execution… and they're almost happy about it!"

"Most people in their situation would be sullen, depressed, trying to cut a deal, anything," Bledsoe said, rubbing his head in astonishment. "These people simply don't care. And Pam Haney, she's the most vicious person I think I've ever seen in my life."

"Now you see why I'm not particularly elated over the day's events. Those three sick clowns in there are convinced that Howard Brennan and Jacqueline Lynch can build and detonate an atomic bomb. And so am I."

"I reckon the next question becomes obvious."

"Yeah. Where… and when?"

Code Name: Juggernaut

The Fourth Horseman

"And I looked and behold a pale horse: and his name that sat on him was Death, and Hell followed with him. And power was given unto him over the fourth part of the earth, to kill with sword, and with hunger, and with death…"

— Revelation 6:8

"…Our Country owed all her troubles to him, and God simply made me the instrument of his punishment. The country is not what it was. This forced Union is not what I have loved…I have no desire to out-live my country…"

— The diary of John Wilkes Booth, April 19, 1865

Three days after the press conference, Rabson had been ordered back to Washington to give a firsthand report to the president and National Security Council on how the investigation was proceeding. Rabson welcomed the order; after weeks of absence, he hoped to have an extended visit with his wife Rachel and children. In the meantime, Bledsoe and the other agents would handle the arraignment of the captured terrorists. At the meeting, the president, the directors of the CIA, FBI and ATF, as well as the Attorney General were present.

Tuesday, July 14th
1100 hours (EDT)
The White House, Washington, DC

"So very nice to see you again Agent Rabson," the president said, extending his hand warmly. "You're doing an excellent job in Denver."

"Thank you, sir."

"The reason that I had George order you back here is to give us a detailed rundown on exactly where things stand on the Rocky Flats case."

"Well, sir, about two weeks ago, a woman was found badly beaten on a Denver street. Through local law enforcement we managed to find out that she was the husband of one of the suspected terrorists."

"Sir, that would be Suzanne Brennan, Colonel Howard Brennan's wife," Director Longstreet interjected.

"Correct. We were able to ascertain that she had been beaten up by her husband. I reasoned that maybe she wanted out, or perhaps was trying to contact us. I managed to interrogate her; and from that we discovered the whereabouts of the terrorist hide-out."

"And from what I understand it was a rather novel form of interrogation," the president said.

"Now, Agent Rabson, exactly what evidence were you able to recover from the raid?" the Attorney General said.

"For one thing, an arsenal — machineguns, assault rifles with silencers, explosives, an anti-tank weapon and thousands of rounds of ammunition. Most of it stolen. I have a list here of everything that we recovered." Rabson opened his briefcase. "If they had known we were coming, it would have been like *World War III* out there. It was almost as if they were preparing for war."

"Any connections to Rocky Flats?" the president said.

"Yes sir. Solid. I got a call from Frank Bledsoe late last night. During the search they came across a detailed map of the facility... we think the same one that disappeared one day before McClintock was murdered. He also said that several computer-generated diagrams of an implosion device were found."

"Anything else?"

"A high-powered Russian-made rifle and several clips of ammunition were taken. Our forensics people say that Jacqueline Lynch's prints were on it."

"You'd think that a professional assassin would know enough to use rubber gloves when using the murder weapon," the Attorney General said.

"Ballistics tests were performed on the weapon; they indicate that it was used to kill at least one of the guard dogs at the construction company," Rabson said. "It has also been tentatively linked to a number of racially motivated sniper killings in Los Angeles, Detroit and Philadelphia."

"What about the three terrorists who were captured?" McCormick said.

"One of them has been linked to the Rocky Flats raid. Her name is Pamela Mae Haney. She's being arraigned on four counts of capital murder even as we speak. She apparently was a Werewolf mole inside the facility. The other two apparently were using their home as a safe house for the terrorists."

"Any of them talking?" the CIA Director said.

"No sir. They've all clammed up."

"What about all that stolen money that was recovered?" the president said.

"It was from the six-million-dollar-armored car robbery in Denver last year. Bank records and serial numbers confirm it. It looks like they recovered about four and a half million of it."

"I understand that there may have been some Werewolf involvement in a mass killing in Greeley," the president said. "Can you elaborate on that?"

"Yes sir. Several pounds of a high velocity explosive called C4 were stolen from a large construction company on the night of the fourth. Some of the material was found in Haney's car during the search, along with the Russian rifle. Bledsoe called me last night and said that Joe Wheeler of the ATF and company personnel have confirmed that it came from the same lot that was stolen."

"Only God knows where these people intend to use it," the ATF director said.

"That's what is so worrisome," Longstreet replied, "high velocity explosives are a necessary ingredient if you want to build an implosion-type atomic bomb. More than ever, we're convinced that the Werewolf intends to build a bomb."

Wednesday, July 15th
0850 hours
The Price residence, Greeley, CO

"Okay, Howie, we're set to go," Mitch said as Howard and Jackie came into the large downstairs laboratory. The poorly ventilated room was filled with complex glassware and numerous bottles of chemical solvents.

"So, these are the ceramic molds you're going to use?" Howard carefully examined the two molds.

"Yup. Made to your specifications. One hexagonal and the other pentagonal. I'll liquefy the C4 in that kiln over there," Mitch said, pointing to a large oven against the wall. "And then pour the molten explosive into the molds. I'll press this form into it for the baratol." Mitch picked up another mold. "Let it harden into the desired shapes. Have to do it slowly to make sure the distribution is even. Simple. It'll take a couple of days for each set."

"Excellent," Howard said approvingly.

"Mitch, you're going to heat up the C4?" Jackie said.

"That's right."

"But won't it explode?"

"No." As if to demonstrate, Mitch picked up one of the C4 bricks and held a lit match up to it in front of her.

"Okay, Mitch, you made your point," Jackie said, slowly backing away.

"That's the beauty of C4. It's very pliable when heated. It's a plastic explosive you know. You can heat it up. Pound on it. Mold it. I can make it into any shape I want. C4 begins to liquefy at about 170 degrees Fahrenheit."

"I see," Jackie nodded. She picked up and examined one of the bricks.

"Okay, Mitch, give me a rough estimate as to how long until the explosives are ready," Howard said.

"Let's see, if anything goes all right, I figure mid-October, Halloween at the latest."

"Perfect!" Howard went upstairs, leaving the pair alone.

"Hey, Mitch, listen," Jackie said softly, placing her hand on his shoulder. "You know I'm real sorry that I was such a bitch the other day. I really didn't mean all those things."

"Forget it."

"Still friends?"

"Sure."

"You know, I stole a hell of a lot more C4 than we need for the bomb. I wonder if you could spare a little of it for something I have in mind."

"What for?"

"I want to kill a cop. This FBI agent called Rabson. Asshole's been tracking me for months now. I think it's time that I got rid of him. Mitch, will you help me do it?"

"How much do you want?"

"A pound or two should more than do the job."

"How you gonna get it to him?"

"Come here, I'll show you." The pair walked over to a telephone. Jackie dialed the operator. "Operator," a voice on the other end said.

"Yes, operator. Can you connect me with the Denver FBI Office? It's most important."

"One moment please." The operator made the connection.

"FBI. May I help you," a female voice on the other end said.

"Yes. My name is Margaret Lynch. I'm a reporter for *Channel Four News*. In light of recent events, we are doing a story on the FBI and I would like to interview Agent Douglas Rabson. Would that be possible?"

"I'm sorry, Miss Our agents generally don't give interviews," the operator said. "Departmental policy. Anyway, Agent Rabson isn't here. He works out of our office in Washington... perhaps I could send you a copy of one of our brochures of the Bureau's activities... Hello?" Jackie had hung up.

"What was all that about?"

"I told you. I'm going to kill this Rabson. First, I had to find out where he is. I'm gonna send him a package in the mail… One that he'll really get a bang out of. So, you gonna help me?"

"Okay. Why not?" Mitch shrugged. "No problem. It might be fun."

"Thanks Mitch." she said, a smile spreading across her face.

0945 hours

Jackie watched with a keen interest as Mitch carefully drilled a half-inch diameter hole, lengthwise, two inches into a one-pound brick of C4. Grabbing a "pineapple" hand grenade, he skillfully removed the fragmentation case, discarding it. Next, he slowly inserted the grenade's detonation assembly into the hole he had drilled into the explosive. "Get me that box over there, will you?" he said, pointing to a table. Jackie returned carrying a heavy cardboard box. Mitch wrapped the C4 brick with aluminum foil and proceeded to dip the package in a series of solvents in large beakers labeled with chemical-sounding nomenclature: CH_3COCH_3, CH_3OH, H_2O, $CH_3(CH_2)_4CH_3$. Next, he placed the charge into the box, with the grenade's safety lever and pin facing upward. Holding the lever firmly, Mitch pulled the pin. He carefully closed the lid down on top of the lever, holding it in place.

"Hand me some tape," he said. Jackie retrieved a thick roll of packing tape and pulled off a long strip. Mitch slowly taped the lid in place.

"There, here's your bomb. It's a nice little booby-trap for your cop friend."

"Why did you wrap the C4 with foil and go through all those washes with those chemicals?"

"You're sending it to the FBI, right?"

"Yeah."

"After all the terrorist scares since nine-eleven, suspicious packages are routinely X-rayed for bombs and the like. I think the aluminum foil should scatter X-radiation, preventing them from getting a good image. The aluminum foil should make it difficult for the FBI's X-ray machines to examine it." Mitch took the package from Jackie. "Also, most explosives today are either nitro-amino or nitro-aromatic-based materials. They've now got sophisticated sensors that can detect traces of these compounds. All this stuff is routinely used at airports to prevent terrorists from smuggling bombs on the planes." Mitch returned the bomb to her and picked up two of the beakers of solvent. "I do the washes in water, methanol, acetone and hexane in order to remove any traces of these nitro-containing chemicals, as well as my fingerprints. You've got to watch for the little things."

"You think of everything," Jackie said approvingly. "Exactly how will it work?"

"It's really quite simple. I took the grenade's detonator and placed it into a one-pound charge of C4. I activated it by pulling the pin. The lid of the box is holding the safety spoon down. When your friend opens the lid, the spoon will fly off; the amatol explosive in the detonator will in turn trigger the C4 charge and KA-BOOM! No more secret agent man!"

"And you're sure that it will kill the person who opens the package?"

"That person and anyone else in the room. Shit, with that much C4, you can't miss."

Jackie proceeded to wrap the package, carefully addressing it to the J. Edgar Hoover Building in Washington, marking it *Attention: D. Rabson.*

"I wonder if you would do me another favor? Take this to the Post

Office for me. I would do it myself but I might be recognized. You know ZOG's got our posters up everywhere."

"Sure, no problem."

Mitch quickly drove to the post office. While waiting in line to mail the parcel, he momentarily glanced at the various FBI Wanted posters hanging on the wall. Among the other wanted criminals, the images of Howard Brennan and Jackie Lynch were prominently displayed. He slowly nodded his head, understanding why she didn't want to go. He paid $8.37 to ship the parcel third class and left.

When Mitch returned, Jackie was waiting for him on the porch. She was wearing an imitation leopard-skin, string bikini thong and matching halter-top. The radio was playing softly. On seeing Mitch return, she suddenly went into the sexy 'bump-and-grind' routine of a Go-Go dancer, her slender hips gyrating to the beat of the music. Smiling, he watched her jiggle show for a full minute.

"Okay, it's in the mail. That FBI guy is as good as dead. You were right. You and Howie got your pictures all over the post office… God, you sure look good."

"Hi Mitch… want to join me? Want a private lap dance?" Jackie purred, wetting her lips while undulating to the beat of the music. She shimmied over to him.

"Huh? No."

"Mitch, why are you afraid of me? Do you wanna touch me? Do you wanna fuck me?" she said while slowly removing her bikini top, revealing her large, symmetrical breasts and ample cleavage. "Here, check out these fine Georgia peaches. C'mon Sweetie. All for you… Enjoy. Make love to me…Fuck me."

"Definitely not a good idea. I mean, you're Howie's woman." Mitch nervously backed away.

"What's the matter, Mitchy? Howie told me to be extra nice to you," she said, now slowly backing him against the wall. "It's okay. He won't get mad. He knows that you don't have a girlfriend. Anyway, Howie's gonna be too busy with the bomb. So, we can have a good time." The bikini top fell to the ground.

"I don't know," he said, nervously adjusting his glasses. Sweat was beading on his forehead.

"Mitch, you know you want me. I can see it in your eyes. Come on, if it feels good, do it. I won't bite. Make love to me." Jackie took his hand and placed it against her breast. Mitch wanted her.

Ridiculed as a 'nerd' in school, he had always wanted a girlfriend like Jackie. Over the last several weeks he swelled with growing sexual excitement as he watched the sleek, nubile blonde, so near and yet always tantalizingly out of reach. He was feeling that he was about to explode.

What am I waiting for? Christ Almighty, Jackie's so fucking gorgeous she makes me cum in my pants! he thought to himself. In a moment of blind desire he surrendered to animal passion.

"Oh, Jesus! You know I want you!" he said, throwing his eyeglasses on the floor. "Let's do it!" The pair went inside and retired to the back room. There, for the rest of the afternoon they made passionate love.

Thursday, July 16th
0803 hours
Greeley, CO

The brief tryst with Jackie had transformed Mitch. Glowing, he felt like a new man. Refreshed and rejuvenated, he could take on the world. He was in the kitchen preparing breakfast when Howard and Jackie walked in.

"Mitch, Jackie and I were talking last night and I—"

"Now wait Howie! It ain't how you think. She came on to me!" Mitch said defensively.

"Relax," Howard said, placing his hand on Mitch's shoulder. "I know all about you and Jackie yesterday. Jackie is a very beautiful Aryan woman. The flower of blonde, Nordic womanhood. It's only natural that you would want to sleep with her. I told her to be nice to you."

"Uh-huh." Mitch was relieved to find Howard so understanding.

"Jackie and I have decided to take you into our confidence. But first, how long have you known about the Werewolf?"

"Couple years. I found out when I was in college. I've done some odd jobs for it over the last few years."

"How much do you know?"

"Well, you and Jackie did Rocky Flats.

You're going to build a bomb to blow up something… or somebody."

"Mitch, I'm gonna tell you something, but you had better keep your mouth shut," Howard said. He took a deep breath and began speaking in a measured tone. "We're going to destroy the government… I'm going to detonate this device in Washington during the State of the Union Address next January. The entire Zionist regime — the Congress, president, and the Supreme Court — shall be eliminated in one great blow."

Mitch's mouth popped open in amazement. Howard continued.

"I've codenamed this operation, *Juggernaut*, after the large vehicle of Hindu religion that crushes everything in its path. I intend this Juggernaut shall be my instrument of mass destruction for personal vengeance against this corrupt government… as well as my tomb."

Mitch swallowed hard. "Howie… I don't know what to say."

"What's more, the Capitol Building and the White House are surrounded by the black inner city urban jungle. Washington is at least sixty-eight percent black. So, I'll be able to kill off an awful lot of them too."

"Howie thinks that we should be able to kill at least four hundred thousand people. Isn't that cool?"

"Four hundred thousand people, so many?" Mitch bit his lip. He was still incredulous.

"Those lives are of no consequence. Most of them are our enemies."

"Hey, Mitchy, if you want to make an omelet you got to break some heads," Jackie said with a laugh. Howard went on.

"With the central government destroyed, I predict the country should fall to pieces, kind of like what happened in Yugoslavia and Russia way back in the early nineties. Smart idea too. A break-up along pure racial lines. Keep all the races pure… the way Yahweh has always intended!"

"But there'll be total chaos."

"Exactly. That's exactly what we want," Howard said, wringing his hands. "Destroy everything! A race war will probably break out. I predict that hordes of the mud races are going to leave the cities in search of loot and rape. We've got Werewolf cells all over the country that have been stockpiling weapons and food in preparation for this great conflict. It's going to be a bloodbath. For sure. That Charlie Manson guy had the right idea… Helter-Skelter."

"Howie, your lip set kind of hard when you spoke of personal vengeance, what do you mean?"

Howard paced over to Mitch, somewhat calmer. "Couple years back, that idiot we have in the White House got me thrown out of the Air Force," he began slowly. "Do you realize that in just a few years this traitor has sold out the white people... his own kind... just to make deals with all those black and Jew animals? The whole government is nothing but a nest for the Jews and the other mud races. I simply spoke the truth and got shit-canned for it. Well, now it's payback time."

"Why not just assassinate the president?"

"Jackie asked me that. Hell, she even offered to do it for me. No. When he threw me out of the service, not a single soul in the government spoke up in my defense. They had their chance," Howard said angrily. He again placed his hand on the man's shoulder. "One thing you've got to understand. There's basically no difference between Republicans and Democrats — just two dogs of slightly different breeds. And even though I hate that lousy sonofabitch mine will be an act of vengeance against the government, and not just one man. It's an act of vengeance justified by political and racial necessity. I believe that this country would be better off without any central authority. Separate states, established along pure racial lines, kind of like what the Russians have done."

"Ain't there another way?"

"No! I mean look, true democracy in this country is already dead. Half the white people don't even bother to vote. The Zionist Jew trickster has reduced my people to a mere flock of sheep. The courts, media and the banks are controlled by the Jews... and the blacks and Mexicans are everywhere! Nobody cares. So, I'm going to bring down the Zionist regime... and I'm going down with it, in a Wagnerian holocaust of fire!"

"I see," Mitch said, slowly turning away.

"Mitch, you ever read *The Carson Diaries*?" Howard retrieved a well-worn paperback book from the kitchen counter.

"No."

"Well I'm not surprised, with the Jews controlling the press and all… The author had to go to a vanity publisher to get the word out," Howard said, slowly shaking his head. "It was written couple of years ago. It's all about this guy named Ed Carson who keeps a detailed diary." Howard began thumbing through the book. "Basically, he's a hardworking white, Christian patriot whose wife gets raped by a colored guy. He's already pissed-off at how this country is run… anti-Second Amendment gun control laws, high taxation, affirmative action, quotas and special rights for the coloreds and faggots and the like, miscegenation with the other races, out-of-control non-Aryan immigration and Zionist genocidal abortion. You know, crap like that."

"Uh-huh."

"He writes in the diary about his dream of establishing a white homeland, *Neu Caucasia*, a pure Aryan People's Republic in the northwest. Starts a racial awareness movement. The Jews try to shut him up. They take his job. The last straw comes when ZOG sends the fucking IRS after him for back taxes… the fuckers try to steal his land." Mitch noticed Howard's voice rising in anger.

"OK. And?"

"Carson finally just can't take it anymore. He snaps. He builds a bomb out of ammonium nitrates from fertilizer and mixes it with fuel oil and puts it on his truck. Drives it to Washington and dies in a suicide attack on the IRS Building in the capital of ZOGdom. Hundreds of the fucking Zoggies die. You see, that's kind of how I'm going to go."

"Sort of like what they tried to do in Oklahoma City way back in ninety-five," Mitch said, slowly nodding.

"And that's the start of the white revolution! The race war!" Howard said, grinning and maniacally rubbing his hands together. "His wife Cynthia bands his followers together into a group called the *Aryan Wolves*. They use his diary as a terror blueprint to blow up integrated schools, churches, a synagogue, shopping centers; they poison municipal water reservoirs with botulism toxin and ricin. Blow up skyscrapers in LA and 'Jew' York City; shoot up a school bus full of little nigger kids with a machinegun and finally bring down a civilian airliner with a surface-to-air missile! It's a beautiful piece of work Mitch, I mean you really should read it." Howard paused and wiped a tear from the corner of his eye.

"Sure Howie."

"White people all over the country finally get the message and wake up." Howard excitedly flipped toward the back of the book. "They take this as a cue to strike, to take our country back… They start killing off the Jews and all other minorities like a bunch of rabbits. They shoot 'em down in the streets."

"Yeah?"

Howard's eyes flashed. "The book finally ends on the *Day of the Rope*… when the oppressed Aryan white masses rise up and march on the capital to overthrow the corrupt Wall Street Jew government in Washington. On that day, ZOG's lackeys and government stooges are strung up from lampposts and trees. You know, kinda like what they tried to do at the Capitol way back in 2021," Howard said, now scowling. He handed the paperback to Mitch and headed for the door. "All surviving non-white mud races are given three choices: confinement on reservations or concentration camps, mass deportation… or extermination. As for the Jews, this time we finish the job… I kind of got my idea from the book. I got Jackie a copy last

Christmas."

"Yeah, I'll sure try to read it."

Howard paused and turned. "One thing more. Now that you know everything, you're one of us. All that Jackie told you a couple days ago is true. If you open your mouth, you're going to fucking die. The Werewolf always deals with those who would betray the cause."

"Sure, I'll remember. I'm cool." Mitch said nervously. He watched Howard leave the room.

Saturday, July 18th
1130 hours (EDT)
J. Edgar Hoover Building, Washington, DC

Aqueous Blank was a first-rate secretary, popular among agents and other staff. In thirty-two years, she had witnessed extraordinary changes at the Bureau. Indeed, she had been on hand when Edgar Hoover himself trod those halls. When she first arrived at the agency as a junior-level secretary, only a dozen blacks were among the staff, mostly in maintenance and janitorial positions. Now, scores of minorities and women were employed by the bureau, many as agents or upper-level administrators. After a career that spanned three decades, she was looking forward to a well-earned retirement.

Blank, a widow for several years, generally came in on Saturdays, making the coffee, catching up on paperwork and distributing the mail. More often than not, she would see Doug Rabson in the office, especially when he was working on tough cases. This particular Saturday was to be an exception: at the insistence of his eldest daughter, Sarah, he was going to her piano recital. Having been forced to break his promise twice before, Rabson considered it the better part of family diplomacy to attend. He had called Aqueous and told her not to look for him until after twelve.

Having gotten a late start, Aqueous made the coffee and went down into the mailroom. Minutes later, she emerged. By FBI standards, there wasn't that much mail on that particular Saturday — mostly letter items for the director and a stack to be delivered to the Counter-terrorism Section Office, including a somewhat bulky parcel for Doug Rabson. Blank always wanted to get the mail distributed before noon. Rushing, she had just dropped off the director's mail and was heading for Rabson's office, when she tripped on a loose floor tile, dropping the parcel. The woman bent over to retrieve it. With a searing flash and loud report, the package suddenly exploded. The force of the blast blew out scores of windows for several blocks. Aqueous Blank was killed instantly.

1335 hours (EDT)

Rabson, having just dropped his family off at home, was heading to the office when he heard on the radio sketchy news of a large explosion at the FBI Building. Nearing the building, he noticed numerous fire, ambulance and other emergency vehicles. As he arrived, he was met by the director.

"My God, what happened?" he said, closing the door behind him.

"We don't know yet. There was an explosion on the third floor. Looks like it may have been a bomb," a dazed Longstreet said. Hearing this, Rabson realized he wasn't going to get any work done: his office was on the third floor.

"Any claims of responsibility?"

"Plenty. The usual number of cranks. The Post is getting all kinds of claims from this-or-that group. Hell, there's even some nut who claims to be Mussolini saying he did it."

"Any casualties?"

Longstreet took a long pause before answering. "One confirmed dead. A woman, that's all I know right now. They found her body parts all over the third floor."

1204 hours (MDT)
The Price residence, Greeley, CO

"Jackie, come in here, quick!"

"What's going on?"

"I'm watching *Faux News*," Howard said, turning up the television's volume. "They just reported about a suspected terrorist bombing of the FBI Building in Washington a short while ago." Jackie ran to the television. The film footage showed smoke coming out of the third floor of the FBI building.

"That's us! I'm sure of it!" Jackie said, enraptured with glee.

"They're saying one person was killed. Guess that was your FBI agent, what's-his-name."

"That's it, we iced Rabson! Hey, Mitchy! We did it! We hit a cop!" Jackie ran downstairs to the laboratory.

1645 hours (EDT)
J. Edgar Hoover Building, Washington, DC

ATF and FBI technicians and bomb experts swarmed over the building, searching for any additional explosives or clues. Minute traces of the explosive, as well as bits of wrapping paper and other evidence were painstakingly collected and rushed to the Bureau's laboratory for analysis. By late afternoon, it had become clear that the explosion had been caused by a parcel bomb. Rabson had been allowed to enter his office, largely undamaged in spite of its proximity to the blast. He started working at his desk, when a somber George Longstreet came to see him.

"Doug, I just got a call from the Medical Examiner at the morgue. We think we know who the dead woman is," the director said in a hushed tone.

"Yes sir?" Rabson slowly rose from his desk.

"The preliminary report says she was a black female, about sixty... We think it was Aqueous Blank."

"Oh no!"

"The bomb was apparently concealed in a package which probably arrived with the morning mail. She must have been delivering it to one of the offices when it exploded. She probably never knew what hit her."

"They're sure it's her?"

"They found enough of her remains to make a tentative identification. Also, her charred driver's license and access key card were found in the hallway. It's her all right."

"How's the rest of the investigation proceeding?"

"The lab thinks they know the type of explosive used. Looks like C4. They say it was probably triggered by a grenade detonator rigged in the package to go off when opened or violently jarred. It was expertly done. Whoever did it, knew enough to wrap the bomb in foil to overcome our detection devices. Traces of paper and aluminum foil are being analyzed right now. Hopefully they'll have something a little more definite in a couple days."

"I wonder how it got past our security arrangements?"

"I don't know. I thought our security had been beefed up since what happened in Oklahoma City."

"Poor Aqueous," Rabson sighed, shaking his head, "and she was going to retire in about six weeks. Has her family been contacted?"

"She's got a sister in Dallas; I've arranged for the Office there to contact her."

1845 hours
Greeley, CO

"Jackie, come look at this. I just caught a segment of the news. Now they're saying that it was some woman who was killed in the explosion. Some colored bitch," Howard said, turning up the television's volume.

"What?" a crestfallen Jackie said. Her face was creased with disappointment.

"You apparently didn't kill that FBI agent after all. He's still alive. You must be slipping."

"Shit! That fucking FBI agent's got more lives than a cat… I'll get him next time."

"Never mind that now," Howard said, "we've got more important things to do right now… How's Mitch and the C4 modification coming?"

"The kiln's working good. Last I saw Mitch had just poured the first portion of the explosive into the molds. Looks great."

"Good."

Monday, July 20th
0923 hours (EDT)
J. Edgar Hoover Building, Washington, DC

"You wanted to see me, sir."

"Yes, come in," the director said. An attractive black woman in a lab coat turned as Rabson entered. "This is Dr. Ethel Methacrylate. She's a forensic chemist in the bureau's laboratory division. I called you in here because I think you should hear this."

"How do you do?" Rabson said to the woman, extending his hand.

"Dr. Methacrylate has preliminary findings on the bombing investigation," Longstreet said.

"The bomb that killed Aqueous Blank consisted of approximately one-to-two pounds of C4 plastic explosive. It was detonated with amatol, a medium explosive used in hand grenades. The device was heavily wrapped in aluminum foil. The bomber was apparently aware of some of the security methods we use to detect parcel bombs. It was shipped in a heavy cardboard container wrapped in brown paper. We managed to collect several large fragments of the paper wrapping.

Enough of the pieces were recovered to provide us with a number of clues. By painstakingly fitting the pieces together, we were able to determine that the parcel was intended for you, Agent Rabson."

"Ma'am?" Rabson said. His voice wavered.

Dr. Methacrylate opened a large file folder and displayed several photographs of the evidence.

"This photo shows some of the fragments we recovered from the wrapper. You'll please note that when pieced together they spell the last five letters of your name."

Rabson carefully studied the picture, nodding in agreement.

"The bomb was rigged to explode the instant the package was opened; a hand grenade detonator was embedded in C4. Aqueous Blank was probably delivering it to your office when it went off. She must have jostled it somehow."

"Any clues as to its point of origin?"

"Not yet, but we're still sifting through all the evidence."

"Thank you, Dr. Methacrylate," the director said. She left the room.

"Well, we're gonna review all of our security measures in the mailroom and maybe the lab will—"

"Sir, I think I know who sent the bomb."

"How do you know that?"

"Dr. Methacrylate said that C4 was used, right?"

"Yeah."

"We know that the Werewolf was involved in the theft of C4 explosive from some construction outfit in Colorado."

"The ATF says there were seven other instances of theft of C4 over the last year, five are still unsolved."

"I led the raid which netted the four suspects. It was all over the news. Don't you see? This bombing is an attempt to get rid of me as an act of revenge by the Werewolf… I'm sure of it."

"Interesting theory."

"On top of that, Jacqueline Lynch contacted me at the Denver office couple of weeks ago. She threatened to kill me."

"What?"

"She knows that I'm the one who's been following her for the last several months. She bragged that she was going to kill me. I'll bet that the bomb was mailed from somewhere in Colorado."

"Okay, go home. We're going to give you protection, both here and at your house. Try to relax, take a few days off. I want to send you back to Colorado to continue the investigation."

"Yes sir."

"I'm putting more resources into this case. From now on, they'll be rigorous surveillance of known white supremacist groups in the country. The gloves are coming off."

"Very good sir."

Rabson took the director's advice and went home. Since he would be off to Colorado again in a few days, it would be better to get in a little quality time with his family.

What would Rachel and the girls do if something had happened to me? What would have happened if Aqueous hadn't inadvertently set off the bomb? Rabson thought to himself during the drive to his suburban Silver Spring home. As he pulled into the driveway, he noticed his wife standing by the door. She had been crying.

"Honey, what's wrong?"

"Come inside." Rabson followed his wife into the kitchen area. She was trembling.

"I came home from the office early today and checked the answering machine. Thank God I got here and checked before one of the girls did!"

"Honey, what happened?" Without answering, Rachel Rabson simply pushed the *PLAY* button on the recording machine. There was no mistaking the voice. To Rabson, it was chillingly familiar.

"Hello, Mr. Rabson. This is Jacqueline. I just want you to know that I was the one who sent that letter bomb. Too bad I didn't get you this time. But I know who you are, what you look like, and where you live. Next time I won't fail. You won't see me coming. You've interfered with me long enough. I'm gonna kill you, and maybe your whole family. You fucker!" Rabson slammed his hand down on the *OFF* button.

"Doug, who is this person? What does she want? Is this some kind of a sick joke?" Rachel said, becoming almost hysterical.

"She's a terrorist I've been trailing. That's all I can say right now," Rabson said, hugging his wife.

"First the bombing, and now this!" she sobbed. "Thank God I got home before the children. I wouldn't want them to have heard this!"

"Please, Rachel, I won't let anything happen."

"But what about the girls?"

"Try not to worry. I'm going to contact the phone company and try to get our number changed. I've already talked to the Bureau to try and arrange for some kind of protection for you and the girls. Nobody's going to hurt us," he said, hugging his wife tighter.

Later that night, Rabson sat quietly in the den, cleaning his weapon. In twelve years as an FBI agent, he had never once had to fire it, save at the shooting range. Now he realized that he was being stalked by a person to whom killing was merely a game. A woman who represented the evil that murdered his great-grandparents during the Holocaust. A female hit-killer who had already left at least twenty-nine victims in her wake.

A sudden knock at the front door jolted him from his thoughts. Looking through the peephole he noticed it was his elderly next-door neighbor.

"Yes? What is it?" Rabson said to the ashen-faced man.

"Doug, you'd better come out here and look at this." Not wanting to disturb Rachel or the girls, he quietly followed the man around the side of the house. There, suspended from a rope on the bough of an old oak tree was a mannequin. Pinned to the effigy was a crude note with a drawing of a skull and the words:

Watch Out! JEW-FBI! THE WEREWOLF IS WATCHING YOU!

"I thought I heard a car pull away and went to investigate," the old man said. "Damnedest thing I've seen... What kind of sick person would do something like this?" Without answering, Rabson cut the effigy down and carried it to the garage.

Tuesday, July 21st
1345 hours (MDT)
The Price residence, Greeley, CO

With eager expectation, Howard and Jackie gathered around a table in the lab. Amid the welter of test tubes, beakers, chemicals and flasks rested the two large ceramic molds.

"Okay, time for the unveiling," Mitch said. He began rapping his fingers on the table, as if performing a drum roll.

"Proceed, Mitch," Howard said, unimpressed by the antics.

Mitch began prying one of the molds apart. A white, irregularly shaped mass of C4 popped out of the mold onto the table.

"Superb!" Howard said, examining it thoughtfully. The explosive was a dull white in color, trapezoidal in shape, with a rounded pentagonal base. A quarter-inch diameter hole had been centered in the middle of the base. On the other side was a concave indentation for the baratol.

Impatient, Howard placed the charge on the table and said, "Okay, now let's see what the hexagon looks like."

"Yes, master!" Mitch said jokingly, hunched over doing a rather convincing Quasimodo imitation. He carefully opened the second mold.

"These are really very good, Mitch... Nice, completely uniform distribution of the explosive. No unevenness anywhere," Howard said, slowly rotating the hexagonal wedge of C4 up against the light. When they're completed they'll form a perfect sphere around the tamper and plutonium core."

"We're going to need about forty-six more of these by the end of October."

"No sweat, I can crank them out at about the rate of four-a-week now that all the bugs are worked out. Also, I made the baratol slurry you wanted."

"Perfect!"

The Juggernaut began to roll.

Stab-In-The-Back

"Et tu, Brute?"

— William Shakespeare, from *Julius Caesar*

Almost since their capture on July 10th, the case against the three Werewolf terrorists had been steadily building. In addition to the Russian sniper rifle, Stacey Manson's MAC-10 machine pistol was positively linked to several of the murders in the Rocky Flats raid. Pamela Haney had already been implicated in three of the brutal murders at the plant because of the discovery of sodium cyanide and dimethyl sulfoxide solution in her abandoned apartment. The presence of stolen C4 found in the back of Davies' car linked him and Haney to the Alliance Construction Company massacre. Faced with the mounting evidence, the initial bravado of the terrorists, that of Bruce Davies in particular, began to wane. By early August his lawyer quietly notified the FBI that he was willing to make a deal.

In the meantime, Rabson had arranged protection for his family. He took the telephone threat and mock lynching seriously. Before he left, he had managed to persuade Rachel and the girls to make an extended visit to her parents in Boston. At least there they would be safe from the vengeance of the Werewolf. This accomplished, Rabson had flown back to Denver. He had no sooner settled into his hotel room when he received a telephone call from an unusually excited Frank Bledsoe summoning him to be in the office early in the morning.

Monday, August 3rd
0900 hours
Denver FBI Field Office, Federal Building, Denver, CO

"What's this all about?" Rabson said upon entering Bledsoe's office.

"It's Bruce Davies. He might be willing to cooperate. I think he wants to cut some kind of deal."

"Oh, really? Never figured that asshole would crack. What about the two women, any chance that they're going to talk?"

"Not a chance. Haney and Manson have clammed up. They're about as mean as they come."

The two men went down to the central holding area. There, a pensive looking Bruce Davies sat with his lawyer, Fred Billings. Billings, nicknamed 'the Anaconda' because of his bombastic, overpowering style, was a graying, somewhat portly western slope attorney of fifty-nine who had defended white supremacists before.

"Gentlemen," Billings said, slowly rising from his chair. "I'll be talking to the DA shortly. My client understands that he has done wrong. He wants to make amends for it; he would like to make some kind of, eh, an arrangement with you. I trust that any cooperation on his part would be looked upon favorably."

"Sir," Bledsoe said, shaking his head. "Yours is an amazing capacity for understatement. This man is accused of involvement in over a dozen murders. Before we go any further, let me state that neither Agent Rabson nor myself are empowered to make deals. We're here only to listen to what he has to offer and then from that make a recommendation to our superiors."

"Fair enough," Billings said, exposing a toothy, tobacco-stained grin. "My client is willing to accept fifteen years imprisonment, with the possibility for parole after ten. He also wants—"

"Whoa!" Bledsoe said, cutting him off. "We've got your client cold. Solid evidence placing him at Alliance Construction at the time of the murders. I'd say that you aren't in much of a position to bargain."

"True, but you don't have the plutonium," Billings said in a tone that radiated confidence. "So you see, we *can* bargain from strength."

"All right, what does your client want?" Bledsoe sighed, suddenly realizing how this lawyer had acquired a reptilian sobriquet.

"I'll let him speak for himself," Billings said, gesturing over to Davies.

"I want solitary confinement," Davies said slowly. "No contact with any of the other prisoners, especially the niggers-eh, colored. Also, it has to be in a federal pen back east, not SuperMax or Marion, that's Werewolf territory."

"And?" Rabson said, tapping a pencil on the table. Bledsoe sat down.

"I got family back in Arkansas. They're going to need protection."

"Well, what do you have to offer for all this?"

"I can give you names and addresses. Lots of 'em! Werewolf safe houses all over the country."

"Sorry, not good enough," Rabson said.

"What do you mean?" Davies said, somewhat surprised. "Shit, you saw all that stuff that we had in Aurora. That's nothing. The Werewolf's got at least a dozen more places just like that around the country. Way I see it, I'm giving up a lot!"

"Like the man said, it's not enough," Bledsoe said, gesturing over to Billings. "I don't know what stories this overgrown rug merchant here has been feeding you, but you're in trouble, big time. If you don't play ball with us they'll strap your ass to the gurney."

"You're a thief and a murderer," Rabson said, joining in, "and there's no way the government is going to let you off with ten years for multiple homicide and theft of plutonium."

"Well, what do you cops want then?" Davies sighed.

"Well, for starters we want Howard Brennan and Jacqueline Lynch... and the stolen plutonium."

"I don't know where the fuck they are."

"You really expect us to believe that?"

"Hey man, it's the truth! Me and Pamie left Greeley right after we done the construction company hit. I don't know where they are!"

"Not good enough! You're going to have to do better than that. Oh yes, we're also gonna want your sworn testimony in court against all Werewolf operatives that we bring in," Rabson said.

Davies started fidgeting in his chair. "I don't know, man. Why I got to testify in court? Nobody rats on the Werewolf... and lives."

"At least you'll have a chance. Even if you manage to snake your way off the gurney, they'll stick your ass in SuperMax," Bledsoe said, rising from his chair and hovering over Davies. "It just opened couple of years back. Already they're calling it the 'Alcatraz of the Rockies'. But don't worry, you probably won't be there long. As you said, that's Werewolf country."

"You must be one of those freaks who actually likes being in the cage," a smiling Rabson interjected. "You know what those yard apes do in prison. You'll probably become some con's girlfriend... Now you want to deal? So deal! We're going to want your testimony."

"Okay, man," Davies said. His throat was dry.

"This abuse has gone on long enough! Not another word," Billings said, cutting off Davies. "My client doesn't say anything else until the Denver DA and the feds hear us out."

Rabson and Bledsoe went to one side.

"What do you think? Think we should take this to the Attorney General and Denver DA? Try to cut a deal with this piece-of-shit?"

"I'd say we don't have much of a choice. Maybe Lynch and Brennan are held up somewhere in one of these safe houses. It may be the only way to find them."

"Okay," Bledsoe said, turning back to Billings. "You go to the Denver DA; we'll talk it over with the director and Attorney General. If they go for all this then we can deal."

"Fine," Billings said, extending his hand. Bledsoe ignored it.

Tuesday, August 4th
1115 hours
FBI Field Office, Denver, CO.

After a marathon conference call to the Denver DA, FBI Director and the Attorney General Rabson and Bledsoe had hammered out the government's position. Billings and Davies were waiting expectedly in the holding area when the two FBI men entered. Rabson got right to the point.

"Okay, Bruce, here's the deal. The state has agreed to let the feds handle everything. You plead guilty as an accessory to civil rights violations in the murders of the men at Alliance and get life with the possibility of parole after a minimum twenty-five years. The grand jury will at that point drop you from the indictment. They'll put you in solitary at the federal pen in Atlanta. Also, we'll protect your family."

Rabson noted that Bruce suddenly looked crestfallen. The

prospect of his remaining in prison until he was at least sixty-five was a letdown. Clearly, he had counted on a better deal.

"That's it? You gotta be kidding!" Billings blurted out.

"Can't y'all get me a better deal than that?" Davies said. "If I'm lucky, I'll be an old man by the time I get out."

"That's the only deal the Attorney General and local DA will accept."

"Bullshit!" Billings screamed, overturning his cup of coffee.

"That's the deal. Take it or leave it," Rabson said with a tone of finality.

"Forget it," Billings said. "My client isn't going to cooperate, not for a lousy horseshit offer like that!"

"Suit yourself," Bledsoe said, "but I think you had better understand something here Bruce. The state's going to push for the death penalty. For sure. We can prove your involvement in the five murders at Alliance Construction. What's more, we can show that the bomb sent to the FBI Building in Washington came from the lot of C4 taken from the construction company. That's another murder…Felony murder."

Rabson joined in. "Bottom line Bruce, when you lose this trial…*and you will lose,* you'll either go to the gurney or rot in SuperMax. And the Werewolf's going to find out about our little conference here. They're probably going to go after your family. You know how they operate. And whether you help us or not, we're going to get Lynch and Brennan."

"That's blackmail!" Billings screamed.

"No… that's justice!" Rabson said with a smirk. The two FBI men got up and slowly headed for the door.

"Wait! Okay, man, I'll take it," Davies said with the hollow voice of resignation.

"Are you sure you want this?" Billings whispered.

"Yeah man. Hey, I'm tired of running."

"Bruce, they're just trying to intimidate you."

"No, man. It's over," Davies said despondently. His head dropped. "I'll take it."

"So, you'll accept the government's deal?" Bledsoe said.

"Yeah. Fuck it, I'm a dead man anyway," Davies shrugged, settling slowly in his chair.

The two FBI men sat back down. Rabson opened a briefcase and produced a small tape recorder. Adjusting the microphone, he began the interrogation.

"First off, Bruce, I'm rather curious. Exactly why did you join the Werewolf?"

"I joined 'cause I'm tired of the niggers always getting things! The government always does things for the coloreds, Jews, Vietnamese, Cubans and Mexicans; ain't doing shit for me! The colored races got to be stopped! They rape our women, steal our jobs! I mean, you're a white man. Can't you see it?"

"I'm also a Jew!" Rabson snapped back.

"Okay, Bruce, fine," Bledsoe said. "Who was with you during the Alliance Construction hit?"

"Jackie, Pamie, Skin-Girl and Night-Hawk."

"What? I beg your pardon?"

"Bruce, don't use nicknames. Give us their full names," Rabson said, retrieving his notepad and pen.

Davies slowly recited the names. "Jackie Lynch, Pam Haney, Ariadne Beausoleil and Jeff Collins. Hey, man, Pamie and me didn't kill those people. I swear. I was in my truck. Jackie and the others done it."

"Tell us what happened."

"Jeff and me took the explosives while the woman watched the guards in one of the buildings. Jeff went back. Couple minutes later I heard the colored guy scream. Jackie came out and handed me another case of C4. She said she and the others killed those people. Told me and Pamie to drive back to Aurora. We was there when all hell broke loose in the FBI raid."

"Where was Howard Brennan at the time?"

"I don't know, man," Davies said, shrugging. "But I think he was with the 'Professor.' Howie lets Jackie do all the killing. I think she kinda enjoys it."

"The Professor? Now who's that? I said no nicknames," Rabson said, repeating his warning.

"Hey, don't know the guy's name. He's some smart college boy. Some four-eyed, Einstein chemistry motherfucker! He's going to help make the bomb. That's all I know."

"What were you going to do with that case of C4 we found in your truck?"

"Jackie said that we should use it for some jobs in Denver."

"We know that your girlfriend killed three people at Rocky Flats back in June. Who else was involved?"

"Let's see… Pamie told me that there was Jackie, Jeff, Becky

Stephens, a guy we call Cyclops Mantooth, Ariadne and a couple really weird skinhead dudes from Utah I ain't never seen before."

"Do you know where these people are now?"

"Yeah. I think so. Some of 'em anyway. Becky's from Stone Mountain, she's one of Jackie's friends; Nat Mantooth, we call him the Cyclops because he's only got one eye; he lives somewhere in Alabama. Tuscaloosa, I think… One of those skinhead dudes is Ariadne's boyfriend. They've been living together, shacking up in Salt Lake City. Ariadne killed some colored guy there. Jeff Collins was in Chattanooga last I heard."

"We know that Lynch and Brennan are trying to build an atomic bomb. What we want to find out is where and when they intend to detonate it," Bledsoe said.

"Hey, man, I don't know where."

"Come on, Bruce, talk to me!"

"Look, Werewolf doesn't tell us everything… it's part of their policy of 'leaderless resistance'… Only a few know where everybody is, that way, if somebody's caught, they can't rat out the brotherhood. Not even under ZOG torture. All I know is they're going to set it off sometime next January."

"January?"

"Yeah, They're gonna set it off in mid-January and start a race war."

"A race war?"

"Yeah, they figure the coons are gonna start rioting; the Werewolf's gonna come out and just start killing them all like crazy. That's why they got all the weapons and shit stashed."

It was getting on toward noon. The interrogation was stopped for lunch. Davies was taken back to his cell in the holding area. During their break, the two lawmen discussed the information obtained so far.

"Well, we got the names of some additional Werewolf operatives. After lunch, you get them off to Washington. I'll be in touch with the director to fill him in on what we have."

"Sometime around mid-January, he said. Mid-January," Rabson muttered.

"What's that?"

"The bomb. What Davies was talking about. They're going to explode an atomic bomb somewhere in this country around the middle of January next year. Frank, what important events occur in January?"

"Well, there's the Super Bowl for one. Say, didn't Clancy write a book along those lines couple years back?"

"Yeah. A best seller. Hell of a book. Something about Arab terrorists who get hold of a nuclear weapon and try to blow up the Super Bowl."

"And the game was played right here in Denver," Bledsoe said. At that, Rabson suddenly went pale.

"Frank, you know what else occurs in January?"

"I don't know. You tell me."

"The Martin Luther King Birthday Holiday… There are celebrations all over the country — with the biggest ones in Atlanta and right here in Denver."

"What are you getting at?"

"Just this. Davies said that they're going to detonate the bomb and start a race war in January, remember? *A race war!* Now the Werewolf is a neo-Nazi gang. Hardcore white supremacist. Over the years, they have committed several dozen racially motivated murders. Picture this, through Jackie Lynch they hook up with this Brennan character, steal the plutonium from Rocky Flats and C4 from that construction company and attempt to fabricate a bomb."

"Okay, and?"

"They build the weapon with the intention of exploding it in a city with a large black population on the Martin King Holiday, figuring that it would trigger a race war."

"Oh my God!" Bledsoe said. He rose from the table, his lunch only half eaten.

"Where are you going?"

"I think you may have stumbled onto the key to the whole plot. I'm going to contact the director right now."

1405 hours

"Where have you been? I've been looking all over for you," Bledsoe said as Rabson walked into the office.

"After I got those names Davies gave us off to the Bureau, I did a little research at the library. I was reading accounts in old newspapers of the various Martin King Holiday events held here in Denver earlier this year."

"Uh-huh." Bledsoe sat down across from him.

"Last January they had church services, prayer breakfasts, speeches by the mayor and local civil rights notables and a parade with over fifty thousand people. If the Werewolf was to set off a bomb in a crowd like that, it would be God awful, a massacre," Rabson said.

"Well, I was talking with Director Longstreet. He's assembling elements of the Counter-terrorism Strike Force under Bill Blaylock."

"Blaylock... he's a good man."

"You know him?"

"Sure, we were in Quantico at the Academy together."

"He's going to coordinate with field offices in the various cities that Davies named as having Werewolf safe houses. We've notified offices in Atlanta, Salt Lake City, Tuscaloosa and Chattanooga to stand by. Maybe we'll get lucky and nab Lynch and Brennan this time."

"Let's hope so."

Wednesday, August 5th
0830 hours

A large document was waiting for Frank Bledsoe when he arrived at his office. It had been sent by courier from the Bureau headquarters in Washington during the night. In it was detailed information, including photographs of all the individuals mentioned by Bruce Davies during the interrogation. Even as he began to study the document's contents, FBI strike teams, armed with search warrants and accompanied by local law enforcement, initiated a simultaneous series of raids on the suspected Werewolf lairs in Stone Mountain, Tuscaloosa, Chattanooga and Salt Lake City. He slowly began reading through each suspect's file.

Rebecca Stephens, a.k.a. "Red Becky" of Stone Mountain is rumored to be a descendent of the Confederacy's only vice president. She's been active in a number of white supremacist organizations before; through her friend Jackie Lynch she hooked up with the Werewolf. Stephens is a suspect in the shooting death of a black Georgia state patrolman during the last year.

Bledsoe continued with the next file:

Nathan Mantooth has been a Grand Exalted Hobgoblin of the

Alabama Klan before joining the Werewolf. He and others are suspected of involvement in a bloody armored car robbery in Denver the year before. Years earlier, he became known as "Cyclops" after losing an eye in a bar fight. According to several of his co-workers, Mantooth has a deep hatred of blacks and Jews and often talked of a desire to kill them.

Next, Bledsoe opened the file on Collins:

Jefferson Davis Collins, originally from Fort Smith, Arkansas, has attracted the attention of both white supremacists and the FBI for suspected involvement in the bombing of a synagogue and the shooting of a rabbi. Collins has a gripe with the government: the IRS is looking at him for payment of back taxes.

Ariadne Beausoleil's file from Salt Lake City was intriguing. It showed numerous arrests for prostitution, illegal drug possession, assault and shoplifting. The police report listed her as a possible suspect in a racially motivated drive-by shooting in April. Bledsoe closed the files.

The federal raids went off like clockwork. Becky Stephens, Nathan Mantooth and Jeff Collins were all arrested at their homes without incident. Piles of white supremacist literature, assorted weapons and portions of stolen money were all taken at each arrest.

Only in Salt Lake City did the bureau fail to get its quarry. Jason Chalmers and his girlfriend Ariadne Beausoleil had moved out of their apartment several days before the raid. At the time, Tom Kelly's assault team was moving into position the fugitives were in fact driving to Greeley, Colorado. Figuring that the pair might be hiding in the nearby Aryan Church of Yahweh, the Station Chief placed an FBI surveillance unit around the church to monitor those who came and went.

On the whole, however, the results of the raids were very

satisfactory. Three additional Werewolf suspects were in custody, weapons and stolen money recovered. As a dejected Becky Stephens was being led away, she was heard to comment that the FBI was "just a bunch of ZOG assassins." One agent within earshot gleefully took up the label telling her, "…looks like the ZOG really kicked some ass today."

1834 hours
Greeley, CO

Jackie and Howard watched the *Evening News* as the lead story unfolded. With growing apprehension, the couple looked at the dejected faces of Stephens, Mantooth and Collins as their comrades were led away by grim-faced men in navy blue jackets. Switching over to *CNA,* they endured a press conference in which the FBI Director was again crowing loudly over the performance of the agency, another triumph over domestic terrorism.

"Well, looks like they got Becky, Night-Hawk and the Cyclops," Howard sighed in disgust. "Shit! First the safe house in Aurora, and now this!"

"I just don't see how ZOG keeps finding all our people," Jackie said, shaking her head. "Poor Becky."

"I'll tell you how. Either Bruce, Pamie or Stace broke under ZOG torture. Or perhaps one of them was corrupted by ZOG gold."

"We should find out on the twentieth. The papers are saying that their arraignment is scheduled then at the Federal Court Building in Denver. I can't believe that any of them would betray the movement."

"Well, it really doesn't matter," Howard concluded. "None of those people know where we are right now; even if one of them is a traitor he can't hurt us… By the way, how's Mitch and the C4 modification coming?"

"Six wedges were complete as of this morning."

"Excellent. Does he suspect anything?"

"No. Nothing at all." Jackie slowly licked her lips.

"You're not getting too involved with him, are you? Remember, we've got a job to do."

"He's just the means to an end, that's all. I like him, but that's not going to interfere with what I have to do."

"Fine. Just keep turning on the sex with him until we're ready to leave. NumbNutZ and Skin-Girl will be here at any time now."

As the date of their arraignment neared, Pamela Haney and Stacey Manson discovered that they had attained somewhat of a celebrity status. Gun-toting female terrorists seemed to provide good copy for the nation's grocery store tabloids. Several investigative reporting teams from various TV newsmagazines had attempted to obtain jailhouse interviews with the women. The Denver County Jail was flooded with fan mail for the two women, including a surprising number of marriage proposals.

Hordes of reporters, several from as far away as Japan and Australia, flocked to Denver for the court proceedings. On the day the proceedings opened the scene at the Byron White Federal Courthouse was near bedlam; newsmen and spectators jostled and fought over passes to the courtroom in the quest for the limited seating. Outside, a virtual tent city arose overnight, as swarms of camera crews from local and national media positioned themselves to cover what promised to be the start of the biggest murder trial since the Menendez and Simpson trials years earlier. Meanwhile, street entrepreneurs did their bit for American capitalism, hawking souvenirs ranging from coffee mugs to screen-printed Tee-shirts. The circus had come to town.

The proceedings themselves were turned into a farce by the defendants. Haney and Manson, angrily proclaiming their innocence, curtly dismissed their court appointed attorneys and insisted on representing themselves. During the reading of the indictment, Pam Haney continuously interrupted, thrusting her arm out in the Nazi salute and screaming "Sieg Heil!" to several local skinheads who were in attendance in the galleries. The courtroom's decorum was restored only after Judge Warren Anders threatened to have the skinheads removed.

As promised, Bruce Davies wasn't included in the federal grand jury's indictment; having agreed to the government's plea-bargaining arrangement, he wasn't to be tried. He sat quietly next to the federal prosecutor, gazing into space while trying to ignore the menacing glances of the female defendants. The government was taking no chances with Davies; he was wearing a Kevlar vest and accompanied by a U.S. marshal. The morning before, metal detectors had been installed at all entrances to the courthouse.

The grand jury's indictment itself was a lengthy one; its reading consumed all of twenty-seven minutes, charging the defendants with sixteen counts of civil rights violations resulting in the deaths of the men at Rocky Flats, theft of government property, bank robbery, criminal trespass, and possession of illegal firearms. The federal prosecutor made it clear that the government was seeking the death penalty for both defendants.

"You have heard the reading of the indictment," Judge Anders told the defendants after the reading. "Do you understand the nature of the charges that the government has made?"

"Yeah," Pam said. Stacey nodded.

"It is the Court's understanding that neither of you wish appointed counsel. While the Court strongly advises against this, the law nevertheless permits self-representation. Do you understand this?"

Judge Anders said.

"Yeah."

"Do you wish at this time to enter a plea?"

"Yeah."

"How do you plea?"

"Not guilty! Death to traitors! White Power!" Pam screamed, again thrusting her arm out in the Nazi salute. The Judge again had to gavel the courtroom to silence.

"Very well. Trial is set for October seventh. Court stands adjourned." On that, Judge Anders rose and departed. As the two women were led out of the courtroom, Pam noticed Rabson sitting behind Davies. They momentarily exchanged glances. In her eyes was a look of raw hate; he smiled at her.

Thursday, August 20th
1845 hours
The Price residence, Greeley, CO

Howard was sitting at the kitchen table, making minor modifications on his design of the bomb. Earlier, he, Jackie, Beausoleil and Chalmers had watched the extensive coverage of the proceedings on *Justice TV*. He was beside himself with rage.

Jackie and Mitch came in from the lab a moment later.

"Davies… he sold us out! Do you hear me? He sold us out!" Howard screamed, turning the television on and replaying a video recording of the event.

"Now, calm down Howie, remember your high blood pressure," Jackie said soothingly.

"But he sold us out! Like Judas, sold out his race… for a lousy handful of silver! Broke the oath! Stabbed us in the back!"

"Yeah. I can't believe that Bruce is a traitor," Jackie said. "And to think that last year that asshole actually tried to hit on me… wish I'd cut his balls off now."

"There! Look! See how he sits there, so smug!" Howard ranted, pointing to the TV screen.

"And that looks like that Rabson guy behind him," Jackie said. "Don't worry, he'll pay for his treason. Yahweh will punish him."

"Goddamn right, he's gonna pay! From now on he'll always have to look over his shoulder. Nobody rats on the Werewolf."

"We could go after his family. Maybe kill them all"

"Never mind that now. Wherever they end up sending his ass, we're going to find him, sooner or later… Thank God at least Pamie and Stace are still loyal to the movement."

"Howie, we're up to fourteen of those C4 wedges completed," Mitch stated, hoping to change the topic.

"Very good. In a couple of days, Skin-Girl and her boyfriend are going to start moving them back east."

"Where?"

"We've got another safe house near Fredericksburg, Virginia. A farm, owned by JR Recke. It's nice and secluded. ZOG doesn't know about it. I'm planning on assembling the weapon there."

"Exactly how are you going to put this thing together?" Mitch said.

"Come downstairs to the lab, both of you," Howard said, gesturing toward the basement. Jackie and Mitch followed.

"See this?" Howard said, holding up an unmarked can. "It's M1 military adhesive paste. I found that if you mix it one-to-three with your standard epoxy resin it makes an adhesive of exceptional tensile strength. I'll simply cement the various sections of the explosive wedges together around the core."

"So basically, you're going to glue the bomb together?" Mitch said.

"That's a rather crude way of putting it, but yes, that's exactly what I'm gonna do. You're doing a good job Mitch. I want you to know that Jackie and me appreciate all that you have done."

The summer wore on. Mitch continued his work, systematically turning out the hexagonal and pentagonal wedges of C4 explosive that were to make up the shaped charge of the bomb. The monotony of his labors was broken only by the joys of frequent sex with Jackie. For her part, Jackie used sex with Mitch as a bonus for the quality of his work, almost as if rewarding an obedient dog. More and more, Mitchell Price began to live for those assignations. Fantasizing about being in love, Mitch would do anything for her. For Jackie Lynch he murdered a sixty-year-old black woman he'd never met. For Jackie he would help kill four hundred thousand innocent people. He was enfettered, and yet he was enraptured. He had been seduced. He had become Jackie's slave.

In the meantime, Bruce Davies had become a fount of information; he continued to rattle off names and addresses of his former comrades; additional Werewolf cells in Florida and Texas were raided. Among the captives taken in Texas were Joseph Horan and Joachim Klimper, both who had been involved in the Rocky Flats attack. The Texas raid also yielded a bonanza of weapons that had been stolen from various military installations. The real prize came in late August when Dagmar Hollander and other Aryans were arrested by the FBI in Coeur d'Alene, Idaho. They were charged with

255

complicity in the murder of cult member Nick Hoover. Reverend Hollander had just given a speech at the Aryan World Congress held at the survivalist compound of the *Apartheid Nation* when federal agents made the arrest.

Rabson was again recalled to Washington to brief the president and NSC in early September. Both the Attorney General and FBI Director wanted another first-hand briefing for the president. For his part, the president, just recently having returned from Moscow after a successful summit meeting with the Russian Federation President, eagerly awaited progress reports on how the investigation was proceeding.

Monday, September 7th
0830 hours
The White House, Washington, DC

"Good morning, Special Agent Rabson," the president said warmly, extending his hand.

"Good morning, sir."

"Jen McCormick informs me that quite a bit has happened concerning your investigation while I was out of the country. Looks like we've finally got the terrorists on the run."

"Yes sir. The good news is that one of the suspects we captured in Denver back in July is talking his head off. He's giving us names, addresses, the works. Based on his cooperation, Bill Blaylock's assault teams made a series of raids on Werewolf safe houses in Utah, Florida, Georgia, Alabama and, most recently, Texas."

"Very good!" the president said, nodding approvingly.

"Two of the terrorists are scheduled to go on trial in about a month."

"Anything on the whereabouts of the stolen plutonium?"

"No sir. Unfortunately, nothing."

"Agent Rabson thinks that he may have an idea on where and when the terrorists plan to use it," the Attorney General interjected.

"Correct. The captured man, a guy named Davies, has indicated to me that the Werewolf plans to detonate a bomb sometime in mid-January."

The President leaned forward attentively in his chair, staring into Rabson's eyes.

"Where?"

"I have an idea," Rabson said while clearing his throat. "Sir, as you know, the Werewolf is a white, racist, neo-Nazi organization. Probably the most vicious in the country. I believe they intend to detonate a bomb in a city with a large black population on or around the Martin King Holiday."

"Based on what?"

"Davies said to me that the bombing was intended to trigger a war between the races. The Werewolf apparently wants to explode the bomb and immediately take credit for it, hoping to touch off a race war. The symbolism is all too frighteningly obvious: thousands of black people slain by racists on a day set aside to honor a black man."

"My God" the CIA Director said. "That could be Chicago, Los Angeles, Atlanta, or even right here. Anywhere. What can we do?"

"It seems that the largest Martin Luther King Day celebrations are in Denver, Los Angeles and Atlanta. I believe that our investigations should center in those cities."

"You're right," the president said. "I gave a speech at the King festivities in Denver two years ago. The National Parks Service estimated that something like fifty-thousand people were on hand."

"Well, one thing is sure," Attorney General McCormick noted. "If Rabson's right, we don't have much time."

"George," the president said, turning to the FBI Director. "What are you and Rabson planning as a course of action?"

"I'm sending Rabson back to Denver in a few days. He and Frank Bledsoe are hoping that those two female suspects break before their trial. On this end we've started interrogating the other prisoners."

"That's it?"

"Yes sir, I'm afraid that's all we can do for now."

Amid tight security, the trial of the two women began on October seventh. The government was taking no chances; in response to rumors of a dramatic rescue attempt, the Byron White Federal Courthouse had been converted into a veritable fortress. Both the defendants and the government's star witness were transported in heavily armored vans surrounded by a phalanx of Denver Police, deputies from the Sheriff's Office and U.S. Marshals. Police sharpshooters lined the route from the jail to the courthouse. Metal detectors had been installed at all entrances. The courtroom itself had been thoroughly searched for explosives by police using bomb-sniffing dogs after a bomb threat had been made the day before. During the preceding two weeks, a twelve-member jury with five alternates had been selected and sequestered under heavy guard in a local hotel.

Meanwhile, scores of reporters had descended on the courthouse; the walkway outside the building was filled with camera and sound equipment. News crews from all the major networks as well as a number of foreign journalists flocked to what promised to be the biggest court case in the country's history, bigger than even the Oklahoma City bombing trials, which coincidentally were held in the same courthouse. More ominously, a group of local skinheads demonstrated outside the court building, eager to show their support for the defendants.

The government's strategy was straightforward: expose the involvement of the defendants in the activities of the Werewolf at Rocky Flats and Alliance, present the formidable incriminating physical evidence, and finally tie everything together by bringing out the testimony of Bruce Davies himself. The two women had been finally persuaded to accept court-appointed counsel. The defense positions of the two women's attorney were divided into three parts: that they were "framed" by the government because of their racist beliefs, that evidence had been planted in order to support the frame, and that Bruce Davies, a man with a considerable arrest record was in fact, a born liar who would easily fabricate a story to save his own neck.

Ira Vance had been selected to present the government's case. A hard-nosed veteran of over twenty years, Vance had handled cases with Jen McCormick while the latter was a federal prosecutor in Texas. The Attorney General had personally picked him to head the prosecution. After a rereading of the indictment and a brief opening statement, he began presenting the government's case:

"Your Honor, ladies and gentlemen of the jury, the government would like at this time to place into evidence before you, Exhibit A; a forty-five caliber Ingram MAC-10 submachine gun and silencer." A hush fell over the packed courtroom. Network television cameras, serving a nationwide audience, focused on the weapon. Vance continued, holding it up for all to see.

"Ballistics and fingerprint analysis shall show that this weapon was used by defendant Stacey Alice Manson in the commission of the savage murders of three DOE security guards, slain on the night of June third at the nuclear facility at Rocky Flats."

For added impact, Vance began holding up the grisly photos of the murdered men, lying in bloody heaps on their cots. Several members of the jury recoiled in horror. "The government would like now to place in evidence before you Exhibits B, C and D, containers of sodium cyanide and dimethyl sulfoxide, both found at the residence of defendant Pamela Mae Haney, as well as a child's water pistol recovered from Rocky Flats. The evidence will show that said defendant used these items in the commission of the murders of DOE personnel George Caldwell, Clarence Gleason and Jon Bent on the night in question."

Before a spellbound nationwide audience, Vance's presentation of the physical evidence went on. In the days that followed, a parade of prosecution witnesses gave their testimony. Rocky Flats Plant Manager George Gillian and Tobias Carlan of Alliance Construction were called to testify, graphically describing the crime scenes. For two weeks, Vance methodically cataloged the government's case, painstakingly outlining a scenario of each defendant's involvement in eleven murders. The two women showed no remorse for the crimes; on the contrary, they sat in the dock, laughing and smiling at the cameras.

The trial had become a media event. After two weeks, it was the most watched television program in history, with more than ninety-seven million households tuned in at its height. It seemed that everybody wanted to see "the two Werewolf chicks." Indeed, a cottage industry had grown up overnight around the two women: "Free Pamie" and "Free Stacey" buttons, tee shirts and other trial-related paraphernalia was doing a brisk business from sidewalk kiosks. Behind the scenes, there was already talk of book deals and even a made-for-TV movie, and still the climax of the trial was yet to come. Everyone eagerly awaited the testimony of Bruce Alan Davies.

Wednesday, October 21st
0830 hours

The moment of truth had arrived. Amid the glare of the cameras, a somewhat nervous Bruce Davies took the witness stand. Beads of sweat dripped off of his brow as an elderly bailiff swore him in and the government's questioning began.

"Sir," Ira Vance began. "Please state your name for the court."

"Bruce Alan Davies," Davies said, looking through the prosecutor over towards the prisoner's dock.

"Race traitor! Yahweh will punish!" Pamela screamed from the dock. Judge Anders gaveled the room to silence and again admonished her against outbursts. Vance continued his examination.

"All right, Mr. Davies, please tell the court about the organization known as the Werewolf."

"It's a group that believes in the purity of the races. It hates blacks, Jews, Mexicans, liberals, gays, and ZOG, you know, stuff like that."

"ZOG?" Vance said, slowly turning toward the gallery. "Please tell the court, exactly what does ZOG mean?"

"It means 'Zionist Occupation Government.' The Werewolf believes that the Jews control America."

"And what was your affiliation with this group?"

"I was a member."

"Briefly, describe for the court some of the activities of Werewolf."

"Arson... extortion... prostitution... drugs... murder. You also have to commit some crimes against minorities to get in."

Vance began to probe deeper. "Describe the activities of this

Werewolf organization on the nights of June third and July fourth."

Bruce paused and bit his lip. There was no turning back. "They attacked the nuclear plant at Rocky Flats and the Alliance Construction Company in Colorado."

"What was the object of these attacks?"

"They was gonna steal some nuclear stuff." A gasp arose from the galleries.

"Permit me to inform the court at this time that the witness is referring to plutonium and conventional explosives. What was the purpose of the theft?"

"They was gonna build a bomb."

"For what purpose?"

"They want to set it off somewhere and start a race war." A collective moan could again be heard in the courtroom.

"Can you identify any of the participants in the attacks at Rocky Flats and the Alliance Construction Company?"

"Yes sir."

"Are any of the terrorists present in the courtroom?"

"Yes sir. Pam Haney and Stacey Manson," Davies said, slowly pointing toward the prisoners' dock. The courtroom erupted into bedlam. Judge Anders again gaveled it to silence. Pam glared at Bruce, taking her finger and drawing it menacing across her throat.

"Pamela Haney was your girlfriend, wasn't she?" Vance said after the room had been quieted.

"Yes sir," Davies said, staring in Pam's direction.

"*Was*... is right!" Pam screamed. The judge again admonished her about her conduct. Vance continued.

"Briefly describe for the court your girlfriend's feelings about blacks and Jews."

"She really hates 'em."

"Why does she hate them?"

"She told me once that a nig-eh black guy tried to rape her."

"Hate them enough to want to kill them? Say, in a race war?"

"Objection. Calls for speculation," Pam's defense attorney said, rising from his chair.

"Overruled," Judge Anders said in reply. "Witness will answer the question."

"Yes sir."

During the questioning Vance attempted to present to the jury a picture of the two women as being cold, vicious, automaton-like killers capable of anything, even mass murder. In this, he was largely assisted by the antics of the two defendants themselves. Their repeated outbursts and threats only served to reinforce the image he had created.

Friday, October 23rd
1030 hours

After two days of intense questioning, the prosecution had completed its examination of Bruce Davies, Ira Vance was well pleased with the testimony of the witness. In addition to implicating Pam Haney and Stacey Manson to the murders,

Davies' testimony had also painted a vivid and detailed picture of the Werewolf itself. He reasoned that this would not only serve to convict the two women, but also provide a platform from which to obtain future convictions of the other Werewolf terrorists.

For several weeks, Robert Denton, the court-appointed counsel defending the two female defendants, sat in silence, carefully studying the government's position and line of questioning. There had been no cross-examination of either Gillian or Carlan; the presentation of physical evidence was not seriously challenged. Instead, Denton saw in the government's star witness, the one weak, potentially impeachable link in the prosecution's case. He reasoned that if Davies could be shown to be lying then the whole government's position might collapse. He resolved to make the most of it. Vance sensed that the defense attorney would open with a punishing cross-examination of Davies. He was right.

"Mr. Davies," Denton said, slowly approaching the witness stand. "Please tell the court how long you were a member of this so-called Werewolf organization?"

"A little over two years."

"You have said that one has to commit crimes against minorities in order to join, is that correct?"

"Yeah."

"What crimes did *you* have to commit?"

"Objection!" Vance said. "Your Honor, the question counsel asks has no relevance in the present situation. The witness is not on trial!"

"Sustained," the judge said.

"Where were you when you joined this group?" Denton said, changing the line of questioning.

"I was in prison at the time."

"In prison, you say? Will you please inform the court what you were in prison for?"

"Armed robbery."

"I see. Tell me, how many times were you convicted of crimes that required incarceration?"

"Objection, Your Honor!" Vance again interrupted. "Counsel is at it again. The question has no relevance."

"Your Honor, the prosecution has presented this so-called star witness to testify against my clients. It is the purpose of defense counsel to demonstrate that said witness is not a credible one," Denton shot back, glaring at Vance.

"I will allow this question... Overruled. The witness will answer the question," Judge Anders said.

"I was jailed thirteen times since I was a kid," Davies muttered.

"Mr. Davies, you weren't at Rocky Flats on June the third, correct?"

"That's right."

"You testified that you did not see the actual murders at the construction company, correct?"

"Yes sir."

"That's interesting. Yet you stated earlier under oath that the two defendants were involved in the killings — killings that you did not witness."

"They told me about it after. Pam bragged about it for days." Denton could see that Davies was becoming nervous.

"I see... Mr. Davies, please describe for the court what you did when you joined this Werewolf gang. Did you, for example, have to take some kind of pledge or an oath?"

Davies paused for a long minute before answering.

"Yeah."

"I see. Exactly what was the gist of this oath?"

"That a member would fight to the death for the race and never betray the Brotherhood."

"All right, so what induced you to testify here today? In effect, to violate your oath?"

"All the killing... I just couldn't take it no more!"

"Oh, come now, Mr. Davies. The government promised to cut a deal with you in return for your cooperation, didn't they?"

"No!" Bruce said nervously.

Denton looked Davies straight in the eye. Their faces were inches apart. "Or perhaps maybe they paid you for this testimony?"

"No! That's not right!"

"You didn't see either of these two women commit these crimes and yet here you are, testifying as to their guilt. You lied, didn't you? I submit that you've been lying all along."

"No! Wait!"

"How much were you paid? Ladies and gentlemen of the jury," Denton said, turning to the jury box. "I say to you that Bruce Davies has admitted to a life of crime that reaches back to his early childhood; that he joined a criminal organization for personal gain, then violated its credo when cornered. In fact, he's attempting to implicate others for his own crimes."

"No! That's not right!" Davies yelled, rising from the witness stand.

"In short, this man is a liar. He didn't see either of these two women kill anybody, yet now he testifies to that in order to save his own skin! I would admonish the jury to ignore everything this man has uttered."

"Objection, your Honor! This is blatant abuse of the witness!" Vance screamed.

"Your Honor, I have no further questions for this witness," Denton said, waving his hand. He turned on the ball of his heel, tucked his left hand into his pocket and sauntered back to his seat. He nodded approvingly to the cameras.

"The witness may step down," Judge Anders said.

Sunday, October 25th
0805 hours
The Price residence, Greeley, CO

Mitchell Price was tired. Late on the previous day he had completed the last of the C4 wedges. For almost three months, he worked diligently in the lab, making the components of the shaped charge that would be used to detonate the bomb. Now his job was finished. Jackie and Howard would be leaving the next morning. After a night of wild sex with Jackie, he sat relaxing in the bathtub.

Everything was going according to plan. Beausoleil and Chalmers had arrived at the Fredericksburg hide-out of Joseph Paul Recke with a load of the modified C4. Jackie and Howard were busy loading the remainder of the explosives, along with the plutonium onto a white truck.

"Where's Mitch now?" Howard said.

"I think he's taking a bath," Jackie said, donning a dark wig.

"Okay, I guess it's time to tell him goodbye. Make it quick. We're in a hurry."

"This won't take long." Jackie picked up her purse and went inside. Barging into the bathroom, she saw Mitch reclining peacefully in the tub.

"Oh, Jackie!" Mitch said, startled. "Boy, you were great last night... You know, I think you look even sexier as a brunette."

"We're getting ready to leave now. Skin-Girl and her boyfriend are waiting for us in Virginia. I've come to thank you for everything you've done," she said, slowly wetting her lips.

"But I thought that you weren't leaving until tomorrow," Mitch said, sitting up in the tub.

"There's been a little change in plans, lover... I wanted our sex last night to be wonderful for you, the best ever."

"You bet... Why?"

"Because it was your last." Jackie suddenly pulled out a silenced Beretta handgun from her purse. She aimed the weapon at his chest.

"Christ Jesus! What do you think you're doing?" Mitch said, now cowering in the tub.

"What does it look like I'm doing, Boy Scout? We don't need you anymore." She smiled and leaned against the doorway. "You stupid, sweet fool, we used you."

"Look! I gave you what you wanted! You're not just going to fucking kill me! Come on, please! I don't want to die! Please... No!"

"I love it when they beg... You're not going to be murdered, Mitch," she said, suddenly spying an electric plug-in razor lying on the edge of the basin. "You're going to die by accident... A tragic, stupid accident."

"No, Jackie, please! I don't wanna die! I don't wanna die!" Mitch shrieked. His eyes started welling up. "When does all the killing stop? You're just not human!"

"Accidents happen... I'm so sorry, Mitch. It's time to go." She picked up the razor's cord and plugged it into a wall socket.

"But Jackie... I love you!" he said. His voice broke into a sob. "Please!"

"I love you too... Mitch, you're fucked. Totally fucked." Jackie tossed the razor into the water near his feet. Mitch suddenly screamed and began splashing about violently as the electricity traversed and seared his body. The lights of the house began to flicker momentarily. Stiffening, his corpse slowly settled back into the water, animated only by a periodic twitch. The victim's eyeballs bulged and then exploded from their sockets, dyeing the water a dark hue of magenta. His red hair stood on end, giving, together with the hollowed eye sockets, the appearance of a Halloween ghoul. A cloud of smoke slowly rose from his mouth. He had been electrocuted. The air had become heavy with the foul smell of urine, feces and burnt human flesh. The room grew quiet, save for the eerie crackle of electricity, which sounded like meat sizzling on a grill. Smiling, and with a morbid fascination, Jackie briefly stared at the dead man.

"Thanks for the orgasm...Lover."

Howard was waiting in the truck. "Well, did you do it?" he said as Jackie opened the door.

"Yup. I did it. Looks like poor Mitchy had a little accident in the bathtub. What a shame." She smiled.

"How?"

"Oh, you should have seen it. It was shocking," Jackie replied, as she suddenly broke into laughter.

"Somehow I never really trusted Mitch." Howard inserted the key into the ignition. "I don't know. He just didn't quite seem fully committed to the movement. We're too close to the end. We can't run the risk of betrayal at this late stage."

"Anyway, we don't need him anymore," Jackie said as she closed the truck's door. "Besides, he was a lousy lover."

With its deadly cargo securely in place, the truck slowly pulled out of the driveway and headed toward the Interstate. Its ultimate destination was Washington, DC.

Code Name: Juggernaut

Shatterer of Worlds

The two-and-a-half-day trip to Fredericksburg, Virginia was an uneventful one, animated only by several rest stops at Werewolf "safe houses" along the way. The pair reached their destination, the farmhouse of Joseph and Cheryl Recke late on the twenty-eighth. Ariadne Beausoleil and Jason Chalmers were already there, having arrived six days earlier with some of the modified C4 explosives.

"It'll be nice to see the Reckes again," Jackie said. "Cheryl had a baby girl late last year. They named her Paranoya. I'm dying to see her."

"Yeah, and JR's done some good work for the Werewolf since Rocky Flats," Howard said as they pulled into town. "He's started a splinter group right here in Fredericksburg. Outfit called the Confederate Brotherhood."

Joseph Paul Recke, thirty-three, was a farmer. The harsh reality of farm life had left him prematurely aged. Difficulty in obtaining loans to expand the farm had made him bitter against all the "Jew bankers" his gravitation to the Werewolf had been a natural one. An amateur writer and poet, he wrote for the Werewolf as its "Minister of Propaganda." His articles, all extolling the "blood and iron" virtues of the Aryans, had already appeared in several neo-Nazi publications.

He lived with his wife Cheryl and infant daughter Paranoya on a small farm overlooking the Rappahannock River just west of the town of Fredericksburg. The farm itself was situated on a rise of land known as Marye's Heights. Rich in history, the town of

Fredericksburg had about 25,000 inhabitants; it was in a battle there that Confederate General Lee crushed Union General Burnside's northern army in December of 1862 during the Civil War. Howard Brennan looked out along the ridge towards the battlefield to ponder and reflect. His great-great-grandfather, Colonel Josiah Brennan, died while leading a Michigan Zouave regiment in a gallant but futile bayonet charge against the rebel army on these same hills during that battle. For his bravery, a grateful nation bestowed upon his widow its highest award for valor, the Medal of Honor.

Now Fredericksburg was to be the scene of history again. The location was perfect: only about sixty miles from Washington D.C., the fifty-three- acre farm was an ideal site for the gang's malefactors. Howard went right to work constructing the bomb's "lens." Under the dim illumination of the barn's lighting, he painstakingly mixed M1 military adhesive with an epoxy resin and began cementing the wedges of C4 explosive together. Working in the cramped space of the truck, the process was a tedious one. The mixture had to be carefully applied to the pieces and then held together to set properly. Slowly the hollow charge mechanism began to take shape.

For his part, Howard Brennan himself was becoming increasingly unglued. As more and more of the Werewolf's operatives were apprehended, his rage and madness became readily apparent. The trial of Haney and Manson finally pushed him over the edge. Whatever frail hold he had retained on his sanity now snapped. As if to justify to himself of the necessity and righteousness of the coming terror, he ranted continuously about the "Jewish conspiracy" in Washington and how much better things would be after it had been destroyed. With a singular purpose of mind, he devoted his full time to the Juggernaut.

Neighbors were becoming suspicious as newspapers began to accumulate on Mitchell Price's front porch. The mail slot overflowed with unopened parcels and unpaid bills. Suspicion became outright concern, when on Halloween night several of the local trick-ortreaters returned to their homes complaining to their parents about a pungent and peculiar smell that seemed to be coming from the Price home. Without realizing the relevance, one of the neighborhood children remarked that it "smelled like someone died in there." Repeated telephone inquiries by his next-door neighbor went unanswered. Finally, on November first, the local police were summoned to the house. Upon entry, they were immediately met with the unmistakably sweet, sickening odor of decaying human flesh. As the bath water was still running, the carpets and underlying floorboards were ruined, completely soaked through. The police activity was closely observed by the beady yellow eyes of a great rat while a cloud of bloated green flies buzzed angrily around the hallway, as if sensing that their feast was about to be interrupted. Anxiously, the authorities followed the sickening stench into the bathroom, where a horrible discovery awaited.

As Mitchell Price's body was removed from the bathtub, detectives swarmed into the house. The rigid corpse, already in an advanced state of decomposition, retained the position it had occupied in the bathtub, *putrefaction* having long since set in. Suspecting foul play, the house was meticulously dusted for fingerprints. Besides those of the victim, in addition to several sets of prints, a veritable cornucopia of other incriminating evidence was uncovered in the makeshift basement laboratory. Amid assorted weapons and piles of racist and anti-Semitic hate literature were the two ceramic molds used for the modification of the C4, as well as several empty crates that bore the black stencil markings of **ALLIANCE CONSTRUCTION COMPANY**. Recalling the theft of high explosives back in July, the Greeley PD summoned the FBI and the ATF in to investigate.

Monday, November 2nd
0745 hours
FBI Field Office, Denver, CO

"How's your schedule look today?" Frank Bledsoe said as Rabson arrived.

"Well, the director wants me back in Washington on the ninth. Today, I was planning on going back to the courthouse. The prosecution is presenting its closing argument in the trial of those two women."

"Well, forget it. Something's just come up, in Greeley," Bledsoe said, getting his coat.

"Oh? What's up?"

"I just got off the phone with Joe Wheeler at the ATF. It seems that over the weekend Greeley PD found some guy dead in his bathtub. He was electrocuted."

"Uh-huh. And?"

"Guy's name was Price, Mitch Price. It seems that they also found several crates in his house had markings of Alliance Construction."

Rabson briefly pondered the statement. "The missing explosives!"

"Right. They're treating his death as a homicide. They dusted his house for prints, sent what they found to the Bureau last night. You want to know what they found?"

"Let me guess, they got a set of prints belonging to Lynch and Brennan, right?"

"Their prints and DNA were apparently everywhere, all over the house. There were also prints from at least two other people we haven't identified yet."

"So that's where they held up all this time," Rabson said. "What about this Price guy? Bureau got anything on him?"

"We don't, but the locals have. He was strictly small potatoes.

They say that apparently, he was fairly active with white supremacists in the Greeley area. Looks like you and I are going to head up to Greeley."

"Yes sir."

The two agents drove the sixty miles to Greeley, arriving there in little over an hour. There, they were greeted by Joe Wheeler and Greeley homicide detective Hal Coates. The house itself, despite a prolonged fumigation, still reeked of decaying human flesh. The sweet, stale odor permeated the furniture, walls and carpets. Donning gauze masks, the lawmen went inside and began sifting through the evidence.

0928 hours
Greeley, CO

"What do you people have for us?" Bledsoe said to Wheeler as he got out of his car.

"They're calling the cause of death ventricular fibrillation," Wheeler said, reading from the medical examiner's report. "Local cops found some guy named Price floating in the bathtub, electrocuted. Jeez, somebody fried his ass like a pot of chicken."

"Right now, they're calling it a definite homicide. According to the Coroner it looks like he's been dead for at least five days."

"Smells like it too," Rabson said while covering his nose.

"Ugly way to die," Bledsoe said.

"Searching the house, they came across these," Wheeler said, pointing to some of the crates in the corner.

"Hmm… So, here's where all that C4 turned up," Rabson said.

"Right. That's when they called us. Their print people came up with the two fugitives you're looking for."

"Brennan and Lynch were here, all right," Rabson said. "From the looks of things, they used all this equipment here to modify the C4 they stole."

"Yeah, here, look at this," Bledsoe said, as he picked up a photocopy of some old papers from a 1947 issue of *The Journal of Theoretical Physics*.

"What did you find Frank?"

"This scientific paper here. I don't understand most of this mumbo-jumbo in it, but it looks like this Professor Neddermeyer person is describing an implosion device."

"I'm afraid I'm lost already," Detective Coates interrupted. "Exactly what's going on here?"

"Last July, terrorists attacked the Alliance Construction Company. They killed five people and made off with at least seventy pounds of C4 explosive," Bledsoe said.

"Yeah, I was part of that investigation," Coates said, nodding. "The case is still open."

"It looks like maybe this Price guy was somehow involved. The C4 was in these crates. From the looks of this setup here, I'd say he probably molded the C4 to a shape that Lynch and Brennan specified. They must've killed him when he finished the work. I guess it's like they say about there being no honor among thieves. Looks like a double-cross," Rabson said as he examined one of the ceramic molds.

"Okay. You said they shaped the explosives. For what purpose?" Coates said, still perplexed.

Bledsoe turned away. "We think they're trying to build an atomic bomb."

"Jacqueline Lynch and Howard Brennan are members of a radical white supremacist gang calling itself the Werewolf," Rabson continued. "They were involved in a raid on Rocky Flats back in June. They took several components of an atomic bomb." Coates simply stood in amazement. Rabson started to go outside.

"Where are you going?" Coates said.

"I'm going to talk to the neighbors and try to find out if anybody saw something."

It turned out that Rabson didn't have to go far to find an observant and cooperative witness. Over the years, the elderly Ginni Moorehouse had acquired a bit of a reputation of being a busybody and neighborhood snoop. Slightly eccentric and a widow for seven years, she filled much of her time staring out the window with her tabby cat, Penelope. Indeed, almost nothing escaped her gaze. Her proximity as Price's next-door neighbor gave her a front-row seat for observing a number of the activities that went on there. When Rabson got to the door Mrs. Moorehouse was standing on the foyer holding the cat.

"Pardon me, ma'am, I'm Douglas Rabson, FBI," the agent said, displaying his badge. "I'm investigating something that occurred at your neighbor's house last week."

"You mean a murder, don't you?"

"What do you know about a murder, ma'am?"

"I knew that something was wrong when Mitchell didn't return any of my calls! It was that evil woman! I figured that shameless slut would harm poor Mitchell."

"You're saying that you think a woman killed Price, ma'am? Please continue."

"Yes! I saw her often. Jezebel! She would be outside wearing one of those nudie bikini outfits and dancing to that rock and roll stuff!

She didn't have any shame at all. I'll bet *she's* your killer."

"Can you tell me about anything that went on in that house?"

"Many strange things. Mitchell did a lot of chemistry-type stuff in the basement after his parents died. A man and woman moved in with him around last August. Making noises all hours of the night. They always seemed to be carrying large boxes in and out of the house."

"Ma'am," Rabson said, retrieving a copy of the FBI wanted poster. "Are these the people you saw next door with Mr. Price?" Adjusting her glasses Mrs. Moorehouse carefully studied the pictures.

"Why, yes, that's the man!" she said. "And I think that this is the woman, but she's a brunette… that's her, all right, but her hair is much lighter in the picture."

"You're sure about the woman?"

"Yes, Mr. Rabson, that's her all right. We didn't get along very well."

"Oh?"

"Yes, she called me filthy names and once even threatened my dear Penelope here with a broom handle. Isn't that right Sweetie," Moorehouse said soothingly, slowly rubbing the cat's head. "She was a very mean lady."

"Anything else look suspicious?"

"Two of their friends arrived back on the thirteenth."

"Can you describe these people?"

"Yes. A pair of teenagers… A man and woman. They were mean too. The man had one of those short haircuts and wore all this Nazi stuff on his clothes; the girl had shoulder-length black hair, parted down the middle. She was always dressed like a prostitute. I just don't know about kids these days. They spent all night loading packages into their car."

"Anything else?"

"No sir... I was glad when they left a couple of days later."

"Did you by chance note the vehicle the teenagers were driving?"

"It was a sports car. Green, I think. Also, I did see the truck the man and woman drove. It was white with a camper shell. I saw them last on, let's see, early Sunday the twenty-fifth."

"Were you by any chance able to get a license plate number or any other descriptive information from the truck?"

"No, I'm afraid not... What did these people do? Are they some kind of drug dealers or something?"

"We're just checking up on things ma'am. Purely routine. I wonder if we could send a sketch artist here. Maybe you can give him a description of the two teenagers."

"All right."

"Thank you, ma'am," Rabson said, sprinting back to the Price house. As he got to the porch he was met by Bledsoe.

"You able to get anything?"

"Yeah, plenty. I got a positive ID on Lynch and Brennan being at the house. An elderly woman next door claims that besides them it seems that two other people arrived here around the middle of last month, probably other members of the gang. Couple of skinheads. Haven't heard anything from the Bureau about those other sets of prints the locals found. I'm going to send Hal Munday here tomorrow to try and get some sketches."

"Anything else?"

"Yeah, about Jacqueline Lynch; looks like our towhead killer is now sporting a brunette wig. The witness is sure that she and Brennan left on or around the twenty-fifth in a white truck with matching camper shell."

"Uh-huh, according to the Greeley PD that jibes with the preliminary estimated time of death for Price... Electrocution in the bathtub, it's a pretty horrible way to die," Bledsoe said, shaking his head.

Yeah, well, Jacqueline Lynch is a pretty horrible killer."

Wednesday, November 4th
1430 hours
Byron White Building, US Federal Courthouse, Denver, CO

After a three-and-a-half-day deliberation, word came that the eight-man, four-woman jury had reached its decision. The proceedings which had gripped the nation's attention for over three months were finally drawing to a close. Under heavy guard, the two female defendants were brought to the courtroom. The two women smiled and joked with the assembled press. News crews jockeyed for the best camera angles. Meanwhile, a horde of curious spectators quickly filled the galleries, competing with newsmen for the limited seating. Several fistfights broke out before guards could restore order.

Ira Vance came in. The federal prosecutor had a look of grim satisfaction on his face. Just that morning he had received a telephone call from Jen McCormick. The Attorney General congratulated him on the quality of his presentation of the government's case. Rabson and Bledsoe quietly came in and took seats behind the prosecutor. Rabson, scheduled to fly back to Washington on the eighth, had been worried that he might not be able to attend the trial's ending; he was delighted by the jury's speedy deliberation. One noteworthy absentee was Bruce Davies. His testimony finished, the government had secretly removed him to an unnamed location. A hush descended on the packed courtroom as Judge Anders entered and addressed the panel.

"Ladies and gentlemen of the jury," the judge opened. "Have you reached a verdict?"

A Denver cabdriver and one of two blacks on the panel answered.

"Yes, Your Honor, we have."

"On the sixteen counts of the indictment of civil rights violations resulting in death how do you find the defendants Pamela Mae Haney and Stacey Alice Manson?"

"We, the jury, find the defendants… Guilty!"

The courtroom exploded in applause. With difficulty, Judge Anders gaveled the room to silence.

"On the single count of the indictment of theft of government property, how do you find the defendants?"

"Guilty!"

"You call this justice? You've just judged yourselves!" Pam Haney screamed at the jury. Her shriek echoed eerily around the courtroom. The irate woman had to be forcibly restrained by uniformed security personnel. Judge Anders continued.

"On the single count of criminal trespass on government property how do you find the defendants?"

"Guilty!"

"On the charge of assault on federal officers how do you find the defendants?"

"Guilty!"

For the next several minutes the reading of the verdict went on.

The two defendants were found guilty on every count. It was a clean sweep for the government. Judge Anders turned and addressed the two women.

"You have been found guilty of the charges indicated," the Judge said. "You shall be brought here for formal sentencing on the seventh of next month. Court stands adjourned."

"Yahweh will take His vengeance… Die! You'll all die! The Werewolf will kill you all! Die! Die! You're all gonna die!" Pam screeched as she and Stacey were taken, being dragged from the courtroom. Rabson, Bledsoe and Vance warmly shook hands and exchanged "high-fives" in celebration. Rabson slowly scanned the audience.

Amid the cheering throng in the gallery, he suddenly thought he recognized a familiar face: it was Suzanne Brennan, now almost fully recovered from the effects of the beating. In her face, he could see a glow of satisfaction and contentment.

Thursday, November 5th
0730 hours (EST)
The Recke residence, near Fredericksburg, VA

Jackie, Howard and the Reckes were in the den watching the *Morning News*. Most of the broadcasts dealt with the conclusion of the trial. With mounting anger, Howard watched the footage of Haney and Manson being led away amid the gloating of the federal prosecutor.

"You see? That's what happens when the Jews are allowed to run this shit country!" he said, yelling so loudly that he woke little Paranoya, who was sleeping in the back room.

"Shhhh, Howie. You're waking the baby," Jackie said.

"Well, she may as well see where this lousy piece of shit country is headed! That's all right, in just over two months I'm going to start to set things right! That kid in there ain't going to have to grow up with all this!"

"Howie, you really going to be able to set this thing off?" Recke said

"That's right. I'm going to send 'em to Hell! I've got sixteen of those C4 wedges cemented together in the back of the truck. They're forming the cradle for the plutonium."

Howard reached into his pocket and extracted a long envelope addressed to the FBI Director.

"Joe, you're going into Richmond today, right?"

"Yeah. I got to pick up some farm equipment there."

"Do me a favor. When you get there, mail this." Howard handed him the envelope.

"What's this?"

"Never mind. Just make sure you mail it in Richmond."

"Sure, Howie."

Rabson had flown back to Washington on the night of the eighth, getting to see his family for the first time in weeks. Although the director had ordered round-the-clock surveillance for the Rabson home, his wife Rachel was still clearly unnerved by the telephone threat. For his part, Rabson, although reassuring, was uneasy for his family's safety. Sarah's *bat mitzvah* was in a week's time, and he had nightmare images of his daughter being abducted by Werewolf terrorists.

After a quick meal with his family, he drove off to his office. He and the director were scheduled to meet with the president and other members of the NSC at midmorning, and he wanted to get his report ready. Pacing down the hallway, he inspected the repair work that had been done since the bombing back in July. He paused momentarily to gaze into the still vacant office of Aqueous Blank, realizing that the sixty-year-old black woman would have been two months happily retired now instead of in her grave but for a twisted, sick individual. A tear slowly ran down his cheek. Heading back toward his office, he was more determined than ever to bring her killer to justice.

Monday, November 9th
1100 hours
White House Situation Room

The President, CIA Director and Attorney General were all in attendance when Rabson and FBI Director Longstreet arrived. As the pair arrived, the president rose to greet them.

"Well, Rabson," the president opened. "Splendid work in Colorado. I see that you got convictions on two of those terrorists."

"Yes sir. Thank you, sir. Judge Anders has set December seventh as their sentencing date. Jury selection for the trial of the others is set to begin, on December twenty-eighth."

"And I've made it clear the government's going to push for the death penalty," Attorney General McCormick said.

"What other new developments have there been?" the president said, getting down to business.

"Well sir, I'm afraid things are worse than we have realized. Bureau and ATF agents have uncovered evidence that the terrorists have been busy modifying the stolen high explosives, obviously for the detonation mechanism for the bomb.

"What kind of evidence?"

"We found several ceramic forms that they apparently were using to mold C4 explosive into the bomb's implosion mechanism. The fact we didn't find any of the missing C4 tells me that they've finished its modification. So far, we know that the terrorists left Greeley, Colorado on or around the twenty-fifth of last month in a white pick-up truck."

"Anything on their probable whereabouts or destination? What about that mid-January date your informant gave you?" the CIA Director said.

"We're still anticipating that they plan to strike on the Martin Luther King Holiday. Next year, the holiday falls on Monday, January the eighteenth. I've done some checking, looks like the largest celebrations are scheduled for Denver, Atlanta, and right here in Washington."

"Hmm, I'm supposed to give a speech about King's legacy in Atlanta that day," the president said.

"Perhaps you should consider canceling it," the CIA Director said.

"Sir, I think we should mobilize all available law enforcement resources in those cities as soon as possible," Rabson said.

"My God!" the Attorney General exclaimed. "How do we find them? Do you know how many white trucks there are on the road?"

"Well, it makes sense that Werewolf would try to construct the bomb close to the target. I suggest that we probably should concentrate our efforts near those three cities."

"Why couldn't we just somehow cancel all the festivities?" the CIA Director said.

"I'm afraid that wouldn't accomplish anything," Longstreet said, "What's to prevent the Werewolf from simply exploding the bomb anywhere? In a crowded metropolitan area, the casualties would be horrendous."

The meeting adjourned. The two lawmen walked up Pennsylvania Avenue to the J. Edgar Hoover Building. Inside his office Director Longstreet noticed a thin brown envelope lying on top of a stack of mail. Opening it, he found a note typed in large capital letters on a cheap grade of printer paper. He began to examine its rambling contents. It read:

AN OPEN LETTER TO ZOG:

IN SPITE OF THE SAVAGE AND UNJUST PERSECUTION BY THE RUMP ZIONIST REGIME IN WASHINGTON, WE, THE WHITE ARYAN PATRIOTS OF THE WEREWOLF, HAVE SUCCESSFULLY ACQUIRED A WEAPON OF MASS DESTRUCTION, A WEAPON AGAINST WHICH YOU HAVE NO DEFENSE. ALTHOUGH YOUR CRIMINAL ABDUCTION OF SEVERAL OF OUR KAMERADEN HAS WEAKENED US, IT HAS NOT SHATTERED OUR RESOLVE OR AFFECTED THE MOVEMENT. SHORTLY AFTER THE COMING OF THE NEW YEAR, WEREWOLF SHALL BRING DEATH TO YOU ALL IN ACCORDANCE WITH THE LAWS OF YAHWEH! YOU CANNOT FIND ME, YOU CANNOT STOP ME. HAIL VICTORY!

GUY FAWKES.

The Director handed the letter to Rabson. "Guy Fawkes? Who's that supposed to be," the agent said upon scanning it.

"It's Howard Brennan. I guess it's his way of having a little joke. Cocky son-of-a-bitch, isn't he? Sending me this letter and all." The director placed the letter in his desk.

"This case is getting stranger by the minute. If he's taunting us like this, it probably means that he's completed the bomb and is confident that it'll work,"

"What's that in your hand?" Longstreet pointed to a file folder Rabson was carrying.

"Oh, yes, this was on my desk when I got back to my office. We finally got a positive ID on the two other sets of prints taken from the house in Greeley. They belong to a pair of skinheads. An elderly next-door neighbor gave us a good description of them. The police department in Salt Lake apparently got to know these people very well."

"Hmm... Ariadne Beausoleil and Jason Chalmers," Longstreet said, slowly reading the file. "Looks like they're just a couple of kids."

"Sir, these *kids* were involved in a variety of crimes back in Utah and Rocky Flats."

"Yeah, I see what you mean," Longstreet noted, flipping through the files of the pair. "Arrests for shoplifting, assault, arson, drug possession; the girl was involved in prostitution... and, Good Lord, is a suspect in a drive-by homicide last April."

"So, you believe that these people are involved with the terrorists?"

"Yes sir, I do. Nick Hoover tried to tell me about them when I was in Utah. They're probably helping Brennan move the bomb's components."

"All right... What's your recommendation?"

"I think we should get their pictures out. Saturate the country with descriptions of this Beausoleil and Chalmers. We're running out of time."

Director Longstreet nodded in agreement.

Sunday, November 15th
0805 hours
The Recke residence, near Fredericksburg, VA

With more than half of the explosive charges, the so-called "lens" now in place, it was time for Howard to begin the preparation of the heart of the bomb: the tamped plutonium core.

"I'm going to start to assemble the bomb's core today," Howard said. He and Jackie went into the barn. Inside, he seated himself in front of a strange, boxlike structure on the bench. Completely enclosed it was made up of heavy Plexiglas panels and had a pair of thick black gloves protruding inward. Inside the structure were the lead canisters holding the plutonium, the uranium tamper and the beryllium/polonium initiator."

"What's that strange-looking thing?"

"It's a glovebox. Rather crude, Rube Goldberg-looking thing that I've slapped together but it'll get the job done. That's all that matters."

"What are you going to do with it?"

"This is where I'm going to construct the core of the bomb."

"Why do you have to do it in there?"

"Two reasons. First, I don't want to be exposed to high levels of radiation while working on the bomb's core. Second, plutonium readily undergoes oxidation in the atmosphere. I'll have to work on it in as near an oxygen-free condition as I can have."

"How are you going to do all that?"

"You see that?" Howard said, pointing to a large gas cylinder adjacent to the glovebox. "I'll purge the chamber with the gas from the cylinder. That's pure Argon. It's inert… very unreactive. Once the chamber is free of oxygen, I can work on assembling the weapon's core."

"But won't the chamber leak when the gas on?"

"No. The Plexiglas walls are very thick and well-sealed. They won't leak."

Jackie watched intently as Howard began his work. He placed the hermetically sealed lead canisters with the plutonium and initiator, partially assembled C4 section and the tamper in the glove- box, tightly clamping its lid shut.

"Turn on the gas cylinder," he said. Jackie slowly began turning the cylinder's knob. A faint hissing sound was audible as the chamber was purged. After several minutes, Howard inserted his hands into the gloves and slowly began prying open the hermetically sealed canisters. The tamper wedges were depleted uranium, light gray in color, and resembled sections of a grapefruit.

"I'll begin arranging the tamper sections on the C4 cradle." He carefully removed the plutonium, depositing a layer of the fine gray material onto the tamper.

"There, now I'm going to place the initiator," he said, carefully holding up the dull gray sphere. "This is the source of the neutrons. It's too bad I don't have a more efficient neutron source... like lithium-6-deuteride, I could get a better explosive yield." He placed the initiator into the hollow of the plutonium, followed by the remaining sections of plutonium and tamper. Jackie watched the process intently.

"There...Done," Howard said, removing his hands from the glovebox. "Now, I'll let that stand under argon for several hours."

1125 hours

Jackie and Howard returned to the house, pleased with the morning's work. Inside, Joe and Cheryl, having just finished their breakfast, were busy watching a football game. The *Washington Commanders* was hosting the *Denver Broncos* in their stadium at Northwest Stadium. The score was 21-3, Washington. Jackie picked up little Paranoya from her crib. The infant cooed with delight.

"Howie built the bomb's core today. We're almost finished,"

Jackie said to the Reckes on entering the kitchen.

"That's great," Joe said in casual response, clearly absorbed in the game.

"Isn't that game being played in Washington?"

"Yeah. They are really kicking Denver's ass today! Look, the Broncos are pinned near their own end zone," Joe said, as a black Washington linebacker tackled the Bronco quarterback on the Denver two-yard line, narrowly avoiding a safety. The player spontaneously broke into an impromptu sack dance in triumph.

"That's right, that's right…now start acting colored," Howard said while watching the lewd celebration. "Look at that… Ever notice how all them colored ballplayers got to start acting like monkeys when they do something right? It's like the old saying, 'You can take the nigger outta the jungle, but you can't take the jungle outta the nigger.'"

"Oh! That's a good one Howie!" Jackie chortled as she carried the baby over towards the television. "Here honey, look at all those niggers in that stadium. See all the niggers?"

"Most everybody in Washington is colored," Cheryl said.

"And just think, in a little more than nine weeks all the coons you see there will probably be dead!"

"And ZOG will be destroyed!" Howard said. "What a target! Imagine a seven-forty-seven being crashed into that stadium right now… Total destruction!"

The conversation paused as an excited sportscaster suddenly announced a big play by the Broncos. All eyes were transfixed on the TV.

"Holy Christ! Look at that goddamned nigger run! You see that?

That coon broke through that line like a panzer division!" Joe said, wildly pointing at the TV as a black Denver running-back ran off-tackle ninety-seven yards for a touchdown.

"That ain't no big deal," Howard grunted, shrugging in reply. "What did you expect him to do? I tell you all them coons are strong as apes! It just ain't fair having Aryan white men to compete against animals."

Washington went on to lose the game, 24-21.

Thursday, November 26th Thanksgiving Day
1030 hours
near Fredericksburg, VA

Joe had just returned from an overnight trip to Richmond with another load of farm equipment. Howard was waiting for him on the porch.

"ZOG's got Skin-Girl and NumbNutz's pictures up all over the place in Richmond," he said as he alighted from his truck.

"Oh?" Howard said, mildly interested.

"Yeah. I also stopped by the Post Office last night to pick up a package… their pictures are right up next to you and Jackie's."

"Forget it, Joe," Howard said, placing his arm on Recke's shoulder. "Come out here to the barn, the others are waiting."

Howard led Recke to the barn. Jackie, Ariadne, Jason, Cheryl and the baby were already inside, gathered around the truck. The building was decorated for the occasion. On the walls of the barn hung a swastika flag and a large picture of Adolph Hitler. Howard climbed up on the back of the vehicle. He gazed upward and began speaking.

"Oh Yahweh, God of Hosts and Light of the Aryans, hear thy humble servant. Thou art a just and merciful God. On this blessed day of thanksgiving, we give thee thanks for thy generous bounty. For on this day, thou hath given unto us the means to smite thy enemies and to establish thy justice. Thou hath given unto us, the Juggernaut."

Howard pulled a large tarpaulin from the truck's bed, unveiling a small spheroid object resting on a crude platform. Next to the device was Joe's old tractor distributor, forty-eight wires emanating from it. Save for the addition of the blasting caps and the ignition source, the bomb was complete. Dull white in color, due to the C4 explosives, the bomb had a diameter of eighteen inches and weighed a scant seventy-two pounds. The alternating array of pentagonal and hexagonal wedges gave the weapon the appearance of a large soccer ball. The assembled throng edged closer to admire Howard's handiwork.

"And now I am become Death! The Shatterer of worlds... ZOG will die!" Howard screamed from the bed of the truck, pleased that the words of J. Robert Oppenheimer's quoting of the Hindu scriptures of the *Bhagavad-Gita* had come to him at the perfect moment.

"Race War! Werewolf! Sieg Heil Adolph Hitler!" Jackie said, placing a record album on an old phonograph player in the corner. She thrust her arm forward in the stiff fascist salute as the strains of the Nazi anthem, *Das Horst Wessellied* echoed around the barn. The others joined in, deliriously chanting and dancing around the bomb. Little Paranoya was lying peacefully in a makeshift crib. The baby watched the spectacle unfolding before her with a quizzical expression on her face, unable to comprehend its meaning.

Its meaning was all too clear. On Thanksgiving Day, the Werewolf had joined an exclusive club: it had become a nuclear power.

Code Name: Juggernaut

Marching As to War

Monday, November 30th
0945 hours
FBI Field Office, Denver Federal Building, Denver, CO

Rabson flew back to Denver shortly after the Thanksgiving holiday. The sentencing of the two convicted female terrorists was scheduled for the first week in December. Although the government was publicly pressing to get the death penalty for Manson and Haney privately, it was hoped that the pair could somehow be coaxed into revealing information about the plot in exchange for a commutation to life imprisonment. The Attorney General, having ordered Rabson back to Denver, instructed him to make such an offer to the prisoners through their lawyer, Robert Denton.

For his part, Denton had become increasingly exasperated with his clients. During the long trial, the two women's bizarre antics were instrumental in the outcome. Now the pair steadfastly refused to cooperate with their attorney while he prepared an appeal of the verdict.

Completely frustrated, Denton arrived in the interrogation room in the Federal Building to meet with Rabson and Bledsoe.

"Mr. Denton, I've come from the Attorney General with an offer—"

"I know what you're going to say, Rabson," Denton said. "You're wasting your time."

"So, you're not going to cooperate?"

"Rabson, those two women are guilty as sin. Don't get me wrong. I would take your offer in a New York minute. Problem is that those bitches simply won't cooperate. Period. They just don't care. You flew back out here for nothing."

"I'm here on the order of the Attorney General. Mind if I talk with your clients?" Rabson said.

"I don't see what good it'll do… Go ahead, to Hell with 'em. I'm washing my hands of the whole thing." Denton stormed out. Rabson didn't think it would do any good either, but orders were orders. Haney and Manson, shackled together and clad in orange jumpers called 'murder suits' in jailhouse slang, were brought up from the holding area to the room several minutes later.

"What do you want, huh, Jew-boy?" Pamela snarled upon seeing Rabson, making an obscene gesture with her middle finger.

"We ain't got nothin' to say, least of all to you!" Stacey echoed. The agent ignored the insults. He got down to business.

"Look, ladies, both of you are scheduled for sentencing in a week. While I don't give a damn about either one of you, I was instructed to come here today. You must understand that the government is going to push for the death penalty during your sentencing. The only reason I'm here is to make you a final offer."

Pamela yawned noticeably. Rabson continued.

"The Attorney General has authorized me to offer you life imprisonment in exchange for your cooperation in finding Jacqueline Lynch, Howard Brennan and the plutonium."

"Hear that, Stace? ZOG must be running scared… You stupid ZOG cops will find it yourself next month, asshole!" Pam said with a laugh.

"Why are the two of you doing this? Don't you two realize that Jacqueline Lynch and Howard Brennan are going to kill thousands — maybe tens of thousands of innocent people."

"That's right," Pamela replied with a shrug, "anyway, who cares?"

"Thousands of human beings!" Rabson shouted angrily. "They deserve to live as much as anyone else! I can't believe that you would just sit back and let it happen!"

"Well, you better believe it, prick. And once the race war starts, you and all your Jew-kind are going into the shitcan along with the niggers and the other stinking pig races!" Pamela ranted.

"ZOG will kill us, but we shall be avenged by the Werewolf and by our God, Yahweh," Stacey said, smiling. "I'm going to join my husband."

"Hail Victory! Sieg Heil Adolph Hitler!" the women chanted.

Disgusted and visibly sickened, Rabson left the room. The two prisoners were taken back to their cells. Walking down the hallway, he met Frank Bledsoe.

"Frank, I just made the Attorney General's final offer to the prisoners."

"Anything?"

"Nope. No dice. I've never seen two people so absolutely consumed with hate. They talk of killing people as casually as if they were watching a football game."

"Well, I'm not surprised. I ran into Bob Denton on my way up here; he told me you were talking with them."

"I had hoped that the threat of the death penalty might make one of them talk. Looks like if we're ever going to find the plutonium it certainly won't be with their help."

"Maybe some of those other Werewolf assholes will crack," Bledsoe said. "Their trials are set to begin December twenty-seventh."

"That may be our only hope, but if the rest of those people are anything like those two, I'm not counting on it."

"If Bruce Davies was right, we've got about six or seven weeks before a major American city is destroyed."

Tuesday, December 1st
1134 hours
The Recke residence, near Fredericksburg, VA

"Where have you been? I've been looking for you," Howard said as Jackie walked in.

"I was in town, at the public library. I got you all the stuff that you wanted. Here, look at this cool map I stole." Jackie pulled out a large, detailed Rand McNally atlas of the District of Columbia and environs.

"What about all those census figures?"

"Got 'em right here." Jackie opened her purse and retrieved a thin stack of folded papers.

"Photocopies?"

"Naw, there was a line at the photocopy machine and I was in a hurry. When nobody was looking, I ripped the pages I wanted out and left."

"Read the figures to me." Howard slowly unfolded the map.

"According to the census figures, there were 646,900 people in the city of Washington as of the last tally — do you want the population figures for any of the suburbs as well?"

"No, just give me the colored population figures for Washington City."

"It says here, that there were exactly 413,951 blacks and 39,358 Hispanics in the city. Looks like a couple thousand gooks as well," Jackie said, reading from one of the torn pages.

"Let's see," Howard pondered, rubbing his chin while performing the math in his head. "That means that about seventy-one percent of the population are minorities. Human garbage. And they're all going to be right in the killing zone when the bomb goes off." Like two shopkeepers counting stock, Jackie and Howard tallied the numbers. The couple sat down to plan mass murder.

1210 hours

Howard was deep in thought when Ariadne and the Reckes came into the dining room. Behind him, a large swastika flag hung loosely on the wall. The large map of Washington DC and its environs lay spread out on the table. Important buildings in the government district had been carefully circled in red, while a route leading across the Potomac into the city had been traced with a green magic marker.

"This is our objective," Howard said as he pointed to the US Capitol building on the map. "The goal which we have long worked for, fought for, and, yes, some of us have even died for. We're going to bring down the government. The State of the Union Speech is tentatively scheduled for Tuesday, January the twenty-sixth. For the Werewolf, that's going to be the Day of the Rope. Downfall. The day of Yahweh's vengeance."

The other Aryans edged in closer to the table.

"On that day, I intend to be in Washington with the bomb... to destroy the government of the United States! Jackie and I are going to take the bomb to Manassas on or around the twenty-third. We'll lie low in a hotel there. From there I'll drive it into the city."

"Exactly where will you have the bomb?" Cheryl said.

"Look here," he said while gesturing to the atlas with a blunt end of a pencil. "I'll have the bomb parked right here in front of the Mellon Fountain at the confluence of Constitution and Pennsylvania Avenues. I've measured the distance on the map. It's a perfect location! About zero- point-six miles… Two and a half city blocks from the Capitol Building where the speech will be delivered."

"Can you really get that close?" Joe said.

"Yeah. I think so. The government now seals off a one-block area around all major federal buildings, especially the Capitol and White House. They want to guard against car bombs and the like."

The others nodded in agreement.

"But will that be close enough to kill the president and wipe out the whole government?" Ariadne said. "You know, ZOG's not taking any chances after what happened at the Capitol riots way back in twenty-twenty one."

"Hell, the Capitol Insurrection was a damned weenie roast compared to the weapon I'm gonna set off! All those people were amateurs; they simply tried to storm the building…" he said, trailing off. "I estimate that the killing zone of my bomb should be about a one-point-five-mile radius. Let's see, comes to an area of about seven-point-one square miles. Total destruction! In short, everybody within that area should be killed by the blast or the shock wave. I should certainly be able to kill them all… the Congress, the president, Supreme Court, everybody. I mean, Hell, we're talking about the power of fifty thousand tons of TNT for Christ's sake."

The others exchanged stares. Howard continued.

"In addition to killing all those people, the whole federal apparatus should be irreparably disrupted… The Federal Trade Commission Building, the Library of Congress, Interior Department, Transportation Department, House and Senate Office Buildings,

Supreme Court Building, the fucking Internal Revenue Service and FBI, the State Department, *et cetera*. Billions of records and files. All these buildings will be in the one-point-five-mile radius... In one great blast, the US government will cease to exist!"

"And what's more," Jackie added on entering the room. "The areas immediately north and east of the DC target area are heavily black and Mexican. So, we're going to be able to kill a lot of them also."

"Jackie's right. The census figures she stole from the library indicate that over four hundred thousand of the mud coloreds reside in the immediate target area." The room was completely quiet. Even little Paranoya was still. Howard got to the point of his diatribe.

"Once the government has been destroyed, the country should fall to pieces, along pure, racial lines, just like what happened in Russia back in the nineties and more recently in Syria. You all are the Aryan *Volkstürm*. Kill without mercy. You must show no pity to the enemies of Yahweh." Howard slowly walked from behind the table over to a large US map.

"In the coming race war, I expect that you and all the others shall continue the fight after I'm gone. Once the struggle commences, the Aryans shall emerge and begin killing." Howard began noting areas on the map with a pointer. "Water treatment facilities, dams, bridges, power grids, communications nodes, airports and transportation hubs... in short, infrastructure must be neutralized, just like it says in the *Diaries*. Then, you will retreat to the fastness of the Alleghenies, the Ozarks and the Rockies, where foodstuffs and munitions are hidden," he said, again gesturing to the map. "From these bastions, you must fight and hold off the black, brown and yellow hordes until our other Aryan brothers relieve you." Howard placed the pointer on the table. "After cleansing the nation of the mud races, you shall begin to establish a pure Aryan People's Republic... Yahweh's kingdom on earth."

Joseph Recke rose to his feet, his arm outstretched in the Nazi salute. "It shall be as you say! White Power! Werewolf!" he shouted.

"Hail Victory! Death To ZOG!" the others echoed in response.

Monday, December 7th
0900 hours
Byron White Federal Courthouse, Denver, CO

The long-awaited day of sentencing had come. Again, barricades had been erected, blocking off portions of Stout Street in downtown Denver. Amid extremely tight security, Pamela Haney and Stacey Manson were brought before Judge Anders to hear their fate. Once again, the two women were the object of the nation's curiosity and fascination. The proceedings were to be televised live on all major networks. Walking through a horde of news cameras and a phalanx of law enforcement officers the shackled pair appeared comfortable, even giddy at all the attention. And why not? The week before the cover of *Newsweek* featured a file photo of Pam and Stacey staring menacingly into the camera. Arriving at the federal building, the press noticed that the two women, in a manner eerily reminiscent of the Charles Manson Family girls in the early seventies, had carved swastikas into their foreheads.

"All rise. Court is now in session, the Honorable Warren Anders presiding," the bailiff said as the Judge entered the courtroom. Pam and Stacey remained seated. The judge glared at them.

"It is customary for all to rise when the presiding officer of the court enters the room," Anders said. "Stand up." The two women ignored the order.

"I said stand up!" he shouted.

"Fuck you, Judge!" Pam screamed back.

"Bailiff!" the Judge said, gesturing to two large uniformed black men seated by the bench. They walked over to the prisoners' dock and unceremoniously yanked the two women out of their chairs.

"You like beating up girls, huh Judge? Feel like a big man? Think you can get it up this time? Get your fuckin' paws off me, black boy!" Pam rasped.

"You two will not play the clown here today!" the Judge said sternly. "Now be seated. Pamela Haney and Stacey Manson," Judge Anders said, adjusting his glasses. "You both stand convicted of having on the nights of June third and July fourth of this year willfully and wantonly deprived sixteen people of their civil rights, resulting in death. In addition, you have been found guilty of criminal trespass on a federal installation, assault on federal officers and theft of federal property. Do you either of you have anything to say in your behalf before the sentence is read?"

"This is a travesty! A mockery of justice! Just remember, we're not the only ones involved, just the only ones who got caught!" Pam screamed.

"Nothing but a show-trial!" Stacey echoed. "Kangaroo court... We're nothing but political prisoners! ZOG murdered my husband!" The Judge ignored the ranting of the two women and continued with the sentencing.

"The people you killed had families, hopes and ambitions, all of which have been abruptly ended." The judge paused and shook his head. "Your complete lack of remorse for these crimes demonstrates to the Court a callous, utter disregard for the lives and property of others. What is more, the extensive criminal records that both of you have amassed further demonstrate that you both are beyond any reasonable hope of redemption or rehabilitation. In short, you are both monsters, pure and simple. Monsters in human form. It is therefore the sentence of this Court that you shall be held over in the federal penal facility in Florence, Colorado. On Thursday, June third of next year you both shall be taken to a place of execution and put to death. While it pains the Court to have to order the execution of two young women such as yourselves, it is nevertheless deemed necessary and appropriate. The manner of execution proscribed by law is death by lethal injection. And may God Almighty have mercy on your souls."

The courtroom erupted in applause.

"Death!" Pamela shrieked in a long tone. The room grew eerily silent as the sound reverberated around the courtroom. "That's just what you'll get! All of you! Eye for eye! Tooth for tooth! Blood for blood!"

"Today you sentence us, tomorrow the Werewolf sentences you!" Stacey yelled, eyes wide with hate. "The Werewolf will have its vengeance!"

"Remember Oklahoma City! You'd better watch your kids!" Pam ranted.

"Get those two lunatics out of here!" Judge Anders ordered, as three deputies from the Sheriff's Office dragged the two prisoners from the courtroom. The long ordeal was over. The local and national press began packing up their equipment; the crowds slowly dissipated. Doug Rabson and Frank Bledsoe congratulated each other and went out into the cold December morning. Meanwhile, Ira Vance was besieged by news reporters.

"Mr. Vance, how does it feel now that this long case is finished?" a news reporter said.

"Finished? It's just starting. In a just few weeks we're going to begin the prosecution of other members of the Werewolf terrorist gang. Let me make it perfectly clear that the government will also seek the death penalty for them as well."

"Do you wish to make a statement?"

"Hopefully this will send a message to any other group contemplating such acts of domestic terrorism. This kind of activity simply will not be tolerated here. For all radical groups, far left or right, my message is that if you engage in terrorism the government will come after you. We will never submit to terrorism."

"Thank you, Mr. Vance."

Rabson and Bledsoe slowly walked back to their car. Suddenly, they heard a woman's voice behind them. It was Suzanne Brennan.

"Excuse me, Mr. Rabson?"

"Ah! Mrs. Brennan," Rabson said, turning around and suddenly recognizing her face. "I'm glad to see that you've made a full recovery."

"Thank you, Agent Rabson. My recovery isn't complete yet. I'm going to need some additional reconstructive surgery," she said. "And my name is Kramer now. That's my maiden name. I consider myself to be divorced from Howard. I never want to be associated with that animal again. It took nearly my being beaten to death for me to wake up. I came here today to see justice done."

"Well, I'm glad you could be here to see this, *Ms. Kramer.* Remember, you made this all possible."

"Call me Suzanne."

"Is everything all right?"

"Yes, I'm staying with my sister. She lives in Arvada."

"I'm going to level with you, Suzanne. The Bureau needs your help again. We have reason to believe that your ex-husband and Jacqueline Lynch have an operational atomic bomb and are planning to detonate it in a major American city sometime next month. I'm afraid if we don't find them soon thousands of innocent people will die."

"I'm sorry, I really wish I could help," Suzanne said. "Howard and I weren't exactly close for these last few years. He never really confided to me about his activities with Werewolf. As it was, I didn't find out about the Rocky Flats attack until later."

"So, you can't give us anything at all?"

"Howard really hated everybody," Suzanne said. "Especially the blacks and Jews. And he was quite outspoken about it. That's what got him into trouble with the government."

"Tell us about it."

"Howard always talked about blacks being inferior. I guess I just ignored it. Several years ago, Howard stated publicly that he felt that blacks should be excluded from the Air Force."

"Please go on."

"The President got wind of this and had him reprimanded. After that, Howard just seemed to go crazy. He said publicly that he wished that someone would crash a seven-forty-seven into the White House and kill the president."

"I remember that," Bledsoe murmured. "He was thrown out of the Air Force after that. We moved to a small ranch in Utah. That's when Howard became active with the Yahweh Church... and that slut Jacqueline Lynch!"

"I see... Well, if you can think of anything else, I'm going to give you one of Frank Bledsoe's cards. You can get in touch with him and he'll pass on the information to me," Rabson said, handing her a business card.

"Yes, I sure will."

1845 hours
The Recke farm, near Fredericksburg, VA.

"Well, it's death. ZOG is actually gonna execute Pam and Stacey," Cheryl said. She wiped a tear away while watching the *Evening News* and the interview with Ira Vance.

"And now comes the Crucifixion," Jackie muttered.

"I just can't believe it," Joe said. "If Jesus was here, I'll bet he'd burst into that courtroom, guns blazing, and set them both free."

"They knew the risks when they took the oath," Jackie said coldly. "But don't worry, they're gonna be avenged. By the time next June rolls around the fucking, Zionist government that persecuted them will no longer exist."

"Where's Howie?" Cheryl said

"He's in the barn with Jason. He told me earlier that we wanted to start arming the bomb."

"You really love him, don't you?"

"Yes," Jackie sighed. "More than anything. Listen, all I have ever known in this life are lousy, two-bit hustlers. Howie's the best thing that's ever happened to me, and I say that we're going to be married."

"But he wants to die when the bomb goes off. You aren't going to have much of a life together."

"It doesn't matter." Jackie shrugged. "After Howie blows up the government, I'm probably going to get killed in the race war anyway. We'll be together with Yahweh in Valhalla."

1910 hours

"Okay Jason, we're ready to start arming the bomb," Howard said. "Hand me some of those blasting caps."

"Sure." He retrieved several boxes.

"You see this?" Howard said while holding up one of the blasting caps. Chalmers watched intently. "Each cap has three parts… an ignition charge of barium chromate, an intermediate lead- azide booster, and the main charge of RDX."

"How does it work?" Chalmers said as Joe entered the barn.

"Electrical current from the blasting machine will be sent to the base charge via the ignition and lead-azide components. The RDX portion will be inside the C4 wedge." Howard inserted a blasting cap into one of the C4 wedges. "When the RDX goes off, that triggers the C4 explosives."

The work was tedious. While Jason and Joe held the bomb, Howard inserted the blasting caps, taking care not to crimp any of the electrical wires. They were taking a break when Jackie and Cheryl came in carrying a large thermos of hot tea and a tray of fruit.

"Howie, we brought you some refreshments."

"Thanks," Howard said, gulping the tea.

"How's it going out here?"

"This is taking longer than I expected. We have to get it right. The arming of the bomb has to be done with great precision."

"You mean the placing of the blasting caps, right?" Cheryl said.

"Correct."

"How you going to set off all the C4 charges simultaneously?"

"Joe's got an old plunger-type blasting machine from when we were removing taproot tree stumps from the farm. I'm going to modify and connect it to a large distributor from his tractor," Howard said, pointing to the corner. "Next, I'll simply run electrical leads from the distributor to the blasting caps in the bomb. Those wires have to be exactly the same length."

"Will this thing deliver enough electricity to set off the caps?" Jackie said, examining the blasting machine.

"It should, after I make the necessary adjustments," Howard said, taking it from her hands. "The current from the blasting machine will enter the distributor and be evenly relayed to each of the forty-eight caps. I'll get you two to test the firing circuits with that galvanometer you stole. It's crude as shit, but I think it should get the job done."

Wednesday, December 9th
0945 hours
The White House, Situation Room

The FBI Director and Rabson arrived for a meeting with the president and members of the National Security Council. Rabson, having flown back from Denver just hours before, scarcely had time to greet his wife when the phone rang with the summons. The President was scheduled to leave on a seven-day, three-nation Asian tour, and wanted a briefing on the course of the investigation before he left. In addition to the FBI Director, the Attorney General, and the directors of the CIA and ATF were all present. There was a growing sense of apprehension among the various federal law enforcement heads.

"I called you all here today to be filled in on the status of the ongoing investigation. Where do we stand on your end, Bill?" the president said to the CIA Director.

"Mr. President, we're all in agreement that the stolen plutonium is still somewhere here in the United States. My agency has no indication suggesting that it was moved to a foreign country."

"What's happening on your front, George?"

"Sir, Rabson and I still believe that Werewolf is planning an attack on or around the Martin Luther King Holiday next month in one of the cities I mentioned."

"George, the ATF has come up with another scenario," Attorney General McCormick said.

"Oh?"

"They think the Werewolf wants to take out the Super Bowl."

"Based on what?"

"The game's being played at Ford Field Stadium in Detroit this year and the city's mostly black."

"I disagree," Rabson blurted out. "I feel that they have another target in mind."

"Agent Rabson, the ATF Director has another reason to suspect that it's going to be the Super Bowl," the Attorney General said. "Howard Brennan was born in Lansing. Our intelligence indicates that before Werewolf he was an active member of the *Aryan Posse*, a Michigan-based, far- right militia group while he was in the Air Force."

"Uh-huh," Rabson murmured.

"The Posse is described as being anti-government, anti-black, anti-Jew, anti-tax and just about anti-everything you can think of. We feel that Brennan and Lynch may be heading to Michigan to detonate the bomb in the Detroit area during the game."

"Sir, I still think they're going to strike on the holiday. And in one of the cities I have indicated," Rabson said, turning to the president. "We're running out of time."

"Don't worry, we're going to try to cover all the bases. A week before the holiday, we're going to saturate Denver, Atlanta and LA with federal agents. Lynch's and Brennan's pictures will be everywhere. It'll be the largest manhunt in US history."

"Everything'll will all set to go on the twelfth of January, sir," Longstreet interjected. "Regional Director Dumbrowski's people are covering the LA area, and Bill Blaylock's got Atlanta; I'm having Tom Kelly send over some of his people to help Frank Bledsoe cover Denver."

The meeting was adjourned. Rabson was right. Time was running out.

Barbarians At the Gate

"For all we have and are. For all our children's fate. Stand up and take the war. The Hun is at the gate!"

— Rudyard Kipling, from *"For All We Have and Are."*

The manhunt was on. Jacqueline Lynch and Howard Brennan, having already been added to the FBI's Ten Most Wanted list months earlier, were now the object of the greatest criminal investigation in the nation's history. Wanted posters, complete with their dated photographs, as well as more up-to-date composite sketches appeared everywhere — post offices, billboards, shopping centers, bus and airline terminals. Interpol was alerted should the fugitives suddenly turn up aboard. Bureau Director Longstreet even made a guest appearance on the popular *Crime Watch 2000* television program appealing for the public's cooperation in finding the fugitives. Hundreds of false sightings were reported.

Meanwhile, at the Fredericksburg hide-out, work on the bomb's arming continued at an accelerated pace. Earlier, while at a Fredericksburg hardware store, Ariadne and Jason had purchased additional lengths of electrical wire that would be needed to connect the bomb to the blasting machine. Indeed, the work had become a group project: while the men painstakingly inserted the bomb's blasting caps, Cheryl and Jackie tested the firing circuits with the galvanometer. Ariadne ran periodic errands or kept an eye on little Paranoya. On a more festive note, with the Christmas holidays just days away, the terrorists spent their spare time decorating a small tree that Joe had picked up while in town.

Code Name: Juggernaut

Wednesday, December 16th
1730 hours
near Fredericksburg, VA

It was Paranoya's first birthday; while Jason, Ariadne and the Reckes gathered in the kitchen to celebrate with cake and ice cream Howard was watching television coverage of the signing of the Pacific Rim Free Trade Agreement during the president's Asian summit. Jackie joined him.

"Come on, let's wish the baby a happy birthday," she said, handing him a piece of cake.

"Later… Here, come and look at this. Makes you sick!" he ranted. "This is why I've got to destroy the government. We're heading for a one- world ZOG dictatorship. Sure as shooting."

"What do you mean?" Jackie walked over to the television.

"We're heading for world government. I'm watching it now. They just signed that stupid free trade treaty; the country is being sold down the river!" Howard seethed with anger. He and Jackie listened in sullen resignation as the president gave an impromptu address to beaming Asian and American trade negotiators.

"The signing of the Pacific Rim Free Trade Agreement Treaty marks a giant, no — rather a historic step forward in the elimination of trade barriers around the world. This is truly the dawn of a new era in world trade. Everybody comes out a winner," the president said as he warmly shook the Japanese Trade Minister's hand.

"Look. You see?" Howard said, a tear slowly running down his cheek. "That idiot there not only sold his country out to the Nips, he's actually boasting about it."

"I know, Honey, I know," she said soothingly.

"We're headed for one world government. Mark my words! Little

Paranoya in there shouldn't have to grow up with all this…It just ain't fair!" he sobbed.

"I know, Shhhh… we'll make it fair."

"Damn right, we'll make it fair!"

"Now calm down, Howie, please. After all, the Senate hasn't even ratified the treaty yet."

"And they're never going to get the chance! Not if I have my way. 'Cause on the twenty-sixth of next month they're all going to be dead!" Foamy spittle dripped from Howard's lip. "By the way, have you and Cheryl finished testing the firing circuits?"

"Yes, Howie, the galvanometer worked real good. We found several faulty blasting caps. We got rid of them. All the ones in the bomb will function properly."

"Good," Howard said, now somewhat calmer. The couple meandered back into the kitchen to join the others.

"Ariadne," Howard said on entering. "Yes?"

"I'm going to need you to run an errand for me."

"Sure, anything."

"I'll need you to carry some money to Lansing. Come on out to the barn." The young woman followed Howard outside. Reaching into the rear compartment of the truck, Howard produced several bulging suitcases. He opened one, revealing a trove of cash.

"Look at all that money!" she said.

"This is more than five hundred grand cash."

"It's part of the haul Werewolf got when we knocked over an armored car in Denver last year. Killed two guards," Jackie said, suddenly appearing in the barn's doorway.

"Yeah, I remember that. The cops said that over six million bucks was taken," Chalmers said.

"I've decided to distribute this money to other, like-minded Aryan patriot groups before the bloodbath begins. They can use it to buy weapons and food. We must share what Yahweh has given us. We're going to start using ZOG's own blood money against it," Howard said, closing the suitcase.

"My mother has a house in suburban Lansing. Here is the address. I want you to take the money there. She'll know what to do with it. You can stay with her at our Lansing safe house."

"What about Jason?"

"I may be needing Jason to help me with the bomb. You can handle this. Now get going."

"Sure Howie, no problem." Ariadne began loading the suitcases into her car.

The approaching Christmas holidays were anything but festive at the FBI Building in Washington. Frustration mounted. As a result of the airing of the *Crime Watch 2000* segment, hundreds of sightings of one or both of the fugitives were reported in California, Nevada, Florida, Ohio, Alabama, Texas and several other states. One couple, dead ringers for Lynch and Brennan, were arrested in Johannesburg, South Africa. Only after a twelve- hour detention was the mistake finally cleared up and the pair released. Werewolf sympathizers and cranks added to the confusion, deliberately calling in false information to send the agency down blind paths.

Friday, December 18th
1000 hours
J. Edgar Hoover FBI Building, Washington DC

"Rabson, the president is coming back next week from his Far-East trip. He's going to want to be briefed on the investigation. Have you got anything new?" Director Longstreet said.

"I'm afraid not, sir. So far, all the leads we're getting are turning out to be bum steers."

"Well, I've decided to act on the ATF Director's hunch. Early yesterday I ordered a surveillance team to East Lansing, Michigan."

"Oh?"

"Yeah. Intelligence confirms that Howard Brennan's elderly mother is living there. It seems that she's as crazy as he is. Local law enforcement reports that she's been active in various far-right wing hate groups in Michigan for years."

Rabson slowly nodded. The Director continued.

"It stands to reason that if the ATF is right and Brennan really wants to take out the Super Bowl next month, he'll probably stop off in Lansing to see the old woman."

"Very good, sir."

Saturday, December 19th
1240 hours
J. Edgar Hoover FBI Building, Washington, DC

As was becoming commonplace for his Saturdays, Rabson arrived at the office shortly after noon to catch up on paperwork and coordinate the bureau's role in the upcoming trial of the other terrorists.

"Doug, come in here," Longstreet called out to Rabson as he arrived.

"Yes sir?"

"We just got a communication from the surveillance team I sent to Michigan. It seems that they apprehended a woman arriving at Doris Brennan's home in suburban Lansing earlier today."

"Who is she?"

"We've tentatively identified her as one Ariadne Beausoleil."

Rabson paused, contemplating where he had heard that name before. "That's one of the two skinhead killers that eluded Tom Kelly's people in Salt Lake City during the sweep. We know that she was at the Price home in Greeley as well."

"Correct. What's more is that she had more than five hundred grand in cash hidden in her vehicle. It was part of the haul taken during that armored car robbery. It's beginning to look like the ATF may have been right. I've ordered the surveillance unit to lie low and just observe. Don't want to spook Lynch and Brennan if they're on the way there."

"Sir, you still believe that the target is Detroit?"

"All the signs are pointing to it being a likely candidate… a large, mostly black city located in a state that's a hotbed for militia and white supremacist activity. What's more, there's the added inducement of the Super Bowl on January thirty-first… You still think they're going to hit somewhere else?"

Rabson paused a long moment before answering.

"Yes sir, I do. I still think that the Werewolf is going to make the strike on the Martin King holiday in either Denver, Atlanta, or maybe LA."

"Well, I realize that this is short notice, but I want you to go to Michigan to question Beausoleil."

"Me sir?"

"You're probably the most familiar with the case. I want you in on that phase of the interrogation."

"Yes sir." The director got up and walked Rabson to the door.

"Try to get her to break. Lean on her. You can offer her the same deal that we gave Davies. Anything. She almost certainly will know where the fugitives are hiding. Bill Blaylock in Atlanta has had no luck in wearing down the other terrorists. This Beausoleil woman may be our last hope."

"Very good, sir."

"But I want you back here by the twenty-third. The President's going to want to be briefed then."

"Yes sir."

Monday, December 21st
1530 hours
Capital City Airport, Lansing, MI

The flight from Washington to Lansing had been anything but uneventful. Michigan's capital was in the throes of a monster snowstorm, and Rabson's flight had to circle the field for twenty-five minutes while plows cleared the runways. The agent was picked up and taken to the Bureau's regional office by Special Agent Arthur Gripp. Agent Gripp had been assigned to the stakeout unit watching the Brennan home. He proceeded to fill Rabson in on the investigation as they drove into town.

"Welcome to Lansing, Mr. Rabson."

"Thanks... Do you people always have lousy weather like this?"

"Oh no, the really bad weather won't get here until February," Gripp said jokingly.

"Sorry I asked... So, what's the status of this Beausoleil woman?"

"This chick is way out. Totally psycho. She was high on crystal meth when we busted her. Can't get anything out of her. Couple days ago, our boys on surveillance picked her up while staking the Brennan house."

"Okay."

"She was carrying three large suitcases with over five hundred grand… all taken in that armored car heist in Denver."

"Anything else?"

"Twenty grams of methamphetamine, some cocaine and a thirty-two-caliber semiautomatic handgun equipped with a silencer were all found in her purse. Imagine an eighteen-year-old girl toting hardware like that," Gripp said, slowly shaking his head.

"What about the Brennan woman?"

"Another nut job. We've got orders to continue the surveillance of the house."

After arriving at the regional office, Rabson relaxed in the interrogation room while the prisoner was being brought in. While waiting, he flipped through her files. The 'rap sheet' from Utah and Louisiana was long: shoplifting, assault, suspected arson, vandalism, drug possession and prostitution. The agent found it hard to believe that someone could amass such a number of run-ins with the authorities by the tender age of eighteen, let alone be involved in a terrorist plot. He began thinking of how his own daughters had turned out and thanked his lucky stars.

He also saw a copy of *The Carson Diaries* among the woman's possessions. Flipping through it, he began reading all the gory details of race war, mass murder and the suicide bombing of the IRS Building. Glancing up, he was startled to notice Ariadne Beausoleil standing in front of him. She was wearing jeans and a black T-shirt with the words "ARYAN PRIDE WORLDWIDE" and a Celtic cross screen-printed in white characters across the front. The SS Death Skull tattoo was prominent on her left arm. Casually smoking a cigarette, the petite brunette displayed no emotion.

"Glad to see you're reading the truth," the woman said as Rabson closed the book.

He leaned slowly back in his chair and said, "Ariadne Tatiana Beausoleil... I'm Douglas Rabson, FBI."

"Oh yeah... Whatever," she said, rolling her eyes. "And my friends call me Skin-Girl. Sexy Skin-Girl." Smoke rings whirled around the woman's head. "But you can call me 'Blowjob,' 'Ariadne Blowjob'." Legs spread open in a provocative pose she flopped down in the chair across from Rabson.

"Oh, you're a real tough girl, aren't you?"

"I'm tough enough... I sure ain't scared of *you*. So you can kiss my ass," she said, blowing smoke into the agent's face. "I ain't got nothing to say, so let's get this shit over so they can take me back to that fleabag they call a cell. Why I gotta eat with niggers?"

Rabson slowly leaned forward and said, "Okay Skin-Girl, lose the gangsta-girl attitude. Listen, you're in a lot of trouble. That money we found in your car was stolen in an armored car robbery back in Denver. Two guards were shot to death."

"That wasn't me. I ain't done nothing... I found it. And you lousy ZOG cops can't prove nothing. Besides, I'm a minor. Only thing you got on me is couple grams of crystal meth they found in my purse... Why all you ZOG pigs always hassling me anyway?"

"We know that you were also involved in the murder of a black youth in Salt Lake City back in April," Rabson said, opening her file.

"Ha! From who? That fucking rat Eight-Ball Hoover? That

fucking asshole's dead, remember?" Ariadne began to giggle.

"Oh, you think that's funny?"

"Yeah. Fucking race traitor had a slight accident, didn't he? Swallowed his balls, I hear. They fished his ass out of Lake Utah couple of months ago. I'm glad he's fucking dead... Anyway, that ugly nigger I whacked deserved it. Honest, it was self-defense, man. Had his dirty black hands all over me... I was fighting for my virtue... Nigger tried to rape me!" Ariadne lounged back in the chair, now smiling. "Yeah...I shot that nigger in the balls. He just dropped... started rolling 'round. I shot him again. Blood was coming up outta his mouth, and the nigger just went dead. It was way cool!"

Rabson could see that this line of interrogation wasn't working. He changed his tactics. He edged closer to the woman.

"Well, Miss Beausoleil... uh, Skin-Girl, we also have a *live* witness, one Bruce Davies, who places you at the scene of a massacre of five security guards at the Alliance Construction Company in Greeley last July fourth." Ariadne sat motionless. She placed the cigarette in an ashtray. Sensing her dismay, the agent continued his attack. "We also have another witness... and physical evidence as well, placing you at the scene of another murder in Greeley on the twenty-fifth of October. Guy named Mitchell Price. You know how he died? He was electrocuted in the bathtub. Kind of like what the Colorado authorities are going to do to you if you don't cooperate!"

"Wait!" Ariadne said, leaning forward with a pout. "What do you cops want?"

"The Bureau wants Lynch and Brennan... and the plutonium."

"Well, what's in it for me? What do I get? What about some kind of fucking reward for me?"

"We can offer you the same deal that we gave Bruce Davies.

Incarceration under an assumed name, protection for your family. That's it."

"That's it? Suppose that ain't good enough?"

"Ariadne, you want to know what two thousand volts of electricity can do to human flesh? Try to imagine for a moment that you just burned a steak— "

"Okay. Okay."

"Have Lynch and Brennan completed the bomb?"

"Yeah. They finished it last month."

"What's the target?"

"They didn't tell me," she said with a shrug.

"I'm getting tired of hearing that from all you Werewolf people!" Rabson shouted, again pulling his chair forward. "Listen, honey, that electric chair is getting closer and closer! And we *do* put minors on Death Row. So, you'd better open up… right now!"

"Hey, *I don't know!*" Ariadne said defensively. Although apprehensive, she feared the vengeance of Werewolf more than the FBI. "I only know that I was sent here with the money. They want to pass it out to other white groups before the race war starts. You know, to buy weapons and shit."

"Where are they now?"

"Don't know that either. They move around a lot, you know, to keep from gettin' caught, but they're coming here in a few weeks. They're going to blow up some black town with the bomb. That's gonna start the race war."

"All right, when are they coming here?"

"Sometime around the middle of next month. That's all I know. Swear to God," the young woman said, raising her hand as if taking an oath. Rabson watched her eyes drift upwards toward the ceiling as she gave her answer. He knew she was lying.

"I've got one more question for you, Ariadne," the agent sighed. "You're an attractive young woman. Undoubtedly you have some potential, why did you throw it all away and join the gang?"

The young woman shrugged and gave a defiant reply. "I don't believe that the races should mix. That's all. I don't see nothing wrong with that. I mean, you gotta protect your race. That's all we got. It says so, right in the Bible. I mean the Jews are the seed of the Devil. They kidnap and sacrifice little white children for their blood rituals. And anyway, they killed Christ... The Aryan Church and the Werewolf took me in. They was the only family I know."

Rabson merely shook his head. He was surprised to find himself feeling a certain amount of pity for the young woman. Ariadne rambled on, becoming more vitriolic.

"Where was all you ZOG cops when my old man was drunk, beating the living shit outta me and mom? Or when my little sister was raped by them three black mud apes back in Slidell? She said they took turns... Like they was goin' to the bathroom in her mouth." A tear slowly ran down her cheek. "Niggers always wanna try to get some of this... and they're willing to commit rape to get it!"

"You know what gets me? All them niggers you see on the fucking TV selling sneakers, diet soda and shit, playing basketball making *beaucoup* money and then they all scream *discrimination*. Talking all this affirmative action shit! And what's up with all this Kwanzaa and Juneteenth bullshit? My boyfriend Jason and me can't even find a job! The blacks and other races get anything they want. When the Aryan does it, he gets slammed down. Pisses me off! Hey, I finally said 'fuck it!' That's when I joined the Werewolf," she finished, crushing her cigarette out in the ashtray.

"And you had to murder that black kid to get in?"

"Hey, I stood up for my race... Told you before that nigger had it coming, talking sassy to me like that. Where I come from, niggers don't dare raise their hand up against a white woman. What was I supposed to do, just let that dirty, shit-colored nigger rape me?"

Ariadne began rocking back and forth in her chair, lost in her tirade. "Somebody said, 'We gotta do something about these niggers'... So, we did. Anyway, niggers don't belong here. They should all go back to Africa... to the jungle." She gave a shrug. "What's all the fuss about anyway? I mean, it was only a nigger... Oops, I forgot. It's not nice to say 'nigger.'"

"All right, that's enough," Rabson sighed, breaking a pencil in frustration. "We're finished for now."

"You know, you're kinda cute. Listen... give you a blowjob, let you fuck me if you let me go," she said while leaning over, gazing into the agent's eyes.

"Look Ariadne, you don't want anything to do with me. I'm a Jew," Rabson said as he pushed away from the table. "Besides, I've got to go *kidnap and sacrifice* some children now." He gestured to a female agent to remove the prisoner.

"At least you're a white Jew," the young woman said with a shrug as she was being escorted out of the room. The agent stared at her in stunned silence.

"Well, I told you so," Agent Gripp said, slowly shaking his head and walking over to Rabson. "Whacko... absolutely shithouse crazy."

"It looks as if all of these Werewolf people are absolute nutjobs," Rabson said in a low tone. He slowly shook his head in frustration.

"Ain't no way any of what she said is going to be admissible in court. She didn't have legal counsel present."

"I know. I'm not worried about that now. She was lying through her teeth. Right now, the Bureau is interested in retrieving the stolen plutonium and getting Lynch and Brennan."

Wednesday, December 23rd
0900 hours
The White House Cabinet Room

"Welcome back, Mr. President," Attorney General McCormick said, beaming. "The Asian trip was a triumph."

"Thank you, Jen, it's very good to be back. By removing all those trade barriers between us and the countries of East Asia, I hope that this trip will be the administration's Christmas present to the nation, and the capstone to my presidency."

"Not to mention worth another seventy-five electoral votes next year when you're up for reelection," McCormick chuckled; the room erupted in moderate laughter.

"Have there been any new developments regarding the stolen plutonium during my absence, George?"

"Sir, I think I'll let Agent Rabson make the report." The FBI Director gestured to Rabson.

"Sir," Rabson began, clearing his throat. "Since last Thursday, a stakeout team has maintained surveillance of the home of Howard Brennan's mother in suburban Lansing. Several days ago, a suspected Werewolf terrorist, one Ariadne Beausoleil, was captured as a result of that surveillance."

The President nodded approvingly.

"I interrogated the prisoner; at first I thought that she seemed willing to cooperate."

"Get anything useful?"

"She indicated that the device has been operational since late last month."

A collective gasp could be heard.

"Let me get this straight, you're telling me that these killers now possess a functional atomic bomb?" the president said.

"According to the Beausoleil woman, that is correct. She also indicated that Lynch and Brennan intend to move the bomb to Michigan sometime in mid-January."

"So, it looks like the ATF was right after all," the Attorney General interjected.

"I'm just not so sure, ma'am."

"Why not? Detroit's a mostly black city. And Michigan is a hotbed for a lot of far-right-wing militia activity. It all looks pretty cut-and-dry to me."

"Too damned cut-and-dry if you ask me… Beausoleil was lying."

"Why?"

"Ma'am, for one thing, I saw this woman's crime record. Besides a host of lesser crimes, she may have been involved in as many as seven murders, honesty just doesn't come across as her strong suit."

"Well, what do you think she's up to?" the president said.

"Deception, pure and simple. Trying to divert our attention from the real target. Frankly, I think she's just feeding us this information."

"Thank you," the president said. "Your concerns are duly noted. But I'm going to order additional manpower to help cover the Detroit area."

"Very good sir," Rabson sighed.

"Don't worry. The cities you named will receive adequate coverage in time for the Martin King holiday."

"Thank you, sir."

"George," the president said, turning to the FBI Director. "How's the preparation for the beginning of the trial for the other terrorists shaping up?"

"Bill Blaylock is in charge of security. He's doing a good job. He's turned the federal courthouse in Atlanta into a veritable fortress. Ira Vance is heading the prosecution team. Everything'll be ready to start by the twenty-eighth."

"Fine." The meeting broke up.

Friday, December 25th
0800 hours
The Recke farm, near Fredericksburg, VA

After three days of intermittent snowfall, Christmas Day dawned bright and crisp. A gentle breeze was blowing across the Rappahannock. The twenty-five thousand inhabitants of Fredericksburg were slowly stirring from their slumber. Here, as across the nation, wide-eyed children raced to the Christmas tree, eager for their presents.

On this Christmas Day there was also a flurry of activity at the Recke farm. The Reckes, Chalmers and Jackie had been told to wait in the den for an important announcement. The night before, after more than three weeks work Howard and Chalmers inserted the last two of the blasting caps: the bomb was fully armed. Now exhausted and triumphant, Howard emerged. He began speaking in a trembling voice,

"I've called you all together to bear witness before Yahweh the solemn union in matrimony of myself to this woman," Howard said, gesturing towards a clearly surprised Jackie.

"Read this," Howard said, thrusting a crumpled sheet of paper to Joe. He stood next to Jackie.

"Do you," Recke began, facing Howard. "Howard Douglas Brennan swear and affirm before Yahweh that you were born Aryan and are free of any Jewish or colored blood?"

"I do."

"Do you, Jacqueline Diane Lynch swear and affirm before Yahweh that you were born Aryan and are free of any Jewish or colored blood?"

"I do," she stammered tearfully.

"Do you, Howard, take Jacqueline to be thy wife, to love and cherish 'til the day of your passing into the bosom of Yahweh?"

"I do."

"Do you, Jacqueline, take Howard to be thy husband, to love and cherish 'til the day of your passing into the bosom of Yahweh?"

"Yes! Oh yes!"

"Then, in accordance with the laws of Yahweh, I pronounce you both married." At that, Howard reached into his pocket and pulled out the wedding band he had taken from Suzanne. He placed it on Jackie's finger. Cheryl brought in a tray filled with cakes and small cups of champagne, while Chalmers put a recording of the bridal march of Wagner's Third Act of the opera *Lohengrin* on an old record player. Jackie and Howard kissed warmly.

1030 hours

"I think that was a wonderful thing you did, Howie," Cheryl noted. "Jackie really loves you."

"Well, Jackie deserved it. She's been loyal to me all this time. I guess it really means something to her to be *Mrs. Howard Brennan.* This is the means I'll reward her," Howard said, displaying no emotion. The "marriage" meant nothing to him. "Let her enjoy herself. In just over a month, she's going to be a widow."

"You really have to die in the blast?"

"I have to, Cheryl. When I push the plunger down on the blasting machine, the bomb goes off. Anyway, this country's government is nothing but a big insane asylum. After I've destroyed it, things can only get better."

"Just what else is left to do before we're ready?"

"Basically, it's set to go. I've just got to connect the electrical leads that will run from the distributor to the blasting caps. I've already started to modify your husband's old blasting machine."

"I see."

"I'm gonna alter it so that it will deliver seven hundred and twenty volts, that's approximately fifteen volts per cap."

"That's enough to trigger the blasting caps?"

"Oh, that's more than enough. Simultaneously, that's very important. The compression of the plutonium core must be uniform. In order for the full nuclear blast to take place, the detonation of all the C4 charges must occur within a matter of milliseconds. We won't have a second chance."

"Now that you got the bomb fully armed, what are the chances of, say, a premature explosion? After all, we don't want to level the town of Fredericksburg."

"Spontaneous fission? Million-to-one long shot. I won't even connect the blasting machine to the bomb until just before I'm going to use it. Don't worry," Howard said.

At that moment, Jackie came in and walked up to her 'husband.'

"So how does it feel, Mrs. Brennan?"

"Feels wonderful. Right now, you've made me the happiest woman in the world."

"Well, I'm afraid that this ain't much of a honeymoon. I'm sorry."

"Shhhh, Howie. I don't want a honeymoon. I only want you, that's all."

On Monday, December twenty-eighth, the trial of the other Werewolf suspects finally got underway. Amid tight security, Nathan Mantooth, Jeff Collins, Becky Stephens and Joachim Klimper were brought to the Atlanta federal courthouse. Sullenly, the defendants listened to the reading of the indictment. The litany of crimes that prosecutor Ira Vance read was a virtual carbon copy of the one presented during the first trial. The suspects displayed no emotion when Vance announced in closing that the government intended to seek the death penalty. Surrounded by US marshals, the government's star witness, Davies, arrived. He was ill at ease at the thought of having now to spend the rest of his life *incognito*. The defendants glared at him with a menacing gaze.

New Year's Day was fast approaching, and the government was intensifying its efforts to apprehend the remaining terrorists. Federal agencies quietly informed city officials in Denver, Los Angeles, Atlanta and Chicago of the possibility that white supremacists might attempt to disrupt observances of the Martin Luther King holiday. Additional units from the various federal law enforcement agencies had already been in place to aid in the investigation. For his part, Rabson had been ordered to help coordinate security arrangements in the Denver area with Frank Bledsoe.

Monday, January 4th
1043 hours
Denver International Airport

"Rabson? Doug Rabson?" Agent Bledsoe said as he saw Rabson emerge from the terminal. "I trust you had a good flight."

"Yes sir, very nice. Looks like I'm going to be here until after the Martin King holiday. I'll fill you in."

The pair walked through the terminal. "Frank, we think they have an operational bomb."

"Oh shit!"

"We're looking for a late model, white Ford truck with a matching shell. Brennan and Lynch may be using it to transport the bomb."

"Well, that narrows it down to about fifty thousand suspects… We'll start checking around. The office here will coordinate with local law enforcement. Right now, we've got Lynch and Brennan's sketches and photographs just about everywhere."

"What about local white supremacist activity? Anything on that front?" Rabson said.

"No. Those sonsabitches have been lying low. Couple skinhead groups and the local KKK are planning a big hate rally at the Capitol building on the holiday. They pull this shit every year. You know, free publicity and all."

"Yeah, I remember that near riot last year. It made the national evening news."

Monday, January 18th
0730 hours
FBI Field Office, Denver, CO

The day dawned clear and mild. The weather forecast had been for snow showers but the weather held off. After more than a week of preparations, the King Holiday had arrived. Bledsoe arrived at his office, exhausted from coordinating the various security details. Rabson was already there.

"Sir, I have here a list of the events scheduled for the King holiday," Rabson said as Bledsoe entered.

"Fine. Read them to me," Bledsoe said, pouring a cup of coffee.

"There's an interdenominational prayer breakfast being held at City Park starting at eight a.m. Something billed as a Brotherhood March down Colfax Avenue is set to begin at nine-thirty; everything culminates at eleven-thirty with a large rally at the Civic Center across from the Capitol Building."

"Okay, anything else?" Bledsoe said as he took a gulp of coffee.

"Some civil rights notables from across the country, plus a number of local dignitaries are scheduled to speak at the rally. I talked to the Park's Service last night. They estimate that maybe sixty thousand people might show up if the weather stays good."

"Holy cow! What a target!" Bledsoe said, spilling his coffee. "Better fill me in on all the security arrangements."

"Since last night, we've had a team of agents working with local police making a series of hourly sweeps of a fifteen-block radius of the downtown area. We'll continue these sweeps up to and during the rally. Already, two suspicious white Ford vehicles were checked out."

"Okay, fine. What else?"

"Local police will be strategically placed along the entire parade route. They'll be ready to intervene at the first hint of trouble. They have orders to keep Klan demonstrators and marchers at least one city block apart."

"Anything on Lynch and Brennan?"

"Their pictures have been distributed at every hotel and motel in the metro area. We've got several agents working undercover at the Hyatt and Holiday Inns. A woman resembling Jacqueline Lynch was taken into custody last night. She checked out clean and was released."

Bledsoe nodded.

"Very good. Now all we can do is wait… Lord, I'll be glad when this day is over."

"How are all the arrangements going in the other cities?" Rabson said.

"I talked to Bill Blaylock last evening. You wouldn't believe the elaborate security precautions they're taking in Atlanta. Besides Blaylock's people, the whole town's literally crawling with Secret Service."

"Well, the president is scheduled to give a speech there this afternoon," Rabson said. "Heard anything from Michigan?"

"No. Not a thing. And the Super Bowl is set for the thirty-first."

Save for some scattered minor incidents with white supremacists, the Martin Luther King Holiday festivities across the country were peaceful. Parades, speeches and marches were the order of the day as the nation paused to honor the late civil rights leader's message. The largest celebrations were in Atlanta, where the president of the United States gave an inspiring forty-five-minute speech on Dr King's legacy to a cheering multiracial crowd.

1645 hours
Near Fredericksburg, VA

The Brennans and Reckes were seated in the living room glumly watching the *CNA Evening News*. The broadcast's first segments dealt with the coverage of the day's holiday events, focusing on the president's speech in Atlanta.

"Look at that! Makes you sick!" Howard shouted. "Listen to all that lousy Brotherhood crap! He's got to be stopped!"

"Shhhh… Yeah, I know Howie. I know," Jackie said, gently hugging him.

"Just look at how that man grovels," he ranted, pulling away from Jackie and pointing at the TV, "and all just to get the no-good nigger vote! That's what gets me, the way he keeps sucking up to the niggers like that."

"And lord-have-mercy he talks for so long," Cheryl yawned.

"Well, in just a few days I'm going to fix all that… I swear to holy Jesus that's gonna be the last speech that son-of-a-bitch will ever make!" Howard screamed. Frothy droplets of foam appeared along the edges of his mouth.

Code Name: Juggernaut

Götterdämmerung

"The President shall from time to time give to the Congress information of the state of the Union, and recommend to their consideration as measures as he shall judge necessary and expedient..."

— Article II, Section 3, United States Constitution

"...How many ages hence shall this our lofty scene be acted out in states yet unborn and accents yet unknown..."

— Cassius, speaking of the assassination of Caesar, from Shakespeare's *Julius Caesar*

"...And a little child shall lead them..."

— Isaiah 11:6

The fact that the Martin Luther King holiday had passed without serious incident, coupled with Ariadne Beausoleil's vague "confession", merely added validity to the ATF Director's theory concerning the Super Bowl in Detroit as the Werewolf gang's intended target. Accordingly, Attorney General McCormick ordered George Longstreet to immediately deploy twenty-five additional FBI agents to Michigan. In addition, greater surveillance was maintained at the Lansing home of Doris Brennan should her eldest son attempt to visit.

Meanwhile, an exhausted Rabson had flown back to Washington on Tuesday evening. During the long flight, he pondered why the terrorists had not attacked. He had been certain that the Werewolf would attempt to strike on the Martin Luther King Holiday. *Was the ATF right after all? Maybe Ariadne Beausoleil wasn't lying. Perhaps Brennan and Lynch were already in Michigan,* he thought to himself.

Although tired, he had promised his eldest daughter Sarah that he would help her prepare for an upcoming test in her English history class. Spent from the long trip, however, he immediately went to bed. Sarah would understand. The next day, still weary from jet-lag, he reported to work.

Wednesday, January 20th
0803 hours
J Edgar Hoover Building, Washington, DC

"Well, looks like the Werewolf was a no-show last Monday," Director Longstreet said as Rabson stumbled into his office.

"Yes sir. Looks like I was wrong."

"Don't sweat it. With that massive show of force, we probably spooked the bejezus out of those bastards."

"No sir, they've gone this far, nobody's going to intimidate them now. They still intend to strike somewhere."

"Well, you look terrible… Take a couple of days off." He could see Rabson's surprise. "The Attorney General wants me to send another group of agents to Detroit. She believes that the ATF may be right… the Super Bowl's the target. I'm putting you in charge of the task force we're sending. Frank Bledsoe and the president both recommended it."

"Thank you, sir."

"In the meantime, try to spend the next couple of days with your family. Try to relax. That's an order. I want you to be fresh for Detroit. Be there by the twenty-sixth. Don't worry, if anything breaks, I'll make sure that you're informed."

"Yes sir… I guess now I can help Sarah prepare for her test. I'll be Public Enemy Number One if I don't. I've already had to break my promise to her once."

"What's the matter, Doug?" Longstreet could see the strain in his stiffened expression.

"Just this, sir. It seems to me that we're putting an awful lot of our resources in Michigan. If the Werewolf's target is somewhere else, we're going to be spread pretty thin."

"Yeah, I know. It's a calculated risk. But that's what the boss lady wants… I'll be joining you there on the twenty-eighth."

"Oh?"

"Yeah, I would come earlier, but the president wants me to be on hand when he gives the State of the Union speech next week," the director sighed. "You know, politics. I think he intends to use McCormick and me as props for when he fights for his crime bill this year."

"Very good, sir," Rabson said, departing.

"Give my love to Rachel and the girls."

"Thank you, sir, I sure will."

1040 hours
Near Fredericksburg, VA

Howard and Jackie were in the barn. Since early morning, the pair had been hard at work making the final preparations on the bomb. Working in the cramped area of the truck's bed, Howard painstakingly removed approximately two inches of the rubber insulation from the ends of each of the wires from the forty-eight blasting caps. Carefully, he spliced them to corresponding wires leading to the old tractor's distributor. Jackie secured each shunt by wrapping it with electrical tape.

"There, it's done," Howard said, as he stood back and wiped the sweat from his forehead. "Now all I'll have to do is connect the blasting machine to the distributor. I'll do that as soon as I get to Washington."

"It's beautiful. Fucking beautiful. And to think that right now we're just *this close!*"

"Jackie, here, get on the truck. I want you to stand next to the bomb. Let's get some cheesecake pictures for posterity," Howard chuckled. While Howard retrieved his camera, Jackie ran back to the house. A moment later she returned, clad in a revealing outfit. Like a fashion model, she began to pose next to the device as Howard snapped off a series of photographs.

Rabson took the director's advice and went back to his suburban home. For the past several months, he had seen precious little of his family; now it seemed a good opportunity to have a little 'quality time.' He was relaxing in the den watching *Congressional News Channel* when Rachel and the girls arrived home. Sarah Rabson, a precocious sixth grader, had an English history exam scheduled for the next day. While Rabson wasn't much on history, he nevertheless had promised his daughter that he would quiz her over the subject matter. Rachel Rabson cleared the living room table while Sarah retrieved her books.

"Okay honey, you're going to have to bear with me on this. You know that Daddy isn't much on history… Okay, first question, who was forced to sign the Magna Carta?" Rabson said slowly, reading from the child's textbook.

"King John signed it in twelve-fifteen, around the time of Robin Hood. At a place called Runnymede," the child said with a confident smile.

Rabson flipped over to another section of the book. "Right… What king started the Protestant Reformation in England?"

"Henry the Eighth did it, in fifteen thirty- four!"

"Good... When was the Spanish Armada defeated?"

"That's easy, it was in fifteen eighty-eight! Come on, give me something harder Daddy!" The child was bouncing up and down on the chair, brimming with enthusiasm.

"All right... Let's see, which Prime Minister served the longest?"

"Ah... Robert Walpole."

"Who led the Roundheads in the English Civil War?"

"Oliver Cromwell, I think."

"Very good Sarah. Boy, you really know your English history. They ought to put you on one of those TV quiz shows so Daddy can retire...Okay, here's a tough one. Who was executed for the Gun Powder Plot in sixteen oh-five?"

Sarah paused briefly and gave her answer. "I think it was a man called Guy Fawkes."

Rabson checked the answer. He froze momentarily, pondering where he had last seen that name before. He closed the book and leaned over closer to his daughter. "Tell me about the Gun Powder Plot, Sarah."

"Guy Fawkes tried to blow up the king and the Houses of Parliament! The English got a holiday to celebrate it. In November, I think... Why are you staring at me like that Daddy?" the child said, drawing back with a quizzical look.

Guy Fawkes... Blow up the king and Houses of Parliament? Guy Fawkes? My God! Could it be? Is it possible? Rabson thought to himself as he suddenly recalled Howard Brennan's chilling letter of last November. "Oh, it's nothing honey, Daddy was just thinking about something else."

The tutorial session went on for another thirty minutes until

Sarah's bedtime.

"Thank you, Daddy! I should really ace my test tomorrow. You helped me a lot!" the beaming child said while clearing her books away.

"And thank you, sweetheart. You may have solved my problem too."

After Sarah went to bed, Rabson carefully began reading her textbook, in particular the part dealing with King James the First and the abortive Gun Powder Plot of 1605. Rachel sat in a stunned silence, incredulous that her husband, who had always hated history, was now suddenly engrossed in his daughter's sixth grade textbook.

The next morning, Rabson went to the public library. There he read several books on the subject of the Fawkes conspiracy. Examining articles from old news magazines, he recalled the events surrounding Colonel Brennan's dismissal from the Air Force. Finally, he thought back to his perusing of Ariadne Beausoleil's copy of *The Carson Diaries* and the chilling description of the IRS bombing. Everything was becoming clear. Convinced that he had solved the mystery, he drove to FBI Headquarters. Director Longstreet had just concluded a meeting with the Assistant Attorney General when a panting Rabson burst into his office.

Thursday, January 21st
1340 hours
J. Edgar Hoover Building

"Rabson?" the startled FBI Director said. "You were ordered to take several days off. What in hell are you doing here?"

"Excuse me, sir. I believe that I may know where and when the Werewolf intends to detonate the bomb."

"Oh?" Longstreet said as he slowly rose from his chair.

"It's been right in front of us all along... I believe that they're going to explode it right here. In Washington, DC... on the twenty-sixth. Next Tuesday. We don't have much time."

"I see. Tell me, just how did you come by this intelligence?"

"I know that this is going to sound crazy, but last night I was quizzing my oldest daughter for an exam and —"

"You were what? You're right about one thing, Rabson, you are crazy. Last week you scared the hell out of us... Remember, you were wrong about Martin Luther King Day."

"My daughter Sarah has a test in her English history class today. I was quizzing her over the so-called Gun Powder Plot of sixteen-oh-five."

The Director lowered his head, trying hard to suppress a smile. "Doug, what does something that happened more than four centuries ago have to do with the Werewolf and the stolen plutonium?"

Rabson approached the desk. "Sir, do you remember that letter that Howard Brennan sent to the Bureau back last November?"

"Yeah, I got it right here. So what?" the director said, retrieving a photocopy of it from the top drawer.

"Please read it."

Longstreet adjusted his glasses and casually scanned the document. "He's threatening us with weapons of mass destruction. Sometime during the month of January... I don't see anything here that would indicate precisely where or when he plans to detonate the bomb."

"Look at how he signed the letter."

"Signed it 'Guy Fawkes.' So?"

"Sir, Guy Fawkes is the name of the man who was involved in the Gun Powder Plot. I was reading a couple books on the subject in the library this morning."

"I still don't get you," the director said, shaking his head.

"The Gun Powder Plot was a terrorist conspiracy to blow up King James the First and the Houses of Parliament in England… See? I think Howard Brennan plans to destroy this country's government in his own twisted version of the Gun Powder Plot! Signing this letter *Guy Fawkes,* he unwittingly gave us this important clue."

The director suddenly seemed to take notice. Rabson continued.

"What's more, remember all those threats that Howard Brennan made when he was cashiered from the Air Force? Wild talk about wanting a kamikaze-like attack on the White House with a hijacked seven-forty-seven?"

"Yes, I remember."

"I also read all that stuff in the press about his dismissal. All those threats."

Longstreet got up and stared out the window along Pennsylvania Avenue towards the Capitol with a worried look.

"And, also, Bruce Davies mentioned to me about the Werewolf trying to start a race war," Rabson said, following the director to the window. "Washington is about seventy percent black. If a bomb in the high kiloton range was to be detonated here, the casualties would be enormous and disproportionately black. Werewolf is counting on that fact to help trigger the racial unrest."

"All right," Longstreet said, turning. "You said that you think that you know when."

"It's simple. When during the month of January does the whole of the US government assemble in one place?"

The FBI Director briefly pondered the question. "The State of the Union speech next week. Is it possible? But Doug, what about the Beausoleil woman and Detroit?"

"Forget her. She was lying. Beausoleil had a racist book on her at her arrest which described the bombing of the IRS here in Washington... I took one look at her rap sheet and didn't trust her. Howard Brennan is a very clever criminal. He knew that we were on to him, that we'd be watching his mother's home in Lansing, and probably sent Beausoleil up there as a decoy, knowing that we'd arrest her."

"All right Rabson," Longstreet said, returning to his desk. "I'm going to inform the president and the Attorney General about this. Consider your vacation over as of now. I'm going to want you to be available to tell them your theory."

Friday, January 22nd
1000 hours
near Fredericksburg, VA

Dawn rose clear and brisk, with the temperature hovering around thirty-one degrees. Overnight, a gentle snowstorm had dumped several inches of fresh powder on the little community. The wintry scene gave Fredericksburg the quaint appearance of a Rockwell painting. To the east, the Rappahannock River had frozen in a few places.

Amid this idyllic setting, Jackie and Howard prepared the Juggernaut for departure. After carefully concealing the bomb and distributor with blankets, the pair covered the truck's bed with the camper shell. The plunger blasting machine and a large electrical battery were inside the truck's cab on the floor of the passenger side. Howard ran a cable from the cargo bed into the cab. While Jackie and

Cheryl prepared sandwiches and soft drinks, Howard took Joe aside and informed him of his intended route on a map.

"Jackie and me will leave and head north on Interstate ninety-five. We'll turn off onto Route two- thirty-four and proceed to Manassas. We should make it before nightfall. We're going to hold up in a hotel there until the morning of the twenty-sixth."

"Why not go straight into Washington?"

"There's plenty of time for that. Besides, I want to see the old Bull Run battlefields once more. My great-great-grandfather fought there at Second Manassas."

"Oh, you mean where General Lee and us Southern boys whipped up on all you Yankees!" Joe said, grinning.

"Yeah," Howard sighed in disgust. "Too bad you Rebs didn't win that damned war. I mean, with the race problem being the way it is and all. The country would probably be a hell of a lot better off."

"We'll do better next time."

"I'm going to leave Jackie at a hotel in Centreville on the afternoon of the twenty-sixth. I'll drive the bomb into the city and park it just where I planned, half a mile from the Capitol building. I'll do the final arming there. Everything should be all set by six-thirty."

"When does the president begin to talk?"

"The speech is scheduled to begin at seven- ten. I guess they got to make time for everybody to get seated. I can listen on the radio. I'll let him get started, let him get into his speech… then I'll send him to Hell!"

"Honey, we're ready to go," Jackie said, emerging from the house with a basket of sandwiches and soft drinks.

"Thank you for all your help," Howard said to Joe, shaking his hand firmly.

"Wish I could be with you," Joe replied, a tear slowly ran down his cheek.

"I know, but you're going to be needed when the race war starts. The Werewolf needs good Aryan men like you. God bless you."

Howard and Jackie climbed into the truck and slowly pulled off. They drove along Marye's Heights towards the Interstate. Cheryl Recke, carrying little Paranoya, joined her husband next to the barn, and waved as the couple disappeared into the distance.

After a thirty-five-minute drive, the couple arrived in the Manassas area. Howard was disappointed to see the battlefield had become a tourist trap, with fast food stands, cheap hotels and other signs of commercialism dotting the area.

"That's the Jews for you," he grumbled to himself, slowly shaking his head. "Anything for a buck."

Howard parked the truck in a garage while Jackie checked them into a Holiday Inn Hotel in Centreville. After settling in, the pair relaxed on the balcony. Gazing off to the east, they could clearly see in the distance the lights of Washington, DC.

Saturday, January 23rd
0830 hours
J. Edgar Hoover Building, Washington, DC

"Doug," the director said, summoning Rabson into his office. "I'm afraid I got some bad news for you. Yesterday afternoon I talked with the president and Attorney General."

"Yes sir?"

"They're not buying into your theory about Washington being the target. The ATF has convinced them that it's Detroit. Werewolf wants to take out the Super Bowl."

Rabson shook his head in disappointment. "My God! Sir, you've got to make them listen."

"I've already tried that, Doug! I argued your point of view with Jen McCormick for over an hour. No dice. I'm sending those additional agents to Detroit tomorrow. I expect you there by the twenty-sixth."

"Sir, I must respectfully request that we redirect our energies here in the capital."

"Dammit, Rabson, you have your orders! Carry them out!" the director shouted.

"Yes sir." Rabson sullenly returned to his office. *Those fools. They're sending all of our resources to Michigan and the real threat is right here. I'm sure of it... Well, I'd better make sure that at least Rachel and the girls are safe,* Rabson thought to himself as he phoned his home. "Hello?" Rachel answered.

"Honey?"

"Yes, what is it?"

"Listen, I can't explain it to you right now, but I want you to pack enough clothes for you and the girls to last you a couple of days."

"What?"

"I want you to go and visit your parents in Boston."

"Doug, why? What's wrong? Did that woman call again?"

"Please, honey, now don't argue. I don't want you to be here on Tuesday. I'm going to make the reservations for you and the girls. I'll tell you the details later."

"All right," Rachel sighed.

"Thanks dear, trust me on this one. I love you." Rabson slowly replaced the receiver.

The Sunday morning news-talk programs all had the upcoming Presidential State of the Union address as subject matter. The day before, members of the administration distributed an advanced "red herring" outline of the speech to the media. On *Meet the Nation* and *Face the Press,* opinions fell pretty much along Democratic or Republican partisan lines. In the outline, the president made it clear that he intended to hail the administration's foreign policy successes of the previous twelve months, namely the Moscow summit with the Russian Federation President and the signing of the Pacific Rim Free Trade Agreement.

On the domestic front, the president made it clear that he intended to renew his fight with the Republicans over his proposed crime bill and economic stimulus, both presently stalled in committee. He specifically asked the FBI Director and the Attorney General to attend the speech. The presence of McCormick and Longstreet, after the well-publicized successes against the Werewolf over the last few months, could only act to strengthen the president's position regarding the bill.

Meanwhile, in Detroit, preparations were underway for that other ritual of Americana, the Super Bowl. The *New Orleans Saints* and the *Miami Dolphins,* both the champions of their respective conferences, had arrived during the previous week and were already practicing for the game on the following Sunday. Without going into specifics, the Bureau had quietly informed the NFL commissioner that the game might be the target of a terrorist attack. Security around the Ford Field Stadium was discreetly beefed up.

Monday, January 25th
1127 hours

J. Edgar Hoover Building

Rabson sat alone in his office, struggling with a weighty decision. He had just gotten off of the phone long distance with Rachel. His family had arrived safely at Boston's Logan Airport and was at his mother-in-law's house. At least his family was safe.

He was scheduled to fly out of Dulles that afternoon to take command of an FBI task force assembling in Detroit. The round-trip, business class ticket on *United Airlines* lay on the desk in front of him. Rabson had a direct order from the director to proceed to Michigan. In his gut he knew that Howard Brennan and Jackie Lynch were on their way to Washington. Perhaps they were already there, making final preparations to annihilate the federal government. *This is why they pay you the big bucks. Somebody's got to make the really tough calls,* he thought to himself. Rabson made up his mind. He got up and left the office; the ticket was still on the desk.

1857 hours
Holiday Inn Hotel, Room 304, Manassas, VA

"Honey, tomorrow at around this time Washington, DC will be pile of cinders!"

"I don't want you to die, Howard!" Jackie said pleadingly.

"Shhhh… please Jackie. We've been over that ground before… You understand what you're supposed to do tomorrow?"

"At five, I'm going to rent a car and drive to our safe house in Baltimore. I'll kill anybody who tries to stop me. Around seven-fifteen you're going to set off the bomb. Right after the bomb explodes, I'll call the radio station and the newspapers there and claim responsibility for the Werewolf."

"That's fine. By morning, the race war will be well underway… One thing though, I want you to take this." Howard handed her a thick envelope with the words *Sic Semper Tyrannis* written on it. "This is my political testament. It's my justification for what I have done. There are two copies. Leave one here in the hotel when you go. It's important that history sees what I'm doing not as a criminal act but rather as an expression of patriotic nationalism. Yahweh alone will judge me."

"I understand," she said, taking the documents.

"I want *you* to be Cynthia Carson. You'll have to rally the Aryans after I'm gone. Just like in *The Diaries*... Listen honey, let's go to bed." Howard went into the bedroom while Jackie slipped into a seductive white negligee and panties.

"I bought this little number when we were in Fredericksburg. I saved it for our last night together. I wanted it to be extra special. You like it?" she said, standing in the doorway.

"You're beautiful" Howard stared into her eyes.

"Howie, I love you so much... Please, give me a baby tonight!"

Overcome with passion, Jackie and Howard collapsed into each other's arms and proceeded to make love with wild abandon. "Married" for only a month, Jackie realized that she was to become a widow in less than twenty-four hours. After several hours of marathon sex, Howard rolled over and fell asleep. Jackie got up and walked out onto the balcony, reviewing her role in the upcoming drama. Wiping a tear from her eye, she opened the envelope and began reading Howard's testament. Re-entering the bedroom a few minutes later, she noticed that it was already past midnight. The Day of the Rope had come.

Tuesday, January 26th, *Judgment Day*
0715 hours
Holiday Inn Hotel, Room 304, Manassas, VA

"Howie, I got us a copy of the paper, here. It says here that all five-hundred thirty-five members of Congress, the nine justices of the Supreme Court and fourteen out of the fifteen members of the Cabinet are expected to attend the State of the Union tonight."

"Very good. Excellent," Howard said as he finished a bowl of cereal.

"The Secretary of the Interior won't be there. He's the 'Designated Survivor'. The paper says that he had some kind of gall bladder surgery last week and is still in the hospital."

"Well, that doesn't matter. After everybody else is dead they won't be able to form much of a government around him."

"Wow! It also says here that besides government officials and press, there's gonna be cabinet undersecretaries, several ambassadors, five state governors, family members and invited guests in the galleries… they're expecting about two thousand people in all."

"Perfect!" Howard replied with a savage grin.

"Howie, what does all that funny writing on the envelope mean?"

"*Sic Semper Tyrannis*? It's Latin. It means 'Thus ever to Tyrants.' It's what Cassius said to Caesar on the Ides of March; Wilkes Booth yelled it at Ford's Theater after he shot Lincoln. I figured it would add a nice touch."

1103 hours
J. Edgar Hoover Building

Mindful of Rabson's warning, the FBI Director had ordered several agents to conduct a sweep of the area around the government district. A number of suspicious vehicles were searched. He was making final preparations for attending the State of the Union speech with Attorney General McCormick. Seeing a light on in Rabson's office, he looked in. He was amazed to see Rabson seated at his desk.

"Rabson, what in Hell are you doing here? You're supposed to be heading up that task force in Detroit."

"Yes sir. I know, sir."

"Then why have you not followed my instructions?"

"Sir. I'm trying to contact local law enforcement here to find the terrorists before it's too late. I'm convinced that they're going to attack here."

"Agent Rabson, for your information I've already had a sweep of the area this morning. Everything checks out."

"But sir, the Werewolf intends to attack tonight. I must insist—"

"Goddammit Rabson, I don't tolerate this kind of insubordination. You've deliberately disobeyed my instructions to proceed to Detroit!"

"Sir, you and the Attorney General have dispersed our resources here. We're wide open. Sir, I repeat the terrorists intend to destroy the capitol… Tonight!"

"Based on what? Your daughter and her English history test?" the director said, livid with anger. "You expect me to make command decisions based on something that happened four hundred years ago? I have to make decisions concerning this agency about the allocation of resources and agents based on analysis and hard facts, not on some guesswork and cock-eyed hunches… You're relieved of duty!"

"Very good, sir!" Rabson replied angrily, heading toward the door.

"And God help you if you're wrong!" the director yelled. Rabson paused at the door and turned.

"If I'm right, then God help us all!" he answered back.

1439 hours

Manassas, VA

"Now, you mustn't cry, Jackie," Howard said as he climbed into the Ford truck. "Today should be a day of rejoicing for us all, the day that we have all worked so hard for."

"Yes, I know," she replied tearfully.

"Today we're going to start taking our country back! I'm leaving now. When we meet again, we will be in the Kingdom of Yahweh. Goodbye Jackie."

"God bless you, Howie. I love you... I love you so much!" she said, breaking into a sob.

"I love you, *Cynthia*." They kissed. As Jackie waved, Howard slowly backed the truck out of the rented garage. He took Route 234 out of town until he reached the old Bull Run battlefield. After a brief pause on the field Howard continued onto Interstate 66 towards the capital, passing the tiny communities of Vienna, Fairfax and Arlington. Washington DC faced its gravest peril since it was burned by the British in 1814.

The trip to Washington took just over forty minutes. It was late in the afternoon when he reached the Theodore Roosevelt Memorial Bridge across the Potomac. As the city came into view, he began merrily whistling the tune *There'll Be a Hot Time in the Old Town, Tonight*.

Along the river, he could catch a glimpse of the John F. Kennedy Center for the Performing Arts as well as the Watergate hotel complex. To the south lay the Tidal Basin, surrounded by its beautiful Japanese cherry trees, not yet in bloom. The street which he was on merged with the city's major thoroughfare of Constitution Avenue. Along the route, he could see to his left the State Department Building, National Academy of Sciences Building, Federal Reserve Building, the Bureau of Indian Affairs and the Internal Revenue

Service Buildings; on his right was the broad open area known as the Mall. Approaching the confluence of Constitution and Pennsylvania Avenues, he pulled onto Sixth Street in front of the Mellon Fountain. Further up the street, he could see access roads being blocked off with barricades. Washington DC police and Secret Service agents patrolled the hastily erected barriers.

In the shimmering haze of a clear midwinter evening, Howard could plainly make out his target: the broad dome of the US Capitol Building less than half a mile away. Just beyond that lay the limestone edifices of the Everett Dirksen Senate Office and the Sam Rayburn House Office Buildings. He checked his watch: it was 4.22 p.m. In less than three hours, the government of the United States would be no more. Opening a small paper bag, he casually began munching on a sandwich that Jackie had prepared for him earlier. His infernal machine, the Juggernaut, was in position.

Howard could not have selected a more ideal site for the placement of the bomb. He noted that, save for the National Art Gallery and an adjacent annex on the Mall, there was no structure of any consequence between the bomb and the Capitol. There would be nothing to impede the shockwave of the blast upon detonation. Indeed, disintegrating buildings flanking the street would act to channel the blast wave down Pennsylvania Avenue towards the Capitol. Finishing the sandwich, he calmly waited for the moment of destiny.

Howard, who spent much of his professional career studying and designing atomic weapons, now visualized in his mind's eye the scene at the moment of detonation. In a fraction of a second, current from the blasting machine would be apportioned evenly via the distributor to the forty-eight blasting caps. The C4 wedges would simultaneously erupt. The detonation blast wave would become concave as it encountered the slower burning baratol, symmetrically compressing the tamper inward onto the core. At the same time, alpha particles from the polonium in the initiator would encounter the lighter beryllium atoms, resulting in the generation of millions of neutrons in less than one-millionth of a second. These neutrons would, in turn, flood the shrinking plutonium core as it went critical, triggering the fission process.

As the chain reaction proceeded, the resultant splitting of the core's plutonium nuclei would increase exponentially, generating more neutrons and becoming self-sustaining, resulting in turn in the release of vast amounts of heat and electromagnetic energy. By this time the core— the fourth state of matter— plasma, originally the size of a large grapefruit, would be compressed to a diameter of less than that of a golf ball. In a searing flash it, now at millions of degrees centigrade, would detonate. A shockwave would radiate out from the bomb's rapidly expanding epicenter at hypersonic speed. It would apply a force, or overpressure, of several hundred pounds per square inch on anything or anyone in its path out to a radius of more than two thousand yards, smashing them flat. No man-made structure within the area would be able to stand that. Hundreds of structures further out, weakened by the rapidly dissipating shockwave would collapse instantly with an earthquake-like effect, trapping and killing their occupants. Shards of metal, wood, broken glass and other projectiles would whirl around and strike any exposed people with lethal force.

Behind the shockwave, there would be a wall of superheated air — a thermal pulse, the fireball — radiating out from ground zero. Its periphery would be hotter than the surface of the sun. At tens of thousands of degrees centigrade, people, vehicles and ruins of buildings would be incinerated, vaporized within seconds up to a distance of two thousand yards. Up to two miles away, people and homes would spontaneously burst into flames. As the air around the fireball cooled to about ten thousand degrees centigrade, it would slowly condense into the characteristic mushroom cloud and rise, hanging like a pall over the stricken city. Its contents would consist of fallout: debris of vehicles, buildings, and tens of thousands of human beings, all burnt to a crisp. This fallout, slowly descending to earth, would carry with it the seeds of a new plague for any survivors, now reduced to a zombie-like, catatonic state: a slow, agonizing death ranging from acute radiation sickness to elevated incidences of cancer and birth anomalies in a polluted environment.

Further out, in addition to the atomic fires, broken natural gas mains and ruptured automobile fuel tanks would feed the growing conflagration. Since fire-fighting personnel and equipment would at least sustain casualties proportional to the general populace, added to the fact that the streets would be blocked with mountains of rubble, the fires would rage out of control. The conflagration would then coalesce into one monster blaze, with near hurricane force winds created as it greedily consumed all available oxygen. *Feursturm*. Fire storm. Dante's Inferno. Hell on earth. Washington, DC, would be a vast crematorium... a charred, blackened city of the dead.

1752 hours

The sudden flurry of activity on Pennsylvania Avenue shook Howard from his thoughts. The roar of police motorcycles meant one thing: the president's motorcade was coming. Two DC motorcycle cops momentarily blocked off Sixth Street as the procession approached. Looking along Pennsylvania Avenue, Howard could see the presidential limousine as it emerged from the White House parking area, Secret Service agents running along either side. Though a gifted speaker, the president always liked to arrive early at speaking engagements for any last-minute preparations. As the car passed Sixth and Pennsylvania, Howard caught a faint glimpse of the president and First Lady in the back seat. For an instant, he thought of quickly connecting the blasting machine to the distributor and eliminating his nemesis right then and there. *No. The President, Congress and Supreme Court must all die together, live and in color on the nation's television sets. This must be a public execution,* he thought to himself.

"Excuse me sir," a black DC policeman said, tapping on the windshield of the truck. "You can't park this vehicle here."

"Oh, I was having a little trouble with it. I called my wife a few minutes ago. She's arranging a tow," Howard said, looking up and in a nervous voice. Luckily, he had just placed his jacket over the blasting machine.

"All right." The policeman slowly turned and walked up Pennsylvania Avenue.

"Stupid, lazy nigger cop!" Howard muttered as the man walked away. "You're going to die with the rest of them!"

The House chamber of the Capitol was already beginning to fill. Camera crews and correspondents from the four major networks had positioned themselves earlier, seeking the best camera angles and testing the acoustics. The First Lady, various invited guests and Congressional staff members all began taking seats in the galleries while the five hundred and thirty-five Representatives and Senators filed into the chamber, the Republicans to the right, Democrats to the left.

1906 hours

Rabson had lingered in the lobby of the J. Edgar Hoover Building after his argument with the director. As the FBI Headquarters was situated on Pennsylvania Avenue almost midway between the White House and Capitol, he had been able to watch the president's motorcade as it roared past. A handful of agents remained in the building, monitoring ongoing investigations including the surveillance operations in Michigan. Director Longstreet had left earlier in the day; he was to accompany the Attorney General that night. Rabson decided to make a swing through the government district. He climbed into his car and drove out on Pennsylvania towards the Capitol. Just before reaching the confluence of

Constitution and Pennsylvania, he noticed a large white truck parked in front of the Mellon fountain. Rabson had no sooner pulled over to the far side of Pennsylvania Avenue when he observed a sandy haired figure emerging from the vehicle. He recognized the individual immediately.

Holy shit! It's Howard Brennan! he thought to himself. The image of Howard Brennan had been etched into his mind for the last several months. Certain of identification, he hurriedly got out of his car, Glöck-17 semiautomatic pistol in hand. He nervously began checking around for any signs of Jacqueline Lynch.

Howard turned on the truck's radio, tuning in the speech. He could hear the applause, whose growing volume meant one thing: the president had entered the chamber. Glancing at his watch, he decided that it was time to connect the blasting machine to the distributor. With a pocketknife, he exposed the copper leads of the wires and looped them around the posts of the blasting machine. He raised the plunger to the fully extended position, then hesitated. In order to ensure better contact with the wires, he decided to crimp the leads onto the posts with a pair of pliers. Remembering that he had a set of pliers in the toolbox in the back, Howard got out and was walking to the rear of the truck as Rabson approached.

"Howard Brennan, this is the FBI...Freeze!" Rabson shouted. Startled, Howard slowly raised up.

"Now turn around and place your hands on your head!" Rabson ordered. He realized that this was the first time in his twelve years in the Bureau that he'd ever uttered those words. Howard slowly turned around.

"So ZOG wins after all."

Rabson, furtively looking around, slowly approached the truck. "That's right. You failed."

Howard managed a smile. "Success or failure... it doesn't matter... Destruction can be an end in itself."

"After all that murder and bloodshed... Oh yes, Howard Brennan, you're under arrest. I'll give you your rights later."

"I was trying to save the country. Are you too stupid to see it? It was the only way! Can't you see?"

"I see that you're responsible for at least eighteen murders. Tonight, you tried to kill more than a quarter of a million people and destroy the government... strange way to save the country."

"It must be destroyed! The government is evil. A tool of the Zionist Jew! A wicked Sodom... It has to be destroyed!" Howard reached down into a toolbox.

"That's why we have periodic elections, workable laws and a functioning Constitution. That's what makes us different. This isn't a goddamned banana republic... Place your hands on top of your head!"

Howard pulled a small caliber handgun from the toolbox and pointed it in Rabson's direction. He squeezed off a shot, grazing Rabson in the arm. He broke around the side of the truck, desperate to reach the blasting machine in the vehicle's cab.

"Drop your weapon!" Rabson shouted, instinctively dropping into a combat stance. The agent fired a single shot. Howard momentarily stiffened and dropped the gun. Wounded in the side, he fell back violently against the truck and collapsed to the ground. Gazing into the truck's rear, Rabson could see the bomb resting on its makeshift platform. The blasting machine, with its handle fully extended, had fallen off of the front seat and was upside down. Looking inside the cab, the agent was horrified to realize that the weight of the inverted blasting machine was slowly compressing the plunger's handle. He broke the front window, opened the door and grabbed the device just centimeters from full compression. Rabson gingerly removed the wires that connected the blasting machine to the distributor. Feeling that the bomb was disarmed, an exhausted Rabson knelt down beside Howard.

"Freeze! Put your hands up!" an unfamiliar voice said.

Startled, Rabson slowly got up and turned around. *Holy shit! Now what?* he thought to himself. To his relief, it was a Washington DC cop, the same man who had stopped earlier.

"There's a wounded man here, get an ambulance."

"I said to raise your hands… Now!" The officer drew his gun.

"I'm an FBI agent," Rabson said, gesturing to his pocket. The patrolman examined his ID and lowered his weapon.

"What the hell happened here? I heard gunfire. I came back here to see if this truck had been moved."

"I can't elaborate now. You have to get an ambulance here on the double. This man is wounded. We have to try to keep him alive."

"This guy told me he was having problems with his truck."

"He's a terrorist, name's Howard Brennan. He's got a bomb in the back that could level half this city."

"Holy shit!"

"Get an ambulance here… On the double!"

"Right." The officer started running towards his unit.

"…And the Army's bomb disposal unit also!" Rabson shouted as the policeman departed. He again turned to Howard. Gazing down, he could see that the man's wound was mortal.

"Well, it really doesn't matter what happens to me," Howard said with a labored breath. He began coughing up blood. "Some revolutionaries are destined to rise to become the patriarchs of new nations, while others suffer only degradation and death. It is the judgment of Yahweh. I wanted to be Ed Carson... like in *The Diaries.* But there are others out there who will take up the struggle. You'll see." The man's breathing became shallow. He was drifting in and out of consciousness. "Make warriors stronger... Bring great army together... Jackie and I showed the way. You cannot stop us... the Werewolf shall conquer!"

"And that's why there'll always be work for people like me... Come on Howard, save your soul. Where's Jacqueline? Howard? Howard!" Rabson pounded on the dying man's chest as the heartbeat became faint. "Goddammit you son-of-a-bitch, talk to me!" Howard grew pale and stiffened.

"*Mein liebe* Jacqueline... *alles zerstört... Werwolf kaput... alles tot,*" he mumbled in German, gasping. His chest slowly rose and remained stationary. Rabson checked for a pulse. There was none. Howard Brennan was dead.

Rabson slowly rose to his feet as an ambulance and the Washington DC Bomb Squad van arrived on the scene. As the body was loaded onto a gurney, Rabson walked over to one of the bomb squad members.

"It's finally over. The plutonium that was stolen from Rocky Flats last year is in the back of the truck. It's been fabricated into an atomic bomb. I've inactivated the detonator."

"Who's the dead man?"

"Colonel Howard Brennan," Rabson said, turning away. *This ain't Iraq or Afghanistan or somewhere in the Middle East... This is the US. This kind of shit ain't supposed to happen here,* he thought to himself as the bomb squad and Army ordnance people went to work removing the device. *Then again, maybe it is.*

Rabson slowly meandered back over to his car and turned on the radio. The announcer indicated that the State of the Union address was about to begin. The agent turned up the volume, pondering how the twisted mind of a madman had brought the country so uncomfortably close to catastrophe, of what a near run thing it had been.

1910 hours
The House Chamber, US Capitol Building

"Madam Speaker, the president of the United States!" the Sergeant-at-Arms announced in a booming voice to the assembled throng. Bearing the mace of the House of Representatives, he slowly led a solemn procession of dignitaries into the hall. Amid the strains of *Hail to the Chief* and a thunderous ovation, all rose as the president entered the chamber, followed closely by the Vice President, Attorney General, FBI Director Longstreet and other members of the cabinet. Cameras from the four major networks captured this timeworn ritual of American democracy, performed almost every January since the days of Woodrow Wilson. For several minutes, the president worked the audience, vigorously shaking extended hands and basking in the adulation of the public eye. He was up for re-election this year and was determined to make the most of the moment. He paused briefly to wave at the First Lady, smiling from the gallery. As the applause died down, a messenger handed him a note. Examining it thoughtfully, he thrust it into his pocket and approached the dais. The hall grew silent. Amid the bright lights he grasped the edge of the podium and began to speak.

"My fellow Americans," he opened. "I'm happy to report to you tonight that our nation is strong and the state of the Union is good…"

It had been a near run thing, indeed.

Epilogue: The Circle Unbroken

"...At what point then is the approach of danger to be expected? I answer. If it ever reached us it must spring up amongst us; it cannot come from abroad. If destruction be our lot, we must ourselves be its author and finisher. As a nation of freemen, we must live through all time or die by suicide."

— Abraham Lincoln, from the *Lyceum Address*

In spite of the successful recovery of the stolen plutonium, the FBI investigation was not completed. While it was true that Howard Brennan was dead, his murderous consort was still at large. Rabson briefly watched the removal of the truck bomb before walking back over to the ambulance.

"I want you to list all personal effects found on the dead man," he said.

"Certainly sir," replied one of the attendants. "What's up?"

"You know the old adage about how dead men tell no tales? Well, sometimes that's not always true."

"Let's see, we found a pair of pliers, a pocket watch, keys, a small knife, a wallet with $230.15 in cash, a small roll of candy, a couple pictures of a woman, a paperback book, and a hotel receipt," the attendant said, sorting through his effects.

"Hotel receipt?"

"Yes. It looks like it's from the Holiday Inn Hotel over in Manassas, eh-Room Three-Oh-Four."

"Let me have a look at that."

2015 hours
House Chamber, US Capitol

The State of the Union speech was over. The President had given a good speech, the best of his political career; the sixty-nine-minute address had been interrupted twenty-one times with prolonged applause. As the crowd dissipated, a congressional page informed the FBI Director of a telephone message to call the Bureau headquarters.

"Rabson? Looks like you were wrong. The State of the Union speech came off without a hitch. The Werewolf didn't strike after all," Longstreet said.

"No sir, I was right. The government of the United States was destroyed approximately seventy-two minutes ago."

"What are you talking about?"

"Sir. It's over. I shot and killed Howard Brennan a little over an hour ago."

"What? I don't understand."

"Brennan had the bomb parked in a truck less than half a mile from the Capitol, in front of the Mellon Fountain. He was making last-minute preparations to set it off when I came across him. I'm afraid I had to kill him."

"What about the missing plutonium?"

"Recovered. An Army ordnance team from Fort McNair have it. Talked to a Major Burleson there. He estimates that the device packed the explosive equivalent of fifty-two thousand tons of TNT. It would have leveled most of the city."

Longstreet paused for a long minute.

"Doug, I'm sorry about our flare-up today. This is difficult for me to say, I was wrong. You did a fine job tonight, and I'll inform the president and Attorney General of that. I want a complete report on exactly what happened first thing tomorrow morning."

"Yes sir... Ah, sir, I think I may know the whereabouts of the Lynch woman."

"Oh?"

"Yes sir. We found a hotel receipt in Howard Brennan's pocket. It's from a Holiday Inn in Manassas. I've taken the liberty of placing several agents at the hotel. I would like to be there when this woman is apprehended."

"Certainly. You've been tracking this woman for the last year. This is your collar. Take all the people you need."

"Thank you, sir."

Rabson hastily assembled a Special Weapons Team and drove to the Holiday Inn in Manassas. On arrival, he found that the stake-out unit was already in place, having surrounded the building. Rabson wasn't taking any chances this time. He recalled how Jackie Lynch had repeatedly eluded him during the past year. As more lawmen deployed, his thoughts turned to his friend Abel Willis, the black FBI agent savagely murdered in Atlanta. He remembered sweet Aqueous Blank, just weeks away from a well-deserved retirement when she died from a terrorist bomb meant for him. And Zach Duncan, the jovial bartender brutally shot to death in a Denver alley. He recalled Jackie Lynch's chilling voice on the answering machine, threatening his own family with death.

2235 hours

"We're sorry to have had to awaken you, sir," Rabson said to the groggy hotel manager. "We believe that a dangerous fugitive may be hiding in one of your rooms."

"Oh?"

"Yes sir, in Room Three-Oh-Four. We'd like to evacuate the adjacent rooms."

"That's not necessary, they're vacant...That's amazing. That couple told me that they were newlyweds on their honeymoon. The woman must still be in there."

"How do you know that?"

"She rented a blue Taurus just this afternoon. I saw her as she drove in with it. It's still here," the hotel manager said, pointing toward the parking lot.

Donning a Kevlar vest and helmet, Rabson and members of the SWAT team cautiously approached the room. Two other lawmen covered the rear. With a baton he rapped on the door.

"Jacqueline Lynch, this is the FBI. The room is surrounded. Come out with your hands in the air!" Rabson said in an almost perfunctory tone. He knew she wasn't going to surrender.

There was no answer. Weapons drawn, the agents kicked in the door and rushed inside. The television was on; a local news reporter was giving sketchy details of a gunfight that had occurred earlier near the Capitol as well as the first political reactions to the State of the Union speech. The agents could hear water running in the bathroom. The team spread out through the hotel room. Rabson noticed that the window was open.

"Looks like she was definitely here, sir," a SWAT member noted, examining her purse and belongings. A silenced Beretta nine-millimeter handgun, a copy of *The Carson Diaries*, old newspaper clippings of several of her murders, a brunette wig and a picture of Howard Brennan lay on the nightstand.

Rabson was seething with frustration. Apparently, the killer had escaped again.

"Doug, you better come into the bathroom. I think you should look at this," another agent said, motioning to Rabson.

Rabson went inside. There, sprawled on the floor of the shower clad only in a brown bathrobe and panties lay Jacqueline Lynch. A broken ampule lay on the floor beside her head. Her lips were a dull purple in color and gave off a strong odor of bitter almonds. She was beautiful, even in death.

"Looks like she's dead, Doug," the agent noted while checking for a pulse. "Smell that? Almonds. Probably cyanide."

"Just like Eva Braun… *die Götterdämmerung*," Rabson murmured as one of the agents covered the body.

"What's that?"

"It's German… means 'the twilight of the Gods'."

"She's still warm… couldn't have been dead more than one hour I'd say," the agent grunted.

"Take her prints. I want confirmation."

While a print team took the dead woman's fingerprints, Rabson looked around the bathroom. A small vial of sodium cyanide rested on the corner of the basin. A large swastika had been smeared on the mirror in lipstick. Rabson momentarily glanced down at the dead woman. Reaching into his pocket, he pulled out one of Jacqueline Lynch's mugshots. He slowly tore the photo in half and left the room, shaking his head. The hunt was over.

Wednesday, January 27th
0830 hours
J. Edgar Hoover Building, Washington, DC

"Well, sir," Rabson said. "Finally over. Last night, we found the body of a young woman in a hotel room in Manassas. It was positively identified by the print unit as that of Jacqueline Diane Lynch. Cyanide poisoning, she committed suicide."

"So that finally closes the file on *the Jack- L*," Director Longstreet said. "All told, we think this woman killed at least thirty-six people, the last one being herself."

The two men gazed out the office window, down Pennsylvania Avenue toward the Capitol. The bipartisan harmony observed the previous night during the president's speech was already long forgotten; with the coming of the new day, the Republicans and Democrats would clash over ideals and policies. Politics in Washington, DC was stirring to life for another typical day.

"The President gave a good speech last night. Reckon things will get back to normal now."

"Yes sir. Caught a glimpse of the political reaction to the speech in the paper. Things are back to normal, all right. The Democrats and Republicans are already at it again like cats and dogs."

Longstreet slowly turned back from the window. "Think they could have pulled it off? I mean, a race war?"

Rabson gazed up at the ceiling and sighed. "I don't know. There's just so much division and hate in this country… lot of pissed-off people out there. It's kinda chilling to see that there are people who are willing to tear the country apart… to give Howard Brennan just what he wanted… even though he's dead. Look at what happened after the Capitol Insurrection and all the turmoil during the last election… I'd like to think that even if the Werewolf had managed to destroy the capital, all the people would come together, unite against the common threat. Like they all did after the terrorist attacks on the World Trade Center and the Pentagon… that they'd turn *to* rather than *on* each other."

"Yeah, I hope you're right," the FBI Director said, slowly nodding. "Oh, yes, before I forget, you and your wife are requested to accompany myself and the Attorney General to the White House on Friday at four."

"Oh? I can't imagine why," Rabson said. He smiled.

"It's a little reception being given by the president. I suspect that he believes that you had something to do with the recovery of the stolen plutonium."

Rabson briefly pondered the request and said, "I'm afraid I'll have to miss it, sir. I have a previously scheduled engagement."

"Oh? More important than a Presidential reception?"

"Yes sir. Sarah is having another piano recital. I've been promising to attend. I wouldn't miss it for the world."

"Maybe she could give it at the White House… By the way, how'd she do on that exam in her history class?"

"She aced it," Rabson said, giving a "thumbs-up" sign.

The Werewolf gang never recovered from the loss of its key operatives. Joseph Horan, Rebecca Stephens, Jeff Collins and Nathan Mantooth were convicted for their roles in the Rocky Flats raid. They were sentenced to death. The sentences of Stacey Manson and Pamela Haney were overturned on appeal. A human rights group convinced a federal judge that the two women were insane. Pamela committed suicide soon after. Ariadne Beausoleil was convicted in federal court and also found guilty in Colorado for her role at Rocky Flats and Alliance Construction. In addition, she was also convicted by an all-white jury and given a life sentence in the state of Utah for the murder of Demetrius Bones. Because of her age and the discovery that she was pregnant, Miss Beausoleil was spared the death penalty. While in prison, she gave birth to a son, Adolph.

Joachim Klimper was extradited back to South Africa where he stood trial and was convicted of a variety of race-related crimes. Jason Chalmers, the boyfriend of Ariadne Beausoleil, was never captured. On April 20th, he was killed during a botched liquor store robbery in York, Pennsylvania. Suzanne Brennan never had a chance to remarry. On July 14th, her body was found at the bottom of the stairs in her home. Her neck was broken. Her death was ruled accidental. Dagmar Hollander, although implicated in the murder of Nick Hoover, was released due to insufficient evidence after an exhaustive investigation. She returned to her role as leader of the Aryan Church of Yahweh the Creator, preaching the gospel of hate and impending race war with the "nigger people" and the "Jews Media." The insanity goes on.

The Reckes were never captured. Depressed over the Werewolf's failure to destroy the government, the couple prepared to take their own lives. Cheryl fed Paranoya a cyanide-laced formula and then took the poison herself. Both mother and child died in agony. Joe sullenly retired to the barn and stood at attention before a large portrait of Adolph Hitler. Giving the Nazi salute, he placed a nine-millimeter pistol in his mouth and casually proceeded to blow his brains out. The insanity goes on.

Bruce Davies was sent to the federal prison facility at Lompoc, California. Despite his *incognito* incarceration, the vengeance of the Werewolf caught up to him. In the first of the so-called retaliation murders, his younger sister Kathy was killed by hooded assailants. The terrified woman was kidnapped, gang-raped and forced to ingest a toxic cocktail of corrosive drain cleaner and roach spray. She died in agony. On November 9th, Davies himself was found savagely murdered in his cell, an apparent victim of "inmate law." He had been castrated and hacked to death with a crude machete. The victim's testicles had been stuffed in his mouth. The words, *JEWDAS-Unsere Vergeltung ist todlish!* were crudely printed on the wall. Three inmates and a guard, all suspected members of the Werewolf, were charged with the murder. The insanity goes on.

Tuesday, April 20th
The Aryan Church of Yahweh the Creator, near Provo, UT

As dawn broke, the denizens of the JerUSAlem compound began a new day. Grim-faced men wearing camouflage patrolled the encampment's perimeter with snarling attack dogs or manned the two guard towers. The normal activities of the JerUSAlem commune were to be interrupted on the account that it was Hitler's birthday. Amid preparations for the evening's festivities, a matronly-looking woman was busy quizzing several small children in the compound's "school."

"Martha, can you tell me what's so important about today?"

"Yes, Reverend Mother, it's Adolph Hitler's birthday!" the child said.

"Mark, who was Adolph Hitler?"

"He's our great leader, the immortal leader of our race!"

"And what happened to our great leader, Mary?"

The little girl pouted and said, "He was murdered by the Jews, Reverend Mother. They're bad. They killed Jesus. I hate them. I hate them all…"

The insanity goes on.

Code Name: Juggernaut

Dedication

I dedicate this work to the memory of my parents, Charles Edward and Wilhelmina Alexandria-Sherman